ROCK GIANT

A BLACK HALO NOVEL

MADELYNNE ELLIS

ROCK GIANT

-Also by Madelynne Ellis-

Scandalous Seductions
A Gentleman's Wager
Indiscretions
Phantasmagoria
Three Times the Scandal
The Viscount, His Lover & I
The Ghosts of Christmas Past
The Serpent's Kiss

Wooing the Wakefields
A Devilish Element

Romps & Rakehells
Capturing Cora
Seducing Sophia
Taming Taylor

Forbidden Loves
The Kissing Bough
Pure Folly

The Black Halo Books
Come Undone
All Night Long
Off the Record
Come Together
All Fired Up
Come Alive
Reflex
Replay
Refrain
Revive
Reckless Beat
Rock Giant

Anything But...
Anything But Vanilla
Anything But Ordinary

Stirred Passions
Cherry Bomb
Black Velvet
Soul Kiss
Mint to Be
Screw Driver

Standalone titles
Tempted
You, Him, & Me
Don't Mess with my Relic
Sharing Adam
Gabriel's Naughty Game
Confessions of a Greedy Girl
Crazy Love
Washed Up

Gothic Urban Fantasy
Broken Angel in Possession: Three Tales
Shapeshifting & Possession
Prophecy
The Demon Way
Shadow Queen

J ODI WOKE TO piercing daylight with a crick in her lower back courtesy of an errant tree root. Hardly something she could complain about since it'd been there first. Best just be grateful for the shelter its boughs had provided her. Honestly, she thought she'd moved past sleeping in the open. Things had been looking good, steady relationship, sensible friends, yet here she was again... Down on her luck... hustling for food... praying the goddamned world would give her a break...

Wait!

Fuck! Wait!

This wasn't right. She was not stuck in that void anymore. Even if everything had gone belly up, she had a tent. A perfectly nice, teepee-like tent with a porch and a sleeping bit, and a soft fluffy sleeping bag, and a nice little stove that ran on camping gas that packed down small enough to fit in her backpack. So, why the hell wasn't she tucked up safe inside it?

Gingerly, she cracked an eyelid. Okay, she was not outside, but within some sort of haphazard structure made of interwoven branches with a canopy of bracken. Flashes of constructing it pierced her woolly thoughts. Had she and Nash built this after the ceremony? Taken things a step further and become one with nature? That kind of rang a bell, even though it didn't seem a very Nash-like thing to do. He was more of a brooding-in-a-dark-corner type than a let's-get-our-hands-dirty-and-construct-stuff one. Then again, here she was. Maybe the occasion had inspired him.

They had tied the knot, hadn't they?

Yes, she could feel the ribbon still bound around her wrist. She raised a hand to admire it, grinning in sheer bliss, her future now secure. Shame the details of it were so thoroughly lost behind a misty shroud. She remembered laughing. Laughing so hard that her stomach muscles were still cramped from it even now.

Or maybe she just needed a decent breakfast.

Her stomach gurgled, hinting it was likely the latter.

A robin chirped overhead. Jodi watched it hop between branches. The roof of the shelter was rather sparsely filled, a testament to its late-night, hasty construction. Why hadn't they gone back to her tent, or, hell, even his bus? The latter would have lacked privacy, but not the former. Instead, they'd opted for what?

A love nest.

At least he was here with her. She'd woken enough now to recognise the heat of a body beside her.

They'd rolled apart a little during the night, because she'd definitely gone to sleep with his arms around her.

"I need food. A nice bacon butty, maybe... That something I can get on your bus?"

She rolled onto her side, intending to wake Prince Charming with a kiss. Only Prince Charming was already alert and observing her, his head tilted contemplatively, his beautiful hazel eyes burning with adoration. Every inch of him was agonisingly familiar: the shape of his face, the strong jaw, the easy smile, that dimple that formed right on the edge of where his stubble grew whenever he grinned. He was grinning at her now.

The hair was different though, buzzed short, where it had previously been longer on top, and nothing at all like Nash's shaggy mane.

"You!" Her heart plunged into her stomach.

"Castle," he said, as his gaze dropped to take in the curves of her semi-naked body, prompting her to cover herself.

He was wholly naked, save for a chain of sadly wilted daisies, the corner of a plaid blanket, a lot of glorious ink...and a ribbon that matched the one fastened around her wrist.

"Oh, shit!"

Jodi hastily put some space between them. No... This wasn't right. It was a dream. A nightmare. She'd wake in a moment. She tried closing her eyes and reopening them, but he hadn't magically blinked out of existence or metamorphosed into the person she prayed he would become. He was still him. Still an inked giant with a heroic jaw and a kindly gaze.

"Oh, God!"

Her heart was going to burst right through her rib cage; it was galloping so much.

Time past, she'd have welcomed the sight of him. God, for months and months, she'd wanted nothing more than to stumble back into him, but not now. Not when she finally had her shit together. When things

were going right for once, and she'd found her feet...
She'd found love. Committed to someone. Tied the
knot...

She raised her wrist and stared at the ribbon
bound around it. Then at the matching one that
encircled his.

No, that wasn't right... That couldn't be... They
hadn't...

"You okay, Castle?"

No, she wasn't fucking okay! Not a fraction, an
iota, or even a tiddly bit. This was bad. Soul-
destroyingly, atrociously, life-shatteringly bad. She
grabbed the blanket, hugging it to herself in a bid to
build a barricade between them. It was too little too
late, of course... And she hadn't given the
consequences of her movement sufficient thought.

The plaid slid off him, revealing him in all his
naked, tattooed, pierced—she blinked—multiply-
pierced glory. Fuck, he was huge, and—"Christ, that
must have hurt!" The words rushed out irrespective of
brain involvement. But also, wow... intriguing, and not
something she ought to be focusing on. She raised her
hand to block the view as she jerked her gaze sideways,
but even seeing him in her peripheral vision was too
much, because she remembered. Remembered just
how gloriously well put together Paul "Rock Giant"
Reed was. And then... then she was hot under her non-
existent collar, and her lady bits were screaming that
they were up for the challenge.

Paul Reed. The larger than life, sometimes vegan,
cat-rescuing, mad as a box of frogs, hippy-trippy,
adventure-loving bass player for goth metal superstars
Black Halo. He was always and always would be, *too
much*.

He was also responsible for making her homeless.

Had she told him that? Was that why she was in a
makeshift shelter he'd no doubt constructed? Had he

tried to counterbalance things by building her a residence? If only a similarly mad explanation would explain away the matching ribbons, or the fact that they were both extremely naked.

And did her body have to react to this vision of godly flesh in quite such a visceral fashion? Her nipples were like two spokes, her heart thumping, and her pussy purring at the thought of rubbing up against that column of barbell-enhanced flesh.

How many were there? Three? Six? More?

God, girl! Get a grip. And stop gawping at his gearstick.

He wasn't even her type, not really. She wasn't into big, muscly men. She liked them all wan and stringy. The sort of guys that a good strong breeze could blow over, not behemoths capable of sweeping her off her feet like she was some renaissance-era waif, not a twenty-something with a food addiction and curves the Sheela na Gig inked on his upper arm couldn't even match.

"What the fuck did we do? Please tell me we didn't..." She wrenched a hand through the tangled strands of her hair. "Fuck!" Tears welled when her fingers got caught.

"Hm?" The noise told her nothing.

She turned to face him again, carefully keeping her gaze focused on his head. "Paul. Did we fuck?"

"Oh. I wasn't sure if you were just cursing or that was a question." He settled his back against the tree trunk, irritatingly at ease, and idly raised an arm to shield his eyes from the rising sun. A smile played on his lips, suggesting he was remembering exactly how their bodies had entwined.

Jodi snatched a handful of leaves from the shelter wall and chucked them at him. "Did we?"

He showed her his wrist. "What can I say? We tied

the knot." As if she wasn't already painfully aware of the damn ribbon and its symbolic trinity knot.

"That's not what I asked you."

"It's kind of fuzzy," he admitted, his recollection seemingly as incomplete as her own. No matter how hard she strained, the memories were no more than snapshots, as if she were flicking through the pages of a book too fast. She screamed and pulled her hair again, neither of which helped.

"Shift," she ordered, scouring the ground. She shoved him, forcing him to budge over.

"What are you doing?"

"I can't see any condoms."

He arched his eyebrows.

"You wouldn't have. We wouldn't have. You're always prepared for anything."

"Also wouldn't chuck them on the ground for some unsuspecting beetle to happen upon."

A sob broke in her throat. She drooped, wilting as if all the life had drained from her. God, she was such a fucking moron.

She ought to have known it was all too good and wouldn't last. Yet again, she'd proved to be her own worst enemy.

"Hey." He was there then. Strong arms around her, cradling her to his chest, and filling her nostrils with his earthy scent. "What's the deal? It's not like it's a first for us, and I don't remember any complaints. And I quote, 'You're an awesome fuck'."

She shoved him away and immediately regretted the loss of warmth. "That was three years ago. We shared one night." A night that remained simultaneously both the best and worst night of her life. It'd upended everything. Ejected her from the bubble she'd been existing in. Shit had needed to change, but she hadn't been ready. She didn't blame him, though. Her choices had been her own. The only person responsible for the dung heap she'd landed in was her. And honestly, the same was likely true now. Curious that he'd been instrumental both times, mind.

"How are the cats?"

"What?"

"I said, 'How are the cats?'"

"I know what you said." She raised her hands. "You don't get to do that. You walked and haven't been in touch since."

"I walked? That's not how I remember it."

"I left you my number."

"The fuck you did."

"I fucking did."

He didn't argue, just shook his head and quietly held his ground. *Bastard.*

"I still have them," she admitted. "They're fine. They're here with me." Were probably grouchy as hell for having been confined for so long. They'd want feeding—her stomach gave another gurgle—and letting out for a stroll. And their litter box was probably stinking out her living quarters —if they hadn't just pooped on her bedding in protest over their neglect.

"Jodi, we didn't," he said, voice soft and utterly calm.

"What?"

"We didn't... shag. Leastways, I don't think so. Pretty sure I'd remember that. I mean..." He shook his head at whatever he'd been about to say. "I'll admit that last night's a bit of a blur, but I'd remember if I'd been inside you... If I'd touched you like that..." He went quiet a moment as if he was waging war with the fog or else redacting portions of the evening he didn't want to share. Eventually, he shook his head. "No condom, because we didn't. Sadly."

The relief allowed her to take one full breath of air before anxiety got her heart in a pincer grip again.

Them not having shagged was something. A good something. A lifeline to cling to, even, and maybe enough that she could bury this... whatever it had been... under a bush and forget about it. The fact that he didn't seem as eager to do so, she chalked up to his ability to thrive in unexpected circumstances. Honestly, she didn't have the capacity to dwell on how unfazed he was.

Also, she *had* left him her number. She'd written it on the glass, and if he'd got the P.S. then he'd got the number. Not that it mattered, other than he wasn't putting their lack of communication on her shoulders.

Breathe, Jodi. Breathe. Remember your grounding techniques. Five... Four... Three things she could hear. Bird song. The breeze rustling the leaves. Her own hammering heartbeat. Two things she could—*it's okay, no hook-ups had happened. No hook-ups were happening. Their past communications or lack thereof weren't of relevance.* —taste. Taste? What could she taste? She couldn't taste anything. Didn't matter. Next one. Next thing. She'd got them the wrong way round. Taste was last. Smell, she'd forgotten smell. What could she smell?

She could smell him. He smelled earthy, of outdoors and summer sun, of dew, and grass, and hedgerows. Apples. She could smell apples.

"Okay, that's good. It's all good." When life bowled a strike, you just had to be rational and logical about it. Tidy things into an order, then work through the list until all was well again. The past three years of her life were littered with such lists. Sometimes, the lists were the only things that had kept her moving forward.

First two items: "I need to go. So where are my clothes?"

She found them fast enough, balled up in the doorway of their makeshift shack, entangled with his, grass stained and crumpled, but wearable with a bit of a shake. She tossed Paul his jeans while he remained on his back, watching her.

"Put them on."

"Okay." He shimmied into them, all snake hips and gloriously lean muscle.

Not that she was looking… Nope, definitely not. Were those abs for real? That Adonis belt? Um, careful with the zip, now.

Stop looking, imbecile.

No man had the right to be that sexy.

Fuck, but he was a sight and a half.

Why was she making him cover up?

"I can't find your shirt."

"It's fine. Castle, it's fine."

"Right. Yeah." She finished pulling her dress over her head.

How was she in a field with Paul Reed? What sort of stars had aligned so that he even remembered her? It was hard not to grin over the sheer fact that he remembered her. She'd convinced herself that she was long in his past, a single snowflake that had melted against his hot skin on a cruel winter's night long— well, three years—ago.

It wasn't like she'd given him an epic jaffle, or a blowjob to end all blowjobs—would she even get all that in her mouth? Did rock stars even consider that sort of shit memory worthy, or were sexual favours so commonplace as to be as noteworthy as a decent pizza?

Why was he here now when she didn't need him, instead of back then when she definitely had? She'd prayed to every deity she'd heard the name of that he'd call. He never had.

Jodi bundled her leggings into a ball and headed outside. Paul emerged from their makeshift nest a moment later. That's what it resembled from the outside—as if two elephant birds had decided to roost at ground level and thrown sticks and ferns together in a hopeful heap. She was tugging at the knot in the ribbon around her wrist but only succeeding in pulling it tighter, while he indulged in a glorious stretch.

"Can you get this?" She held out her wrist to him.

"Yeah." He broke off saluting the sun and flashed her a glimpse of the identical binding around his own wrist accompanied by a worrying smirk.

"I mean, can you get it off? I want it off. The knot's pulled too tight. Can you snap it, or something?"

He tested the tightness by sliding two fingers between the ribbon and her skin. "It's fine."

"No, it's not. I want it off." She gave one end another ineffective tug.

"Keen to be shot of me so soon, Castle? I was banking on a longer honeymoon period."

The proof was right there. It was mocking her every attempt to pretend otherwise. Jodi just wasn't ready to acknowledge it. Nothing good would come of that. "We can forget about those, rig—"

Before she realised what he was about, Paul was leaning in. Kissing her. His lips caressing hers, firm but gentle. Then his tongue swept against hers, and his free hand closed around the back of her neck, drawing her to him, holding her where he wanted her.

Shock coupled with arousal and sent sparks through her body. She groaned. Her fingers curled against the springy muscle of his bare chest. One of his nipples tightened against her palm. She felt his cock stir too.

She tapped out, and he eased off a fraction. "Good morning, wife. Sure I can't tempt you back into this love nest before I find you breakfast?"

White noise ate up the sounds of the festival around them. Jodi's vision tunnelled in on his face. Wife! "Don't say that. I'm not. We're not. We did not get married."

This was rural England, not Vegas. There weren't any quickie ceremonies around. They were therefore not legally bound. Couldn't be. It wasn't possible.

Paul clasped her hand in his, drawing attention to the twin ribbons, like he was making the oaths all over again. Worse, she could hear the echo of those promises in her head. Could hear herself reciting those ages old vows of bonding.

They might not be legally married, but they had got hitched.

"Wife has a certain ring to it though, don't you think?"

"Paul," she said firmly, looking up at him. Not wanting to meet his eyes but knowing that she had to. She needed to make this point absolutely. "I'm really sorry, but I can't. We're not. This isn't... We need to cut these off and forget this was ever a thing. We weren't thinking right. We were high, or drunk, or something. We need to rewind. This is going to fuck up our lives so badly, and unnecessarily."

Were there witnesses? Had there been witnesses? Someone must have officiated, but that was just one random bod, who probably couldn't even remember what they looked like now.

Paul's puzzled frown said he didn't understand. One long finger stroked her inner wrist beneath the ribbon, creating shivers. Jodi snatched her hand away.

"Cute, Castle, but it's not something we can just forget. We swore sacred oaths to one another."

"While tripping our arses off on 'shrooms."

She remembered that now, trawling the field with a host of other idiots. Trying to tamp down her fucking anxiety by focusing on something, eating them because she'd read something and someone had told her about something, and it'd seemed like a bright plan in the heat of the moment, even though she hated any kind of mushrooms.

"No." She batted him away or at least tried to. God, any minute her knees were going to give way, which was why she didn't completely shake off his hold when he clasped her forearms and held her in place, lowering his head so that he could look her in the eyes and forge a connection that had no business existing.

"Doesn't matter if we were drunk, or high. A vow's a vow."

"Shit, you don't get it. You don't understand. I can't be bound to you. I'm not free to be bound to you."

"You are bound to me. We're bound to each other."

"This is going to ruin everything."

"Like what? What's it going to ruin, Castle?"

They'd had this conversation. She was damned sure of it. She'd fucking told him. The memory flared—comet bright. She'd been trawling the field. Passing time. Waiting. Focusing. Never intending to actually partake. She hadn't even been looking for mushrooms. She'd just been trying to keep her head together while she waited for Nash to turn up. But then, he...Paul, had appeared, like some faerie lord sliding between one reality and the next. He'd lifted her off her feet, spun her around like she was a child. "Jodi," he'd said. "Jodi Castle," as if it were a blessing. Then, "I've been looking for you, Castle."

He'd kissed her. He'd brought those generous lips down on hers and breathed fire into her veins, and dumbstruck fool that she was, she'd let him. She'd let him claim her, let him stamp his taste all over her, let his heat permeate her body. The memories of him dissembled in her mind. Around them, people had cheered and catcalled. It hadn't slowed him. He'd been thorough, and she'd been bewitched.

She'd wobbled when he finally put her down, lightheaded and near breathless. Still, with the presence of mind to raise her hand and stop him before he'd completely enchanted her. She remembered the soft brush of his stubble against her fingertips, how his lips parted in a way that made her want to graze her thumb across them. She hadn't though, because she wasn't a cheat.

"Don't. I can't. I'm sorry." She'd raised her other hand to show him the ring. "I got engaged, see."

TWENTY-FOUR HOURS EARLIER

"JEEZUS, IS THERE nowhere on this bus free of shagging? I swear you're all at it 24/7. I'm trying to *fucking* sleep."

Paul "Rock Giant" Reed slumped back in his bunk and pulled a pillow over his head. It failed to block out the *bafumpering* noises coming from across the narrow aisle of the tour bus bunk room.

"I've not done it anywhere on the bus," Ronnie, the band's keyboard player, replied.

Paul turned his head so he could see from beneath the pillow and jerked his curtain open. Ronnie was leaning over the edge of his bed on the adjacent top bunk, his dark hair spilling forward as he looked down at the bunk below, whose curtains were closed, but from which the noises were coming.

"Bravo." Paul gave him an insincere clap. "Doesn't really counterbalance the rest of them. What the fuck, Ash!"

"Quit whining 'cause you're not getting any," Ash, one of the perpetrators of the noise, said. His curtains began rippling rhythmically.

"We're being as quiet as we can," his wife added.

Paul groaned. That was the problem. They were trying to be stealthy, hence they were being ten times louder than they would have been if they'd just got on with it, instead of communicating in stage whispers, and giggling every time the bed groaned. Now, admittedly, if you were up for a masterclass in dirty talk, then there was plenty on offer here to get your teeth into, but what he wanted was another hour of blissful slumber. He folded his arms over the pillow, folding it around his head so that it blocked his ears, but it barely deadened Ginny's appreciative squeaks or Ash's indulgent groans, and his noise-cancelling headphones had gone walkabout again.

"Fuuuck, can't you just bloody get on with it and ejaculate?"

"Don't come yet," Ginny countermanded.

"Not gonna."

Course not. Mr Stamina here was going to continue making the walls vibrate for eternity. Bastard. That is, it was great that he finished these days instead of dishing out pleasure for no discernible reward, but still... give a guy a break. He needed his zzz's, they were playing a gig tomorrow.

"Right there. Yeah... Just like that. You're so fucking good, Mr Gore."

"You're so fucking hot, Mrs Gore."

Now they were just messing with him.

He endured another few minutes while contemplating alternative accommodations, but it wasn't like there was anywhere else on the tour bus he could safely take a quiet nap. Their frontman and drummer, Xane and Luthor, had co-opted the back bedroom, along with their girlfriend, Dani, and he was pretty sure that their rhythm guitarist, Spook, was next door in the bus's tiddly entertainment suite with their sound gal for the weekend. That pretty much left their minuscule kitchen as a no-sex zone, and the seating area there wasn't remotely big enough to comfortably house his limbs. Then again, he'd take silence over comfort at this point.

Ronnie had started narrating the session like he was a sports reporter for the Sexual Olympics.

Paul dropped to the floor and plodded downstairs. Turned out he was wrong about Alle and Spook. Alle was handcuffed to the kitchen table, bent over its surface with her naked, cherry-red arse in the air. At least Spook had manners enough to plant a brew in his hand as he scooted between them and the fridge, heading for the front exit. It seemed the only place he was going to find any tranquillity was in the great outdoors. Maybe he could find a hedge to snooze under.

He'd forgotten to pick up a T-shirt, so he claimed one from the merch box balanced on the fold-down second driver's perch. Ginny could scold him later. Like he gave a shit.

The shirt barely stretched over his chest and sat right on his waistline, proving the XXL sizing to be an outright lie. No doubt she'd tell him it was babydoll fit or some other shit. Like babydolls were anything but adorably soft and chubby.

The world outside was a blank white canvas. Mist swaddled most of the surrounding countryside, but it seemed fields stretched in all directions, save one thick with woodland. Paul stretched and curled his toes against the sodden grass as he supped his brew. Tea. Green. Just the right strength too. Utter bliss in a mug. Spook was a fucking saint. Gold star, Mr Mortensen. Gold star.

A couple of sheep bleated at him from the other

side of a hedgerow. "Morning to you too. Best make the most of it, mate. It's not going to stay this peaceful for long. There's a bunch of metal heads on the way." Within a few hours, the mist would have burned off. He could already feel the hint of sun, and the place would be swarming with people, and tents would crop up like mushrooms to litter the horizon. Between the constant burr of voices and stomping feet, there'd be the kick of drums and bass slicing through the air and vibrating underfoot. He lived for it, but that didn't mean he didn't appreciate the chance to absorb a little silence.

He'd stopped yawning by the time the bus door opened behind him, and Spook's girlfriend, Alle, came down the steps, no longer showing off any flesh. "Sorry about that. We didn't think anyone would be up and about this early, otherwise..." She shrugged.

"Best laid plans, eh?" He preferred walking in on Spook and Alle to any of the others. He wasn't sure why. Ultimately, sex was sex, and generally not that much fun unless you were actively involved, and it certainly wasn't because he was likely to witness anything less risqué between them than any of the others. The tamest option was Ash and Ginny, but simultaneously, Ginny was likely to bite his head off if his gaze roamed, and Ash turned into a scrappy terrier likely to savage your ankles if he thought you were ogling his woman. Xane and Luthor didn't fucking give a toss who saw anything, and Spook... Spook was as likely to invite you to kneel as hurry you along.

He wasn't interested in kneeling, but he didn't mind seeing the odd bit of skin, and of course, there'd been that time in their early days, when they'd asked him to join in. Not that he was angling for a reprise, much as Alle had the sort of curves he very much appreciated.

"Hey," Alle leaned her head against his arm.

Despite being taller than the average woman, she still only came up to his shoulder. "You okay?"

"Awake too bloody early, but otherwise peachy." He wrapped an arm around her shoulders and gave her a squeeze. "Suppose I can get some yoga practice in."

She nodded. "Sorry."

"Nah, you didn't wake me."

"But we did get in the way." Alle was very much about not getting in the way. "Spook's making breakfast. He said to ask if you wanted anything."

"What's he making?"

She peeped up at him through pale eyelashes. A wild mass of freckles decorated her nose and cheeks. "Pretty much whatever you want. He's in a good mood."

"And you too, by the sounds of it."

"Yeah." She flashed him a dimpled grin. "A few orgasms before breakfast will do that for a girl."

"Even when you earn yourself a sore arse in pursuit of them?"

She put her lips together, smirking. "Silly. Those are the best kind."

And that was why she was hooked up with his bandmate, despite him considering her a very good friend and deliciously sexy. "You don't need to kiss me better, Paul. I'm good. He's good to me. He gets me. You can have a hug though, if you need one."

"Away with your flirting," he said, removing his arm from her shoulders and giving her a gentle push back towards the steps.

"Jealous that you didn't get two orgasms before breakfast?"

"Profoundly."

"Give it a few hours, and I'm sure you'll have no trouble getting laid."

"Aye, maybe." Likely true, if he wanted a random

hook up. Black Halo were one of Equinox's headline acts, and while he might only be the lowly bass player, he was also the only remaining single original member of the band. Not that fans ever gave a shit about relationship statuses. The thing was, increasingly, he didn't want that. Fun in the moment didn't counterbalance the post-release emptiness. He needed to find himself a partner in crime. One who was up for madcap adventures, was undaunted by his towering height and other quirks, and preferably had curves for days. The first two, their keyboardist had more or less covered, but Ronnie was skinny as a rake, and in the immortal words of Brian Molko, did not have breasts and all the rest.

"So, full English?" Alle prompted.

"Sounds great. So long as he's not using the same spoon to cook with that he used on your arse."

She laughed, and about turned to the steps again, pausing one foot on the bottom one. "We vegan this week or not?"

"Ish. No faces, and lots of mushrooms, please. And absolutely no pussy juice."

She shook her head at him, prompting him to offer her a salute, but she was snickering as she closed the door between them, leaving him to the mist and dew and the bird calls, and she was no doubt inside repeating his request verbatim to Spook. Who was probably contemplating adding a side of pussy juice to breakfast, but ultimately wouldn't because he wasn't an arse, just a sadist.

Thank God he and Alle had worked out a way to be happy together.

Maybe a hook-up wasn't such a bad idea. It'd beat wanking in the bus's miniscule shower in which he regularly bruised his elbows attempting to shave.

Paul had finished his tea by the time Spook knocked on the window to let him know that food was ready. The three of them sat down together around the tiny kitchen table Alle had previously been bent over. He didn't ask about sanitiser. Spook was a stickler regarding consent. He appreciated that Alle sat next to him too, rather than them both sitting opposite like some sort of symbiont. He followed the conversation for a while until they drifted into a discussion about tech stuff. Ulf, their usual sound guy, had taken a leave of absence to deal with some sort of family crisis at home, so Alle was filling in during the festival, and for a couple of the subsequent tour dates.

"You okay, big guy?" Alle nudged him with her elbow, having caught him staring out of the window.

The mist had already lifted some.

"Yeah. Fine." He offered her a smile until she tucked into her food again. Her boyfriend took more convincing. Spook wasn't looking directly at him, but Paul sensed his attention. Insightful bastard never missed a trick, but he didn't probe. He knew how to be circumspect and respect privacy.

"We're celebrating tonight, right?" he said hoping that'd dial back the scrutiny.

Spook gave a nod, followed by a head toss to send his swathes of blond hair back over his black T-shirt-clad shoulders.

Paul scratched his scalp. The summer had been brutally hot, so he'd buzzed his scalp short and decided he kinda liked it, both from an ecological perspective and a less stressful personal grooming one. He didn't want to be contributing to the hole in the ozone layer every show. Well, he still was, just not as much. They all were, just by virtue of existing and being part of modern society. It was fucking hard to avoid it, but if they all at least tried to minimise their impact, maybe the planet would stay green and blue a wee bit longer.

"Celebrating? What are we celebrating?" Alle put

down her knife and fork and pushed away her plate. "Shit! It's not someone's birthday, is it? Whose? I still haven't recovered from Xane's. That was frickin' wild. Not helped by the fact that someone forgot to mention that we were supposed to bring gifts."

"Gifts. Birthdays. Kind of a given," Spook muttered around forkfuls of scrambled eggs.

"If they're your bestie, sure. When it's your lover's confidant and sometimes bit on the side, it's not quite such an obvious call."

"Presents, always," Spook confirmed. "And he's not my bit on the side. We're just... comfortable with one another."

"He's totally your bit on the side. Pass the juice, Paul."

He did.

"Are either of you going to give me an answer as to what it is we're celebrating?"

"Mabon," they both replied.

"And what exactly is that?"

Paul stabbed the last of his mushrooms. "The autumn equinox. The middle of the three harvests."

Alle considered this with her lips pressed to the edge of her glass. "Are you actually Pagan, Wiccan? Sorry, I don't know if they're the same thing or different, or if there's another term I'm supposed to use. Please tell me if there is. Are you?"

"No."

"He just follows the old ways," her boyfriend said, throwing him a glance. "Blame his folks and his upbringing. It stems from the same place as his almost vegan, outdoor loving, mushroom foraging hippy traits."

Like Spook was any less of an adherent to the old ways.

"It's the point in the year when day and night are in perfect balance."

Point made.

"It's also when the door to the underworld opens," he added. That bit always made people sit up and pay attention. Sure enough, Alle cocked her head and made an 'ah' sound. "So, it's a celebration similar to Valborg in Sweden?"

"Ish," Spook replied. "Not really."

"Fewer fires, I hope."

"There'll definitely be a campfire," Paul said. Campfires were one of the best bits. "And as we're not performing until tomorrow night, there'll also be weed, booze, and naked mud wrestling with an orgy to follow."

For a moment, he swore she took his deadpan delivery entirely seriously, then she gave him a friendly shove.

"Oof!" he complained as his shoulder collided with the window. "Okay, okay... scratch the mudwrestling."

"Xane's a one-man orgy in waiting. I don't think you need to encourage him. And I've never seen any of you smoke or even vape. What's the actual plan?"

He and Spook exchanged glances. He cracked first. "Foraging, campfire, cider, and storytelling, in precisely that order."

"Damn." Spook got up and knocked the kettle on for another round of brews. "I was really psyched for the mudwrestling. It's good for the skin, you know."

"I'd totally mudwrestle you." Alle's gaze followed her boyfriend's movement.

Paul leaned into her ear. "That's because you're obsessed with getting him naked."

She grinned broadly. "Have you seen him? Of course I'm obsessed. He's fucking gorgeous. He's my elven prince."

"More like your cruel prince."

"Not a prince," Spook muttered. "Same again?" He nodded at the now boiling kettle.

"Not for me." Paul nudged Alle, so she'd rise and let him out from the table. After two cups of tea and a pint of orange juice, the thing he needed most was a piss. "Reckon it's safe to venture through and use the facilities?" He pointed towards the rear of the bus.

Spook glanced at the microwave clock. "Odds aren't in your favour."

"Fine. I'm going to find a bush."

"There are Portaloos." Alle pointed towards a blue plastic box in the middle distance.

"Yeah, no thanks."

Not even on day one of a festival.

CHAPTER 2
Jodi Castle

REATHE GIRL, BREATHE. If you don't, you're going to wind up hyperventilating, and then where will you be? Sitting on the damp grass breathing into a paper bag, that's where. It's not a look that's going to impress anybody, especially not your future husband's people.

Cat carrier tucked under one arm; Jodi Castle stepped off the shuttle bus into the sprawling chaos of the Equinox Festival camping zone. A canvas city of greens and blues with the odd garish eyesore filled the horizon. Behind her, to the right, stood the main festival stage. She'd got a good look at that on the way in from the comfort of her bus seat. It resembled an alien spacecraft, and honestly, if it didn't sprout legs and tentacles by the end of the weekend, then she'd demand her ticket money back. Not that she'd paid for a ticket. She'd got in for free, which frankly, considering the cost of festival tickets these days, was the only way she could afford to be here. Knowing the right people, that was the key. And boy did she know the right people.

Speaking of; it was past time she tracked them down and presented herself. She'd meant to arrive mid-morning. Only there'd been a slight problem with her train ticket and then a delay. Mysterious leaves on the tracks, or something like that.

The three moggies imprisoned in the oversized cat carrier yowled at her, reminding her to move. "I know, I know," she said, attempting to soothe them. "We'll get right on with finding him so that you can stretch your legs. Look, it's not going to be an issue. We're going to have a fab time." There were only five to ten thousand people here. No probs. It wasn't as if he was going to be milling about with the masses. There'd be a band enclosure somewhere. She just needed to find it. A quick glance at the orientation board told her the area wasn't conveniently labelled. Not really a surprise. If it was marked, every bugger would be trying to blag their way in for a chat with their favourite artist.

She fired off a text.

Jodi: I'm here. Where are you?

Nash: In a meeting. Can't talk atm.

Yeah, great, but where are you?

Nash was her saviour in so many ways. Thoughtful. Intelligent. Handsome in exactly the way she liked her men to be, hence smallish and kinda skinny with big eyes and pouty lips, and shaggy ink-black hair that softened all his sharp-edges. Obviously, he had his faults, everybody did. Was singlemindedness a fault? It could be, when it made you unaware of everything else outside of that narrow focus. Out of sight, out of mind. She shrugged; it was just how he was. Luckily, he had her to keep on top of all the other things.

Jodi: Not asking you to meet me, just need a clue where to head...

She left the message in draft a moment, then deleted it, and trooped over to one of the hi-vis wearing officials instead. It was likely what she'd wind up doing anyway, and she didn't want to make things difficult for Nash. Not now, when things were going so smoothly.

"Hey. Hello." She rested the cat box by her feet, then raised a hand to shield her eyes from the afternoon sun. "I'm with one of the bands, can you point me in the right direction?"

Somehow, this was always easier when you were arm-in-arm with a musician, rather than flashing security a smile while carrying a rucksack containing all your worldly belongings and simultaneously trying to hush a carrier full of yowling moggies.

"And they're expecting you?" The officials craggy face folded in disbelief. The guy had to be sixty and didn't look as if he wanted to be here in a field full of predominantly twenty-somethings, listening to their awful music while they drank too much, and forked over astronomical amounts for some lungfuls of fresh air.

"Should be." She offered him her brightest smile. Nash had promised her he'd make sure that security was notified, and his band's manager had been present for the conversation, so fingers crossed. There'd been a few hiccups in the past.

"What did you say your name was?"

"Castle. Jodi. I'm with the Ghost Boys."

"I've seen at least a dozen girls walk past with

bands around their wrists that say just that in last five minutes.”

Shit, did that mean he wasn't going to help her? What the fuck did she do then?

Not panic, that's what. Didn't stop her heart doing a wild gallop.

She would just have to find herself a quiet spot and hang until Nash was free to correct the oversight.

It'd get easier over time. It would. The people surrounding the band would get to know her. Would recognise her. Nash would introduce her, or one of the other guys. Finding herself fenced off from them had never been a problem before they signed with Stormland, but she'd been a part of the team then. Not so now. Now she was just their lead singer's cuddly fiancée. The person who, just like this guy, got looked at and dismissed.

“What does he see in her?”

“That's who Curtis Nash is engaged too?”

“She's all tits and arse and not in a good way.”

She'd heard it all. Mostly let it wash over her. It was that or dissolve into a puddle of anxieties. Six months ago, nobody even knew who Curtis Nash or the Ghost Boys were and the shape of his girlfriend hadn't mattered to anyone.

The guy began talking into his radio. He repeated her name. Good, he was doing his job rather than just discounting her.

It was crazy how fast everything had changed. How one miserable night on a farm in rural Valencia had birthed something so significant, and all because a bunch of fruit-picking nomads had saved her from an over-zesty orange merchant and wound up jamming together in a communal camping barn.

As the sole non-musical participant that night— she played about as well as Bob Dylan sang—she'd become their de facto manager. Well, more like a booking and merchandising assistant. She'd been a whizz at designing gig posters and merch. And zines. She'd created a whole string of them, although only the first three issues made it to print, because the word about them spread fast and their audiences kept on doubling in size.

They'd been playing together six weeks when Harry Storm swooped in and bound them all up in contracts. All of them except her. Girlfriends weren't part of the package deal. Future merchandising would be outsourced. Thank you. Goodbye.

The guys had all been shipped back to England to a recording studio the moment the contract ink was dry, leaving her to see out the rest of the picking season alone. She'd mourned the loss, convinced that the distance would put an end to their relationship. Then Nash had only gone and surprised her with a goddamned ring. Paid for it with his very first royalty cheque and had written, with a lot of help, a song that referenced it that was still dancing up and down the Spotify top ten.

The engagement ring glittered on her finger as she waited on security making their necessary checks. She didn't often wear it that way. Mostly, she kept it on a chain around her neck. It always felt alien on her finger and stressed her out over the possibility of losing it.

Plus, it caught on things, like all the time.

"Yes, she's here with three cats," the site official said into his radio. He turned to her. "Someone's going to come and collect you, but you're not supposed to have pets onsite. Guide dogs only."

She shrugged. What was she supposed to do? Abandon them at the gate? "They go everywhere with me."

The look she got in return made it clear if he hadn't already branded her a crazy cat lady he had now. She'd tried the emotional support line before. It never washed, even though it was true. Those cuties were her family.

Thirty seconds later, a guy in a golf buggy arrived. "You Jodi Castle?" he asked, not bothering to get out from behind the wheel. "Climb in. You can put your luggage in the back. I'm to take you to the band enclosure."

She struggled with the weight of her rucksack.

"What have you got in there, a tent?"

As a matter of fact, she did. For two reasons. She'd learned not to rely on others for her well-being. That included a guaranteed bed beside her fiancé. Secondly, it was where she lived, as in it was her permanent abode. Not everybody had the luxury of bricks and mortar. She'd been pitched in a patch of woodland just off the M62 until yesterday. Last night, she'd slept in the train station waiting room. Tonight, would hopefully be a bit more comfortable, although if the guys were to be believed, tour bus bunks left much to be desired.

Nash didn't like it, of course. Her roaming. Right after he'd put that rock on her finger, he'd insisted she move in with him and advocated for a ceremonial burning of her tent. She'd said she'd feel trapped if she did that. Poor Nash, he meant well, really wanted to do his best for her, but he didn't really understand where she'd come from. He thought her "troubles" were down to the episode in Valencia. It was hardly his fault; all she'd told him about her family was that she wasn't in touch with them anymore.

She suspected he was secretly pleased that he hadn't been obliged to do a meet and greet with them or ask her dad's permission to wed his daughter.

Did people even still do that? She supposed some did. The notion kind of revolted her. Smacked too much of being someone's property, and she wasn't and would never be that. Even if it meant humping her home around on her back.

Of course, nothing was as straightforward as it ought to have been. Golf man deposited her right by the Ghost Boys tour bus and immediately whizzed off, at which point the band's security, a snotty cow she didn't recognise, informed her she'd have to wait until one of the band confirmed her identify before letting her on the bus. This, despite the lanyard the bitch was holding with her name and picture on it.

Jodi: They won't let me on the bus.

Nash: Who won't?

Jodi: Your security. Not until you've vouched for me in person.

Nash: WTF. Okay, soz. Gonna be a while yet. Hopefully not too long though. Maybe get a brew somewhere?

Jodi: Yeah. I'll do that. Xx

With only two pounds thirty-seven in her pocket buying a drink was out of the question. It might have got her a drink on the high street, but the festival mark-up was eye-watering. Who the fuck paid nearly seven quid for a cuppa? Seemed that if she wanted a brew, she was going to have to make one for herself.

Jodi found herself a pitch in a quiet corner of the enclosure that no one else fancied, probably because it bordered both the recycling bins and a line of Portaloos. Also, it wasn't a very big space, but then, she didn't have a very big tent. If any of the bands were camping, they were doing so in style. The field was predominantly buses, along with an assortment of vans; everything from big white transits to ancient VW campervans. There were various pavilions scattered about too, clearly intended as chill out zones rather than for sleeping. Seemed, given that even the well-known acts had opted for sleeping aboard their buses rather than under canvas, that tour bus bunks weren't really so bad. Maybe Nash had just been thinking about how squashed up they'd be if they were sharing.

He turned up four hours later with a stupid grin on his face, wearing a shirt that looked like something someone's nan would own. It was off white, an odd choice for a field, and striped with muddy orange and black lines. Severely smudged eyeliner circled both his eyes, and he was wearing jeans that did absolutely nothing for his delicious butt, which was one of his better features. He'd also grown a considerably longer beard in the fortnight since she'd last seen him. Thick and dark like his brows. It served to pull your gaze down to his lips and away from his eyes.

"I see the stylist got to you." She bounced to her feet to greet him and accepted his tight hug. He smelled different too. Gone was the earthy citrus spice replaced by something sharper, cleaner, and considerably more manufactured.

"Babe. I'm sorry..."

"It's fine." She'd people watched, not that she communicated that. There didn't seem much point. "I got settled."

His brows knotted, and he cast her abode a suspect glance. "You're moving onto the bus though, right?"

"It gives us options, and the cats needed to stretch their legs."

"The cats... Aye, right. Always forget about your monsters."

He gave her another squeeze, pressing a kiss to the

top of her head. Nash wasn't a cat person. He tolerated her wee bundles of fluff but had never wrapped his head around her enduring love for them, or how she'd spend her hard-earned pennies on making sure they were fed, watered, and wormed ahead of her own comfort.

"What kept you? And what's with the eyeliner?"

While his hair had always been on the longer side, particularly on top, she'd never seen him even moisturise before, let alone don make-up.

"I'm just trialling it. The fans go wild for this sort of thing, so…"

She'd figured that much. "As long as it's still you underneath it."

"Course." He gave her what she interpreted as a shoulderless shrug, then beamed at her and went so far as to snatch her up in an unexpected hug. "We've hit the sodding jackpot, Jo. You're never gonna believe who we're touring with."

She wouldn't guess because she was still hopelessly out of touch with the music scene beyond a couple of favourites acts. "Who?"

"I told you we all thought Harry had something up his sleeve. Turns out it was bigger than we imagined."

His grin was eating his face now, prompting her to smile too even as her insides roiled with anxiety. If they were touring, and he'd only just confirmed that for definite, then what did that mean for her… for them? More time apart?

"It's not just gonna be UK dates." They'd been hoping for some European shows too, but apparently, they weren't quite so easy to score post Brexit.

"We're going worldwide, Jo! Us. Me, you, the guys… It's major. It's fucking amazing. We are so made."

"So, who is it you're supporting? Not Hammerjang or Trollforge, like you thought?"

He made a rude noise. "Small fry. We're bigger than both. Harry's only gone and fucking secured us a ride with Black Halo. Black *fucking* Halo, Jo! Not just for a few shows either, the rest of their European tour, with the possibility of it becoming the whole last leg. Eight months of dates across the globe." He rattled off a string of countries. "What do you think to that?"

Her heart made a panicked flutter, like it wanted to break out of her ribcage and fly off. "That's amazing," she croaked, and buried her face against his chest so he wouldn't see her panic.

Black Halo. Of all the bands... Of all the fucking bands in the world it had to be that one. Not that it mattered. She wouldn't meet them, and it wasn't like the other party was likely to remember her. He'd probably forgotten all about her and their adventures together. Black Halo's bass-player, Rock Giant...Paul Reed...He'd certainly never attempted to get in touch despite her leaving her number. Not that it mattered, or that she'd expected any other sort of treatment from a rock star. She'd been a night's entertainment, no more. But she'd liked him. Genuinely liked him. That was the real kick in the teeth.

Fact was, half the population were complete arseholes, and being a rock star didn't exempt you from that. It probably made you an even bigger one. Not that it mattered. That was the past. One she'd moved on from. Her future was set. Her and Nash. Nash and her. As evidenced by the hulking great rock on her finger.

Nash had been saying something, and she hadn't caught it.

"...wedding. I don't want to, but if we're touring..."

"Eight months isn't that long. There's no rush." Even as she said it, she got an itch in her bladder. It'd be hell. It was an eternity.

"Babe, it's an age. Too long by far until I can make you Mrs Nash."

Actually, she was planning on being Mrs Castle, but that was a conversation for another day.

"I've an idea."

Was she ready for ideas? The tour news was still reverberating and causing her stomach to cramp.

"There's a ring of standing stones just over there." He nodded his head in a vaguely leftwards direction. "Seems it's the equinox or something tonight."

Duh. "It's in the festival name."

"Yeah, all right, brains. Anyway, there's a guy conducting handfasting ceremonies, and I figured..." He raised his dark eyebrows suggestively.

Reckoned what? Wait. "Us? Get handfasted? But neither of us believe..."

"Come on. That part doesn't matter. It'll be fun, and we can tell people we've tied the knot. It won't be officially recognised, but it might shut Harry up." He nudged her elbow with his. "Come on, what do you say?"

"Harry? Shut him up about what? About me?" Harry Storm scared the fuck out of her. He stank of privilege, though she wasn't certain he realised that. He seemed to think he was one of the guys, but that's because he was a rich boy who couldn't conceive of not being universally loved.

Nash sighed and brushed his fingers through his hair leaving the top strands mushed in a way she loved but would probably upset whichever stylist had had their hands on him. "Apparently, we're a hotter commodity if we're all single. Don't get hung up on that. It's irrelevant. You're my girl, and it should be about the music anyway, not whether I'm available or wearing the right stuff."

She nodded, but the Nash she knew mooched around in T-shirts with stretched out of shape necklines, and either cargo pants or joggers and was forever losing socks so that virtually every pair he owned were mismatched.

"So, what do you think? We should do it, yes? Yes?"

She gave a tentative nod.

"Yes!" He smacked a kiss against her lips. "Cool. We'll have some drinks, have a chill, swear some oaths and..." He pulled her closer to his body, an arm around her neck, so that his breath whispered hot against her ear, laden with promises. "Then you and me are gonna enjoy some good old-fashioned rutting."

"In your tour bus bunk?" she wondered aloud.

"Maybe. Or maybe I'll have you right there in the middle of that there sacred ring of stones."

"Not sure Harry will approve of that."

TWO OF THE remaining three Ghost Boys drifted in their direction a few moments later.

Lee, typically head to foot in green, dirty blond hair resting loose about his shoulders, stopped five or six paces off and opened his arms wide. "Jo..." Duly prompted, she ran to him. The moment they were toe-to-toe he wrapped her in a killer embrace, squashing her tight against his chest and accidentally giving her a mouthful of his hair. As Jodi wiped the strands clear of her mouth, Balin embraced her from behind, his stubbly cheek colliding with hers. She scented beer on his breath.

"Good to see ya, Jo-Jo. Has Curtis here told you the news?"

"Just. It's amazing. Congrats. You guys are going to be so big. You're not going to want to know me." She summoned every scrap of enthusiasm she could muster to put into her expression. It seemed to do the trick. They all started backslapping one another again over their good luck. Not that it was pure luck... They were talented. That had been obvious from the off. Still, she loved these boys. They were her world, her family. She prayed fame wouldn't take them from her.

"...nah, it's our frankly audacious talent that's won us a cushty gig..."

"It's deserved," she said, nodding at Balin, the Ghost Boys bassist.

"It's down to you, Jo-Jo."

Sweet but untrue.

"You brought us together."

Ish. In circumstances she preferred not to dwell on.

"And you sort us all out."

She did her best. They were a shambles if left to their own devices.

Interestingly, both Balin and Lee were draped in their usual attire of cargo pants and washed-out T-shirts.

"How come you two haven't been made over?"

Balin scoffed. "What's the point in designer denim and shirts that cost two hundred quid a pop but don't look any different to the ten-quid knockoffs? Besides, they were probably made in the same sweatshop."

"What he said," Lee echoed. "Also, we're just the backdrop."

"Fuckers," Nash muttered.

"Man, there are limits to what I'm prepared to sacrifice to the gods of fame and fortune. They'll be prying my lucky shirt off my cold dead corpse. Plus, we're not toddlers, man. We don't need our mammies to dress us."

"Considering the shit mine used to pick out..." Lee shook his head.

Nash threw a bunch of shade at them, but it didn't

penetrate the shield of their mirth. If anything, his scowls made them mock all the harder.

Lee still had his arm slung around her shoulder. "You should come and see the bus. Height of luxury, it is. All mod cons. You'll be amazed." She didn't have the heart to tell him it wouldn't be the first tour bus interior she'd seen. That would necessitate diving into a part of her history she'd never shared with anyone. Still exerting his claim on her, Lee turned her about and nudged her towards their new home on wheels.

"Wait! I need to zip the tent up."

She wriggled free of his hold. While it was unlikely that anyone around here would be interested in her stuff, the weather might change at a moment's notice, and she'd rather her things stayed dry. The cats she confined to the inner pod. They'd be fine until she got back. They had everything they needed all set up how they liked it, and they were used to her wandering off. As long as they got their kibble and she didn't howl over the occasional mousy-froggy-baby birdie supplement, they were no bother.

Lee reclaimed her, despite Nash's attempt to snag her by the hand. "Where's Jez?" she asked after the band's drummer as they walked.

"You mean Pee-ter?" Nash said in a ridiculous voice, prompting chortles from both Lee and Balin. "Probably gone back to wallowing."

"Wallowing?"

"Oh, shit! Hasn't Curtis told you?" Balin stuck his head between them, only to about turn and level a tut at Nash. "How could you not tell her, man?"

"When?" Nash raised his hand in his defence. "I've barely had time to say hello before you two mugs arrived and commandeered her."

"He told me about Black Halo," Jodi said, and even managed to sound normal despite how jangly it made her feel inside. Shit! Did that mean they were here?

"Didn't tell you about Rune though, did he? Fuckwit only went and dumped him, didn't he?"

"No! No way. You're shitting me?" Rune was Jez's Norwegian boyfriend… ex-boyfriend. Painfully beautiful and painfully awkward. The pair of them had been inseparable the entire time she'd known them. They were so hopelessly in love with one another it hurt her head to think of them as separate entities.

"Why?"

She shot Nash an irritated look. Unless it'd literally happened in the last four hours, there was really no excuse for him not telling her.

"Wouldn't we all love to know?"

Lee rubbed his smooth jaw. "Claimed it wasn't going to work out, what with us being on tour and shit."

"Rune would never have minded that." Rune was the sweetest, gentlest, most amenable man she'd ever met, with one possible exception, but she wasn't thinking about him. Especially not now. Were Black Halo here? "Please tell me Harry Storm didn't have a hand in it."

"Harry? Why would Harry have anything to do with it?" Balin asked.

"Nah, it's all Jez," Lee said. "Maintains he didn't need anyone around cramping his style and that it'd been on the cards for a while, but let's just say he's not entirely convincing. Whatever the real reason, he's keeping schtum about it. So, to answer your question, he's probably knocking the hell out of a drum kit somewhere."

"Or banging something else," Nash said.

That was just horrid. Absolutely sickening. It made her belly flip-flop. And what did it say for her future with Nash if the hottest, sweetest couple around hadn't survived even five months of one of them hitting the limelight. The echoes of all the snarky remarks levelled at her when people learned she was with Nash circulated in her thoughts again.

"He's not actually out there shagging your fans though, right?"

Silence.

Damning silence.

Coupled with some awkward looks from Balin and Lee. Yeah... Seemed they'd all been scoring themselves some easy action.

"You're gross. Yuck." She shrugged Lee's arm from her shoulders.

"Why, 'cause we've indulged in a few hookups? How's that any different to before? I wasn't gross when I banged that barmaid back in Valencia—"

"Or when I had that three-day bender with the chick from Heidelberg and followed it with a blowjob from that lass from New Zealand—"

"And her sister, or was it her cousin, two days later? Think you must have hit the bass playing jackpot that week."

"Nah, it's just my natural charm and charisma."

"Stop grossing my fiancée out." Nash clouted them both around the head, which took a bit of effort given they were both way taller. It silenced them though, not that that was necessarily a good thing. It left space for her to think.

Jez and Rune had been a fixture way longer than her and Nash, and they'd done the whole long-distance thing on and off for ages too. Was this what she could expect in the future?

Nash dropped an awkward kiss on the top of her head as he pulled her away from Lee and claimed her hand. "Fuck me, you're actually wearing it." Nash lifted their clasped hands, so that the sun scintillated in the oversized rock on her finger.

"I resent that. I always wear it."

"You know what I mean."

"Well, I need to let all your new fans out there know what the score is, don't I?"

They reached the bus, and the security girl who'd given her a hard time earlier scowled at her as she handed over her lanyard.

"On which subject, guys, Jo and I are getting hitched tonight."

"Handfasted," she elaborated, in case they thought the actual wedding was this evening.

"You're seriously hitching yourself to this tosser?" Lee quipped. "Nah, I'm pleased for you, course I am." He slung an arm over her shoulder again. "Well, here it is. The old home on wheels. What do you think?"

"Wow." Hopefully, she'd instilled the appropriate amount of enthusiasm into her voice. Behind the driver's perch, the space opened out into a curved seating area, at the rear of which a cupboard-sized kitchen consisting of a microwave, fridge, and a cooker no bigger than her camping stove. The layout was nothing like the one on Bertha. Didn't stop her imagining a certain figure charging towards her with soap suds in his hair and the titchiest towel in existence secured around his hips.

"Bunks are back here." Balin opened the door to the rear section. A dark space with a single thin horizontally set rectangular window. There'd been a full-sized bed in this area on the Black Halo bus.

"Eight bunks?" she said.

"Yeah, and nine of us, ten with you." Balin shrugged like that didn't make for a mathematical inconsistency. "Us, you, the driver, our guitar tech, the tour manager, and two roadies stroke security bods."

"This one's ours." Nash patted the bed second up on the left.

"Great," she squeaked. She was definitely going to

have to persuade him to spend the night under canvas. If she stayed here, they'd be squashed together like corpses in a coffin. Plus—a tickle in her nose made her sneeze—beneath the blossomy scent of air freshener, there was an odour of blokey smells and dirty laundry. It didn't seem like anyone had thought to install any ventilation in the place or do any laundry. No skylight either to allow access onto the roof. She backed out of the space and settled on the oddly curved seating.

"So, what time's your ceremony?" Lee asked. He opened the fridge, thus confirming her suspicion that it was packed with beers with a few food items tucked in around the cans and bottles like an afterthought. Having dished them out, Lee lifted one of the seats to replace them with cans from their stash.

"Quarter to eleven," Nash confirmed. "Figured it'd still be quiet-ish. Tonight's headliners will still be on stage. People's attention will be pointed in that direction, not at us." He claimed Jodi's hand and sat right by her. "It's our moment. Not something we need to be sharing with the masses."

"There'll be other couples too though, right?" she asked.

He settled back more comfortably, legs falling apart. Maybe because he wasn't blessed in the height department, he always spread himself out. Another reason sharing his bunk might not work. "A few, maybe, I guess. But they're going to be focused on what they're doing, not that Curtis Nash is saying 'I do' to his fiancée."

"Is that what we say?"

Nash wriggled about so that he could fish something out of his back pocket. It turned out to be a folded piece of paper with a loose order of the ceremony and some example oaths. "We can amend them, make them personal to us. They don't have to be exactly as written." He'd already jotted a few such amendments in the margins, reducing his vows to:

These are the hands of your future husband, strong and full of love for you, that are holding yours, as you promise to love, cherish and obey him today, tomorrow, and forever. She smudged the pencil marks with her thumb, obliterating the obey part. It gave her shivers, reminding her too much of her father's dictatorial approach that had blighted her teenage years.

"You don't like that part?"

"It's a bit old-fashioned. We're entering into a partnership, we should be making the same vows, not setting it up to be lopsided from the start."

"Guess," he muttered, before stuffing the paper back into his pocket. "We can figure it out."

Balin announced he was going to chill in his bunk, and Lee muttered something about tracking down Jez, and left, taking his beer with him. Nash snuggled her closer. "Just us left."

"Yeah."

His lips pressed to the side of her neck, while his hand landed on her leg, then slid into the space between her thighs.

"Nash, is this really the place and time?" Lee hadn't even closed the bus door after he'd left. Anyone could walk in. Balin was still only next door, and the mean security lady was in earshot.

"What other time is there? This is going to be our life for the next eight months. We're going to be constantly on the road and surrounded by people."

"You say that like I'm going to be with you."

"Of course you're going to be with me. Why wouldn't you be?" He seemed genuinely puzzled. "Need you to keep me sorted."

"Nash, you know I'm shy about..."

"About the fact you're not as skinny as some

women. So! I don't mind, and it's not as if I'm asking to livestream you going all reverse cowgirl on me or anything." He curled a strand of her hair around one fingertip and used it as an anchor to draw her nearer, while his other followed the inner leg seam of her trousers upwards. Jodi shrugged him off.

"Is this because you had to wait around?"

"No."

"It is, isn't it? We were meeting Black Halo. Harry made sure we got a decent stretch of time with them. We're hot right now, but we're still small fry next to them. I don't think you get how important it was that we put in the work sucking up to them."

"It's not about you meeting Black Halo or the fact I couldn't get on your bus. It's not about anything. It's just... It's... this is too exposed. The door's open, anyone can fucking see in. It's not sexy. It makes me anxious."

"You know Balin got a girl off in a packed club the night before last. Put a hand up her skirt and frigged her in front of us and all her mates. And your bestie, Lee—"

She didn't want to hear it. "It's irrelevant, Nash." She wasn't some other girl, and she wasn't engaged to either Balin or Lee, much as she loved them both. She stood. "I'm going to take a walk."

"A walk?" He watched her from beneath his dark brows but didn't get up from the seat. "I thought we were going to hang together."

"You can come with me. I thought I might take a look at this stone circle. Make sure I know where I've got to be later while I stretch my legs."

"It doesn't seem like you're all that committed to the idea. Don't like the vows. Don't like the timing. Not interested in anything intimate, which is saying something considering absence is supposed to make the heart grow fonder."

Everyone knew that was a myth.

"I said yes, we should do it. I'm literally about to go and suss out the place. How does that make me not committed? Don't be an arse, Nash. Just because I said no to sex in a public location doesn't mean..."

He muttered something that she didn't quite catch and couldn't be bothered to ask him to repeat. "Maybe Jez has the right idea," he huffed.

Great, now he was having a full-on strop. She knew better than to argue with him when he got like this.

She left him to get over himself.

Give him an hour and he'd be all Jo-Jo, please can you do this for me? And have you seen my thingamabob, and my hoogeewotsit. And, argh, my lucky marble's missing, and I've looked everywhere, and I need you to work your lady magic to find it.

And because she loved him, she probably would.

AUL MADE GOOD use of the nearby treeline, then took his time strolling back to the bus. With the sun having burned off the morning mist, he could see more of the band enclosure. Plenty of buses were still shut up with their curtains drawn, but there were pockets of activity, and the site management were already in full organisational flow, waving in additional buses and trucks full of gear. Roadies for various groups were trotting about, or else whizzing past on push bikes. A few had golf buggies and seemed to think that made them it. He spotted Ronnie's manager setting up her deck chair under the awning of her camper van. He liked Lyra. Found her easy to relate to. For different reasons, they'd both had nomadic youths.

"Morning, Lyra."

"Mr Reed." She gave him a wave. It amused him that she always called him that and never anything else. "Hope you've not been leading my boy astray." She always reminded him to look out for Ronnie too. No leading him into temptation and that sort of stuff. Not that the kid needed his hand held. He had a nose for trouble. Not for getting into it, but for sniffing it out before it began, so he was there as an eyewitness to all the important events. If he wasn't also such a blabbermouth, then MI6 would surely have been on the phone by now eager to employ him as a secret agent. That, or Reuters. He'd have all the scoops.

"There was someone around a little while ago looking for you."

That brought him to a halt. He turned his head to regard her, unused to being a person that anyone looked for. "Really? Who?"

"Didn't leave a name. Looked like she was channelling Siouxsie Sioux circa 1982."

Chair sorted, Lyra pulled her laptop onto her knee, while Paul chewed over possibilities. The description narrowed it to any one of a number of people, most of whom, if he was being totally honest, he wasn't desperate to see. That is, he'd love to see them, but his bowels weren't so happy with the notion. "I'll keep an eye open. If she turns up again, you could always point her at the bus."

"I could, but as Graham is keen to remind me at every opportunity, I'm not your manager—"

"Just a splendid human being."

He startled a grin out of her. She shook her head. "And I'm not in the habit of pointing random ladies at rock stars. Nothing good ever comes of it. You're all bad news."

"Me?" He turned his hand towards his chest. "Bad news?"

"The worst sort."

He didn't take it personally. He knew she was generalising, and likely she'd seen enough during her years in the business and as a kid on the road with her dad to have solid evidence for the opinion. "Later, Lyra." He gave her a salute.

"Later, Mr Reed."

He'd barely gone twelve paces before said Siouxsie Sioux wannabe materialised. Although to be fair, he'd have said Patricia Morrison rather than Siouxsie.

"Well, if it isn't Paul Reed in the flesh," said the woman. "Found you, you elusive bugger."

She was accompanied by another figure he knew only too well.

The sun caught him straight in the eyes leaving him temporarily blinded to the waif he nevertheless opened his arms to. She dived into his embrace, legs wrapped around his hips, clinging on tight for a solid minute. There was barely anything to her, hardly a weight in his arms, but the press of her lips against his cheek was real, as was the familiar jasmine scent of her, and that made him smile.

"Hello, E. How are you doing?" he said after he'd started to feel rather like a stately oak being assaulted by a druid.

"Do you know how many laps of this dung heap I've done trying to find your giantness?"

"No more than two, I reckon."

She tipped her head back to look at him, legs still wrapped around his waist as she clung to him like a baby monkey. "Four. Four laps. I've been heckled, I've been propositioned, I have the names of three guys who can get me anything, and had the worst tofu burger I've ever had the misfortune of encountering."

"It was like toasted carpet with a side of woolly bears," her companion added.

"Eloise." He acknowledged her with a nod, but she leaned in for a kiss, even though he still had Elspeth in his arms. No doubt he now had a black lip print on his jaw.

"Tell me your brekkie was equally shit," Elspeth said.

"Spook cooked. Thus, it was perfection." He smacked his lips in appreciation.

Elspeth groaned in frustration.

Eloise gave a sigh. "To be expected, I suppose. The rest of the man's divine, so, of course his cooking is too. Although, he's also now taken, if the gossips are to be believed." She gave a sorrowful sigh. "Dish, Paul. I mean, what's that about? I thought you were putting in a good word for me." She crooked one sharply winged eyebrow.

"For you?" he gasped in mock horror as Elspeth finally relinquished her grip on him and slithered down his body onto terra firma. "I swear it was Sev who asked. I gave him the full spiel, not that he bit."

"You did not mistake me for my sister," Eloise huffed, then poked his midriff, where his babydoll fit T-shirt was showing an inch of skin between its hem and the waistband of his jeans. "Still bouncy, I see."

"Yup, and you're still—"

"Fantastic. Gorgeous. And the fairest of the three."

He laughed along with her. As one of triplets, there was always a competition of some fashion being waged between her and her sisters. They hadn't seen one another in a hot minute, not since the birthday get together his folks had organised right around the time Spook took his leave of absence. He'd aged another year since then. But that was time for you, it had a way of eating up moments, so before you knew it, that promise to catch-up was at least eighteen months overdue.

"So, how are you doing?"

Eloise laughed at him. "I'm in a soon to be muddy field that looks exactly the same as every other muddy field I've ever had the pleasure of occupying, how do you think?"

"Bloody awesome."

"Bloody awesome," she returned in a deadpan tone, before they both cracked smiles.

"And you E?" He winced even as he asked, afraid of the answer. That night, two years gone, was forever etched into his brain. The dark shadow of Xane's body silhouetted against the night sky; her limp body cradled in his arms. The two of them soaked through and her as pale as if she'd been drained dry. An involuntary shiver tickled his spine. Hard not to recall how clammy she'd felt, or to hear the insistent *drip...drip...drip* of the water. The noise had been due to the water falling off their clothes, but his brain, then and now, said otherwise.

She stuck her tongue out at him, before wrapping her tiny sprite-like form about his person again. Warm and very much alive. He was pleased to see she'd gone blonde again, and was rocking some colours, be they rather autumnal tones. In fact, she seemed to be leaning into the hedge witch aesthetics. It was different to what he'd grown used to, harkened back to a time before Black Halo, before the gothic aesthetics took over, when they were just kids, and he hadn't felt like there were brambles between them. But she looked better for it, and that he liked. The last few times they'd met in person, she'd resembled a walking corpse, but there was a blush of colour in her cheeks now, and her smile was honest and broad. "I'm good, Paul."

"Good. It's fucking good to see you, E." He gave her another squeeze, emotions still conflicted.

Eloise coughed.

Prompting him to amend his remark. "It's fucking good to see both of you."

"You've been missed. We thought you'd have made it to Mayfest at least, after you failed to show your face last Christmas."

And there it was, the scrape of thorns and the reminder that he hadn't been doing his duty. There'd just been such a lot on. Things to contend with; Spook's disappearance, his return, and them then being holed up to record their latest album.

"You know how it is."

"I do. You're avoiding us."

"As if."

She gave him a stern look that said, *ha*, you don't fool me, but at least she didn't go all prosecuting lawyer on him and make him stage a defence.

Elspeth linked arms with him, prompting Eloise to claim his other arm, which wasn't comfortable for any of them, given he was tall, and they were both titchy. He wriggled out of their holds and looped his arms around their shoulders instead. They all started strolling because standing still at a festival was never a good idea. Someone always asked you for something, offered you something, or else you sank up to your shins. Lyra saw them and shook her head. He guessed he was living up to the rock star stereotype, at least to an outside observer. The dew was barely dry, and he already had a girl on each arm. Shame that he had no intention of ever banging either of them. They were practically his sisters.

"How are they all, or shouldn't I ask?" Elspeth ventured after a few paces. She didn't look at the Black Halo bus parked behind them, but he knew who she was enquiring about.

"Why shouldn't you ask?" While it was true that she hadn't departed the band on the best of terms, they'd still been her friends, her family for years. "They're good. Not gonna lie, things were rough for a while, but they're good now." The major turning point had come at the end of February, and then again as the Beltane fires burned. "It's all become weirdly settled and domestic."

"All coupled and throupled up, so I've heard."

Precisely. He gave a nod. It was on the tip of his tongue to say that she'd started the settling down trend, but he didn't want to bring a blight upon the moment by reminding her of her loss. She and Steve had been married barely five days before his tragic death, and this was the first time he'd seen her and thought she might eventually climb out from under the blanket of grief that had been smothering her ever since.

"At least you're still reliably nomadic and unattached."

He cocked a brow.

"Oh, come off it. Don't try that shit with me, Paul Reed. I know you. And what would I do if you were pre-occupied with some other lass?"

"E, I love you, but..."

She cackled, and dug a pointy elbow into his middle, before straining onto tiptoes to plant a kiss on his cheek. He still had to lean forward obligingly for her to manage it. "I'm pulling your leg, mate, and you know it. Also, you need to shave. You've a chin like sandpaper." She hooked her arm around his again, making it difficult for him to test his bristliness.

"Where we going?" he asked after a moment or two. They seemed to be steering him, subtly, but purposefully, towards the opposite end of the band enclosure. There were fewer big buses at this end of the field and more tents nestled between the trees. Numerous people nodded to them as they passed by. He recognised a lot of old-timers from his parent's generation, which honestly was a little odd, this being a rock festival and his mum and dad traditional folkies.

He nodded at guys from a few other bands and exchanged a passing hand slap with Mikey Ruin of Wrath & Ruin who he'd met while touring with Ronnie the previous year. The bit that struck him as really odd were the number of young kids hanging around. Most of them on phones, a few kicking a ball around. He'd always toured with his parents, but that wasn't usual.

"Where did all the kiddies come from?" he asked.

Eloise gave a tut. "Didn't your mummy and daddy explain about the birds and bees to you?"

Honestly, they hadn't. There'd never been a need. He'd been surrounded by people and animals his whole life. Seemed there was more than a little bit of domesticity going on outside of Black Halo too. Then again, the rock business wasn't the same scene it'd been in the past. The rebelliousness of it largely quashed by the men in suits. It was all about bleeding as much money out of a song or artist as you could these days. The decline in the number of new bands coming through or even being signed being the most depressing indicator of that fact. The industry would rather deal with individual artists than bands, much easier to negotiate with one person than five guys with often contradictory views, and use samples, computers, and session musicians for the rest.

"They're the result of getting laid. You remember what that is, right, big guy?" Elspeth said.

"Vaguely." Hard not to recall when he was surrounded by his constantly fornicating band mates.

"Dry patch?"

He shrugged. The other thing about being surrounded by people in committed relationships, was that there were a lot fewer random backstage visitors these days, therefore a lot fewer opportunities for scoring some fun. While he'd never been the sort of manwhore that Xane had been, his sex life had been pretty rockin'. Not so much now. He wasn't about to send the roadies out to snag him some ego boosters. If he was going to end up in some lass's knickers, he wanted it to be due to a genuine connection not because Cave Troll had given her a lammy.

Elspeth tugged his arm a little harder, leading him toward the smell of wood smoke and mead. "Come on, let's see if we can't get this rock legend laid."

"Less of the legend, please. It makes me sound decrepit, and I'm not old. Reserve the legend thing for mine and Eloise's folks, eh?"

"Aw, not so much a dry patch as a dry season."

He squished his lips into a pucker, which made her laugh. God, how amazing was it to hear that sound, and to see her smiling rather than wafting around like a stiff breeze would scatter her composite parts? He'd forgive her the jibes, the same as he'd forgiven her for pretty much everything since she stole a stash of pinecones from under his nose when they were five.

"You look good, E. You seem…"

"Don't," she warned, cutting him off. "I'm taking each day as it comes, and it's mostly working, but it's a micron-fine cushion seeing me through that won't take much bursting."

"Sorry."

"The drugs don't hurt either."

He pitched her a wary stare not sure if she was being serious. Shock ricocheted through his innards when he realised she probably was.

Elspeth levered her elbow again. "Watch it, Captain Uptight, that looked horribly like a judgy face."

Drugs were another of those things that had circled around him endlessly the whole of his life and had failed to entice him simply by being so ubiquitous and easily obtained. He valued rarity, the unobtainable, not shit that was as common as bread. Mind you, there'd been times when bread had definitely been harder to come by than an easy high, and it wasn't as if he'd never partaken.

"For depression," she said, setting him straight, "although Eloise has a string of numbers if you want something harder."

"They're in my little black book." She patted a virtually invisible pocket in her gothic ensemble, mostly black, with a few white stripes and a flash of muddy purple. "So handy when you need a number for those pesky scam callers."

"You give telemarketers dealers' numbers?"

"Only the ones who try. I don't give my numbers out to just anyone, you know. I like to make them work for it."

"It's impressive," Elspeth confirmed. "She had some guy the other day convinced she was going to refurbish her whole kitchen."

Eloise cackled in glee. "I had to let him down in the end. He just couldn't accommodate my electric cauldron and didn't seem to grasp that I spend ninety per cent of my life in other people's houses, so probably didn't need a thirty grand do-over, or that vinyl oak effect laminate would look shit in my thatched shepherd's hut."

He grinned along with the girls' laughter, even though it didn't seem that funny.

Time to change the subject. "Why are you two here?" Of all the festivals they might have turned up at, why here and now? Not to mention they were in the band enclosure, and to his knowledge neither of them were currently in a band, so they had to be mooching along with some other outfit.

Eloise chose that moment to skip ahead a few paces. She started walking backwards. Honestly, if he hadn't known her so well, he'd have said she was channelling her sister today. It was the hair. Definitely the hair. Lulu normally did the hairsprayed spikes, Eloise usually ironed her hair straight, and Sev, the last he'd seen her, was sporting a red and black two-tone effect complete with heavy fringe.

"The fact you need to ask shows how out of touch you are. Dad got the band back together, *pfft*, eight months ago. It'd be embarrassing, if the world didn't think watching a few old geezers play was so fucking cool."

"Toys in the Attic reformed?"

"Yeah!" She raised her arms for emphasis, which also served to show off her batwing sleeves. "Mad, eh? Sev's helping dad out with the logistics, and Lulu's about somewhere, doing something. I'm the official spokesperson, and Elspeth here—"

"Is tagging along for the ride and reminding them all this is no longer the eighties, or even the nineties, and things are done a little differently in the modern age."

"The epic falling out is all forgotten, then?"

Both women shrugged. They all knew why goth pioneers Toys in the Attic had split. It'd been regurgitated at every gathering they'd attended since being small. The gist was that the D'Amon brothers couldn't agree on something or other that forever remained vague, and weirdly, they'd kept talking while the third member of their line-up had disappeared into the weeds. He'd never met her.

"So, what's Nellie Strife like?"

"Cool," they both replied without pause, and laughed.

"She is cool," Eloise added. "I like her a lot. Both Dad and Uncle Damon fawn over her like a couple of schoolboys. It's cute, and weird. But you can see for yourselves if, you know, you find time in your busy rock star schedule to hang out with your besties."

"Is that not what I'm doing now?"

Both women considered this with their heads tilted. Then, having reached a decision, they dragged him toward a fortress-like pavilion made of black canvass and trimmed so it looked like it had turrets. Eloise wafted past security without pausing and ushered them in. He almost wished the guy on the door had insisted on carding them. It'd have given him an excuse to make an exit.

It wasn't that he had anything against the D'Amon clan. In fact, he was rather fond of them. They were his people. Slightly wacky, outside the norms of society, but not so strange that you were left battered by the experience of hanging with them. He'd shared a moment or two with the middle sister, Sev, back in their teenage years. Nothing serious; even by fifteen they'd both realised holding on too fast to another person was a recipe for heartache. No, what concerned him here was the possibility of surprises of the unwelcome kind. The kind that would put him on the spot and crush the carefully constructed cocoon he'd created.

Thankfully, his entrance didn't prompt any sort of scream, or hug cavalcade. Thus, he could shove his justifications to the back of his mind again and purge his unease with a shake.

Inside was carpeted and cosy. A bit gloomy, but that was goths for you, and it wasn't like the Black Halo colour palette was all that different. Eloise's sister, and his one-time kissing friend Severina, stood off to the left, hunched over a tablet pointing out something to their Uncle Damon, while their father Steve D'Amon lounged on a plush velvet couch near the central pole, nursing what looked like a pint of swamp juice. He gestured them over and they exchanged hand clasps, before he offered Paul a seat, and a spinach smoothie.

"Good for colonic health. I can have one of the girls rustle you one up. Swear by them. Not bad with a splash of vodka, either."

"Dad!" Eloise settled in beside him, her fishnet stockings brushing his denim-clad legs. "Is your liver not pickled enough?"

Steve sighed.

Paul said, "Yeah, I'm good, thanks."

"Haven't seen your face in a bit. Busy schedule?"

Paul nodded. He was genuinely busy. He'd gone from touring with Ronnie, to recording Black Halo's latest album, to touring again with barely a break between. So, sure, he'd missed a few semi-important gatherings, and a wedding, but these things happened. Evidently, his absences had totted up enough for people to have started wondering though. He'd have to make sure he quietened their interest before anyone started inventing reasons for his absence. One thing he'd learned young and learned well, was that people loved to gossip about anything and everything, but about each other most of all. So, if you didn't want speculative rumours spreading about your doings, you had to make sure to feed them just enough of what they wanted to hear so that they felt in the know enough not to make shit up in your absence.

As he lacked both a watch, and currently, his phone, he turned Eloise's wrist to check the time. Today was mostly for chilling, except for a couple of things Sally had lined up with some internet creators and a meet and greet with their support for the next leg of the tour. The music press wouldn't get time with them until tomorrow. It'd be mundane stuff, all platitudes, and no substance. *Yeah, great line up, rocking atmosphere, album's doing well.* All that stuff. The only excitement would arise from Ronnie opening his mouth at the wrong moment and blurting something they'd have strangled anyone else for saying. He was armed and ready for that though. He'd found a supply of life-sized jelly toads in a service station when they'd stopped for a slash and because

Ash wanted a sticker book. Who'd even known those things still existed?

"So, you're back," he said to Steve. "I thought you were retired from this gig."

Steve, white rather than blond these days, refreshed himself with another slurp of swamp goop. "Aye, but there's no helping it when the muse comes calling."

"You're releasing new stuff?" That did surprise him. He'd figured this reunion was just a victory lap to relive their heyday before they settled into true retirement.

"That's the plan. The core fans are psyched for it, and we've picked up a ton of new listeners since *It's No Treason* got featured on that Netflix show last year."

He wasn't much of a TV watcher, having grown up without one, so he hadn't understood why the track had started getting so much airplay again until Ronnie had brought him up to speed. Actually, how the fuck had Ronnie not been aware of the reunion?

Or maybe he was and just hadn't thought it worth mentioning. He guessed he'd never said anything to allude to him having a connection to them. Just as well or he'd have had a running Ronnie-style commentary about their every move.

"When are you up?" he asked Damon.

"Tomorrow, six-ish," Severina answered for him from across the tent. "No use asking him, he can't tell the fucking time."

"Tomorrow at six," Steve echoed. To his daughter he said, "Mind your tongue, young lady."

She shot him a middle finger the moment his head turned back to Paul. Some things never changed. Steve had taught all his daughters how to swear effectively. If they were gonna do it, they were gonna do it well, being his reasoning. The lessons had run right alongside how to properly kick idiots in the nuts. He'd called it life-skill 101 and forbidden any of them to ever fuck a musician. Naturally, they all did the precise opposite. Just as well. Steve would have been beside himself if he'd learned they were fucking tech bros.

"Cool. I should manage to catch it, then." As headliners, Black Halo weren't due on stage until ten past nine and knowing how these things usually panned out it'd be more like quarter or even twenty past.

"I tried to get your folks to come." Steve leaned forward, swamp juice still in hand, a smear of it clinging to his upper lip. "They couldn't make it work. Saw them a couple of weeks back."

Inwardly, Paul jolted, though he took pains to keep his reaction off his face. A rock festival wasn't their scene. His folks weren't even goths or goth adjacent like Toys in the Attic, they were traditional folkies. Steve and Damon making a comeback was hardly enough to bring them here, even if they had all been hanging together since the late seventies.

"Debs seemed keen to see you. Mentioned you've not been around for a while."

Aw fuck, here it came.

"Yeah. I need to eke out time for a visit. You know how it is. This last year's been insane, and we've not got a real break coming up until the end of the tour."

"That so?" Steve's blue eyes burned him with the intensity that had won Toys in the Attic scores of fans ever since their first intensely atmospheric music video.

Elspeth circled her arms around his neck from behind. Her lips brushed the crown of his head, followed by her hand. "Oo, soft," she said of his buzz cut. She leaned in closer, mouth to his ear. "What's with the knots in your nuts?"

"Excuse me?" He knew what she meant. He'd been wound tight from the moment he stepped inside this tent. How she knew that he was less certain about, but she proved her point by digging her fingers into his shoulders. His muscles were indeed full of knots that resisted her massaging. "I slept like shit. Bus is loud. You know how it is. Probably need to go for a run and work it off."

She made the appropriate noises, but he sensed she was unconvinced. Felt they were all viewing him like he was flashing up an anomaly warning. Honestly, it was a relief when Damon wandered over and started grilling him about recording studios. Where was still open? Who was the best for what? He gave Ric's Liddell Island studios a plug. They both waxed lyrical about Rockfield for a few minutes, before he got asked about Stormland, but couldn't offer anything constructive having never been there. At the end he gave DeathScythe a plug too, purely because Allegra had worked... still worked there on and off.

Forty minutes passed before he figured he ought to make a move before someone came looking for him. He'd done two rounds of goodbyes and reached the tent entrance, only for Damon to pull him to one side. "How are you set for October?"

He regurgitated the stuff about his tour schedule.

"Not too far away, then," Damon insisted, one hand fast around Paul's lower arm. "Make sure you get to the Samhain Fire Festival. I can't say why, but I'm telling you, you need to be there. No excuses. If you miss this..." He finished by shaking his head.

"I'll do what I can, man but—"

"Nix that right now. They'll be fucking gutted if you're not there, so make sure you fucking are, and don't be a whiny arse about it. I don't give a shit why you've been keeping your distance, get over it. In fact, if you've any fucking soul, show your face before then too. They don't deserve this, Paul. They taught you better than this."

He wasn't sure he had a response that didn't just dig him into a deeper hole, so he kept his mouth shut, and left with his cheeks burning.

The fact was, Black Halo had a five-day break scheduled right after the Norwegian leg of the tour, but he and Ronnie had some sightseeing planned, and he'd snagged a cabin that promised an entirely off grid experience. Besides, his folks were probably busy swimming with pigs, or grooming alpacas, or contributing to some rewilding project somewhere.

He hadn't realised that Elspeth had followed him out until he was halfway back to the bus.

"E?"

"Paul." She swallowed, then offered him a terse smile. "Don't be a stranger because of whatever Damon said."

Yeah, he didn't see himself making time to hang out. Was no longer sure he even wanted to watch their set. "You know where to find me."

She snorted.

Okay, fair. She wasn't about to breeze aboard her former band's bus for a random catch up. Leastways, not uninvited by one of them that wasn't him. Too awkward. He knew the gist of what had been said the last time she and Xane had spoken, but that hadn't pressed reset on all the pain. There remained slights on both sides that wouldn't easily be forgiven and that would make any sort of gathering they were both at distinctly uncomfortable. Nor did he have a grand plan for how to go about changing that. Time, he guessed. It was supposed to heal all. He wasn't sure that was true. Meanwhile, maintaining distance made for less drama, and even though he relished a bit of excitement after Damon's lecture, the band wouldn't benefit from more Elspeth drama.

"I'll see. Who knows how things will pan out. You know how it is."

"I do." She stretched up on tiptoes again to press a kiss to his jaw. Then gave him a hug. "Miss you," she said, as she pulled away. "I miss our adventures."

It'd been a very long time since they'd shared what he'd describe as an adventure. "Me too, E. Me too."

He left her there, just about in sight of the tour bus, but certainly not close enough so that anyone would ever think she was interested in or connected to the band to which it belonged. He only looked back once he reached the bus steps. By then she was gone and miraculously, the shower on the bus was free. He stayed in there until the water ran out.

FORAGING HAD TURNED up one old boot, three tubs of ripe blackberries, fourteen random plastic items, now deposited in the site's recycling bins, seventeen sloes, some chanterelles, and a bag of rosehips courtesy of Ash and Ginny. Ronnie having been responsible for the old boot, Spook the sloes and chanterelles, and Xane and Luthor the blackberries and plastic.

"Not bad, not bad." Paul offered the congratulations as he dished out bottles of Welsh cider in reward. "Not sure the boot really counts though does it, mate? It's not exactly edible or even useful. If it were a pair, then maybe."

Ronnie stuck out his tongue, but his expression soon twisted into a pout when Paul continued to shake his head.

"You need to do better."

"I couldn't find anything, and I wasn't sure about

the berries. Didn't want to risk killing anyone," Ronnie whined.

"There's a shed load of nettles over there," Luthor helpfully waved a hand in their general direction.

"Nettles. What use are they? Plus, I'll get stung."

Nettles had loads of uses.

"Gloves," Ash helpfully offered a pair, be them of the fingerless mitten variety that at a guess someone had handmade him. They were baby-shit green with a motif of flamingo pink mice and had Danger Mouse written across the knuckles. He was going to remark upon their ugliness, but suddenly thought, what if Ginny had crocheted them? Then the remark would land him in deep shit, and he didn't feel like wallowing in poo. Bad enough that he still had Damon's lecture noodling about in his head.

Ronnie sniffed at the offered gloves, and continued to pout, which made him look cute rather than sour faced. He turned on the puppy dog charm too, rounding his kohl-enhanced eyes. Paul remained resolutely unswayed.

"Sorry, but rules are rules. You need to do your part. This is not an acceptable contribution. No cider or s'mores for you."

"But...but..."

"Just offer him a blowjob," someone called.

Xane, Paul suspected, but it might have been Cave Troll who was lurking around in the background like some sort of hulking bodyguard making sure their campfire didn't attract any unwanted visitors. Honestly, a few extra visitors might have been a welcome distraction, providing they came bearing the appropriate offerings of course. Things were feeling rather insular. Maybe he ought to have sent invitations over to some of the other groups. Except, it would have been difficult to do that without putting

Toys in the Attic at the top of that list. And he... Well, he didn't wanna.

"Do blowjobs count?" one of the ladies asked. He wasn't paying enough attention to notice who. "I wasn't told that was an option."

"Do you really want to be wrapping your mouth around the monster he's harbouring?" Cave Troll replied.

"She's not wrapping her mouth around his cock," Ash said over the top of various mutterings. Ah, so Ginny, then.

"Already did, hun. Sorry to remind you, and all..."

Ash grouched. Ginny gave him a pat on the head, then hugged his arm. Within a couple of seconds, they were smooching. And that was all it took for the rest of his band mates to start getting cosy with their lovers too, leaving him and Ronnie trying to find neutral positions in which to focus their gazes.

Okay, Ronnie was outright gawping, but he didn't need a ringside view of all the tongue sandwiches. It was great that they were all happy, but man... He pried the top off one of the ciders and flopped onto the blanket he'd laid out. For several minutes, he did nothing but swig his drink and stare into the flames. Gawd, he didn't half miss the old days, when the guys were up for shits and giggles of an evening, and everyone would have been in if he'd suggested a daft game or... Or maybe he was pinning that on them. What was to say they wouldn't still be up for some silliness? It's not like he'd asked, and lord knows when you were on the road, you needed those moments of levity.

Which was why that dumb remark about the blowjob sprouted legs and ran wild right through multiple rounds of storytelling, when it ought to have been forgotten. It was like an echo doing its thing in a bloody loop. Xane's creepy as fuck ghost story somehow referenced it. Same with Spook's headless man offering that had them all howling so much, there were tears glistening on people's cheeks. He decided they'd just unanimously decided it was pick on Paul night, which mean the best option was to roll with it, and accept it as intended, as a bit of harmless fun.

It did niggle though. Maybe because it'd been so long since anyone had blown him. Ronnie started squirming around beside him, too. Hard to tell if that was due to the convo though, or just typical Ronnie restlessness.

Paul cracked open another bottle and offered him it. "Suppose I can let you have one, in the spirit of community and whatnot." Mabon wasn't just about harvesting. It was about forging community and sharing your bounty with those around you who weren't so fortunate, because maybe they'd be around for you when you needed support too. Values his parents had drummed into him from an early age. His upbringing might have been atypical and excessively free range, but his parents had never left him in any doubt about the things that mattered. It boiled down to: if you could make someone else's life better in some way, by sharing your time, or something you had and they didn't, then that's what you did. And they'd do the same for you when you needed help. It's why he never wasted energy worrying about them. Karma, or whatever you wanted to call it, would make sure they were taken care of.

Ronnie closed his fist around the neck of the offered bottle and beamed at him. "Sure I don't need to blow you first?"

Like he said, legs that wouldn't die.

"Not necessary, Ron."

"Sure? I don't want you thinking I'm not contributing properly."

"I don't."

"Well, the offer stands."

"Let it go, Ronnie. I'm not so desperate for a shag that I need to accept blowjobs from a bandmate." Just over yonder, there were literally hundreds of pretty ladies who'd probably be only too happy to make him happy. If he could be arsed to go schmooze them. Which, honestly, he couldn't. He wasn't in the mood. Cider normally lifted his spirits, but tonight, it felt like he was stuck in the sediment.

He pried the top off another bottle for himself and let the taste of mouldering fruits settle on his tongue.

"Is that a no, then?"

"Yeah, it's a no."

Ronnie's grin remained firmly fixed in place, while he consciously or unconsciously made suggestive hand movements around the neck of his drink. If it'd been one of the other guys, he'd have confidently said it was deliberate. With Ronnie, hard to tell. The boy was forever fiddling with things. Take away the bottle and he'd be squishing and eating one of the multiple bags of gummy sweets secreted about his person.

"Is that cause your knob's still sore?"

Good grief! "Give it a break, eh?" While he'd been abstinent for a stint while his most recent set of piercings healed, they'd done so nicely weeks ago. "You don't even want to blow me."

Ronnie's head came up immediately. "Says who? I never said. Did someone else? I don't like it when people speak for me."

"Ron, chill."

Too late, Ronnie had already fixated on the idea.

"Yeah, but I don't want you to think—"

"I'm not thinking anything."

"Except you obviously are, because you wouldn't have said no, definitively no, if you hadn't thought about it, and you wouldn't have said that I didn't want to, if someone hadn't given you that impression. That wasn't me. I've not implied that."

"Okay. Got ya. You know Xane was joking?"

"Yeah," Ronnie said in a way that left him uncertain if he did actually know that. "But maybe I wasn't. What if I've been harbouring secret fantasies and psyching myself up to this moment, and now you're crushing my sweet little sugar heart with your offhanded dismissal?"

"Am I?"

Ronnie could talk the legs off a spider while simultaneously writing a hit single. He was a confusing sod, and frequently contradictory. The question though, made him pause long enough to give it some actual consideration.

"You might be. That is, I'm curious. I've not blown anyone with a pierced knob before."

"There's a darn sight more than one bit of metal ribbing his cock," Alle remarked from over to their right, where she was sitting snuggled under Spook's leather jacket, or maybe it was Xane's jacket that Spook had commandeered. When the heck had they all started borrowing clothes like they were teenaged girls?

"Should we ask how you know that?" Xane's petite girlfriend asked.

Alle blushed beneath her freckles. "Um..." She turned to Spook. "You don't mind that I've seen his cock, do you?"

Spook shrugged. "You'd already seen it."

"Hands up anyone who hasn't seen Rock Giant's cock?" Ash said.

A quick show of hands proved that was precisely zero out of the people currently present.

"Do the bars not catch on stuff?" Dani asked. She'd come out of her shell recently and was more likely to speak up than hide behind a pair of Xane's shades and hope nobody noticed her. "I'm curious whether Ronnie will be risking his teeth."

Ronnie had particularly nice teeth. Lord knows how, given the amount of sugar he consumed.

"Irrelevant. He's not blowing me." Why wouldn't they let this die? Did he have 'I'm desperate' stamped across his brow? He rubbed his forehead just in case someone had inked it there and he hadn't noticed. And he really wasn't desperate.

"I think I should be offended." Ronnie fetched out his pet lip.

Goddess, save him! He rolled his eyes skyward.

"Plus, who can resist that much cute?" Xane remarked.

Proving that his crush on their lead singer was still alive and strong, Ronnie immediately made flirty faces across the fire at Xane.

"He can." Dani shot Ronnie a death glare. "What have I told you about propositioning my boyfriend?"

"That you'll pull my arms and legs off and bury me in a shallow grave," Ronnie dutifully recited.

"And she's not joking, mate." Xane gave his girlfriend a cuddle and kissed her upturned face.

"I think the question is can Rock Giant resist?" Ginny said, contributing yet more sticks to the fire.

He needed to knock this on the head, or it was going to run forever. "Guys, he's hardly my type. No offence, mate."

"None taken this time," Ronnie settled his head on Paul's lap. "Unless you're saying you wouldn't get it up if it was me. Then I might be hurt. I'm not that unattractive."

The cheeky imp was the exact opposite, and he knew it.

"Don't you think it might be a bit weird tomorrow, when you're not wasted on cider?"

"When isn't he weird?"

"Shut up, Ash. I'm not wasted. I've barely had a drop." Ronnie had in fact only had a couple of swigs from the one Paul had opened for him. He, on the other hand, was possibly a little bit tipsy, because he was currently at fifty-fifty on saying sod it, fine, get on with it if it's going to make you happy, and only his recent brush with Elspeth was really stacked on the against side. Now, when things were finally settled, he wasn't about to do owt that'd jeopardise the internal stability of the band. P.S., he ought to mention she was around but couldn't face the inevitable downer that would result.

"It's just a friendly bro-job you're offering, right, Ronnie?" Xane was stirring again, evidenced by the fact he was completely straight faced.

"Right," Ronnie chirped from Paul's lap. "Just a friendly bro-job between friends. Where's the harm in it?"

"Fine. Look, if you wanna blow me, blow me."

"For real?" Ronnie rolled onto his stomach. His pointy chin dug into Paul's thigh as he gazed along his body.

"Wait a minute." Alle whistled. "I thought you were straight, or at least rock star straight."

"What the fuck is rock star straight?" Ash asked.

"He just rolls with the flow, don't you mate?" Xane laughed and flashed everyone a glimpse of his tongue-stud. "Also, I give fucking good blowjobs, which is why no bugger in their right mind turns them down. Even 'straight' boys."

"What I want to know is when this blowjob between you and him occurred?" Ginny asked.

"Way back," Xane replied.

It had been a tidy while ago, back when they still had their original line-up, before Xane's stint in rehab, and Bertha's drowning. His memory got snagged up in the recollection of Bertha's demise. Those twelve or so hours of him being a hostage lived rent free in his head as a top tier experience. Not that any of the guys knew about it. Three years on, and he'd never breathed a word about that night. They all thought *he'd* stranded them at the services and drowned Bertha, and he was good with that. It was his little secret. His and his hijacker's—crazy, captivating Jodi Castle. Plus, Bertha Bus II was way nicer.

What was Jodi Castle doing with her life now? Something equally demented? She'd been a catastrophe on legs. Maybe that's why he'd liked her. And he'd liked her a lot. She'd needed someone to fucking save her from herself, and he'd enjoyed stepping up for the few hours they'd spent together. Maybe it was nostalgia, but his cock got perky at the thought of her, and not just because she'd been blessed with huge tracts of land.

"Paul?" Alle prompted.

"Where? Huh? Oh, what, me and Xane?"

Conveniently, Spook stepped in and answered for him. "It was at the festival where Ash and Steve got stuck in a Portaloo and it rained so incessantly the stage was practically floating."

Yeah, that was right. No one bothered asking how Spook knew. He probably had photographic evidence of the event stuck into a scrapbook.

"And you?" Ginny nudged her hubby in the ribs with an elbow. "When and where was it? I know it happened."

Ash sighed.

Spook helped him out, too. "The Chetwode near Milton Keynes. The night before Paul dearest rolled the bus down that embankment almost killing everyone on it, which happened to be everyone but Xane and Ash.

Ronnie, having smudged his already smudgy

eyeliner, was patting down his pockets in search of sugary comfort. "Well, I feel completely left out."

Alle leant over and gave his belly a pat. "Function of joining this crazy train ADL—after Dani and Luthor."

"Luthor's being very quiet," Ginny remarked.

That's because Luthor knew when to keep his gob shut.

"When did you two get together?" Alle asked Dani.

"Wasn't it while the rest of us were cosied up with Ginny in your hotel room?" Paul said, prompting Ash to drop the beer crate, so it landed with a thump. He glared at Paul, lock jawed. "That's twice that's been referenced now. Drop it, you lot. In fact, never mention it again."

Ginny barked out a laugh, then tickled her hubby's cheek. "Aw, you're getting all possessive. It's so cute."

"Give over," he tried to bat her away, but failed. "I'm not cute. Nor am I a possessive arse. I just don't need reminding that you've wrapped your lips around my bandmate's trouser snake."

"Yeah, but you were eating me at the time, and that's the part that sticks in my head."

"It does?"

"Absolutely. Your licking skills are legendary. Want to remind me how good they are?"

He took her by the hand immediately. "Let's go."

Ash and Ginny wandering off into the night prompted the rest of them to start exiting. Alle and Spook soon followed. It seemed the party was over, and fucking hell, it wasn't even five past ten.

"Wanna tag-team Luthor?" Dani asked Xane, and off they trotted too.

"Guess that leaves thee and me," he said to Ronnie, who was staring at the departing figures with his brow furrowed. He had a row of jelly rings lined up on his middle finger, which he proceeded to suck off one by one and chew contemplatively.

"It's not very rock and roll, is it, turning in this early?"

"We're a metal band." He didn't know why he'd said that.

"It isn't very metal either."

Paul meant to clap him on the shoulder and say something glib about finding some bites to bat the heads off... bats to bite... or something like that. Virgins, to willingly sacrifice? But wound up patting him on the cheek instead. "You're not wrong, mate. Not wrong. We'll just have to make our own fun."

"Blowjob?"

"Maybe in a bit." He cracked another bottle open for Ronnie, who proceeded to decorate the neck with more jelly rings. His own, he poured straight down his throat. Was he possibly a teeny bit sloshed now? Maybe. The trees weren't dancing yet, but he was seeing all their pretty auras. Moreover, he didn't like how quiet it had become, nothing but the whisper of leaves and the crackling of the wood in the fire. It perked up the fine hairs all over his body.

Ronnie sat up and considered him with his head tilted over to one side.

The way he was currently staring, with his lips parted, made Paul suspect he might be about to attempt to kiss him, and he hadn't yet decided where he stood on that.

Hell, maybe he muttered as much because Ronnie said, "I'm not convinced you're all that onboard with the idea."

Honestly, he wasn't sure how into the idea he was either, but he did know he needed to stretch his legs. His left calf was half-asleep, and he hated pins and needles.

"Get up. Need to move."

Turned out he wasn't *that* wasted, as he stood without any bother. After the two of them had pissed on the fire to help put it out, he cracked another bottle, and they struck off in an arbitrary direction away from the bus.

"DON'T REMEMBER if it's the ones with yellow legs or the trumpet-y ones I'm supposed to be picking," Ronnie said. After he'd expressed remorse over his earlier foraging efforts, Paul had agreed to give him an impromptu lesson.

"Both," Paul said from where he was leaning against a tree. He and the beech had been having a heartfelt one-to-one. He just couldn't remember entirely what about. "Just not the ones that look like parasols. They'll make you sick."

"What about these?" Ronnie leaned against the bark alongside him and shone his phone torch over the collection of fungi in his hands.

Paul picked out and chucked the objectively dangerous, and not so dangerous but definitely not worthwhile mushrooms, which left them with a grand total of... one. One weedy looking Horn of Plenty.

"I don't get how Spook found all those…what did you call them…chanterelles, earlier."

"Bought them."

"When did he go to the shop?" Ronnie pointed out quite reasonably. He could be as irritatingly logical as he could be inane.

"Ages ago." Paul didn't know that for sure, he just had a suspicion. Nah, Spook wouldn't cheat like that. Ash, maybe. More likely, Spook had grown them from spores specifically for the occasion. That'd be a very Spook thing to do. He waved his hand vaguely, which unfortunately knocked the last mushroom from Ronnie's palm. Neither of them bothered to bow down to hunt for it. Weren't worth it. "Probably growed…grow-ed…grew them *espesh-ully*."

"I didn't know that was allowed."

He patted Ronnie's clean-shaven cheek. "It's a harvest. Course stuff you've growed's allowed."

"Right." Ronnie touched his cheek where Paul had just patted him. "Only problem with that is that I'm shit at growing stuff. I even managed to kill the cactus I had. It went all brown and shrivel-ly."

"Know what else is brown and shrivelled?" After drinking the bottle or two he'd brought along with him on this stroll, his head was full of fog. He'd had a nip or two of *boom-boom* from the flask tucked into his boot too.

"No, what?"

He paused, trying to remember and had to shake his head. "Don't remember."

"That's a shit joke," Ronnie said, laughing anyway.

"That's it," he recalled. "A turd."

"Dude, there's something up with your innards if they're coming out like that."

"A flinty graveller – a turd after a festival," he elaborated. "You've never experienced that after a bit too much to drink and active avoidance of the festival bogs?"

Ronnie shook his head, seemingly bewildered by the notion. "I'd never been to a festival before I started playing at them."

"Never?" That was mind-blowing. He'd attended his first festival aged three weeks. Not that he could remember it, but he imagined it had been like every other festival. They were much of a muchness, and at least to him, a familiar sanctuary. It made his current twitchiness all the more remarkable. Drinking hadn't shaken him of it, and honestly, trudging around with Ronnie was probably making it worse, all that nonsense about blowjobs having created an uncomfortable tether between them that would need to be disposed of sooner or later.

Sooner, based on the way Ronnie was looking at him, concentrating on his lips when he spoke and checking him out in a way that was probably meant to be subtle but definitely wasn't. The boy had sex on the brain.

Paul definitely didn't have a sudden boner for Ronnie Bush. On the other hand, there was a charge flowing between them, and he wasn't averse to having a bit of fun.

He would quite like to get laid.

He had that itch.

Though, what he really desired was a pretty plump maiden with breasts so big he couldn't encompass them with his hands, and a nice soft tummy that made folds when she sat, and thick thighs to wrap around him as he explored the cavern at their apex. But, failing that, and because he was an opportunist, and open-minded, and always up for an adventure, he'd take what was on offer. If it was still on offer.

"Bushie."

"Yeah."

"About that offer you made... Are you still good for it?"

Ronnie coughed and spluttered and made a show of patting himself on the chest. He brushed his long hair behind one ear and peeped up at him from beneath dark eyelashes. "Um, yes," he said drawing out the syllables. "I mean, sure, that is, if you are too."

It was cute the way he was trying to play it cool.

Trying, because he was failing utterly. His smirk made his lips pucker, and his eyes lit like fucking lamps.

"I was thinking maybe now."

"Now!" Ronnie choked a little. Then he started patting down his pockets for his jelly sweets. The moment they were in his hands, Paul took them off him and pushed a jelly ring onto the end of his rolled tongue.

Result—rabbit in the headlights. Ronnie stared at him. "You're shitting me, right?"

"Nope."

He watched the man's Adam's apple bob as he gulped. "You're seriously gonna let me? You're not just fucking with me like earlier?"

"Didn't want it to feel like peer pressure. You had a whole gaggle of them egging you on. If you're gonna, I'd rather you did it because you wanted to."

Ronnie's teeth dug into his lower lip, then he blurted, "I really fucking wanna."

"'cause of the ladder?"

"Not just that." He gave a funny little squirm. "Though I am fascinated by it. Kind of terrified too, to be honest."

"Why? It doesn't bite."

"Yeah, but..." His hair fell forward as his gaze sank to Paul's loins. "We're not really gonna, are we? I mean, if we do, Lyra will give me such a fucking bollocking for doing shit while drunk."

Except, neither of them was drunk. They were still upright, still compos mentis, and he could still see in straight lines. Ergo, not drunk. "Fuck Lyra."

"Wouldn't dare."

"No wonder you never get laid if you're constantly being oppressed by Lyra's thumb." Paul pressed his thumb against the centre of Ronnie's brow.

Ronnie swiped at him. "Maybe I've not been interested until now."

"Kiddo, you have not been holding a torch for me."

All he wanted was some no strings action. An orgasm or two. No remorse. No rewriting the occasion after the fact as anything more than what it was, namely, two mates having a bit of fun together because they were—he scratched the word lonely from his mind before it took root. He was never lonely. He was always surrounded by friends. If there was one thing besides playing bass, and foraging that he was truly epic at, it was making friends.

"Need me to swear I'm not in love with you?" Ronnie asked. "I'm not. At least, I don't think I am. Although, I do love you, and I've a literal wedge in my pants over the possibility that I might get my hands...tongue on the barbell-enhanced monster dick you possess."

"Anyone ever tell you that you talk too much?"

"All the ti—"

Paul grabbed Ronnie's T-shirt front and reeled him in, cutting him off.

"You're not really my thing, Bushie, but if you're really offering, and this isn't just a lame game—"

"I'm offering. We can be like Xane and Spook."

"No," he said. That was not the vibe here. Not that anyone besides Xane and Spook really seemed to understand what the fuck their relationship was. He just needed to get the hell out of his own headspace for a bit. He still had the fucking D'Amon brothers twittering away in his skull like a chattering of starlings, not to mention Elspeth's presence weighing on his shoulders like a lead balloon.

Dwelling on shit wasn't him. He never did that. If he had a mantra for life, it was easy come, easy *fucking* go.

Nothing that anyone had said ought to have left him feeling this fucking off kilter.

Getting laid would surely sort him out.

"I'm like ninety per cent straight, Bushie. This is strictly a one-time deal, and I'm laying out the boundaries. No butt stuff, and it's not tit for tat, so don't go expecting it."

"Aw, you're not gonna get on your knees for me after?" Despite the droopy faces Ronnie made, the lack of reciprocity didn't seem to be a dealbreaker, given the guy was still buzzing with excitement. "So, your bunk or mine?"

"Here," Paul said. Hadn't he already said that? "It's not like there's anybody around, or is that too wild for you? Maybe you're frightened Lyra will cancel your Haribo subscription if we're caught."

Personally, he thought a little danger ramped up the fun. Also, he and this tree were like soul mates now. He had no intention of parting company with it until it told him to piss off and stop stealing its oxygen. Hang on, no that wasn't right. Trees made oxygen. Wait, so technically all the oxygen belonged to the trees. Humans should be worshipping them like fucking gods.

Ronnie leaned in closer, a smirk playing over his mobile lips. "Is this what you're like when you're anxious? Dickish?"

"Not anxious."

"I think you are."

"No."

A warm hand pressed against his upper thigh, shifted to caress the inner seam of his jeans.

Paul encircled his hand around Ronnie's slender wrist and moved it so that it was sat over his rapidly thickening cock in order to make his point. "You're not my first guy, Bush. You're not even the third or fourth."

"Ninety per cent straight?" Ronnie repeated, both eyebrows raised. "I think you're fooling yourself, mate. Where I come from, they call that being bisexual."

"Whateves..." Ronnie could label it anyway he liked... Bisexual... Bi-curious... Rock star straight... Heteroflexible... Opportunistic... It didn't matter to him. He knew what got his heart thumping, and it wasn't guys, even if he did sometimes say yes to them getting him off.

"Kiss me, dare ya."

"I dare. Don't know why you think I wouldn't."

"'cause you're a good boy."

"Not that good," Ronnie replied, right before his brow collided with Paul's nose, which left him blinking away stars. "You all think you know me, but you don't."

His mouth finally found its actual target and *fuck me* the man kissed real nice. His lips were soft, and he tasted...sugary and a little fruity. And while he was eager, he wasn't at all aggressive. Nor did they end up sticking to one another like Velcro, because while he still needed a shave, Ronnie was fastidiously clean chinned.

Fuck! Seemed he'd genuinely missed the old lip locking stuff, because it was lighting sparklers in his chest and doing a number on his dick. Then again, that kind of was the purpose of making out.

And they were doing tongues. Okay, fine. He was cool with that. Didn't mind how Ronnie was leaning against him either, occupying the space between

Paul's hips and pinning him so that the tree bark scratched his back. Ronnie's hand remained wedged between them too, his thumb making subtle, teasing stroking motions against his thickening shaft.

Okay, he took back all his previous thoughts about Ronnie's lack of sexual nous. The guy clearly knew what he was about. Almost irritatingly so, because he was doing just enough to make Paul hard, but not enough that it was satisfying.

"Open my fly, you fucking tease."

"Ah, dunno." Ronnie said with a clack of his tongue. He rolled sideways so that his back hit the tree trunk, but his head turned so that he was still looking at Paul slumped against the tree beside him, with a hump distorting the front of his jeans. "Why don't you do it, and show me what you've got? I feel this is something I need to see before we get to the touching part."

Paul grumbled but complied. What was it with folks always insisting he did the honours himself? Did they think his trouser snake had fangs or something? Once in a while, it'd be nice if they were eager enough to be super handsy with him, rip his shirt off, wrench that zip down, not do the whole bug-eyed thing and the gulp when they got a glimpse of his cock, with or without his jewellery. It wasn't like it reached to his armpits or anything. It was a standard...slightly above average...sized cock for a man of his proportions. Yeah, okay, maybe it was the length of his forearm when it was erect, but it's not like it was anything near the same girth.

He shucked his jeans and underwear down to his thighs. As he was still wearing the babydoll T-shirt from that morning that left nothing to the imagination, the moonlight twinkled in the silver of his piercings.

Ronnie did his best not to wig out, but wound up

doing a tree-frog impersonation, nonetheless, all eyes and tongue. "My God, that thing's huge. And how many barbells? I was expecting like three not..."

"Nine," he said saving Ronnie the effort of counting. "Ten if you count the Prince Albert."

"Damn! I don't know if I'm turned on or about to piss myself." He'd already crossed his legs. As Paul watched him, he swiped a hand across his eyes, proving they were watering. "I didn't think it'd look... be... so compelling, but it's not just aesthetically pleasing, there's something hardcore sexy going on too."

"It...I'd appreciate some hardcore action."

The remark passed Ronnie by. He was still laser focused on drinking down the vision of flesh and metal.

"What does it feel like?"

Paul crooked a finger. "Why not take hold and tell me?"

Instead, Ronnie sucked a jelly ring off his thumb. He reached out but stopped shy of making contact. Glee dug dimples into his cheeks.

"You're not gonna bug out on me, right?" Paul asked.

"Nah. I was just thinking it's a good job I've got a big gob." His grin stretched wide again, this time painting stars in his inky pupils as it spread. And then there was contact. His hand closed around Paul's shaft an inch or so up from the base. He gave the whole length a tentative upwards and hopelessly back-to-front stroke that ended with his palm sliding over the crown so that the friction caused the Prince Albert piercing to shift.

A shiver of bliss rolled right through him, so that he drew his next breath through his teeth. Goddamn, yeah. The piercings weren't just for show. They did wonders for his sensitivity.

Ronnie repeated the motion, which soon had him weeping pearlescent tears from his slit. Fascinated, Ronnie caught them on his fingertips, then brought those digits to his mouth. His tongue peeped out, pink and moist as he tasted first his thumb then his index finger. The sight made Paul groan.

"I think I've found a toy I could play with for hours."

He did not have the fucking patience for that. The only way he tolerated any sort of lengthy teasing was by being restrained. Paul pushed away from the tree, made a sharp turn, and smashed Ronnie up against the trunk. Enough with the getting to know you bollocks. If they were doing this, they were doing it now.

He went all in on grinding them together at hip level while a kiss battle commenced. Not that they properly aligned. He had half a foot on Ronnie, and the guy was slight where he was corded with slabs of muscle. Didn't matter. He was used to having to perform contortions, most women were shorter still, and the pressure was right. The feelings prickling through his chest and swirling through his groin, too. He'd left it too long since he'd last got intimate with someone, that was clear, because he was ready to hammer nails, and his balls started lifting, ready to fire within minutes. And that wasn't because Ronnie's wrist action was that spectacular.

Probably...

Still, it was a relief of sorts when Ronnie decided he was serious about the oral thing and dropped to his knees. Much more of what he'd been doing, and it'd have been fifty-fifty over whether Paul spilled in his fist or jacked Ronnie off the floor and got intimate with his lily-white arse.

Ronnie was making much of the chance to explore

Paul's piercings. He kept tracing the skin between and around them with his lips and tongue.

Paul braced a hand against the tree, then wrapped the other around the back of Ronnie's head. "Please, Bushie."

Ronnie surrounded his crown in sweet, wet heat.

He'd had many a blowjob in his life. Some furtive, some indulgent, some worthy of celebrating, others best forgotten. Xane had been memorable. He'd never deny that, but skill wasn't everything. It'd been about mechanics not emotions. The same ought to have been true now, only there was something about this that was doing an absolute number on him on a visceral level.

It didn't make sense.

Probably something to do with the apples in the craft ciders he'd been pouring down his throat.

It certainly wasn't because he was catching feelings for the man on his knees sucking him like it was his purpose in life.

Fuck, but that was good.

Needed to cool it though, or it was going to be over too fast.

That was the thing, when it was good, you wanted to fucking savour it, and savour it... Simultaneously, he couldn't bear to slow things down. Not when Ronnie was curling his tongue so that it whipped the flat of his crown, not when all the knots in his brain and in his shoulders were finally unravelling.

Gawd, yes! Right there. Like that. Exactly fucking like that.

Should have realised his professed talent was real. Ronnie couldn't lie to save his life. He was brutally honest and lacked any sort of filter. If anything, he tended to underplay his talents, rather than hyping them up.

"Fucking hell, man..."

While he might not want this to be over in a flash, pretty soon there'd be no holding it back short of having some kind of medieval torture device clamped around his bollocks.

"Gonna come," he huffed, easing his grip on Ronnie's head, in case he didn't want a mouthful of baby fluid.

Insane bugger only went and upped the ante. Seemed he was eager to sup down every drop.

"You don't have to," he grunted.

There was still no let-up, meanwhile he was losing the ability to think coherently, let alone compose or voice sentences.

Ronnie clamped his hand around his arse, digging his fingers into Paul's flanks and using the leverage to take him deeper. He couldn't take him all. He bottomed out at the back of Ronnie's throat with inches to spare, but it was enough. More than enough. The main source of joy was concentrated around the head, anyway.

His ears were buzzing. His head was buzzing. Every goddamned nerve cell in his body lit up with pleasure. Then there it was. No stopping it. The pinpoint of time when everything was just perfect and simultaneously too damned much. His balls emptied, and Ronnie, bless his sugar heart, sucked down every damn drop like it was fucking nectar.

Of course, when the high was that high, the come down was a bummer. The chill of the night air painted his flesh with goosebumps. Wind rustled the trees and made his ears cold. He rubbed his scalp, wishing the spikes he'd sported for years were still there. Then, of course, there was the cold of his cock slipping free of the hot cavern of Ronnie's mouth.

He ought to say something, he just wasn't sure what. Thanks, kinda didn't cut it.

Ronnie gazed up at him, still on his knees. He

hadn't even unzipped, but he was slack-jawed and dazed looking. The amber of his eyes almost coppery in the filtered moonlight.

"Need to take it out and show me?" Oh, God, what was he saying? *Engage brain. Engage brain. Reboot. Reboot.*

"You said no tit for tat."

"Never said owt about sucking you. Only asked if you wanted to show me it."

Someone silence him with gaffer tape.

Ronnie continued to stare up at him slack jawed and wet lipped. Then, he gave a decisive nod and carefully unzipped. It paid to do so when you were negotiating anything with teeth while sporting a boner that big.

Paul wasn't any sort of cock connoisseur, but Ronnie had a nice one. Cut, which was a novelty in this landscape. It was long, but skinny, same as its owner, only flushed an even deeper shade of crimson. "I'm not going to touch you," he said. "But I'm good to watch if you want to finish off." That seemed somewhat unjust, and he strove to be fair in his dealings, so he added, "Tell me what's on your mind while you do it. How does the fantasy of this night end?"

If he'd been a little more sober, he'd have realised that was a can of worms probably better left closed, but he had cider sediment fuzzing up his brain.

Ronnie, naturally, had zero qualms about blabbing his innermost thoughts. He went at it without a second prompt.

"You shove me down among the leaves and rail me. You don't touch my cock, even though I'm desperate for you to do so. You just tug me into the position you want and fill me up. And you make me take every single rung of that ladder." He groaned, like it was actually happening. "I feel every one of them as they slide past my ring on the way in and on the way out. I'm kind of terrified what'll happen when you start grinding... whether my arse will survive, but that just makes me even more desperate for you to do it."

Horny bugger was well into this. Paul felt a twitch of desire himself. If he hadn't literally just come, he'd be wanking along to the fantasy, too.

"God, every time you shift even a bit it takes my breath away. It's like you're stabbing me in the chest with that monster. I need... I need... But, when I try to touch myself, you slap my hands away and growl stuff about your cock being all the stimulation I need to get there.

"Maybe it is. You up the tempo. God, it is. It's going to be. You're pounding me so hard I lose my balance and face plant into the leaves. It doesn't stop you. You don't even slow down. I'm pinned beneath you, the whole of your weight on my back, and you're ploughing me good now, driving me right into the earth. You're using my hole, taking what you want, and it's not about me. It's not about me at all. You could be fucking anyone, but you're not. You're fucking me. You're fucking me."

Ronnie gasped, then came with a cry, spilling joy over his hand and onto the leaf mulch between Paul's feet.

Spent, he sat frozen, fist still wrapped around his shaft, eyes closed and mouth open until Paul bent to haul his jeans up his legs. He didn't like awkward moments, and this had the makings of a particularly awkward one.

He ought to have kept his mouth shut, left Ronnie to jerk off against his thighs or offered him the use of his fist instead of inviting him to share his thoughts. What the fuck had he been thinking? This stuff was going to be echoing around in his head henceforth. Shit! Bad call, Paul. Words had the power to shape the world. He knew that. That was the whole basis of the affirmations trend. Putting it out there was like flipping quantum switches. You could fundamentally alter reality.

He hadn't needed to know that it was about more than mechanics for Ronnie.

Too late, it was done now. Well, maybe they could bury it in alcohol amnesia.

"You okay?" he asked.

Ronnie shook off his daze and buttoned himself back up. Paul offered him a hand up, which made things weirdly uncomfortable the moment Ronnie regained his feet. Neither of them seemed to know quite what to say or where the lines on physical contact were now drawn.

"What shall we do now?"

"I can see lights," he said simultaneously with Ronnie's question. He could hear voices too. Familiar voices. Voices that belonged to people he didn't want to encounter right now, and not because of who he was with or because his skin was still hot from the flush of orgasm. "This way." He led them away from the chatter, deeper into the thicket, only realising he still had hold of Ronnie's hand when Ronnie used that fact to bring their exit to a halt.

"Are you freaked out?"

"No. Why'd you think I would be?"

"You're just... You're being weird."

"Am not."

"You asked me to tell you what was in my head."

He shrugged. "I know. It's fine. We're fine."

Were they fine? Something certainly had his hairs on end. And while it'd been a dumb call to ask Ronnie to share like that, it was hardly a reason to sweat. He'd fucked guys before, actually fucked them, not just stood and listened to them blurting out a fantasy while they wanked. They'd been temporary friends, though, the sort he loved for a week or a weekend and then left behind. Ronnie was rather more long term and present.

Wait, he was sweating over this for no reason.

Spook had tea-bagged him that time on the journey over to Sweden and then had him fuck his lady. He'd never lost sleep over that or worried what he'd got himself into.

Ronnie wasn't Spook though… and he wasn't Xane… Ronnie was far more squishy, and he didn't want to hurt him.

"We don't have to share the fact that I did it with the others," Ronnie said, as if that was the issue here.

"They'll find out."

Realistically, there was zero chance of it staying under wraps. Ronnie was the biggest security liability going. Forbidding him from talking about something just meant it circled in his head until, generally, at the most inconvenient moment, he'd bark it out.

"Paul? Did I screw up?"

He turned and faced Ronnie. There were leaves caught in his hair as if he *had* been railed amongst the leaf litter. There wasn't a trace of his trademark elastic grin on his face. His nose was wrinkled, which put a series of furrows between his eyebrows.

"We're still friends, right?"

Paul playfully punched him in the arm. "Course."

"You're sure?"

"We're all good, Bushie. Promise."

Ronnie's brows stayed knotted, and only slowly unravelled when Paul slung an arm around his shoulder. "What'd you say we get back to hunting 'shrooms, eh?"

"Sure, if you like. I don't think I'm going to be miraculously better at it though." Ronnie patted himself down and finally located a packet of sweets in his back pocket, that he frowned at, but peeled open, nonetheless. They were squashed and chewy and not even vaguely jelly like. While his jaw worked, his fingers made spidery movements against his thighs. "Should we try somewhere that's more open?"

"Like... like a field? Good thinking. This way, right?"

He led. Ronnie followed. They eventually found the edge of the wood, and a wide expanse of a moonlit paddock. It wasn't the field they'd come from, or any of the fields by it. It was occupied, not with tents, but with people. All of them bent over and pacing.

Seemed they weren't the only ones looking for mushrooms that night. Of course, the presence of so many foragers told him precisely what sort of mushrooms they were likely to find. He started humming an old folk tune. He knew better than to mix booze and 'shrooms. Then again...

"Just talking in hypotheticals, how are you with breaking the law?"

Ronnie shot him a quizzical frown. "Depends on the context. I mean shagging outside is kind of..."

"I wasn't thinking about that." He nodded his head towards the foragers. "It's like totally illegal to pick those things."

"What? How can it be illegal to pick something that just sprouts naturally?"

They might have got into the ins and outs of it, but he didn't feel like having a debate. "Snack time," he announced.

"OH! All alone."

Even Bushie had gone away. Where'd he gone? Where was he going? Paul had a vague notion that he was heading to meet someone. Who, he couldn't quite recall. A friend... maybe? No, he'd met his friend... his friend had... He grinned at the memory of a dark-haired individual's head bobbing. Xane... right? No, that'd been years ago not recently. He was getting mixed up. Had probably stumbled over a stray sod... oops, like that... and wound-up pixy led.

Paul picked himself up off the grass, where he'd landed face first, pausing on all fours to get his bearings. He was still in the field. Of course, the field. Failing to straighten his feet out, he rolled onto his back. Above him in every direction the jewelled blanket of space stretched out. He lay there for a while until it occurred to him that the grass was cold.

Around him, scarecrows were still grazing. Where was Ronnie?

"Bushie?"

Where'd he go? Off with some BushBaby, probably. Never mind. He could find a new friend. He never had trouble making friends.

The first few people he tried were genial, but not very interesting. He ambled on, a smile on his face. The world was beautiful... and vast. He threw his arms out to encompass it but couldn't quite manage it, even though his arms were long... and they had these funny things at the end of them... fingers. He could do all sorts of shit with his fingers. Fingers were cool. He played bass with his fingers.

Music...

Man, he loved music...

That's when he saw her, like she'd solidified right from the lyrics of the song that he was mouthing. Twenty or so yards away, stooped low, hair loose about her shoulders, dressed in a grey-blue smock that emphasised her considerable assets. He was running before he realised it.

Had swept her up in his arms before *she* realised it.

Jodi Castle.

Nothing could make him forget curves like hers. Even if they hadn't shared a particularly memorable night, she'd have lived rent free in his head. She remained exactly as he remembered her. Waves of dark blonde hair that settled on her shoulders, an acreage of bust and that defensive but sassy scowl that pinched two lines between her eyebrows.

She squealed right into his ear, but he didn't mind that.

"Found you," he said.

Like he'd mislaid her.

Which he kinda had.

Still holding her off her feet, he smacked a kiss on those delicious lips of hers. She made another surprised squeak but didn't fight him off. Oh, no, her mouth was eager under his... welcoming... The taste of her gave him shivers. Hell, yes. Yes, he needed more of that. Kinda needed to take a breath too, though. She was tapping him on the arm.

Carefully, he set her back on her feet, but kept a hold of her, worried he'd conjured her out of thin air, and she'd evaporate into the ether if he let go.

"You," she said, gazing up at him all wide-eyed astonishment.

"Yes, me."

"How?" She cleared her throat. "I mean, you're here. That is, I knew you were performing—"

Already done with the small talk, and ready to just bask in this fateful moment, he leaned in for another kiss. Alas, she wedged a hand between them and held him back with her palm flat against his chest. She might as well have been holding his heart in her hand. "Jodi Castle," he repeated, undaunted. His gaze fastened on her lips, which were crooked in amusement.

"Wait, I can't."

"Can't?" The words didn't compute.

"I got engaged." She raised her hand and flashed him an ugly oversized rock sitting on her finger.

"Why the fuck would you do that?"

"Duh, love," she replied, sassy as ever. "Same reason as most."

"Right. Love." The notion positively sobered him. *What the fuck! His kidnapper was getting hitched.* He looked around at the nearby foragers, expecting to find her prospective spouse glaring daggers at him, but while there were certainly a few speculative glances being levelled their way, they seemed to belong to the neighbourhood nosy parkers rather than an irate fiancé.

He meant to ask who, but what came out was another "Why?"

"Why'd I love him? Um, 'cause I do. Or do you mean, why'd I find someone else? Well, duh, you'd pissed off." He thought she'd intended that as a joke, but it rang with all too visceral hurt.

"Definitely didn't. You left me."

"I left *you* my number."

"Nope." If she had, he'd have called, even if only to check up on the kittens and make sure she hadn't got herself into more trouble, but she hadn't, so he couldn't...

Still, accidental collisions like this put a different spin on things. In these circumstances, it wasn't chasing, it wasn't not taking a hint, just amazing good fortune or the universe trying to tell you something. Like, *Girl, you and me belong together. How about we lie down right here and I give you a green gown?*

He cupped his hand over hers where it still lay against his chest. She was looking at him funny, like he'd sprouted antlers or something. Oops, had he offered to bang her? Well, it was a splendid idea.

Except, she had that rock on her finger.

Stupid rock. Ugly and ostentatious, but probably very useful if you wanted to put someone's eye out. Still, he'd better mind his manners. "Okay, congrats," he said and smooched her like crazy again.

She pulled free of his grip and smacked him across the cheek. "Paul! I said I can't."

Right, yes. Jodi Castle, sexy curvy lady, human magnet, disaster on legs, mean slap —he rubbed his jaw. And now apparently off limits.

Fuck, he hated limits.

EARLIER...

THE STONE CIRCLE was... Well, it was a stone circle. Grey rock, mostly upright, some of them a teeny bit tilted after centuries of the bracing British weather. On the other hand, there was something serene about the location. And it was blessedly quiet. No people, no noise, not even the distant hum of traffic. Just grey sky and grey rocks and bird song.

Was this what had prompted Nash's suggestion that they tie the knot? Had he come up here earlier and felt the calm seeping into him too? Okay, so he'd been an ass, but that didn't change the fact that she loved him. She did truly love him. He was good to her. They were good together. But nothing was ever perfect, so that meant accepting that someone could light up your world and simultaneously be a complete arse on occasion.

Was it making excuses for him to acknowledge that tensions were high right now?

The Ghost Boys' meteoric rise from nobodies to somebodies had changed all their lives, and she was so proud of them all. She'd been giddy all week thinking about seeing them perform for a crowd this big. They'd never played a stadium, nothing bigger than a club, really. How many people were here? Thousands? Tens of thousands? Yeah, it made sense that he had jitters, and that he'd seek out security by further cementing their bond with a handfasting. That was Nash through and through. He wanted the limelight, the spectacle, but if it was possible to get all that from beneath the security of a weighted blanket, he would've. How many times had he told her she was his anchor?

At least as many as the times she'd told him the same. He was. Her life had improved immeasurably since meeting him. He and the guys had made her feel wanted, when no one else wanted her. They'd made her a part of their world, made her realise there were good people out there, and sometimes you had to be brave and let them in.

Not everyone was out to hurt you. Or to use you. Some of them were set on showering you with all the love and security you'd craved. She hadn't enjoyed much of either of those things prior to meeting Nash et al. Even now, there were days when she woke expecting it all to evaporate.

She ought to have been kinder earlier. Maybe Nash was right. She had been shirty because he'd left her in the lurch for hours, which was unfair, because there'd been nothing he could do about it.

She'd head back in a moment, straighten things out with him. Suggest they decamp to her tent, or if he really felt the need to prove his rocker credibility by shagging her on the bus, they could cosy up in his bunk.

Only, when she got there, Nash was no longer on

the Ghost Boys' tour bus. She found their drummer, Jez, in his place scrawling words into a tatty notebook.

"Hey, I heard about you and Rune. Sorry, it didn't—"

"It's for the best," he mumbled, then took off towards his bunk leaving only the smell of his aftershave behind.

Jodi fidgeted a while, then bracing herself for a snotty reply, climbed down the steep entry steps to where roadie girl was still on duty. "You don't happen to know where Nash is?"

"Who are you again?"

"Don't be a bitch, Krista," a bald guy wearing a crew vest called. "She's Nash's fiancée, and you're perfectly aware of that fact. Give the woman a break." He finished fishing something out of the under-bus locker and drifted over to them. "They're doing an interview."

"Without Jez?"

"You've seen Quill?"

She nodded. "He's in his bunk."

"Give me a moment, I'm supposed to be rounding him up, and then I'll take you over to them."

"Thanks. What's your name?"

"Brian."

"Thanks, Brian."

Jez stared daggers at her as he was herded off the bus. He looked wrung out. Eyes hollowed out by too many late nights and probably dehydration. He had a beer in his hand now, and there were tangles in his wild mane of curly brown hair.

"Right, lets hook you up with the rest of them." Seemed Brian was their tour manager, who'd obviously seen it all before. A sour-faced drummer mooching along with a beer in his hand and probably a broken-heart wasn't anything to fuss over. "Honestly, hen, the romantic relationship nosedives are nowt to fuss over. Happens every other day. Then a girl offers to blow their mind, and they inevitably move on. It's when the band start plotting to murder one another, that's when my job gets wearing."

That'd never happen. The guys were besties.

The band were leaving a shack as they arrived. It looked like a larger version of the wooden stalls that populated European Christmas Markets, only festooned in promotional advertising for the conglomerate of influencers it was housing for the weekend instead of overpriced marzipan pigs and nutcrackers.

"Where the fuck were you?" Balin asked, barrelling past her without so much as a nod to lay into Jez. "You're not taking this very seriously, man. We've finally got our break, don't fuck it up. You barely said a word at the meet and greet earlier, and then you skive off the interview."

"I'll do the next one."

"That's the spirit." Brian clapped Jez on the back. "One missed interview ain't gonna crumble your cookies, guys. Our boy here was composing, not slouching, so dial it down a little. All is well."

"Yeah, all right." Balin gave their drummer a friendly punch. "It's not like anyone gives a shit about drummers anyhow."

Jodi left them to their snipping over whether drummers or bassists were at the bottom of the pecking order and drifted towards Lee and Nash who were still in the shack doorway talking to their pretty interviewer. Lee was laying the charm on thick, but the girl's gaze kept straying towards her man. Nash, of course, was lapping it up. The boy was a sucker for attention. Still, it was a blessing when the woman sent them on their way and returned to her shack.

"She's got to prepare for her next interview," Lee explained.

"Hey." Nash planted a kiss on her cheek. "Sorry about earlier. You know what I'm like."

She did. "It's fine. I took a hike up to the standing stones for a look see. I think we should do it."

It was like she'd struck a match inside him. "Yeah?" He positively beamed. "You wanna get all pagan with me?"

Jodi nodded, amused by his giddiness. He was all tentacle arms and smoochy cuddles while Lee tried to ignore them. "God, you're amazing, Jo. Can't believe how lucky I am to have you. Guys, Jo-Jo and I are gonna tie the knot."

"We know," they chorused. "We've seen the fucking rock on her finger, and you remind us at least twice a day."

Nash scowled. He leaned into her all conspiratorially. "I say we don't invite them."

"Just us," she whispered back. That shouldn't get her in the chest, but it did. Whenever the wedding came up in conversation, he'd start rattling off names of relatives they'd have to invite, and she'd start dreaming about the two of them eloping to a beach somewhere.

"It's a date. Midnight up at the stones."

"Midnight? It was quarter to eleven, earlier."

"Yes. Quarter to midnig...eleven."

"Which is it Nash?"

"Eleven. Definitely, eleven. This is why I need you. You never forget anything. What else am I supposed to be remembering?"

She shook her head. "I don't know. I haven't been at any of your briefings."

"You'd better come to the one tomorrow. Laundry. That was it. I'm completely out of pants. You should be our official girl Fri—"

"Are you the thieving wretch that stole my boxers?" Balin grabbed him by the shirt.

Nash gave him an innocent look while shaking his head and attempting to uncurl Balin's fingers. "Probably the latest girl you banged."

Balin pursed his lips and released him. "Better have been."

"Any chance you could stick a load in for me?" Nash said out of the corner of his mouth to Jo. "And, guys, what do you think, should we make Jo-Jo our official Girl Friday?"

"You mean pay her to do your laundry?" Lee remarked.

"Honestly, that's a task that requires danger money." Jez said, droll as ever.

"Laundry and other things. For all of us, not just me. We all want her to stick around, right?"

"Aye, but she doesn't have to play at being a domestic to do that, she can just come along for the ride."

"But having an official role would be better, right, babe?"

A weirdly excited fizz permeated her veins. Who the heck got excited by the prospect of becoming a dogsbody? Her, apparently. But an official role, would also make her a legitimate part of the tour. Needed. Essential. Not just a hanger-on. "I don't have to wash anyone's underwear who'd prefer to wash their own."

"Wouldn't you rather just hang out?" Lee asked.

"Honestly, I'd rather earn my place."

"Okay."

En masse they started back towards the tour bus, only to detour part way lured by the smell of food from various stalls and tents. "Hungry?" Nash asked. Her stomach rumbled right on cue. Breakfast had been long ago and hadn't been anything substantial. She'd opened a tin of tuna once her tent was pitched, but the cats had polished off most of that. After this, she ought to check up on them. Flugwhump, the little scoundrel, could be an escape artist. He wouldn't wander far, and he always came back, but she didn't want him sneaking onto someone's tour bus and winding up far, far away. He was her favourite. Not that she had favourites.

Nash, still with his arm around her shoulders, guided her between the lines of people. "Choose whatever you fancy. Lee's paying."

"Why's Lee paying?"

"He just is."

She looked back at the Ghost Boys' guitarist, who shrugged. "I'm the one that Harry and Brian trust with the funds."

Ah, so he wasn't paying. He just happened to be overseeing the expenses. Made sense. Lee was fair, if he wasn't always sensible. But at least with him in charge they'd all get the same deal. No one person would wind up living on Pot Noodles because one of them had blown the budget on caviar to spread over a groupie's tits and then lick off. Nope, it'd be Pot Noodles or caviar all round.

"What do you fancy, Jo-Jo?" Lee bumped up against her arm as she was reading through the various versions of chips, burgers, and kebabs.

Honestly, what she wanted was some decent home-cooked grub. She'd worked at too many fast-food places to ever want to eat from them, and none of the associated memories were good.

"We can try another booth if nothing's grabbing you."

"Chicken tikka kebab on a naan, with pickles and salad."

"That it?"

She gave Lee a nod. Balin and Nash had already ordered enough food to keep her going for a week, so she was sure there'd be plenty if she wanted something extra. Sadly, there weren't many vegetables. Damn, what she craved right now was a nice crunchy apple, or a peach. Yeah, a nice fuzzy skinned peach.

"Quill, what about you?" Lee asked.

Jez stuck his pointy nose in the air and gave a sniff. "I'll pass. Not hungry. I can pick up something later if I want it." He did a one eighty and headed off.

"He's not doing so good," she observed.

Lee blew out a long sigh. "It's the fucker's own fault. He shouldn't have given Rune his marching orders. Fuck knows why he did it."

"He hasn't said?"

"Just some bollocks... Whatever the real reason, he's keeping that to himself."

Whatever it was had to be big, surely, given how much it was clearly hurting him. She hadn't believed in the notion of soul mates until she'd encountered them and had her opinion resoundingly altered.

The food arrived fast. Nash bounded over with her order, and the four of them found a patch of grass to sit on while they ate. The site had grown busier over the course of the day, and now the sun had gone down the music had started. Bass and drums from both the main and second stages reached them, creating a strange, amalgamated medley. Out on the main site things were obviously rocking; even within the band enclosure a party atmosphere was building.

Scores of scantily-clad girls walked past in cutoff shorts and microscopic tops, some of them in wellies, others in sandals, one or two in ridiculous heeled boots. They pinched chips and kisses off the guys, but soon wandered on in search of more prestigious offerings. In contrast, the guys strolling about fell into two camps: band and crew, identifiable by the expensiveness of their jeans and tees as in stupidly overpriced versus seen better days.

The guys pointed out various famous faces and exchanged hellos with one or two. Eventually, Balin got to his feet and announced he was going to head over to the main stage to catch that night's headliners. Nash hastened upright too but faced her with his mouth turned down when he realised she'd stayed seated.

"You can go, Nash. I'll be fine. I can hang with Lee."

"Well actually." Lee flipped onto his feet too, winning him applause from various passer-bys, and mutterings of "show off" and "wanker" from his mates.

Jodi stood too, rather than straining her neck looking up at them.

"Do you mind, babe?" Nash pleaded, hands clasped together and looking downtrodden. "You could come with us."

She wasn't much for crowds, nor was she a fan of the band they were heading over to check out. They were all growl and doom. *And I say DOOOOOM!* If it were tomorrow night, then she'd be there to check things out, but she'd be there anyway to watch the guys, and maybe... just maybe, she'd stick around and see if she could catch a glimpse of Black Halo live. She'd do so from a distance though. No point in putting herself in a position where she was likely to embarrass herself, or the guys, or more likely be plain old disappointed when Paul "Rock Giant" Reed failed to remember he'd met her.

Yeah, best to keep her distance.

Would Rock Giant have actually forgotten her?

Maybe she was just one of many crazy girls who'd kidnapped him, drowned a bus, sailed down a river and rescued kitties with him.

Was that likely?

Best she worked out some spiel in case his memories of that night were as vivid as hers. If he said, "Hey, if it isn't my kidnapper," she'd use that as a means of establishing her connection to Nash, whose heart she'd kidnapped, rather than his person. She'd be all look at me with my shit together and he'd be all look at you with your shit together, and they'd go their separate ways and that would be it. No remembering, no reminiscing, nothing to cause anyone any alarm. She wouldn't have to explain to Nash that she'd accidentally absconded with a tour bus and drowned it in a previous life, or that she'd sailed down a river on a boat coat with one of metal's favourite bass players, or that he'd named her kittens, made her the best brew ever, and screwed her so good with his pierced rock giant that she'd been walking bowlegged for days after.

Yeah, none of that, because that was past Jodi, not present Jodi. She'd found her feet. Found her way to Valencia. Found Nash. Hell, she'd discovered the Ghost Boys. Without her the band wouldn't be, they'd said so themselves, and Black Halo wouldn't be about to rock a score of nations accompanied by a stellar support act.

"No, you three go enjoy. I'll check on my cats and maybe see what Jez is doing and put some laundry on. See you later," she said to Nash, squeezing his fingers as he leaned in to give her a parting kiss.

"Midnight." He winked.

"Quarter to eleven." She sighed.

"I'll be there."

HE WASN'T THERE.

Now, admittedly she'd turned up an hour early, but she liked to be punctual. Arriving late for things, especially important things brought on her anxieties. Although so too did standing around in the dark on her own looking like a moron.

Maybe she could walk back towards the band enclosure and meet Nash en route, suggest to him that they invite some witnesses after all. She'd like for Lee and Balin to be there. Jez too, if they could winkle him out of his hole. She'd have liked it if Rune had been present too. Deeply romantic, he'd love this. Beautiful too, both inside and out. What on earth had gone wrong between him and Jez? She couldn't figure it.

Jodi turned the carnation in her hand. Now where had that come from?

Maybe she'd get changed. The other couples had been dressed up. Some in their Sunday best, others in a carnival style, one pair were kitted out like mediaeval nobles. None of them had rocked up in the old clothes they'd spent the day in. What if Nash put on a shirt, and she still had her ancient rags on? Maybe she could find more flowers and make herself a crown, so it seemed as if she'd tried.

Not that it was about appearances, it was about the vows they'd exchanged.

Damn, she still needed to think about those, too.

Maybe rushing into this wasn't the best of plans. All the other couples seemed to know exactly what they were doing.

There were people roaming the pasture downhill of the standing stones. Well at least she wouldn't look out of place while she hunted out some flowers. Daisies... there were bound to be daisies. She could weave them into a chain, maybe add in a few buttercups and this lovely carnation. Not that she was seeing much other than clover and some pointy-hatted mushrooms. No doubt Rock Giant would have been able to tell her what they were.

Duh, people were picking them, and not, she suspected, to throw into a pan with some bacon in the morning.

A shadow appeared before her. She'd barely had time to lift her head before someone had scooped her off her feet and she was being kissed.

The moment her lips were free of the onslaught, she squealed.

"Found you," he said.

Nash! Fuck, her heart was pounding. Fuck, wait. Nash couldn't lift her. Nash did not smell like this or taste like this or have beautiful hazel eyes that were peering at her as if she were a long-lost treasure.

Rock Giant!

He kissed her again igniting memories and sparking fireworks in her veins. Damn that man could kiss. Still, yes, Rock Giant. This wasn't appropriate. She wriggled free of his grasp, or at least enough that he set her on her feet again.

"You," she said.

"Yes, me."

"How are you here? I knew your band were playing but..." But Black Halo were a big deal, she figured they'd be staying off site somewhere posh. Also, quelle surprise, evidently, he did remember her.

"Jodi Castle." The way he said her name sent a pleasurable shiver through her limbs. He kept on staring at her, like he couldn't quite believe she was real, and if he let go of her, she might vanish. Seeing the way he was eyeing her lips, she planted her hand in the middle of his chest.

"I got engaged." She waved her ring at him, so he'd understand.

"Why the fuck would you do that?"

Okay, that was a non-standard response. Most people opted for congratulations. Then again, most people weren't Paul "Rock Giant" Reed, or ought that to be Paul "Rock Giant" Reed wasn't most people.

"The usual reason – love."

"*Riiighht!* Why?"

Why was this so confusing for him? "Well, you'd pissed off, so I had to write that possibility off." She meant to sound jokey, but the crackle in her voice nixed that.

"You left me."

"I left you my number." She'd scrawled it on the glass along with a farewell message. Sticking around hadn't seemed such a stellar plan in the cold of the dawn. His band had been bound to turn up, and then she'd probably wind up in handcuffs, and not the sort with fuzzy linings. Not that it'd been easy to go either.

Before Nash, she'd often dreamed about how

things would have worked out if she'd stayed tucked against Rock Giant's side, head on his shoulder.

Fantasies that had seen her through a few low points, that's all. Reality would likely have been way crueller.

Still, "I thought... I figured you might call to check up on the kittens." And other reasons. There was that false hope rearing its head again.

Paul mumbled something that sounded suspiciously like *if he'd had her number, he'd have totally hit her up*, and that made her heart hiccup. "...but seeing as we're both here now, fancy making up for lost time?"

Cue him cupping his hand over hers where it still rested on his chest soaking up the thunder of his heartbeat and bowing his head again. And her, despite her galloping pulse, having to remind him that she was engaged, ergo, off limits, again.

"I'm meeting him in half an hour to tie the knot. I was just looking for some things to put in a flower crown."

Traitorously, her mind conjured an auditory hallucination of him saying, "Then that's half an hour I have to prove how big a mistake you're making." What he actually said, was, "What are you using as a base?"

A base? Oh, for the crown. "Um, I haven't got very far." She showed him the carnation and explained about her hunt for daisies.

"Hawthorn, and maybe some rosehips," he said, taking her by the hand and leading her across the field to its western edge where it was bordered by a hedgerow. "Maybe some harebells, too."

"I'm not sure what they look like."

"Bigger bluebells." He plucked a few and handed them to her, before returning to his hunt through the hedgerow.

"Paul are you high?" she asked after observing him for a few minutes. He seemed to be alternating between states of obsessive focus and standing still staring at nothing in particularly with a dreamy expression on his face.

"Hm, maybe a little."

"On what?"

"Life," he jogged on a few steps seemingly in pursuit of something in the hedgerow that was making a getaway.

"Not mushrooms?"

"I do like mushrooms."

"I know."

"But you don't. You're very strange, Jodi Castle. Strange but very, very bounteous." Usually, she'd have shrivelled inside if someone had described her in such a way, given she'd worried about her weight her whole life, but how Rock Giant said it? It was like he was bestowing her with a mark of excellence.

"Well, I've never tried the sort you've obviously been eating."

"Can't claim they're tasty. Better made into a brew, but..." He shrugged, then hunted through his pockets. Having failed to find whatever it was he was searching for, he bounded back across the field a way, before bending and plucking something from the grass. "You didn't see me do that," he giggle-whispered into her ear when he returned. "Got some *boom boom* in here somewhere, to help wash them down."

He produced a metal flask from inside his boot.

"Yeah, I'm not sure that's gonna help," she said as he added the mushrooms to the assortment of foliage and berries in her hands.

"Help with your anxiety."

"I'm not anxious."

He scoffed at that. "Course you are. That's why you've been through my pockets three times already."

"I have not."

Paul just smiled. "There, I think we have enough. Just need a bit of... Where's my knife?"

Jodi handed him the multi-tool she found in her pocket, which he used to cut the thorns off some twigs he'd harvested. He sat cross-legged where they were and began weaving the bits of foraged hedgerow together, even including a few mushrooms in her crown.

"Have you figured out your oaths?"

"Not yet." She joined him on the grass. She'd forgotten how magnetic he was, and how he seemed to suck her closer purely by being present. He'd changed. There was a seriousness coupled to his practicality that hadn't been present three years ago, and a harder edge to him, as if someone had taken a chisel to his softer edges.

"Cutting it a bit fine, aren't you?"

Apparently so. Although there was still no sign of Nash. She was keeping half an eye on the path up to the stones. Then again, he never worried about punctuality. He sauntered through life, and no one ever seemed to mind if he was a bit late or a little early. She wished she could say the same about herself, but everyone—literally everyone—mentioned it and never let her forget it if she was late. It happened more often than she liked, which is why she always set out to be early.

"What would you say?" It was interesting seeing him without the spikes of coloured hair he usually sported. The shorn look suited him though. He had the bone structure to carry it off, plus, it looked invitingly soft.

"Me?" Rock Giant lifted one brow. He smiled at her when she ran her hand over his head and leaned into the touch just like Flugwhump did when she scratched between his ears. "You'll have to be there when I get hitched to find that out."

Just the idea made her heart pang.

Stupid really. Of course, some girl would snatch him up someday. The real miracle was that no one had done so already.

"No hints that could help a girl out?"

His smile withered a little, though his pupils remained dilated. "Hints at what you should promise a guy I've never met. It is a guy, right? It's not a sapphic snuggle party I'm making this for?"

"Nope," she confirmed. "And you have met him."

"Really? He can't have been very memorable."

It might have helped if she'd mentioned Nash by name and explained their connection, but she got distracted watching him weave in the daisies she'd collected, only to remove them again immediately. Jodi retrieved them and made them into a necklace. It gave her something to do with her hands that didn't involve touching him.

"Here you go. I think I've got it the right size."

Paul knelt to place it on her head. Jodi put the daisy chain around his neck as a thank you.

He stood back to admire her. "Now you look like a faerie queen."

"Waiting for my knight to appear. It's always knights they marry, ain't it?" She stood and did a little twirl and gave a curtsy.

Paul nodded his approval. "Not sure about elven knights, mind. They're wily buggers. All the songs agree on that." He started singing one she didn't know the words to, full of longing and loss and rich with meaning. Even sung in his somewhat off-key tenor it raised goosebumps across her skin.

"What are you seeing?" she asked him a little while later. They'd moved over nearer to the track uphill at her behest. His gaze kept darting in the direction of the standing stones, while hers focused downhill.

"Ah..." He wagged a finger at her. "You have the means of determining that right here in your crown." He plucked a bunch of mushrooms from the assemblage and almost had them in his mouth before she stayed his arm.

"Not sure you need anymore."

He considered; lips pursed. "I remember you. You like contradicting me. Jodi Castle, the girl with heavenly thighs, wandering hands, and an inferiority complex."

"Nice to know what you think of me."

"Just saying what I see, but go ahead, tell me I'm projecting."

"Are you?" In response he brought the mushrooms to his lips again. Jodi redirected his hand and bit the heads off them, leaving him with just the stalks. "What's shitting on your parade, Paul Reed?"

"Well, there's this girl I know who's getting hitched..." He watched her chew. Damn, these things were bitter. "Nah...Just the usual. You know how it is. Sometimes pernicious little hobgoblins come and hang out on your shoulders and fuck your shit up."

"Is your shit fucked up?"

"Evidently not as fucked up as yours."

"Mine isn't fucked up at all. Things are great. I'm getting married."

"Your shit is fucked. I can see your aura."

"My what?"

He squinted so that one eye closed completely, then focused just right of her ear. "Yup, it's totally emo—pink, but like shot through with black."

It was? He was probably just hallucinating, although, honestly, he wasn't being much different to how he'd been the previous time they'd met.

"What colour is yours?"

"You tell me?" He offered her another mushroom, and then his flask. "A little boom-boom to wash it down. Probably green. It's usually green, sometimes orange."

Jodi swallowed, attempting to wash away the foulness that lingered on her tongue. Not that the boom-boom tasted much better. And if she'd expected the world to burst into colours, then she was sadly disappointed. If he had an aura, she couldn't see it. "What is that?" she complained of the flask's contents.

"Absinthe."

"Fucking hell, you're like a one-man party. Isn't that stuff illegal?"

"Nope that's a myth, and I happen to like aniseed. Damn, I could go for some nice aniseed balls. Did you ever have them as a kid?"

"Can't say as I did."

"Bit like mini gobstoppers. Tough on the teeth. Nicer than chewing sticks."

"Huh?"

"Liquorice...liquorice sticks. Not the same but they taste similar. You've never had one of those either? Woman, you've been living under a rock. Say, is that why I couldn't find you? Should I have turned over more rocks?"

Had he been looking for her? If so, why? The cats, probably.

She was past the point in her life where she needed the likes of Paul Reed to swoop in and save her. Things were on track. Nash's band was on the rise. The stars had aligned. She wouldn't be spending next winter outdoors huddled under canvas... They'd have a home, somewhere safe and dry...

Wait, was that what she wanted? When she thought of Nash's place, all white walls and guy furniture she felt like a cat trapped in Schrodinger's box waiting to find out if it was alive or dead. Why did nobody ever ask the cat? She'd often wondered Surely, it knew.

In any case, she was going to be The Ghost Boys' Girl Friday and tour the laundrettes of the world.

"You okay, Castle? You're looking a bit wan."

"Fine. How long is your tour?"

He shrugged. "Not sure, another six to eight months, maybe? It has legs. More legs than it probably needs, and it's not like there's any real down time between them, or any decent pussy nestled there like there is between yours."

"What?" His logic was hard to follow. What had legs to do with her pussies?

"All I'm saying is that I hope he appreciates you."

Of course he did, if they were talking about Nash. Were they talking about Nash? Why did she feel like someone was walking over her grave? Maybe she was just cold. That was probably it. It was late. The sun had turned in hours ago. She didn't have a coat on, not even a jumper. Nor did her companion, but he didn't seem to be affected by the elements. Nothing ever seemed to faze him. He just took everything in his long-legged stride. Why did part of her want to grab him by the hand and yell lets go on a bear hunt together? There weren't even bears in the UK. Maybe they could hunt a Gruffalo instead. They lived in the woods. The woods were right over there. But no, wait... she had to be somewhere. Running off with him wasn't an option. It was a fact that one did not marry the goblin king... Except, Sarah should have.

Damn, what time was it. She managed to locate her phone. Thirteen o'clock. No, that wasn't right. Twelve thirteen. Shit, she was late. Nash must have engaged stealth mode and slipped right past her.

Why did her legs feel so leaden? Her centre of gravity swished from side to side as she started making her way uphill.

"Hey, where are you going?"

"Feel a bit sick," she said.

"Normal when you're nervous." Her giant slung an enormous, tattooed arm around her shoulders. The action crushed her to his side and swaddled her in warmth and that gorgeous earthy scent of his. It was almost impossible not to feel fine when he cuddled her in this way, so warm and... happy. She was happy. This man, he always protected her. Protected her with his big giant body and made her feel good with his rock-hard cock.

THE STANDING STONES came into view. Grey stooped pillars in a ring like a dozen cowled figures. Why were they here? That's right, she was meeting Nash. She loved Nash. Where was Nash? Had he come and left already? She slipped free of Paul's hold to dart around the circle of stones in search of her betrothed, in case he was concealed behind them, but a full loop of the circumference failed to locate him.

"I can't find him," she said, taking hold of both of Rock Giant's hands. He had a ring on his thumb, that she ran her thumb tip against. It wasn't cold like metal usually was. "I guess I just wait, right?"

"It's one option."

"YOU'RE THE LAST pair," the man said. He had a crabby face and funny forked beard and a moustache like a man out of a fantasy movie, only taller. Everyone seemed to have grown really tall today. Her neck got a crick in it each time she looked up, so she looked down instead. The grass was pretty, and very green.

"If you're going ahead, it needs to be now." Fantasy man looked pointedly at his watch as he spoke.

Jodi couldn't quite recall what the delay had been about, but sure if he needed them to get on with it now, that was okay.

What was it they were doing?

Vows. That was it.

She'd been having trouble fathoming out what to say. The guy went first though, right? So, she could wing it based on what he said to her. That's what she'd do. "I'm ready," she told moustache man.

Damn, she wished she could focus properly. Time kept jumping around and there were colours swarming around the standing stones like tiny luminescent insects. They were very distracting. Not as distracting as the sounds though. Whenever anyone spoke, she could taste their words like they were putting them right on her tongue. She kept trying to wipe them off, but ribbons held her wrist in place, and whatever she was tied to was as immovable as one of those standing stones.

"Your turn," someone prompted.

Turn tasted of oranges. All zesty and sharp. She figured that was what sunshine probably tasted of, too. It was night right now. She wasn't sure what night tasted of. Someone was talking a great deal about hands and that kept overwhelming the taste of night.

"Jodi..."

"Yes," she said.

"Jodi..."

"Yes." Maybe he hadn't heard her over the taste of hands. "Yes."

Hands tasted of Armagnac.

"May this knot remain tied for as long as love shall last. May the vows you have spoken never grow bitter in your mouths. Hold tight to one another through good times and bad and watch as your strength grows. In the joining of hands and the fashioning of a knot, so are your lives now bound.

PRESENT

P AUL, RIGHTLY OR wrongly, insisted everything would seem better after breakfast—unlikely—thus he waltzed her onto the Black Halo tour bus, when what she really wanted to do was crawl into her tent alongside the cats and sob into a pillow. At least on his bus, she could tidy herself up a little before she faced Nash, and maybe...maybe, she wouldn't have to make a big deal out of it, if, once he had some food inside him, Rock Giant became more amenable to the notion of sweeping the whole nonsense under a bush. They had, after all, both been off their heads. Plus, all they'd actually done was agreed to some shit she couldn't even remember. Well, except for the forever part. She distinctly recalled that part. In fact, it kept echoing around her head in a particularly nettlesome way. She must have been looking him in the eyes during that part, too, because the memory came complete with a vision of his pretty hazel eyes and blissful grin.

A kitchenette occupied the space directly behind the driver's berth, complete with a diner-style table and padded bench seats.

"Who's this?" A guy with floppy brown hair looked up and asked.

"My wife, so keep your sticky mitts off."

"Your what?" The guy continued to scratch at his morning stubble.

"Wife," Paul replied. "I got married. Oops, sorry, forgot to invite you."

His band mate's—she assumed—interest morphed from one of bored amusement to full-on scrutiny.

"Yo, guys. Rock Giant's hitched," he called, prompting other figures to creep out of various crevices. Two sets of booted footsteps hurtled down the stairs that emerged just behind the dining area. A waif-like woman in fishnet tights and a band tee came out of the back room and perched on the worktop, while an ogre uncoiled from the driver's seat and leered at her as if he was eyeing her up as his next lunch.

"You got married?" The question came from one of the two men who'd come downstairs. He peered at her intently, like some prince of darkness inspecting the latest offering left at his altar.

"Yep."

"No. We're not married. It was a handfasting."

"Same thing," Rock Giant muttered.

"It's not. It isn't legally—" She'd meant to say it was merely a ceremonial union, not legally binding or recognised, but based on the looks the guys and girls were now giving them, that didn't seem to matter. To them, to Paul, they were official.

Shit! This was going to require far more explaining, now, than when it'd simply been a matter for her and Rock Giant to work out.

"Congratulations." A guy she'd not noticed yet pushed his way forwards. Long blond hair fanned around his shoulders, and a wealth of leather bangles covered his forearms. He offered her a hand, then pulled her into an embrace. "Welcome to the lunatic asylum. Hope you realise what you're letting yourself in for..."

"Jodi," she supplied, realising he was waiting for a name.

"Jodi," he repeated as he looked her over again. Some sort of illumination seemed to strike him as sparks lit inside the hearts of his eyes. "Of course."

Of course, what? She didn't get a chance to ask as various people swaddled her in hugs and spat names at her, among them an Ash, and a Spook, and a Troll. A nickname she hoped. Also, a Mrs Ash, and the prince of darkness, whose name she didn't catch but maybe started with Z, and a guy with strikingly different coloured eyes called Luthor.

"I thought you were hanging with Ronnie last night," said the latter.

"Hanging," said the ogre-troll, "I thought Ron was slurping his giant."

"Where is Ronnie?"

"Still in bed," Mrs Ash said.

There were so many of them cracking jokes and making remarks she couldn't keep up with it all. Paul removed a guitar pick from her hand then laced their fingers again.

"So, how'd this come about?"

The prince of darkness seemed to be their leader. "You ditched Ronnie and found yourself a lady friend..."

"Careful," Rock Giant cautioned.

"I'm just pointing out that you weren't betrothed at the start of the night. What did you do, make a pact with some old-world deity?"

"I suspect mushrooms were involved." A red-haired woman entered. She lifted her hands in a shrug when Paul glared at her. "Soz, Ronnie told me."

"Blabbermouth strikes again," Ash remarked.

"Mushrooms! As in 'shrooms!" Evidently, the Prince of Darkness didn't approve. "Are you fucking kidding me? You got married because you were tripping your bollocks off. What happened to being mister clean living, huh?"

"Fuck off, Xane. Besides, fungi are the natural bounty of Mother Nature. And don't fucking lecture. It's not like you've never partaken of anything. We've all been naughty a time or two on tour."

"Naughty?" Xane blurted. "Mate, shagging isn't illegal. 'shrooms definitely are."

Now instead of smiles, everyone was giving them serious stink-eye.

The bus's axle groaned as a large man entered behind them as if summoned by the spectre of trouble. He had on a suit, though it appeared to be wearing him rather than the other way around, and his bulk instantly made the bus seem narrower. "What's illegal?"

"The bogs in this place," Ash replied without blinking, proving that when it mattered these guys had one another's backs.

"That is true," the new arrival said. He noticed her and gave her a quick up and down glance, before returning his attention to the band. "Useful to find you all up and gathered. Saves a summoning. You know I only like to say things once."

Yet another figure stumbled in from the back, this one in llama pyjamas and blinking sleepily. "What's all the noise, guys? It's like two hours until rise and shine time. Oh, hi, Graham." He gave the suit a nod, then attempted to open a cupboard, prompting three of the guys to duck their heads. Having retrieved a packet of custard creams, he set about laying waste to them. Jodi's stomach rumbled. She'd been promised breakfast. If she'd realised it'd involve meeting forty-three people; she'd have given it a hard pass.

Mrs Ash leaned into the biscuit-crunching new arrival, and hand over her mouth whispered, "Rock Giant got hitched while tripping his bollocks off last night. Thought you were taking care of him."

Graham either didn't hear her or pretended he didn't hear her.

Ronnie's sleepy eyes widened. "Um...well, yeah, I was... I did... we got parted." He squinted at Jodi, evidently realising she was an unknown, then at her and Rock Giant's clasped hands. "Wait, did you say hitched? Like married, hitched?"

"Who's hitched?" Graham turned his head in a two-seventy-degree arc to laser each of them with his glare. "Yeah, I know about you," he said on reaching Ash, before bouncing his gaze back to Spook, who shook his head, and then Xane and Luthor. The former of whom rolled his eyes, while the latter pressed his knuckles to his mouth, which barely contained his mirth. He didn't even give Rock Giant a glance.

"Obviously not you," he said to Ronnie. "Given that like usual you're the one running their mouth. *Pfft*, you're not my problem, anyway."

"I did," Paul confessed.

"He got handfasted, last night," Spook elaborated. "Plighted his troth to this lovely lady here." That drew all the attention back to her, right when she'd been contemplating a swift exit down the steps.

"And you are?" Graham asked.

Rock Giant stepped between her and their manager. "My lucky bride, that's who. She's not your concern. You're in charge of band management, not our private lives. Being hitched doesn't affect my ability to play bass. Therefore, not your problem."

Their manager grunted, then pulled out an enormous handkerchief and blew his nose into it. "Allergies." He stuffed the soiled cloth into a pocket. "Do I at least get an introduction."

"Sure." Scary how lit up it made him to show her off. "Jodi, this is our manager, Graham Callahan. Graham, this is my wife, Jodi."

"Congratulations, Julie, was it? I suppose I'm going to have to look into getting you lot a bigger bus."

"We're fine, Graham." Xane stepped forward and patted him on the shoulder. "There's still an excess of bunks. There's only nine... ten of us when we're all here, and not all the ladies want to ride along with us all the time. Now, why don't you tell us why you're here, then Ronnie can get back to his beauty sleep."

"Oh, no, I don't need to sleep anymore. I want to hear about everything."

Curiously, she wasn't the only one who groaned in response.

"Yeah, right, it's nothing major, just been asked to ask you all to keep a look out. Seems your new support act has mislaid someone," Graham said.

"Someone," Xane echoed. "One of the band? You promised us some decent support who weren't going to cause havoc. That's not a good sign if they've lost a member."

"Singer's fiancée. Not one of the band."

Xane's gaze flicked to her then back to Graham.

"Probably just got sick of the bugger or got wasted and is sleeping it off under a bush."

Jodi's cheeks burned. She'd have protested the description of herself, if it didn't ring a little too true. She had spent the night under a bush sleeping off the aftereffects of doing something dumb, and now on top of that, Nash was worried enough to have organised a manhunt for her. He must have checked her tent and realised she wasn't there. Hopefully, he'd at least fed the cats.

"Description?" Spook asked.

"Female..."

That was apparently it. She was missing, and the best description out there of her was female. Great going, Nash. Graham gave a semi-apologetic shrug, which caused his shoulders to collide with various storage cupboards.

"I'm not expecting you to produce her. If it were a bit back, then I'd have come straight here, and no doubt laid my hands right on her." He stared pointedly at Xane, provoking the prince of darkness into sucking on his eyeteeth.

"You say that like I shagged anything that moved."

"Pretty much did," Troll-guy muttered, before squeezing his way back into the driver's bay.

"Shut it," Xane snarled at his back. "Ash was just as bad."

Ash refuted this with a shake of his head. "I only slummed with half the population, you were there a hundred per cent, and before you argue, I'm sure Spook will be happy to confirm exact numbers."

"Not completely exact," Spook said.

Having evidently decided his duty was done, Graham about turned and left the bus. The guys all watched his descent down the stairs. The moment the door closed behind him they all started yelling at once.

Jodi jammed her hands over her ears, but it didn't block anything out.

"Are you fucking kidding me? We have to go on the road with those bastards..."

"We've barely exchanged hellos, and you've already fucked it up..."

"His fiancée. His fucking fiancée..."

"We can get a different support act."

"No, we *fucking* can't, Paul." Xane got right up in

his face. "Leastways, not without a heap of aggro and a massive financial hit, and let's not talk about what it'll look like from a PR perspective."

"I'm not sure anyone is going to lose sleep over the visuals, Xane." Mrs Ash dropped to her feet and got in between the two guys. "Rockstars swapping women… That's routine any day of the week."

Jodi felt their eyes again. Rock Giant tucked her neatly behind his body.

Mrs Ash patted him on the chest. "You've really stolen their frontman's fiancée?"

"Married their frontman's fiancée," her husband corrected her.

"Couldn't you have made do with a fucking shag?" Xane asked.

"Handfasted," Spook amended.

The sheer number of voices and opinions here was going to make her head explode. Allowing him to bring her here had been a mistake. She'd known it would be a mistake, but she'd gone along with it because it meant she didn't have to face Nash quite so soon.

"It's not legally binding," she said again, but as before no one was listening. Or maybe they were; Mrs Ash stepped around Paul to look at her, her friendly smile scrunched into a moue. She reached out and clasped Jodi's hand that wasn't being squeezed by Paul's increasingly sweaty palm.

"Oh, sweetheart. I'm sorry. If we were talking about any other fool, then that might wash, but you've tied yourself to Rock Giant here, who I guarantee doesn't give a shit whether your vows come with legal documentation. You're his, and he's yours. He swore it in the middle of some standing stones, right? In a ceremony that dates back to the dark ages."

"Damn right," Paul confirmed.

"No," Jodi whined. "Paul, I'm engaged to be married."

"And I told you, that's okay."

Evidently, what he'd meant by that okay was not what she'd taken it to mean. What she now suspected it meant was he was okay with being part of a polycule. She, on the other hand, was not, and nor would Nash be. How had she fucked up this badly? This was way worse than when she'd accidentally managed to kidnap him, and he'd refused to let her escape.

Paul Reed seemed to delight in holding her to account for her actions. Although, in this case, she barely remembered what she'd done, let alone what vows she'd sworn to him. Evidently not fidelity, or to be his obedient housemaid. She guessed that was something. Indeed, what the hell had he sworn? A lot more than she had, she suspected. From the conversation still raging around her, it was becoming increasingly apparent that in his eyes, a handfasting was a very serious matter. The very fact that it was steeped in tradition that spanned centuries made it more binding than any legitimate marriage. He was still proudly wearing two of the trinity ribbons around his wrist. The third, still around her own, was creased and frayed and dotted with tooth marks. She irritably shook off his hold on her hand, determined, now more than ever, to take it off.

Of course, doing so wouldn't mean anything, but...

"Here, let me help. I'm Ginny, by the way." Mrs Ash offered her some scissors from the kitchen drawer. She slapped her hand against Paul's chest and bared her teeth when Rock Giant made protesting noises. "You need to give her some breathing space, Paul."

"She's right," the red-haired woman agreed. "It's just a ribbon. It's symbolic, not the be all and end all. Neither of you are going to be wearing them forever. It's like you've been saying: it's what you put out into the universe that matters."

The mention of forever was apparently the tipping point because Jodi burst into tears.

"What do you say us girls go somewhere quiet and give the guys some space to finish yelling at one another?"

Jodi allowed herself to be led. She wasn't as nimble or thin as the woman leading her and hence couldn't glide between various bodies with quite the same degree of grace, but the guys were incredibly obliging about making space, all except llama pyjama boy who stumbled over his own feet and then into her, before Luthor physically picked him up and moved him out of the way.

Beyond the kitchen sat a bunk room, and beyond that a bedroom with a double bed. Ginny pulled her down onto its end.

"It's freshly made. I just made it." Indeed, the laundry sat bundled up in the corner. "Want to tell me what happened?"

She slumped onto the mattress and wrapped her arms around her head. "Fucked my life up, that's what. Don't do drugs. Dumb shit happens when you do drugs." She'd heard that mantra way back as far as primary school; too bad she hadn't fucking heeded the goddamned message. Why the hell had she eaten those 'shrooms?

Because he stood you up, whispered the imp on her shoulder. *You were there, and he wasn't.*

He hadn't merely stood her up. He'd stood her up *again*!

So sure, she was the self-sabotage queen, but Nash was at least a little to blame. All he had to do was be where he'd said he'd be at the right time. For fuck's sake, it'd been his sodding idea.

"What do you want to do?" Ginny asked kindly.

Jodi wasn't usually a crier. Her sobs hadn't turned into a torrent, but they were catching in her throat making it difficult to get her words out. What did she want? How about a do over? One where she endured some shitty music instead of tangoing with fate. She should have gone to watch the DOOOOOM! band with Nash and the others. That way, the only problem she'd be dealing with this morning was perforated eardrums.

Ginny provided a tissue, and after she'd sniffled into it a bit, Jodi dried her eyes and shook herself off. "I need to go speak to Nash."

"Dark hair, short? I met him yesterday," Ginny said, when she nodded. "Seemed like a reasonable human being."

"Yeah, he is." Having shredded the tissue over her lap, she moved on to, "I don't know what he's going to make of this, though. I don't even know how I'm supposed to tell him."

"Stick to the facts."

The facts sounded like a particularly unfunny joke. *Hey honey, I got cabbaged last night on 'shrooms and accidentally exchanged vows with the bass player of the band you're ridiculously excited about supporting over the next eight months, but it's okay, he's happy to be part of a polycule.*

A hysterical laugh escaped her throat.

Ginny gave her shoulder a squeeze.

"I keep hoping this is all a hallucination and that I'll wake up in my tent with a cat's arse in my face and all will be normal."

"How did you wake up?"

Jodi groaned. "In a fucking love nest. Though he swears we didn't... you know... I don't think we did. Oh, God, but if we did..."

"Pretty sure your pussy would know if it'd been entered by that barbell-enhanced truncheon."

"True." She didn't feel as if she'd taken that sort of ride. Although, why did her inner muscles have to clench in quite such a longing fashion at the mention of his cock?

"I'm so fucking dumb. I can't believe I've manged to screw up this much. It's record-breaking even for me."

"I think you're being hard on yourself—"

"I'm pretty sure you've never done anything this dumb."

"Oh, I dunno," Ginny mused.

"Why did he have to walk back into my life now, rather than all the fucking times I wished he would?"

"Wait up," Ginny raised her hands. "I figured you'd just met. You were already acquainted?"

Jodi sucked a breath through her teeth realising her mistake. She'd predominantly been talking to herself. "I guess," she admitted. "I mean, barely. We met once, years ago, and haven't kept in contact."

"Right..." The way Ginny drawled the word implied she got the picture. One-night stand from the past... "But he remembered you?"

"I guess. Yeah."

"And you obviously remembered him." Ginny was beaming now.

"He's pretty hard to forget. But look, it wasn't like you're thinking. It wasn't a hookup, even though, I guess we did. That was kind of a side quest." She raised her shoulders. "It was a bit of a wild night, actually."

"Adventures are what Paul does best."

An adventure... Yeah, it had been that. Sailing down that river on the boat coat he'd claimed to have invented. Losing his phone overboard, rescuing her kittens, then afterwards, their impromptu campfire, and him singing to her in his low gravelly voice while playing an accompaniment on two teaspoons. A grin tugged at her cheeks over the memories. And, yeah, her astride him and his Prince Albert piercing hitting her in all the right spots was part of what made it memorable.

"Happy memories," Ginny observed, one eyebrow quirked. That instantly sobered Jodi. They were happy memories. Her life had changed completely owing to that night. It'd given her the impetus to leave home and all its shittiness behind. To start over, start again, travel, better herself. And what do you know, things had improved once she'd escaped from the tyranny she'd hardly realised she was living under. Of course, there'd been one or two low points, but... But nothing. Dwelling on those things now wouldn't get her out of the mess she'd currently blundered her way into.

"How do I convince him to forget about this?"

"Not gonna happen," Ginny said, confirming her own suspicions.

"It has to."

Ginny gave her another gentle pat. "If it was any other fool.... Let me tell you about Mr Reed. He's a big softie, despite appearances. Tenacious. Protective. The champion of anyone or anything he perceives as weaker than himself. He's completely laidback, but he's also hardcore about his beliefs. They and his ethics are sacrosanct. Violate either at your peril. Which boils down to this. Last night he swore an oath to you that's steeped in tradition. He made it beneath the stars, with the wind as a witness and...he's not going to shrug that off and let it go just because it creates difficulties. Not now, and not in a day or two. Whether you want him or not, he's yours."

"It's not legally binding," she tried again, knowing it was futile.

"I can come with you, if that'll help," Ginny offered, drawing her thoughts back to the real problem—communicating her fuck up to Nash.

"Not sure that's..." She shook her head. "Thank you, but it's probably better if I speak to him alone. On which subject, I should really..." They both looked towards the door. Judging by the rumble of voices still coming from the front of the bus, things hadn't settled any.

"Back door." Ginny got up and opened a curtain shrouding the back window of the bus. "It's a sort of fire exit. Reckon you can squeeze through?"

It'd be a wriggle, and it was a much bigger drop than she'd really have liked, but it'd be worth it to avoid walking through the argument raging out there. Also, if she attempted to exit via the front, then it was ninety-nine per cent certain that Rock Giant would hound her like a shadow, and the last thing she needed while breaking the news of her stupidity to Nash was Rock Giant leering over her shoulder.

T TOOK ALL of three minutes to walk between the Black Halo and Ghost Boys buses. Curiously, there was no security posted outside today. The why of that became apparent the moment Jodi mounted the bus steps and got a whiff of the interior – sex and weed. Seemed she hadn't been the only soul who'd succumbed to escapism last night. While her absence may have been noted, it sure didn't seem like anyone was overly worried. Lee and Jez were sprawled across the banquettes that curved around the front section of the bus, three girls a piece draped over them in varying stages of undress. The detritus of a booze and sex filled night littered the area, necessitating her stepping over an assortment of empty cans, discarded prophylactics and roaches en route to the rear.

"Jodi, you're alive," Lee reached a hand towards her. His fingertips brushed her hip as she sidled past trying not to touch anything. "Nash was looking for you. Where'd you get to?"

Where'd he get to?

"Where is he, Lee?" Not out scouring the campsite, she'd warrant. He'd probably only noticed that she wasn't here because the rest of them had companions to cuddle and she'd not been on hand to pull onto his lap.

Sure enough, Lee tipped his head in the direction of the back of the bus. It had to be said, that while this bus was newer and slicker in some regards, it felt sterile after what she'd seen of Black Halo's home on wheels. It wasn't down to the layout difference either. That bus had felt like a home, whereas this was basically a corporate sex shack on wheels, and it still smelled of the showroom beneath the spilled beer and body odour.

"Anything I should know before I go in there?" she asked, hand on the bunk room door handle.

The question seemed to momentarily confound Lee.

"He's not a cheat." Jez removed his nose from some girl's cleavage to spit out that observation. A sight she'd like to remove from her eyes with bleach. Besides tits, what did that woman have that he couldn't have got in a far more meaningful way from Rune?

"So, I'm not going to walk into a roomful of naked bodies?"

Lee *hmn-ed*, and Jez *hah-ed*.

"Can't say for sure," the latter eventually admitted. "Balin's back there, too, and you know what Mr Karunarathne's like about shedding his attire."

Actually, she didn't. She'd never seen Balin anything other than fully clothed. Well, okay, minus a shirt a time or two.

"Doing?"

"What do you think?"

Using his newfound fame as an ego booster. Okay, she'd just brace herself for the possibility that humping was happening. Although that begged the question, what was her fiancé doing back there?

Nash wasn't shagging.

That wasn't much of a relief, given that he was watching Balin fuck some lass and had obviously been doing so for some time. He was still in the same clothes he'd had on last night, and his hair was limp with sweat. "Babe, you're here," he said, pulling her onto his lap and shoving his hands up her top to fondle her tits. "I've missed you. Where've you been?" His lips were already heading towards her ear when she jerked back out of his lap, where he'd clearly been hoping to fasten her.

"I think the more important question is *where were you*?"

Not the note she'd wanted to get off on, but her insides were aflutter, guilt eating her, and he was watching his band mate fuck a stranger.

"Me? I've been right here, keeping an eye on this dirty pair." He grinned at that, which further provoked her. She was sorely tempted to call him a wanker, except, which of them was truly in the wrong here?

"It must have been a stellar performance, since it slipped your mind that you were supposed to be elsewhere."

"Huh?"

He continued to glance around her to the pair on the bottom bunk. Her arrival hadn't impacted the performance, Balin's naked arse clenching with each thrust into the girl whose legs he had braced against his chest.

"Nash!"

His attention snapped to her face, eyes wide.

"You were supposed to meet me."

It took a moment. Then, "Oh, shit! Oh, God. Sorry. I'm sorry. Did we agree to that?"

Did they... He'd sodding made the arrangement. Suggested it to her, not the other way around. "Quarter to eleven. Up at the standing stones. Remember arranging that?"

He gave her a blank look.

"We were supposed to get handfasted, Nash, and you fucking stood me up."

"Hey. Hey," he reeled her in. "Where's all this hate coming from? It's been crazy, okay. I forgot. Maybe." He shook his head. "Are you sure we fixed a time? I know we were discussing it, but we hadn't even been through our vows."

"You arranged it."

"Right. Well, no biggy. We can do it tonight."

"You're performing tonight."

"Tomorrow, then, before we leave."

"No, Nash. That's not what it's about. You're not just supposed to rock up when you feel like it. It's supposed to symbolise commitment."

"Right, and aren't I committed to you?"

"You stood me up."

"I don't think I did. Look, I gave you that ring, yeah?" He straightened out her fingers, so the ring was prominent on her hand. "Along with my promises, and my heart." She was practically on his lap again, only straddling him now. It was an odd time to notice it, but his fly was undone. More than that...

"You're fucking hard."

"Well, yeah. Of course I'm hard. You're here. You do it for me, baby, you know that."

"Bullshit, you're hard because you were watching a live fucking porno."

"Tone it down, folks, I'm trying to shag here," Balin said from the bed, in a breathless voice.

"Yeah, Jo-Jo, what's with? You've never had an

issue with me indulging in a bit of voyeurism before. It gets me hot, so what? I'm not sticking it anywhere, apart from in you."

"Gee, you're so romantic. I feel so wanted. You left me on a hillside in the dark, but it's okay because you did it so you could watch porn to get it up for me."

He shook his head. "Not what I said. You know I think you're sexy. You're my sexy snuggle pug."

She knew he intended it to be cute, but objectively pugs were pretty ugly. Sometimes, ugly enough to be cute, but still...

"Babe, what's up? Why are you so upset by this? I said I'm sorry. And we can sort something out about the handfasting, promise. I'll figure it all out. You won't have to worry about it. Let me take the weight. You know you like it when I do that for you."

"I can't, Nash. It doesn't matter what you organise or how it fits in your schedule anymore, or even if you remember. I already... Shit!" She bellowed the expletive so loud the girl on the bed wriggled out of Balin's grasp, and taking the bedclothes with her, exited the room.

"Fuck," Balin swore, attempting to chase after her with a still raging hard-on.

"Babe," Nash finally rose from his perch. He tried to reach for her, but she was too upset to be coddled in the usual way.

"You didn't come, Nash. Do you know how much that hurt? I kept telling myself that you'd show, eventually. Told myself punctuality has never been your thing, but—but then..."

Then she was right back in the moment. Rock Giant stepping in like he was who she'd been waiting for all along. Taking her hand, making her all those promises, and looking her right in the eyes as he did it. It'd been kind of perfect. The heavens, the woodland scent, him smiling down at her. The flower crown. His hand enveloping hers. His grip so solid, so utterly reassuring. Her throat closed up as the memories bit her hard.

In the binding of our hands, I give you my strength when you need it. I will passionately love you and cherish you through the years, and with the slightest touch, will comfort you like no other. I will hold you when fear or grief fills your mind. I'll wipe the tears from your eyes, tears of sorrow, and tears of joy. I give you my heart, forever and always...

Oh, God! Oh, God!

Her heart didn't know what to do with itself. Had he really promised her all that stuff?

She pressed her fist to her mouth, to hold in the sob that threatened to break free.

"But then, what?" Nash demanded, not even looking at her as he asked, but focused instead on zipping his fly.

"Someone else stepped in."

"Say what?"

Now his attention was on her.

"It was our turn, and everyone else was done, and he—he stepped in, and they did the thing and..."

"So, like, you did a practice run with some tool?"

It prickled. It prickled bad to hear him describe Rock Giant in that way.

"No, I got handfasted to him. There's no practice run. You exchange oaths, and they tie the knots."

It took a moment for it to sink in.

"You fucking what?" Nash's eyes bulged and heat licked across his cheeks and temples. "We're engaged, Jodi!"

"I'm aware."

"We're fucking engaged. What do you mean you said, I do with some bugger else?"

"It's not legally binding, Nash. A handfasting is a traditional ceremony, symbolic, but—"

"You exchanged vows with someone else! Who the fuck is this bastard?"

"—he's insistent that we respect it. He's not going to let it go."

Maybe this wasn't the best time to mention that, but then again, wasn't it best to just get it all out there at once?

"I'm going to fucking kill him."

In a show of support, and because they'd evidently been eavesdropping, the rest of the band barrelled into the room, jeans, and shirts in hand, as they tried to dress while moving. "We're here. Whatever you're thinking, we're—"

"You're not going to do anything," she said, finding some measure of strength. The last thing she wanted was for this to escalate into something more than it needed to be. "You're going to let this lie and let me sort it out. It's my problem. My mistake to correct."

"The fuck I am," Nash spat. "You're shit at sorting your problems out. Give me his name right now, so that I can make sure he doesn't set foot near you or this bus. And forget shacking up in that tent of yours. You're staying here from now on."

Happened that she liked her tent. It was hers. Her sanctuary. Her home. Shit, the cats... They obviously hadn't been fed this morning... Nash had been here, watching Balin dipping his wick. They'd be distraught.

Nash's hands circled her upper arms, and for a moment it seemed like he intended to shake her. Instead, he growled, "Who the fuck is he?" right into her face.

It made him ugly. Uglier for the memories it invoked of both her father and her youngest brother, Cam, yelling at her from a similar distance of approximately two inches, making sure she knew exactly how worthless, how big a nobody she was. Emphasis on big. She was so caught in that recollection, that when he demanded a name for a second time, she blurted it right out.

"Paul. His name's Paul, but you're not going to do anything. Nash, don't."

"Sounds like a tool," Balin observed.

"You might not want to say that to his face," she retorted, getting defensive on her... whatever he was's behalf, and because old habits died hard. She'd never learned to shut up. She always screamed back...fought back. It was an automatic response. One she thought she'd conquered. Truth was, she'd just not been in a situation that had tested it. At least not since Valencia.

"Oh, and why's that?" Balin asked. He was still naked; save for the socks he paused in the act of putting on to await her answer.

There were various grumbles and groans. "Who is he?" Nash demanded, still too close, looking murderous, and blasting her with stale beer breath.

"Paul Reed. His name's Paul Reed. You might have heard of him."

It took maybe a millisecond for the penny to drop.

"Rock Giant." Nash blurted. "You have got to be fucking kidding me. You hooked up with Rock Giant? And you have the temerity to lash out at me for watching Balin."

She hadn't hooked up with him. They'd got handfasted. Big difference. But looking at her four closest friends and the disgust on their faces, all the heat drained out of her, along with her fight. She hadn't meant to fuck things up, and now she'd made it worse. She'd meant to explain it all calmly, play it down, rather than launch it like a grenade.

"Tell me this is a fucking joke."

If only she could. "You think I'd make something like this up?"

The F-bomb explosion Nash let off was probably loud enough to have been heard on the Black Halo bus.

He peeled away from her and sat with a thump on the unmade bunk. When she followed, and knelt before him, he slapped her hands away. "Fuck off," he said. "Just fuck off, Jodi. I don't even want to look at you right now. I can't believe you've done this. Why would you be such a thoughtless cunt?"

AFTER PAUL REALISED that Ginny had assisted Jodi in making a getaway, he was all ready to go on the hunt for her to make sure she was safe and to retrieve a dozen things that had no doubt ended up in her pockets. That plan was promptly thwarted by Xane, Ash, Spook, and Luthor all sitting on him, which in turn netted everyone some bruises until Alle got in on the act. He wasn't going to risk hurting her, for all that she was hurting him by planting herself on his lap.

Jodi, his Jodi had just walked off to face a battle alone, and he ought to have been there to protect her. He'd promised he'd do that, and he kept his promises.

"You can love her without hounding her like a deranged stalker." Alle turned sideways so she could look at him as she spoke. She was wearing a dress today, knee-length, and bare legs. "Just shaved," she said, observing his line of sight. She rubbed a hand along one shin. "All silky smooth. Unlike you, you're practically beardy."

"Am not." He tried his palm against his cheek and... And maybe he was. Leastways, his stubble had grown long enough that it was soft to the touch rather than spiky.

"I kinda like it."

"I should shave." He lifted his hips prompting her to move, except she didn't.

"Do you really think I'm that dumb, Paul Reed? Any personal grooming you want to do will be happening right here."

"I'll fetch his electric," muttered Ash, who alongside one of the newer roadies, was standing guard at the front entrance in case he tried to make an exit, which, by the way, was complete bollocks. Black Halo were supposed to be doing interviews right now. Xane, Spook, and Luthor had gone. Ronnie had tried to sneak off with them, but Xane had magicked his manager, Lyra, out of thin air and she'd whisked him off to keep him busy meeting his army of adoring teenaged fans. The last thing anyone needed was Captain Blabbermouth blabbing about blowjobs or bride thefts. Even Paul agreed with that, although, curiously, no one, and that included Ronnie, had mentioned the whole bro-job thing in the face of his impromptu wedding—small mercies.

"How about you tell me what the hell happened?" Alle said, stroking his furry chin. "How'd you get from the prospect of a Bushie blowjob to tying the knot with a lass you've just met?"

"He hasn't just met her." Ginny squeezed her petite derriere onto the vinyl-covered bench alongside them. "They shared a night of unbridled passion in the past, ain't that right, Paul?"

That wasn't quite how he'd have described it. The passion part had only taken up a fraction of the evening he and Jodi had shared. Not that he was downplaying that part. He had some very fond memories of her tits jiggling above him. He did always love a woman on top. Especially one with cushiony thighs who didn't freak out over the fact he was ribbed for pleasure. It was too bad they'd both passed out last night before things got as far as consummation. Then again, considering how freaked Jodi had been about everything first thing, maybe that was a good thing.

He hoped her fiancé wasn't giving her a hard time.

Actually, he hoped she was ditching the lousy sod. He fucking deserved it. Only a complete monster agreed to marry someone and then stood them up. Unless he'd been in a freak accident and was now in a hospital bed incapable of speech or motion, he had no fucking excuse for failing to honour his intentions. None. Seriously, none.

Not that Paul had minded stepping in.

His gain. The fool's loss.

Jodi had been all kinds of gorgeous in her flower crown.

"When was this?" Ash asked, returning from upstairs with Paul's electric razor. He skidded it across the table, misjudged the slipperiness, so that it wound up in Alle's lap. She picked it up and turned it on.

"Ages ago," he muttered, and left it at that. The details of that night were his and Jodi's and would stay that way. No one else needed to know that it'd been her who'd drowned Bertha I. He smiled recalling the panic in her eyes when she'd first clapped eyes on him and realised her joyride had come with a passenger. She'd tried to get away from him then and hadn't stood a chance. He certainly wasn't planning on letting her run for the hills now they were oath-bound.

"Want me to do the honours?" Alle waved his vibrating razor under his nose.

"Are you trustworthy with that thing?"

"I am if she's not," Ginny insisted. "I'm gentle, aren't I, Ash?"

"Mostly."

That earned him a pout.

In the end, he let Alle shave him out of sheer boredom, both his chin and his armpits, plus some annoying tufty bits that had a habit of sprouting on the tops of his shoulder blades. After that, and multiple switcheroos that saw him playing chair to both Ginny and Dani in addition to Alle, the ladies realised it wasn't actually necessary for them to sit on his lap at all, because there were handy dandy handcuffs attached to the table, courtesy of Spook and his sadistic ways.

"Honestly, ladies, this is highly unnecessary."

"The guys say otherwise," they replied, all smiles. "Just think of us as your own set of angels. We'll be right here keeping you company until you have to be on stage."

"I need a slash," he said.

Ginny promptly planted a pint glass in the centre of the table. "We'll look the other way if you need us to."

"This is bollocks." He tested the cuffs, but there was no give in them, or the chains by which they were attached. Seemed unlikely he'd manage to wrench the bolts out of the wall either. He'd just have to hope that Jodi was fairing okay alone. She'd better be okay, or he was going to cave-in some heads the moment he was free.

If they didn't think he'd do it right on stage in front of the thousands-strong crowd, they were being blind to reality.

"So, did Ronnie blow you?" Ginny asked, facing him across the table with her chin in her hands.

"Fuck off."

"Now, now, no need to be grizzly. I just wanted to know if he was better at it than me?"

Paul clamped his mouth closed, then settled back against the chair back and closed his eyes. If he was going to be stuck here, he might as well take a fucking nap.

EE PULLED JODI off her knees and dragged her into the bus lounge. They all knew too well what Nash was like when he was pissed off, and currently he was at the mighty end of that scale. The sound of the bolt being thrown turned both their heads.

"Hey," Balin protested, and banged his fist against the door. He was still stark bollock naked apart from his socks, his clothes somewhere on the floor of the bunk room.

In a surprising show of sense, Jez ushered the ladies that they'd been entertaining off the bus, while Lee backed Jodi onto one of the banquettes. She sat heavily, bruising her arse on a stray beer can.

Stupid...stupid...stupid...

What had she done? How did she make this right?

Balin began raking amongst the bits of discarded clothing on the floor, and turned up a T-shirt, possibly Nash's. No, Jez's. Who took it straight off him and handed him a hoodie instead. Who that belonged to was anyone's guess. It made him less distracting, but still meant he was flashing his naked butt cheeks left, right, and centre.

Lee stood before her rubbing the knuckle of his thumb against his lips. "Tell me if I have this right. Despite being engaged to Nash, you've started something with Rock Giant, the bass player of the band we're supposed to be supporting on a world tour?"

She swallowed the hard lump in her throat, but her voice still came out hoarse. "I haven't started anything. Nash ditched me last night to watch you lot fornicate. I might have reacted a little irresponsibly in response and got a tiny bit... wasted." She wasn't about to admit she'd been tripping her arse off on magic mushrooms to them all. It was easier to let them believe she'd drunk too much. Excess drinking they'd be less judgy over. Maybe.

"So, what was all that shit about a handfasting?" Balin asked. She couldn't look him in the face, but the sight of his hairy legs and Mr Tickle socks made her want to giggle. That, and had she really just seen him fucking some woman?

God, they were all disappointed with her. She hadn't just fucked things up with Nash, she'd dented her relationship with the rest of the Ghost Boys, too. If Nash dumped her over this, they'd ditch her, too.

"Nash arranged for the pair of us to get handfasted up at the standing stones last night."

"No one invited us."

"It was supposed to be a romantic thing between the two of us, before the official exchange of vows. We were supposed to meet there at quarter to eleven... or midnight." Whatever. "Except, he didn't come."

"Oh, he came plenty," Jez remarked flippantly from the other end of the seating.

"Not helping, pal." Lee levelled a scowl at him. "And don't muddy things unnecessarily. Nash didn't cheat on you, Jo. Can you say the same?"

"Fuck you." Fuck him for even suggesting she'd been unfaithful. "I didn't sleep with Rock Giant if that's what you think." Well, technically, she had slept with him, or at least next to him, but she…they hadn't shagged one another. At least, not last night.

"What are we supposed to think? Seems clear cut from where I'm standing. Nash allegedly failed to show, so you retaliated by buddying up with Black Halo's bass player and made pretty promises to him instead. There's no way that went down without some action."

It hadn't been like that. Actually, it hadn't been anything like that. What he said implied pre-meditation, and there'd been none. It'd all been the very opposite of that.

"I'm not proud of what I've done, Lee, but I'm no cheat. What happened is that I got wasted. Same as any of you would have done in that situation. Ever been stood up? It sucks. Now imagine it wasn't just any date; it was a fucking significant date. The person you're fucking engaged to and are supposed to be spending the rest of your life with, stood you—he stood *me* up."

She guessed her words hit home, because sympathy started creeping into their expressions. "I don't even remember what happened properly."

An ever-increasing number of snapshots were coming back to her, enough to piece a line of events together, beginning with Rock Giant kissing her, and ending with them constructing that ridiculous bird's nest to sleep in.

"I know I've fucked up big time when drunk." To her surprise, Balin flopped down beside her and leaned his head over until it met her shoulder. "Nash'll calm down eventually, and it's not like you made out with the guy or actually tied the knot with him." He laced his fingers with hers and gave her hand a squeeze.

Actually, tying the knot was precisely what she'd done, but she got what he meant.

"So, you just need to stay away from him."

Yeah, who was going to keep Rock Giant away from her? To him, those vows they'd made were apparently eternal.

"Really it's just like the pair of you role-played getting hitched."

Kinda. But not really.

"I'll talk to him," Jez offered. She wasn't entirely sure who he meant to speak to until he moved towards the backroom door. Right, Nash, not Rock Giant. Good, because frankly she was probably better off handling Rock Giant herself. Sitting him down, and having a nice, sensible, adult conversation with him. Once she made sure he really understood what was at stake, then maybe they could figure something out like the grown-ups they allegedly were.

She'd never felt less like a responsible adult.

But nor did she want this to turn into a high-school drama with people being jerks to one another and assaulting one another in grimy bathrooms.

Lee intercepted their drummer. "Sit back down, Jez. Nash's better left to stew. If you try to reason with him now, it'll just make it worse."

Jez pitched a sigh in the direction of the door. "I'd rather he didn't trash the place and land us with some bollocks bill for the damages. We're not made yet, guys."

It seemed to her they'd managed to trash the place successfully already. She wasn't about to make that point though.

"The worst he can do in there is massacre a few

pillows." Balin gave her hand another squeeze. "He did miss you last night, Jo-Jo. He made us all swoop by your tent to try and find you, and he asked that security bird and Brian about your whereabouts."

It sucked some of the hurt out of her to know Nash had hunted for her. And the handfasting had been a maybe, not a definite.

"Said he was going to carry you back here and roll you onto his bunk."

"That's what we were gonna do?" Jez said. "I thought we were going to have a Valencia style snugglefest. Remember those?"

She did. Back when the digs they were staying in had accommodation that consisted of one enormous bed, and a bunch of cribs that were barely long enough for her, let alone the guys to sleep comfortably on. There'd been many a night when they'd all crashed together on the big bed, snuggled up, legs entwined, no covers because their combined body heat was more than enough to keep them all cosy. It hadn't been sexual. Just friendly. Although, looking back, she guessed Nash had always managed to wind up spooning her.

She missed those times. Missed the closeness, and how they'd been like a family. It'd been like having four—five with Rune—big brothers who gave a shit about her, the total opposite of her relationship with her actual brothers. Nash putting a ring on her finger had kinda tempered all that. Stopped the late-night chats with Jez and Lee snuggled together under a blanket, and the early morning ones with Rune. Maybe things hadn't changed so much with Balin. He still licked her if he wanted to, and licked Nash too if he dared to protest. But she hadn't minded the changes too much.

Except if things truly went tits for up them what

would happen, would she lose all the guys as well as Nash... Lose her family?

"You've gone awful pale," Jez observed.

The three of them peered at her closely.

"Need some rescue remedy?" Lee asked.

She shook her head. "I'm really sorry, guys. I know how jizzed up you all were about touring with Black Halo, and now I've gone and fucked it all up for you."

Balin punched her in the thigh. "Hey, less of the past tense. We're still hitting the road with them. What's a bit of fucking between friends, right?"

Lee slapped him around the back of the head. "She didn't fuck him."

"Hey! All right. She didn't fuck him, but come on, we're looking at this the wrong way. Shared experiences are how friends are made. It's something we can all bond over."

Neither Lee or Jez seemed convinced, and while Balin's optimism was endearing, Jodi couldn't see things working out that way either. Black Halo certainly hadn't shown signs of seeing the funny side while she'd been on their bus, and it was more likely that Nash would attempt to chew Rock Giant's face off than laugh about it over a pint.

She'd fucked up.

Completely and thoroughly.

Just like she always did.

Best thing she could probably do right now was get the hell out of here and hope they managed to pick the pieces up.

"I ought to feed my cats, guys."

Excuse meet reality. There was nothing to be gained by sitting here. It could be hours before Nash emerged. Days... He'd come out for their set later, wouldn't he? But would he want to see her right before that? Probably not.

"I'll walk you back," Lee offered. It didn't take him

long to do so. He stuck around while she fed the kitties and let them stretch their legs. Even went and filled up her water carrier. She wished he'd stop being so nice. It made her feel twice as bad about how she'd fucked things up for them all. Maybe it'd be okay, like Balin suggested, but it was just as likely that it'd all go tits up.

"You should be on the bus, not sleeping over here on your own. It's not very safe."

Now didn't seem like the right moment to be making that move. Not when the chances were high that Nash would chuck her straight back off and demand his ring back too. She said as much to Lee.

"He loves you, Jodi. That's why he's pissed off. He's not going to end things with you. He won't—"

"Jez broke up with Rune, and what did he do?"

Lee gave a sad sigh. "Nash isn't Jez. It's going to be fine, Jo. You know what he's like. He always goes up like a rocket but give it an hour or so and he'll be back to his usual self."

Maybe. She could only hope. If only everything else would miraculously be back to normal by then too. Maybe the rest of Black Halo would talk some sense into Rock Giant. Make him see that it'd be best all round if he just forgot about the whole knot tying, vows thing.

She could dream, right?

After Lee left, she found some fresh clothes and ate some peanut butter out of the jar, and a banana that was two days past its best. Stomach, at least quelled in terms of its rumblings for food, but not remotely relieved of the acute case of anxiety butterflies, she curled up on her camping mat and pulled her sleeping bag over herself for comfort. God, you're such a screw up, woman. If it all implodes, it's your own damn fault for being such an idiot.

J ODI AWOKE IN a stifling hot tent with a raging thirst, and three cat arses in her face. She hadn't intended to sleep, only to hide. Of course, now she was conscious, reality came crashing in and bludgeoned her with all her fuckups, recent and historical, so that despite being bathed in sweat and desperate for a drink, she lay stupefied, salt tracks drying on her cheeks.

Sometime later, the sound of the tent zip being drawn alerted her to an arrival. Fresh air seeped in through the flap as the inner compartment door opened. All three cats made an immediate exit. Shit! Now she'd no choice but to rise.

"They're contained."

Nash filled the doorway. His hair was crushed flat on one side, and creases lined the cheek on that side too. Seemed they'd both been attempting to sleep their woes away.

"Can I come in?"

"Of course."

Nash lay down behind her. After a second or two, he looped an arm around her waist and pressed his nose to the back of her neck. "You're lathered," he said. "It's like an inferno in here."

He'd left the inner door flap open, so at least it was cooling.

"Aren't you speaking to me? I'm sorry. I shouldn't have said those things, Jo." He found her hand and curled his palm around it. "You took me by surprise. You know I didn't mean it. You forgive me, right?"

"I shouldn't have done what I did," she croaked. "I should have seen the band with you, instead of taking mushrooms."

"You were tripping on 'shrooms?" There was almost a chuckle in his voice. "Babe, what the hell? You don't even like the normal kind."

"I know," she said, and he squeezed her tight, letting her know she was forgiven. Tight enough to squeeze out a few more tears that trickled along familiar salt tracks. "I don't know...I just..." She didn't have even a halfway decent explanation for her behaviour, so she could hardly blame him for his initial reaction.

"Did you fuck him?" he asked, voice still soft. "The guys said not, but..."

"No. God, Nash, no." She tried to turn, but he held her fast against him. "Not last night. I would never—"

"Not last night?" he seized on her qualifier. She guessed she owed him the truth.

"I—I met him ages ago, and we..." She gave a one-shouldered shrug. "It was just one time... Long before we met."

She didn't want to get into the details. Nash knew bits about her past, but mostly she didn't talk about it, because she'd worked hard to leave all that shit behind. That night she'd spent with Rock Giant had started her transformation into the woman she was now. Still a screw up, but far less of one than she had been back when her home life was toxic, and she routinely did dumb shit just to attempt to exert some control over things.

"Okay."

"Okay?" she echoed.

"We both had lives before each other, and we agreed when we first got together, we'd never hold stuff we'd done in the past against one another."

Right, yes, they had. Although, there'd been some caveats for illegalities. Did her first encounter with Rock Giant fall under that? She had kidnapped him, be it accidentally when she'd borrowed his tour bus. Technically, borrowing buses was illegal too, but Nash wasn't acquainted with her joyriding past. It was a part of herself that she'd left behind.

In any case, the details of that initial hook-up with Rock Giant were irrelevant. If he wanted to imagine she'd met him in a club somewhere, or that she'd finagled a backstage pass out of a roadie then she was fine with that. The details weren't important, nor the fact he'd been a pretty epic lay. Nor did she need to share anything about how that night was a cherished memory. A favourite memory.

"We're still a team," he said, bruising her shoulder with his chin. "You believe that, don't you? You're the most important person in my life."

She sniffed, and gave a nod, not trusting her voice to hold, or herself to say the right things. Nash loved her, and he was going to forgive her. Everything was going to be all right.

"It's so hot in here." He let go of her for a moment and took off his hoodie. Only when he lay back down did she realise he'd shed his T-shirt too. Warm, bare skin pressed against her. He put his arm around her again, only this time his hand pushed up under her top. Having found her breast, he rolled her nipple between his thumb and index finger.

Evidently, they'd reached the point of make-up sex. So where was the rush of relief? Instead, her throat felt thick.

Nash's breath warmed the shell of her ear. "What's this interesting little thing I've found?"

He kept on plucking at her nipple, coaxing it to steeple.

"Nash," she said uncertainly, straining her neck to see him.

He lifted from where he was nuzzling the side of her throat, and rolled her onto her back, before straddling her legs and snatching up the hem of her shirt. He pulled it up her body. The fabric clung to her in the sticky heat, but he soon wrestled it over her head, leaving her naked save for her knickers.

"Let's get these off, too, eh?"

She didn't much enjoy her own nakedness in daylight. Too many wobbly bits for that, even though she did her best not to cave into the brainwashing that the media portrayal of womankind bombarded everyone with.

Nash didn't wait for a response but tugged her underwear down her legs before casting them into the jumble of items around the tent's inner walls.

"Naked, and wholly, mine." He licked his lips. "Come here, nymph."

He practically face-planted down on top of her, sealing his lips to hers, while he ground his denim clad loins into the groove formed by her hipbones.

He was calm again. That was good. Wanted her again. That also was good. She accepted his kisses, kissed him back, waiting for her anxiety to dissolve into flames. Usually, she could rely on sex to quash her fears. Probably something about feeling wanted. Few people in her life had ever made her feel truly wanted. Nash clearly wanted her. He was all over her, his cock bruising her through the layer of heavy cotton that still separated them.

"I don't want to lose you. You're too important, baby. Best thing in my life."

"I'm sorry," she whispered back. "I'm so sorry, Nash."

"Show me. Help me, baby." He guided her hand to his fly. "Prove to me it's me you want."

If this would make it right… If it meant they could put the argument behind them…

Jodi dutifully slid his button and zip. Seemed he hadn't bothered with underwear. He'd showered since she'd last seen him. The peppery scent of his shower gel lingered on his skin. His cock sprang up eager between them. She took him in hand.

"God, yes. That feels so good. Want you so much, Jo. You and me, we're a perfect fit. You're so sexy. Touch me, baby, please."

He reared back, watched her stroking him, stretching, and preening as she shuttled her hand up and down his shaft, and slid her thumb around his tip in the way he loved. His skin was so pale, his body slight, almost half the size of hers. Usually, she loved that slenderness. The way his muscles were evident beneath his skin, without him being in any way muscular. Today, tension had her in too tight a grip for her to get lost in his beauty, and the heat made her feel trapped inside a too tight skin.

"Come." She beckoned him to close the gap between them.

Nash kissed her, all tongue and hunger. Then nibbled her chin before returning to nuzzling her breasts.

"Best bits," he muttered. "So soft. I could just squish them together and fuck them until I'm silly.

What do you think, Jo? Should I give you a pearl necklace to go with your ring?"

"Not sure it'd suit me," she said. She needed closeness, something that made her feel they were connected right now. Cuddles. Caresses. Maybe even some long sultry looks.

Nash clearly had other ideas. His cock bobbed before her, then poked her in the chin. "Give him a little kiss, eh?"

He stretched right over her and pushed into her mouth. Jodi clasped his arse, to stop him driving too deep. He was here battling his own doubts, too, seeking reassurance in the way that appeased his inner voice. Nash needed to know she was still his, and what better way for her to prove it than by sucking him off?

He groaned with increasing urgency as she sucked and tangled his fists in her hair. "You do that so well, baby. You slay me."

She did all the things she knew would make him happy, and a few of the things he protested about, but inevitably made him squirm with excitement, like resting her fingertips against his arse crack. The one time she'd properly touched him there; the top of his head had almost blown off.

Suck and retreat.

Suck and retreat.

Squeezing his arse when he groaned.

"God, I'm getting so close."

Jodi released him with a smack of her lips. "Why don't you show me what you can do with this magic wand?"

He chuckled but obligingly slithered down her body again. Jodi widened her legs, giving him all the room he could need.

"Are you happy to see me?" he said to her pussy. He swiped his thumb over her entrance to check that she was wet. Gave her clit a little pet. Her heart sped in response. Was he... would he maybe go down on her? His head dipped. He was gonna. But he turned away, falling to the side of her instead, so that he could kick free of his jeans. Once they were shed, he returned to his former position over her and lined them up.

Jodi pressed a palm to his abs to slow him down. She needed to know they were still in love. Still connected. "We're okay, aren't we, Nash?"

"Of course, we're okay." The implication being that they clearly wouldn't be doing this otherwise. "Let's just forget about him. Let's not let one shithead come between us. We're forever, babe. You and me."

"You and me," she echoed. Not that Rock Giant was any kind of shithead.

"I'll talk to Harry, make sure he doesn't give you any trouble. Make your Girl Friday role official, too."

She'd really rather he didn't talk to Harry, at least about Rock Giant. "Is that practical? I don't want to cause any trouble, Nash. I can sort it out myself. I don't want this to create friction between you and Black Halo."

"Don't want him near you," he grunted into her ear, while reaching down between them to line them up.

"Guide me in, yeah?"

Instead, she used the head of his cock to tease herself. Rubbing his crown up against her clit, so that her breath caught, and heaviness infiltrated her womb. She'd have kept it up for longer, but Nash started croaking and shaking, then making whining noises deep in his throat. "Need you, babes. Need you so bad. Gonna fuck you so good."

"Yeah. That so?"

"You know it."

It was one of their little routines. Him promising. Her crooking a brow and challenging him to make good on those promises.

"You know how good my cock makes you feel." He put his hand over the top of hers, signalling that it was time to stop playing about and get on with putting it in. He met her gaze, eyes all sultry and hazed with lust. "You're making me weep, babe."

True. She caught the silky pearls of precome leaking from his slit and spread them over his crown. It made him shiver, and his eyelids drop. He rolled his hips, letting her have her way with him. "So...good. But I really wanna fuck. Come on, Jo. Let me inside you. If you don't let me soon, I'm going to blow."

"Yeah?" She swiped him again with her thumb.

Nash grabbed her by the wrists and pulled her hands up, so they sat either side of her head. "Naughty, babe. Bad girl."

"You like it," she said, and licked his nose.

"Not half as much as I like this." He filled her. Sinking in deep, then drawing back slowly so that only the tip of him remained lodged. "You feel so fucking perfect. Like you were made for me. We were made for each other." He linked their fingers together either side of her head as he continued to slide in and out, gathering speed until their bodies were meeting with a slap each time. "So good. You're so fucking beautiful, baby." He smooched her lips, then pulled away breathless and buried his face in the side of her neck. His bottom kept rising, their hips grinding. The sheer driving tempo of it made her moan.

A tear leaked from her eye and ran around the back of her ear.

Nash didn't notice.

She sniffed, trying to hold it together, concentrate on the good. How nice it all felt.

Nice. Such an insipid word. *Nice is for bake sales,* Rock Giant of three years gone said in her head.

Sweat coated Nash's back. His chin kept banging against her collarbone. He was close, and there was a cat... a fucking cat in her hair. Mel flicked her grey and white tail before Jodi's face, so it swept in front of her like a wiper blade.

Sexy, nope.

Distracting, absolutely.

"Not now," she tried to bat the cat aside, and succeeded only in slamming the back of her hand into something hard sat on the floor. She squeaked in pain. Her muscles cramped.

"Oh, fuck!" Above her, Nash arched backwards. "Oh, fuck. I'm there. God, Jodi, I love you."

He pumped into her deeply and another twice, then shuddered, and cried out as he ejaculated.

Exhausted, Nash collapsed over her.

He lay lathered and still, his weight restricting her lungs. Jodi bit her lip.

"Sorry I couldn't keep it together longer," Nash said directly into her ear, and gave the lobe a little nip. After a minute or so, he rolled off her onto his back, allowing her to suck in some needy lungfuls of air. "Once we're dressed, we'll get your gear moved onto the bus. It'll have to be soon, our set's..." He trailed off and raised himself on one elbow to look at her. "You okay? You're not saying much."

"Fine. Just really thirsty," she croaked.

Nash searched amongst the jumble she always seemed to accrue. "You've a flask here." He lifted a small metal flask. Rock Giant's boom-boom. How had that got here? She shook her head. Then, sat and stretched forward to stick her head into the outer compartment to reach the water carrier Lee had filled for her. She stuck a mug under its tap and waited for it to fill.

Nash clapped a hand against her bottom where it was raised aloft. "I'm gonna want to do you all over again if you keep jiggling your arse in my face like that."

"You've a set to perform," she pointed out. Then, downed the cup of sadly warm water. "You wouldn't want to be late for that and disappoint all your lovely new fans." He could bang her afterwards. That is, if he wasn't too knackered. Which he frequently was. He never ate or drank enough, so his after show buzz inevitably left him within fifteen minutes and rendered him practically comatose within another half an hour.

"Later, then." He gave her bottom another pat, then pulled on his jeans.

"SHOWTIME, LOVER BOY," Ginny announced, sitting on Paul's lap while Dani dealt with the handcuffs. As if her weight were any sort of real impediment to him making an escape. If he wanted to, he could lift her up and walk off the bus still carrying her. Hell, he could have Dani hanging off his back too, and it still wouldn't slow him down much.

Allegra had already headed over to the stage area with Spook, and honestly, she was the only one of the ladies who might have stood a chance of pinning him down if he decided to make a freedom bid. He reckoned the girls were aware of that. But what would be the point? He had a stage to be on, and he'd had time to think during his imposed rest break. The most likely place he'd find Jodi was in the vicinity of that there stage, given that the Ghost Boys were performing right before Black Halo. That was assuming she and her fiancé were still all loved up and hadn't had a dreadful falling out.

And no, he didn't wish that. It was true that he didn't have a lot of respect for the guy. What sort of idiot stood up the woman he was supposed to be exchanging vows with? One who wasn't nearly as committed as he claimed, that's who. He had no time for that sort of insincerity. None. Ergo, Curtis Nash was a human waste of space.

On the other hand, he wasn't going to sabotage Jodi's relationship with the fool, because he believed in personal freedom. He could wish she'd choose otherwise, but wishes rarely impacted reality. If they did, he'd have a pet dragon by now, Steve Matlock would be playing house with Elspeth in Happy Happy Land, and his parents... Scratch that, his folks were fine, and anyway, the whole point of bucket lists was that you never reached the end of them. They were about adventures, and who the fuck wanted a life devoid of those? Not him, and not his folks either. They dreamed big. And so did he. So, he hoped, did Jodi, which is why, even though it was fucking torment accepting that she was likely out there choosing a life with some waste of space rather than him, his promises to her—to love, honour, cherish her, and be the friend she needed from now until forever, stood. And would stand, for as long as he stood on this earth, and beyond.

"I'm not sure I like the look on your face," Ginny remarked from kissing distance. "What are you plotting, Paul Reed? It'd better not be ways to sabotage a relationship. You can't have her. She's committed to someone else."

"Your arse is really bony," he said.

If Jodi's relationship with that tosser who'd stood her up ended, it wouldn't be down to him. Well, nothing deliberate, anyway. If she happened to wake up and realise he was an obvious knob, that was a different matter.

Ginny wriggled on his lap, making him wince. "My arse is perfect. How dare you slight it?"

"Sure," he agreed. "It's a wee sliver of loveliness. Now get off me. I'm not hitting the stage in this getup." He was still wearing a baby doll tee and wilted daisies.

Ginny gave him the sort of penetrating stare that might have put a blush on a lesser man's cheeks. He just cocked a brow, and eventually she relinquished and slid off his lap. After Dani finished with the cuffs, he stood and massaged the red marks around his wrists.

"That's not going to impact your ability to play, is it?" She worried her lower lip with her front teeth.

"Bit stiff, but nothing that won't wear off in a minute or two."

"We did it for your own good, you know."

He realised that they believed that which is why he was being so amenable. They were trying to save the band a heap of aggro, and him potential heartache. Too bad the heartache was guaranteed at this point. He and Jodi were forever. The universe had witnessed it. Nothing would change that. He was hers, regardless of whatever distance or restraints were placed on him.

Ginny turned him towards the stairs and gave him a prod. She and Dani followed him up to the bunk room.

"Are you planning on watching me change?"

Dani turned around. Ginny's gaze didn't dart away for even a second. "It's not like we haven't seen it before." She flashed him a lewd grin.

He gave her a two-fingered salute in return, then pulled what he needed out of various cupboards. It was far too cramped in the aisle between the bunks to get kitted up in his stage gear, especially with the two girls leering at him from the doorway. Dani had given up trying not to look, so he bundled everything he needed into a knapsack. There'd be some form of green room set up for them backstage. He'd get dressed there. "Let's go."

The girls clamped onto either of his arms the moment he set foot on the grass, as if he were about to leg it. "Really?" He rolled his eyes. "Ladies, I've an audience to entertain. I'm not about take-off." And them clinging to his hands wouldn't anchor him in place for more than a millisecond if he had a mind to break free.

"You're not?"

"You promise?"

He crossed his heart and offered them both his pinkie fingers. After they'd shaken on it, both women breathed sighs of relief. Paul grabbed each of them by the hands, lacing his fingers with theirs, Dani on the left, Ginny on the right, and refused to loosen his grip. Sweet revenge. They were walking at his pace, too, no dawdling, and yes, that meant they were taking three steps to his every one.

"So, we'll meet up after the show for that threesome later," he said to them, à propos of nothing, right as they caught up with their respective other halves. Ash's jaw immediately clenched, and his gaze shot to Paul's hold on his wife's hand. Xane's pierced brow rose behind his dark glasses, and his lips pursed.

Payback, wankers.

"If you so much as touc—"

Ginny shushed her hubby. "He's just trying to provoke you. I thought we could have a threesome with that Balin bloke instead. He's quite hot."

Ash's jaw dropped. Ginny smacked him in the abs, as she lapsed into giggles. "Honestly, you know you're the only man for me. It's why I said yes, remember?" She wiggled her fingers before him, flashing off her wedding band, before clasping his hand, where he wore a similar gold band. "Come on, DM. Let's get your eyeliner fixed."

Paul cuddled Dani to his side. "Just you and me then, maid." He even risked a sore nose by leaning in to give her a peck on the cheek.

"In your dreams, mate." Xane claimed his girlfriend, who immediately leapt into his arms and straddled his hips. Rather than stay and watch them smooch, Paul barged past them into their canvas dressing room. Luthor was occupying one corner, and Ronnie sat cross-legged on the floor before a bench, lining jelly tots up in rainbow order. Paul unpacked his stuff, making sure to take up as much space as humanly possible. Given that he was a giant, that was a lot of space.

Xane eventually wandered in, his throat marked by a brand new hickie. He eyed Paul's territory and gave his head a shake.

"By the way, Elspeth's onsite. She says hi," Paul informed him.

"What?"

It wasn't Xane who groaned, but Ash.

"Was she best man at your nuptials last night?" Xane asked, strangely calm.

"No. She's hanging with Toys in the Attic. I'm just letting you know, in case you want to avoid them and a scene."

Xane squinted at him. "Right. Thanks, I think."

Paul left him exchanging various mutterings with Spook and Ash.

PAUL FOUND JODI right where he predicted she'd be, standing in the stage wing, at the head of the ramp that led from the mat-covered grass at the back of the main festival stage. Ear defenders covered her ears, and her messy blond hair sat in a knot at the back of her head that left her neck exposed. She was dressed in cutoff trousers and a Ghost Boys T-shirt, swaying her hips in time to the racing drumbeat, her attention on the stage. It wasn't the greatest view of the performance she could have found. All you could really see were a bunch of arses.

Feeling naughty, and because the guys were all far too busy preparing to go on to notice what he was doing. Paul slipped up behind her, stood a moment, breathing in that summer child smell of fading flowers and sunshiny salt and sweat, before bowing to press a kiss to the little stretch of skin between her hairline and her collar.

Shocked, she jolted and gave a squeak, then turned to face him, pulling off her headphones.

"Hey," he said, offering up a grin.

"Rock Giant!" She swallowed hard, before throwing a wary glance at the stage.

The Ghost Boys were mid-number, so no cause for worry there. He guessed words had been had, and he'd be villainised. Sure, he'd roll with that part, if she needed him to.

"If he's any sense, his attention is focused on the mad bastards out there, not what's going on in the wings."

She glanced again at her fiancé singing his nuts off for the crowd. He was no Xane, and Paul said that as a Xane sceptic, but he did have the audience singing along with him. He vaguely recalled exchanging a handful of words with the guy yesterday, now that he got a look at him.

"Are you in deep shit with him, because, honestly, it's ninety per cent his fault. Dumb fucker shouldn't have stood you up. Did he have a great excuse?"

She swallowed again and peeped up at him warily. Damn, he hated the unease he saw etched into her face, wanted to lean in and kiss the lines around her mouth away.

"I don't want you to badmouth him. I'm still engaged to him. That's not about to change."

He made an *hm* sound in acknowledgement.

"Please. I don't want my mistake to cause trouble between your band and his."

"Your mistake? What mistake did you make, Jodi?"

He knew what she'd intended to say. It pleased him immensely that she couldn't say it. The vows they'd exchanged had been no mistake. "There are no current plans to boot them." Unless she gave him one. "Are they going to bail on us?"

She shook her head vigorously. "No. I don't think so. It's a big deal for them. A huge honour. I'd hate to be responsible for mucking it up for them. They're my friends. Good friends. You do know that I'm taken, don't you, Paul? I know what you were implying earlier, but we can't be anything to one another. Nothing more than friends, that is. I'm engaged. I'm planning my wedding to Curtis Nash." She pointed to him as if he needed identifying.

"Still committed to the man who stood you up. You're either loyal or stubborn."

"Paul," she chastened. "I'm in love, is what I am." Her gaze sank down to a spot between their feet. "I know he's not perfect. Nothing in life is, but he's said sorry, and he's been there for me, when I needed someone. Look, we've forgiven each other, and what I did was far worse than what he did. I wasn't in a position to be making promises to you. It was wrong of me, and the fact I was off my head isn't an excuse." She snatched an upward glance at him. "What promises did I even make? I can't remember. Do you?"

He tilted his head. He remembered every word.

"Surely not being able to remember means it's best forgotten? We were both out of control and not thinking rationally."

"A vow's a vow. I keep my promises, Castle." Plus, he was pretty sure if that sort of argument worked as a get out of jail free card, then murderers and other unsavoury sorts would have been routinely using it to escape punishment.

She held up her hand to his mouth. "I know you feel like that, but really, we're not anything to each other. We barely know one another, and I don't want one foolish promise to wreck what it's taken me three long years to find, especially not when you're the one who made it possible in the first place. I like my life, Paul. I'm happy—predominantly happy. I'm rather keen to maintain that. There's been plenty of fucked up shit in the past. I don't need any more trouble."

"I made it possible?" Interesting.

She clamped her lips together tight.

Paul traced the curve of her cheek, then rested his hand on her shoulder. "Come on, Castle. You said it. Of course I'm gonna ask. How exactly did I make it possible?"

"You didn't have me arrested," she said, but he knew that wasn't it. That was a diversion. He folded his arms, but kept his gaze levelled at her. She wriggled a little, then delved into her pocket and started turning a familiar flask over her hands. "I left home after that night. I couldn't have kept the cats, and I promised you" —she gave an awkward shrug— "I'd take care of them, and I didn't want to break my word."

So, she was a woman who kept her promises, even if that made things difficult.

Paul scraped a hand over his scalp. Speaking to her and not cocooning her in his love was proving harder than he'd anticipated. He was literally itching to pick her up and explore that mesmerising mouth of hers again. Tangle their tongues, knock hips, talk, and talk, and talk, until they were comfortable enough that silences didn't set them on edge. "So, you're saying I was the catalyst for you getting your shit together?"

"I guess. Yeah." She tugged her hair loose, then bound it again, in an even messier knot.

"Mind if I..." He took the flask from her, and swallowed a slug of the contents, before handing it back. Jodi peered at it confused.

"This is yours, why are you giving me it?"

"Why don't you hold on to it for me? I've not really got anywhere to put it."

His guitar tech appeared, though he remained at a respectful distance. He had minutes at most. She wouldn't be here when he came off stage. Nor was he sure when he'd get the chance to see her again. That didn't make him happy, nor did it change anything, and he wanted her to understand that even apart, they were together.

"Hey, hear me out a minute."

She gave him a wary nod.

"My state of intoxication last night doesn't change anything. I'm here for you." He raised his hand and stopped her flailing at him, as if she could waft him away like a bad smell. "I realise you don't necessarily appreciate or want that right now, but it is a fact—an unchanging one. You can rely on that."

"I'm with Nash."

"I know." He touched her face again. "Got to respect your choices, maid. You know your own mind, and I'm no misogynistic arsehole who thinks he knows better. I'm not going to make things difficult for you."

"You're not?"

He was memorising the curve of her cheek. "Of course not. I am, however, going to point out that if we're going to be on tour together, we're going to be in one another's pockets, and I refuse to be a stranger."

"You accept that we can't be more than friends, though?"

He withdrew his touch, and scraped his fingertips over his own chin, before agreeing with a nod. "Message received. Friends." He offered her his hand.

Jodi scraped her teeth over her lower lip and threw another of those wary glances towards the stage. He didn't like that one bit. Hated that she was wary of even accepting an offer of friendship, because Curtis Nash might not like it.

Now, admittedly, they both understood that he'd like them to be more than friends, but he'd promised to respect her boundaries. Really, that ought to be the end of the matter. "Friends," he reiterated.

"Friends." She shook his hand and released it. "And not the kind with benefits."

"Well, damn," he said standing by her as they watched the end of the set, pleased to see she'd relaxed enough to make a joke out of an obvious loophole. "If you ever change—"

"I won't."

"—your mind, there have been exciting developments to the equipment."

She blushed. "I saw." Her tongue peeped out between her lips as she grinned. "Going to pretend from here on that I didn't though. No cock talk from this point on."

"But I talk about my cock to all my friends," he lamented. "Guess we'll just have to stick to convos about pussies."

She looked as if she was about to berate him, but he said, "How are the cats?" So, she poked him instead.

"They're fine. I'm sure you understand why I'm not about to invite you over for a visit."

He folded his arms. "Will we have to go to court over cat daddy visitation rights?"

That made her laugh. "Not sure that'll go in your favour. You've not been a good father. Very absent."

True. He'd have to make up for that.

The Ghost Boys set was over. Nash was talking smack to the crowd, while the audience showed their appreciation. Their bass player added a few lines, getting the crowd hyped for Black Halo hitting the stage. It amped the noise levels up exponentially.

"Give me your number."

She shook her head. "That's not a good idea."

"Fine, then at least let me give you mine. I want you to be able to get hold of me." He rattled off the digits of his mobile. "Need me to write them down?"

"Paul..."

He stretched an arm out towards the technician. "Got a marker, Jake?"

"Yeah, um, sure here." He dug one out of a pocket and handed it over.

"Paul, I'm not sure—"

"Is your relationship that unstable it's going to dissolve over a phone number?" He pushed up her sleeve. "Not where I'd like to stamp my mark, but it'll do." He wrote his number on the inside of her forearm, blew on it to make sure it was dry, then pulled her sleeve back over it. He handed the marker back to Jake.

"I love him."

"Yeah, you said."

Xane tapped him on the shoulder. "You set?" He offered him a set of earbuds, before giving Jodi a thorough once over, like they hadn't already all seen her that morning.

Paul slipped the earbuds in and checked they were working. He could hear the rest of the band just fine. "Let's rock these bastards." He finally gave his guitar tech a break and claimed his bass.

Ash went on first, followed by Ronnie and Luthor, then Spook. He was next.

"Break a leg," Jodi said.

"Later, sweet lips."

He wanted to lean over and kiss her, but he suspected Xane would knee him in the nuts if he did. That's if Jodi didn't do so herself. He'd said his bit, agreed an arrangement, now he needed to man up and live it.

He couldn't resist looking back at her though. Doing so left him with a horrid lump in the centre of his chest. The sort that formed when you had to say goodbye forever, except that wasn't how it was going to be. He made a V of his fingers and pointed them at himself and then her. "You and me, forever, Castle."

"Non-kissing friends," she mouthed back.

"Proud kitty parents."

Nash brushed past him as he came off stage lathered and red-faced. "Good set," Rock Giant muttered in as friendly a growl as he could manage. What he wanted to do was rip the fool's head off and shit down his throat, but he'd promised not to upset the apple cart—much.

Nash ignored him and made a beeline towards Jodi, proving he at least had some priorities straight.

He didn't kiss her though, so points for and against.

"Thanks, man," their bassist replied, in lieu of Nash.

Paul acknowledged him with a nod. Bassists were usually the soundest blokes in a band. Seemed the Ghost Boys were no exception.

On stage, Ash was saying something about how good the Ghost Boys had been, and how they were stoked to have them supporting them on the next leg of their tour. The crowd seemed happy enough to hear it. He warbled on a bit longer, then the stage lights dropped. Outside, darkness had swallowed the field, a hushed whisper rolled through the audience. A sharp note pierced the veil, then a familiar riff kicked in— Ash. Then Spook, complementing him. Drums followed, then keys, then him on bass, and finally Xane strode on, pinpointed by multiple spotlights, and the six of them gave their audience exactly what they were there for—a fucking killer show.

"YOU WERE TALKING to him. What did he want?" Nash demanded, leaning in to embrace her, despite his shirt being soaked through with sweat. It didn't make for a very pleasant hug. His hair, also drenched, lay plastered to his brow, and his lips which he pressed to her brow, seemingly as an afterthought, were rough, apparently chapped by his onstage efforts.

"He was just saying hello. Shall we?" She turned towards the ramp that the rest of the band had already exited down, even though she'd have loved to stick around and watch Black Halo play. She'd never seen them live. Hadn't known anything about them prior to meeting Rock Giant. She never recognised all that much of him in their music, except the occasionally killer bass line. He just wasn't really very gothic or metal, in her head. When she thought Rock Giant, she thought of folk songs and country footpaths.

"Well, I'd rather you stayed away from him."

"Nash, that's going to be difficult if I'm coming on tour with you." Harry had miraculously agreed to her taking on a dogsbody role for the band. "And it's unnecessary, too. There isn't anything between me and him."

"Is that what he thinks?"

"It's what he's agreed."

"Lighten up, shithead, eh?" Balin clapped him on the shoulder from behind. "If Jo says everything's cool, then everything's cool. No sense making an issue. I for one am grateful we haven't just been turfed."

They met Jez and Lee at the bottom of the ramp.

"Yeah, Balin, I think your opinion might be a little different if he was trying to fuck your—"

Jez prevented him from launching into a regurgitation of earlier, by accidentally on purpose treading on his foot and then sticking his tongue out in lieu of apologising, before legging it across the field. Nash gave chase. Balin followed. Boys were weird. Though she was grateful for the distraction.

"They're full of it," Lee said, putting his arm around her and guiding her in the same direction the others had sprinted. Towards the band enclosure. "Don't worry about Nash. He'll settle down, once it's evident there's not an issue. There isn't one, right?"

She shook her head and dearly hoped that Rock Giant had meant what he'd promised. "We agreed to be friends."

"And forget all that bonded shit?"

Not entirely. "He gets that I love Nash. That I'm with Nash."

That seemed enough to appease easy going Lee, who gave a nod of approval. "So, what did you think of us live? The crowd fucking loved us, right? So many people, Jo. I need to find out how many. It was mad looking at them all. Seeing them singing our lyrics.

Not that I could see or hear them that well. The spots are blinding, especially once the sun set."

"I thought you were fantastic, obviously." She bumped her head against his shoulder and breathed in the familiar comfort of him. "I knew you were all going places the first time I heard you, and you've improved astronomically since. It was awesome, Lee. Really fucking amazing." They paused for a moment, arms clasped, and did a stupid little jig together.

They began walking again.

"Make sure you tell Nash that too, eh? Or hell, even show him."

She stopped and stared at his back until Lee turned to see where she'd got to. He sighed on seeing her frown.

"I just mean that he's feeling a bit insecure after— after what happened."

"I'm not exactly feeling secure myself right now." Was this a good point to mention Rune's dismissal at this point?

Lee strode back to her and took hold of her hands. "It's gonna be all right, Jo. This will blow over, but maybe you and Nash should grab some time for yourselves for the rest of the evening, rather than hanging out with the rest of us."

"Maybe." Honestly, she had the most fun when they were all together. The guys were just as important to her as Nash, and she wanted to celebrate their achievement this night with them. Playing a festival this size was a major achievement, especially given they'd only been a real band since earlier that year.

When they caught up to Jez, Balin, and Nash, The Ghost Boys' drummer had her fiancé in an uncomfortable-looking headlock. "Want to take this fucktard off me? Fiver and he's all yours."

"Five pee, more like," Balin quipped.

Jez gave Nash a friendly push towards her,

whereupon he wrapped both arms around her waist and attempted to lift her but failed, and hence just kissed her instead.

"Ah, look at the *boo-ti-ful* love birds," Balin crowed. Both her and Nash flicked him an array of fingers. For a moment, everything seemed to slip back to how it had been. The two of them loved up and surrounded by a tight-knit group of friends, marriage on the horizon along with the promise of years of togetherness and happiness. Then she saw Jez's gaze sheer away from them, and Nash stiffened in response to the sound of Rock Giant telling the festival audience a story about a fair maid he'd once happened upon, before launching into a short section of a traditional folk song.

It was a love story cemented by mushrooms.

Nash stiffened, his arms still around her.

Rock Giant sang a whole verse and chorus in his low rumbly voice, accompanied by their keyboardist, before their frontman interrupted and steered them into their next official song. A song she just happened to know the lyrics to and hence sang along to without thinking.

"Didn't think you knew who Black Halo were prior to yesterday," Balin said.

The scowl was back on Nash's face, even though she was sure she'd heard him playing this song before too. She shrugged. "Everyone knows who they are." And luckily for her, this was one of their biggest hits. It was hardly a surprise she'd be familiar with it. People without any interest in metal knew this one. More explaining might have been necessary, if it'd been something off an obscure EP.

"You're headed back to the bus, yeah?" Lee said to her and Nash.

"That's right." Nash grabbed hold of her hand.

"Where are the rest of you going?"

Cue numerous sidelong glances. Okay, dumb question. Female festival attendees beware. The Ghost Boys were going on the prowl.

"Your knobs'll drop off, you filthy beasts," Nash called after them, then added, "Except I hope they don't, cause it'll bollocks up the band," under his breath. "You realise they're going to end up back on the bus with whoever they pick up?"

She'd figured as much, which meant they wouldn't find any privacy there. Then again, she didn't really want to head to the bus. The place reeked of beer and air freshener, and even falling into the bigger bed in the bunk room involved a certain amount of ick. She'd bet actual money she couldn't afford to lose that no one had changed the sheets since she'd witnessed Balin banging that girl there earlier. "We could go to my tent."

There hadn't been time to move her stuff earlier, so it was still pitched and cosy.

Nash made a noncommittal grunt. "We shouldn't have to sleep in a pokey tent."

"It's fine."

"It isn't. I've worked for this as much as they have. I'm entitled to enjoy it just as much. I shouldn't have to worry about having my fiancée disturbed by my band mates and whatever pea-brained fuck toys they bring back."

"They're just enjoying the moment, Nash. The novelty will wear off soon enough."

"Yeah, sure," he scoffed. "They're all going to wake up in a week or three and decide they're done with screwing whoever they please when they please. I think maybe you're still tripping if you believe that, babe. What fool turns down the offer to have his cock sucked as often as he fucking likes?"

"You sound jealous, Nash."

He sniffed. "I'm not. Obviously, I'm not." Irritably,

Nash swished his tongue over his front teeth. "Fine, maybe a little. I'm not going to bail on my relationship in exchange for mindless fucking like Quilly's done though. That is what they're doing, Jo. It's emotionless... Soulless..." It sounded like he was trying to convince himself. "It's not a patch on what we've got." He lifted their paired palms and pressed a kiss to the back of her hand, before grinning, and adding, "Besides, it's not like you won't blow me if I ask."

"Hmm..."

He made pretty eyes at her from under his feathery eyelashes. "If I ask nicely, right?"

"Well...maybe."

He dragged her into the shadowy alleyway formed by two parked vans and pushed her up against the side of the nearest one.

She hadn't meant now.

"Lovely, darling, Jo-Jo. My beloved fiancée. Beautiful, bountiful goddess of my heart." He crowded her against the cold metal. "Will you get on your knees and worship my cock?"

"Can we not do this right now, Nash?" They were out in the open, where anyone could wander past at any moment. She didn't need to give the world reasons to make her feel ashamed of herself, and they would, if they were caught. Not so Nash. It'd make him a fucking folk hero.

"No one is going to come around here."

"You don't know that."

"This is a performers' only area, and everyone is watching the gig."

Not everyone. They weren't. Scores of roadies weren't. "Let's just go to my tent."

"Let's not."

They stood at an impasse for several increasingly uncomfortable moments.

"Jo." He slid his hand between her legs.

"Nash, no. Not here."

"God, woman!" He relinquished and thrust the same hand through the damp locks of his hair. "I could be forgiven for thinking you don't want to be seen with me."

"I'm fine being seen with you, obviously." What she didn't want was to be caught on camera doing something that was best enjoyed in private and wind up as the star of some viral TikTok. "But I'm your fiancée, not some groupie you've picked up to fan your ego and discard after a quickie. It matters to me how I'm perceived. It should matter to you. I'm trying to make it as a children's author."

He showed her far too many teeth as he snorted. "You've written one cat book that no bugger's read, babe. You couldn't even get a publishing deal for it. It's only in print because—"

Because Rune's family were in the printing business. Yes, she was a failure. He didn't need to point it out.

"Bet it'd be a different story if Paul Reed was here begging you, wouldn't it? Bet you wouldn't hesitate in dropping to your knees for him. How do I know for sure that isn't what you did last night? Got all starry-eyed and gobbled his prick like a proper groupie slut."

He had not... He had not just said that.

Her mouth goldfished open and closed, while her brain tried to catch up with all the implications of his words.

"You entitled arse! If that were true, Nash, I'd have ridden his monster pierced cock to multiple orgasms last night, and I'd be at the side of that stage now," – she made a jabbing motion in that direction— "watching him, instead of standing here with you being insulted. But maybe—maybe you'd actually prefer that. Maybe you'd like to get rid of me, so then you could go screw whoever the fuck you wanted."

Tears welled as she snarled, but she rapidly blinked them away.

Scarlet heat flooded Nash's pale cheeks, while anger glazed his eyes. "And how the fuck do you know he has monster fucking cock, pierced or otherwise?"

That—of all things—was what he fixated on. Not the fact he was acting like a prick. "Well, if you ever actually listened... He and I had a one-night stand years ago. I told you that, earlier."

"And maybe I believe it only happened in the past, earlier."

"I didn't sleep with him last night, no matter what you think." She shoved him again, but he held his ground, immovable, keeping her trapped against the van.

"Whatever."

"I fucking didn't." Right now, she wished she had. Her hands curled into tight fists. "Know why I didn't, Nash? Do you?" She thumped him hard in the centre of his chest again. "It's because I chose you. I fucking chose you. You stood me up, Nash. You fucking stood me up, and you haven't even apologised for it, not properly."

"Jo," he soothed, apparently realising he'd hit a nerve. "Come on. I did."

Jodi slapped his hands away. "Don't you fucking touch me."

"Jo-Jo." He struck a conciliatory tone, addressed her softly, like she was child amidst a meltdown. "What are you getting yourself so worked up for and making such a scene? Honestly, all this 'cause I asked for a blowjob? It was just a fucking joke."

Had it been?

"Calm the fuck down—"

"Back off."

He shuffled back a pace. "—or you're going to have security over here."

That was what he was bothered about.

"Jeezus, what the fuck is up with you tonight? You're being proper irrational."

No, she wasn't. She was pissed off. He was belittling... demeaning her. "I know my book didn't do very well, Nash, but I thought you at least had some faith in me." She'd been about to say she'd stood by him, cheered him on when the Ghost Boys started out, but it wasn't a good comparison. They'd hit it big from the off.

"There you go, you're just looking for reasons to be pissed off," he said. "I do have faith in you. Of course I do. I helped with the launch, remember. And I'm the one who took you out and made everything better after no bugger turned up."

A few people had. She'd even sold some copies.

"I'm the one who made sure you didn't starve after you blew your savings, remember that? I'm the one who's always here for you. The person who looks out for you, when you forget to look after yourself. I leave you unattended for a few hours and you wind up tripping your arse off and throwing yourself at some guy."

That wasn't quite... She guessed it kinda had happened like that. She did often wind up in trouble when she was alone.

Nash lifted her chin with his fingertips. "A little appreciation of my efforts, eh?"

"Maybe."

"So, can we stop arguing and enjoy the night?"

"Guess."

He kissed her. Except within seconds, it had stopped being conciliatory and turned sexual.

"Nash." She wriggled, trying to extract herself from his hold.

"Oh, come on, Jo-Jo. Please, be a doll, just this once. It's a special night."

"Nash, no."

He gave a frustrated huff and raised his hands in surrender. "Why'd you have to be such a fucking prude?"

"I'm not. It's just..." She'd already explained it. How did she make him understand? "It's not like you're going to get on your knees and get me off."

"What the fuck?"

"You wouldn't...You don't."

"Do."

She shook her head. She could count on one hand the number of times he'd gone down on her since they got together. It wasn't remotely comparable to the number of times she'd sucked him off.

"Well, you never ask me to."

She had. Plenty of times.

"You never want anything in bed. I ask you what you want all the time. Fine. You want your pussy licking in exchange for a blowjob? I'll do it now."

That wasn't what she'd been saying at all.

"Actually, I think I'd just like to go back to my tent."

"The fuck," he muttered. "Give a guy a break. You can't throw this back in my face later. I offered, and you've snubbed me."

"I just don't think this is a good place or time."

He stared at her so hard his eyes were in danger of bulging free of their sockets.

"Actually, I think I'd just like some me time." She managed to extract herself from his hold by ducking beneath his arm. "I'm gonna go back to my tent."

Nash followed her to the rear of the two parallel parked vehicles. "Seriously? You're leaving? You better not have fucking well arranged to hook up with him."

If only. The possibility of Rock Giant swaddling her in an all-encompassing hug and making all the ugly things in the world disappear was more appealing than it ought to have been.

"No. I have not arranged to meet him. I just told you, I'm going to my tent, because I need some quiet."

"Right. And where the fuck am I supposed to go?"

"Your tour bus."

"My bus. You mean, my bus on which my bandmates are screwing groupies, that one?"

"Like that fact actually bothers you, Nash." She'd seen him earlier. Cock in hand, watching Balin. It was burned into her memory in a way she didn't much like.

She got four paces before Nash snarled, "Maybe this time I won't just watch," at her back.

She froze, lead weights settling in her stomach. "If you do that, we're done," she said without turning.

"Whatever."

He deliberately barged into her as he stormed past, jarring her shoulder. Jodi flipped two fingers up at his back, then her knees gave out and she sank onto the grass into a pitiful heap. "Shit!" she hissed into her clenched fist. How had everything fallen apart again so fast? He wouldn't really buddy up with the guys and fuck other women, would he? Part of her wanted to stalk after him, peer in the tour bus windows and ensure his words were just shit thrown around for effect, but she wouldn't demean herself in that way. She'd take herself back to her tent, exactly as she'd said she'd do.

Back in those canvas quarters, she cried to her cats about it.

The two girls, Mel and Zar were about as comforting as a barbed wire elephant, but Flugwhump rubbed his black furry face against her cheek and licked away her tears with his rough kitty tongue.

The worst bit was she couldn't figure out whose fault it all was. Hers, most likely. It usually was.

CHAPTER 18
PAUL "ROCK GIANT" DEED

N HINDSIGHT, THE confrontation was inevitable. Now, Paul would have done the accosting in a far less public place, such as the nice section of scrubby bushes to the left of the khazis, thus avoiding unnecessary witnesses. Then again, he wasn't a weedy shrimp with more attitude than brain cells.

Curtis Nash chose a well-lit backstage area with plenty of witnesses, probably because there was safety in a crowd. Or maybe booze had just loosened his vocal cords. Or not. Because while he strode up like he was on a mission, it seemed to occur to him that Paul could snap him like a twig once they were approximately face-to-face, for what came out of his mouth once he was staring up at Paul was far less abrasive than it might have been. It didn't start with fucker and end with wanker, and there might even have been a please involved.

Hence, "You need to stay the fuck away from my

fiancée." Not: keep your hands off her or I'll chop them off with a blunt cleaver and then violate you with your own right hand.

Definitely the line he'd have taken if their situations were reversed. If it wasn't that for some unfathomable reason, his missus insistently maintained she was in love with this cockwomble and his singular mission in life was her pleasure, then he'd be taking that line now.

"Na, don't think so, mate. I made vows to her, I ain't going against them because it's putting your nose out of joint that I'm willing to make her happy."

"I make her happy, you arsehole."

"That so. Must be why she was so eager to tie the knot with me instead. She knows I keep my promises."

"You got her fucking high and took advantage."

"Why don't you say that a bit louder so security can hear you?" Spook muttered from beside him. Paul hadn't noticed that half his band had fallen in behind him. Not that he needed backup.

Nash gave a hard sniff and straightened his spine. It still barely brought him to Paul's shoulders. "This has nothing to do with whatever sick shit you offered her. She was in a suggestive state and you—"

"Promised to honour and protect her, love her until the heat death of the universe and beyond and to be by her side come what way. Not sure how that's taking advantage."

The guy's eyes bulged, and a nervous tick started firing under his skin, right in the centre of his forehead.

"If I'd been there to take advantage, I wouldn't have stopped after knotting a ribbon around her wrist, would I?"

"He'd have gone for the full-on knotting," Cave Troll, who'd appeared out of the scaffolding of the stage, remarked.

That wasn't quite what he'd been about to say, but it got the sentiment across. It was hard not to grin, both at the look of horror on shit creek's face, and the mental pictures Troels' remark was creating in his imagination. He wouldn't mind being stuck inside Jodi's gorgeous pussy for an indeterminate length of time. Damned if he wasn't turned on by the notion of it. He was sad they hadn't consummated their bond with some rabid fucking. Was sad too that his tongue wasn't strained from licking, and was hence working well enough to talk to this gobshite.

"You think you're clever. That this is all a joke. It's not fucking funny. We're engaged. We're getting married. She's mine. Have some fucking decency and stay the hell away from her, or are you that much of a prick you get off on destroying relationships?"

"Pretty sure you set that mantrap yourself. Maybe try not standing her up. I mean, if you'd showed, I wouldn't have had to step in, would I? At least now she knows she has options and doesn't have to settle for someone who clearly never puts her first."

"Of course I put her—"

Rock Giant laughed loud enough to drown him out. "Where were you? What were you doing that was so fucking important that it clean escaped your mind that you were meant to be exchanging vows with the woman you're allegedly in love with? Huh? No answer? Anyone around here know?"

"On-bus entertainment," one of the now significant number of observers muttered.

Paul lost significantly more respect for the guy, because that wasn't anything like a good enough reason to abandon the woman you love at the altar. Now, maybe dickbrain wasn't bright enough to realise that's what he'd done, but Paul knew, and a significant number of their current observers could work it out given the details, and most important of all, Jodi knew, and even though she was apparently deeply forgiving, he hoped she'd filed the slight under events to refer back to when deciding if she actually wanted to spend her life with this fool.

Evidently, even Nash realised he didn't have a decent argument, because he bleated, "Just fucking stay away from her," and turned tail and beat it. No doubt he was currently reworking the exchange in his head so that his bravado stood up to scrutiny, and Paul was thoroughly put in his place.

"What a complete carrot," Spook muttered, giving the phrase a particularly British bite that he'd definitely learned from Ash or Xane. He raised his middle finger at Curtis Nash's retreating back. Beside Spook, Xane quirked an eyebrow, his lips puckering into a smirk. Paul had expected a reaction, just not that Spook would be the one to voice it.

"What do you want to do?" Xane asked Paul.

Their vocalist's gaze kept sweeping the crowd, on the lookout for further trouble no doubt. Not from the knobwaffle, so much as other quarters—Elspeth. "It's your call. We're behind you, whatever you decide."

That was a change from earlier. Then again, earlier they hadn't had to endure a public confrontation with a halfwit. "About?" he asked, mostly to make sure they were in fact talking about what he thought they were talking about and not something else entirely.

Ash bent over his splayed knees to reach the water bottle between his feet. "Whether you want to continue touring with gobshite or not. What the fuck does she see in him? He's like the antithesis of you."

Paul wasn't sure he had an answer to that. Happened he was on team Spook when it came to opinions on Curtis Nash. On the other hand, he didn't want to toast the rest of the Ghost Boys's dreams because they happened to be saddled with a prick of a lead singer. Where were the rest of them? Seemed significant that they weren't in tow, backing up their friend. But mostly, ditching their only-just announced support act at zero notice was going to create ructions. Major ructions. None of them needed another legal wrangle. Or worse, a media circus.

"I can stomach him if the rest of you can."

Also, if they ditched the Ghost Boys, that would mean losing his missus from the tour right along with them. So, no, best option available was to tolerate dipshit, and hence keep Jodi in his orbit.

Where was she now, while dog-breath was waving his bollocks around?

He doubted she'd be impressed.

He was tempted to text her and find out, until he realised while he'd given her his number, she'd refused to hand him hers.

Xane passed Ash the bottle he was still straining to reach and sat his arse on the sofa Ash was occupying the back of. "I'm thinking we contact Graham and apprise him of the situation, so he's at least aware of it, and doesn't wind up blindsided if Harry Storm gets on his case."

"Think he will?"

"If his reputation is anything to go on, yeah."

"Text him," Spook agreed. "Makes sense, just in case anything further kicks off."

"I'm sorry," Paul mumbled. "I didn't mean to create hassle."

Xane patted him on the back. "If she's the one, then she's the one. It'll work out."

That didn't sound much like Xane.

Their lead singer sucked on his lip-piercing, then flashed him a grin. "I'm trying to take a leaf out of Luthor's book and be more zen about stuff."

"Do we not need to consult him and Ronnie before

we make any decisions?" Ronnie had been accosted by Lyra and dragged off to do a late-night meet and greet.

"They're going to roll with whatever you want. I can vouch for Luthor, and we all know Ronnie's your bestie."

He wasn't so sure of that anymore.

"Where is Luthor, anyway?" He'd only just realised their drummer wasn't with them.

Xane made the universal sign for phone call, then rested his head against the bench back and blew out a long breath. "Family shit."

"Oh?"

Xane shook his head, clearly not wanting to get into the weeds of it. "Same shit that called Ulf home. I'm not sure of the details, I just know he wasn't best thrilled with whatever decisions seem to have been made in his absence, but let's stick with the current issue, eh? So, to confirm, we're going ahead as planned?"

"We are."

"Fun, fun, fun," Ash drawled. "Right, we packing up and getting out of here?"

"Now?" Paul asked. He didn't recall an immediate departure being on the agenda.

"Now," both Spook and Xane confirmed.

Maybe he oughtn't to have mentioned Elspeth.

J ODI SLID BENEATH the curtains enclosing the bunk she and Nash were sharing to search for her jeans and failed to find them. Gentle snores came from the bunk across the aisle, and a hairy leg dangled over the edge of the topmost bunk above where she'd slept. Balin had her jeans tucked under his head.

Damn.

She blew out a breath and tugged the shirt down lower. It'd be fine. It wasn't like any of them were awake.

The Ghost Boys had played four gigs across Belgium and Germany, before taking the ferry from Kiel to Oslo to rendezvous with Black Halo for the next eight months. Their label owner cum manager, Harry Storm had insisted the extra shows would ensure they were on top form ahead of playing to the bigger crowds Black Halo pulled.

While Equinox had been a highlight for the guys,

Jodi had enjoyed the more relaxed atmosphere of the smaller venues they'd played since. Everything was just a little more ad hoc, a little more down to earth. Also, it'd given the guys a chance to adapt to their new situation, and her a chance to get to grips with her new role as their personal assistant. No more dragging their own amps out of the back of a van or replacing broken strings for themselves. There were a team of roadies to do that. Of course, there were downsides too. None of them could just run to the shop anymore—that was now her job—as there was always a tidy group of fans around no matter the time of day. It kept their two security guards busy.

The last ten days had also given her and Nash the time they needed to work through their insecurities and spend some quality time together. Hopefully, catching up with Black Halo later today wouldn't unravel them again.

She tiptoed through to the tiny bathroom, fixed her hair and face, and scrubbed her teeth, before heading up front to give the cats their breakfast. Mel and Zar were draped over different sections of the banquette, with Lee stretched out between them, while Flugwhump was sitting in the sink of the tiny kitchenette waiting for her to turn the tap on. He'd taken to drinking straight from the source since their arrival on their new home on wheels. "Weirdo," she chided, giving his furry head a scratch.

"If you're making coffee, yes please," Lee called.

Dutifully, she picked out the last two mugs in the cupboard. By the time she'd finished making their drinks, Lee had rolled onto his front and was leaning over the edge of the seat, playing phone games one-handed.

"Anxious about later?" he asked, as she sat on the floor, level with his mobile, and pulled her shirt over her knees.

"You're the one playing."

He wrapped his hand around the mug and took a big swallow before letting out a contented sigh. When he put the cup down, it was half empty. Jodi blew on her own drink, as the cats came up and rubbed against her. Lee insisted on having so much milk in his brews, they barely remained warm for more than a minute or two. She, on the other hand, had mostly got out of the habit of adding milk. It wasn't the easiest thing to transport when you lived out of a backpack, and she'd had a couple of accidents in the early days with spillages that left everything stinking for weeks.

"Rock Giant," Lee prompted.

Yeah, she knew what he'd meant. Rock Giant was never far from her mind. She was antsy about seeing him. How could she be anything else? She'd woken the night after the festival gig, to find Black Halo had already departed. Seemed they'd come off stage and left within the hour. The guys had helped her strike camp and dispose of the stuff she seemed to have accumulated, then, she and Nash had found their way back to one another about an hour after that. She'd been up at the standing stones, hanging with Jez as he jotted down lyrics, saying a sort of farewell to them while the roadies packed the last of the Ghost Boys equipment up. She'd been beheading daisies, when Nash crouched down before her, and holding a buttercup beneath his chin asked, "Do I like butter?"

There was indeed a golden glow visible on his skin. "It's down to the anatomy of the petals," she told him. "Nothing to do with whether you like butter or not."

"Right." He sat cross-legged before her. After a moment, he stole one of the daisies. "She loves me. She loves me not. She loves me. She loves me not." White petals scattered on the breeze.

"He loves me. He loves me not," she countered.

"He loves you," he insisted, delivering the

denuded disc florets of his daisy to her as proof. Jodi lifted her gaze, meeting his muddy blue eyes. He offered her an apologetic smile. "Oh, Jo. I'm sorry about last night. I don't know what the fuck got into me. No, that's not true. I do. I'm a jealous arsehole, and apparently, I don't take care of my woman properly. Assuming you haven't decided to be done with me completely, I promise to do better on that score."

Beside them, Jez shot them a glance over the top of his notebook, but dropped his gaze again the moment he figured they'd noticed him.

"How are you going to do better?" she asked, chewing on her lower lip. Honestly, it was a relief to know he was still speaking to her, and that they weren't breaking up. She hated discord, but she also knew better than to try and talk to him before he was ready. Also, she'd be lying if she said she hadn't been panicking over the possibility of them all leaving without her. Sure, the guys had helped her pack up her stuff and had merrily bad-mouthed Nash to her, but if it came down to it, Nash and the band would totally win over her and the cats.

"Tongue exercises?" Nash stuck his tongue out and contorted it several impressive ways.

Jodi showed him, that she too could roll her tongue. "I was overly harsh. It wasn't unreasonable for you to seek reassurances from me considering everything that's happened since we got here."

He licked her on the nose. "It's okay. I forgive you for picking a fight. And I'm sorry I wasn't where you expected me to be the other night." He nodded his head at the standing stones as if her memory might need jogging. "I'd probably have chomped a shed load of mushrooms too, if I'd been noodling about this place for hours. It's bleak."

Actually, with the dappled autumn sun over it, it

was rather lovely, especially within the circle, where the breeze only tickled, and the world beyond seemed out of phase with that within.

"You should make him grovel more," Jez remarked, eyeing them over the lip of his book.

"Cheers, mate."

"Any time, arsehole."

Jodi snorted at their snipping. "I'd rather get along than draw things out," she said to Jez.

He shrugged.

Nash dropped a kiss on her brow, then moved in for more of a smooch.

"Urgh! If you two are going to get soppy..." Jez's shadow fell over them as he stood. "It's more than my stomach can handle." He made puking noises. "See you back at the bus. We leave in forty, remember."

Things had been okay since then. They'd gone back to making vague wedding plans. Hadn't quite agreed on a date yet. The whole of Nash's family had to be consulted, and their availability tallied with the Black Halo tour dates, plus promotional appearances, a video shoot for an upcoming single, plus Harry had the Ghost Boys booked in to start work on their second album the moment the tour ended. Their lives seemed to have been timetabled into the distant future.

"It's usually the constant travel that wears artists down," Brian had told her the day before, but the Ghost Boys had all been digital nomads/fruit pickers/ backpacking wanderers prior to becoming a band. Travelling wasn't the hard part. Sticking to a set schedule, *that* was the tricky bit.

She, Nash, and Balin had taken off yesterday afternoon while they were in Kiel to see the U-boat submarine museum and arrived back a teeny bit late. Result—they'd almost missed the ferry across to Norway. Had been forced to board as foot passengers, as the tour bus had left ahead of them, and thus, had been yelled at by Harry Storm over Zoom, and given an in person ticking off from both Brian, and the overall tour manager, a scary guy named Samson.

She'd been mortified. The guys—not so much. Balin and Nash had spent the rest of the evening mucking about, spying on people with a cardboard periscope they'd picked up in a tourist gift shop.

"I'm sure it'll be fine," she eventually said to Lee. "We'll probably barely see Black Halo. I bet it's a myth that bands on tour hang out together. And he's probably forgotten all about me. He's a world-famous bassist, after all, and I'm just me." She shrugged.

Lee met her gaze. "That's just it, Jo. You're you. You're amazing. It's not a surprise that the guy's into you, only that he's being so chill about it."

Both their heads turned towards the door to the bunk room as Nash emerged, yawning sleepily.

"Piss off, Lee," he demanded. "I want some private time with my woman."

"Should I stay, or should I go," Lee asked her out of the side of his mouth.

"Go," she mouthed back. "And give us half an hour."

"Okay, girl." He rose, giving her shoulder a squeeze, then brushed past Nash. "Morning, cunt."

"Still opting for the bum fluff, I see."

Lee had started growing a beard, but it barely constituted stubble yet. He rolled his eyes. "Least I know how to find a woman's."

"Women don't... Fuck off."

Lee laughed and closed the door between them. Within seconds, music was blaring loudly enough there was no chance of anyone in the bunk room overhearing whatever she and Nash said or did.

Jodi rose from the floor. "Morning," she greeted Nash with a kiss.

"Let's make it a good 'un, eh?" He grazed his lips against the shell of her ear. "Fancy kneeling for me?"

Jodi knelt on the banquette, facing the window. It absolutely wasn't what he meant, but...

"Babe!"

She wiggled her arse at him.

"Oh my, God, are you bare under that?"

"Someone stole my knickers last night. Can't think who or why, mind."

His reflection in the window while faint was visible enough for her to make out his grin. He'd insisted on her undressing and touching herself on their bunk with the curtains drawn, while he watched through the periscope he'd picked up from the museum. She'd been shy about it, but when Nash had finally crawled into the bunk alongside her, he'd been seriously hyped.

The rest of the band hadn't turned in until long after they were done and dozing. Thank God.

"You were so fucking hot last night, Jo. I woke thinking about it." That would explain why his hand was straying inside his shorts. "Are you planning on staying there?"

The windows were tinted. From outside you couldn't see in, which meant it was safe to watch the world rolling by without fear of being observed, even if it seemed like they were rolling by in a fish tank on wheels.

"In the arse or the pussy?" he asked, chin prodding her between the shoulder blades.

"Bit presumptuous, aren't you?"

"My cock needs its Jo-Jo fix. Are you wet?" He wrapped an arm around her hip and slid his hand over her mons. "Or do I need to frig you a bit?" He gave her clit a pet.

"Nash, we'll be arriving soon."

"Right. I'll just stick it in, then."

She gave another wiggle, eager to get this over with. "Be quick, yeah. I don't want to get caught." Nor did she want to reek of him when they met up with Black Halo.

"WHAT DID I do wrong?" Ronnie Bush asked for the fifty-first—fifty-second time. It wasn't the repetition that was the issue, so much as the question that was grinding Paul's gears. Fact was he hadn't been able to produce a suitable response at the time of the first asking—right after they'd come off stage at Equinox—and he still didn't have one now. Leastways, not one that Ronnie wanted to hear.

Another two hours until Jodi-ville. He was still sore that he'd never got to say a proper goodbye. It was his own fault. He'd mentioned Elspeth being about, so of course Xane arranged for them all to make a swift departure. He'd dressed it up and presented it as some extra hours of R&R so no one had protested. But Paul had wanted a few moments. Time to say, 'Bye for now' and 'See you again soon', along with the chance to breathe in the scent of her, maybe wrap his woman up in a full body embrace, and maybe squeeze a phone number out of her.

"Fucking just tell him, please," Ash muttered from across the other side of the table.

Paul would say one thing for the Norwegians, they'd put some serious effort into their hospitality. The catering they'd arrived to was a major step up from pretty much everything else, and of course they were all famished, so here they still were, two hours later, filling up the corners after a truly impressive lunch.

"Nothing," Paul said to Ronnie. It conveniently covered most of the things he was potentially being asked. The blowjob, what he recalled of it, had been fine. The issue was that Ronnie seemed to have got it into his head, that Paul had run off and got hitched to Jodi as a direct response to his own oral sex inadequacies. Thing was, that was hard to debunk, when he was banned from talking about Jodi, after days of talking about Jodi, and they weren't talking about the bro-job for the obvious reason that the guys didn't know about it.

How they didn't know was almost beyond comprehension, but he was clinging to that minor miracle like a life vest. He certainly wasn't going to be the one to change that. Yes, he'd almost had to smother Ronnie once already to make sure he didn't blab. Mind you, he'd also woken up earlier to find Ronnie arranging Haribo bears along his spine and on his butt cheeks. That'd been slightly odd even by Ronnie standards. "Bored," he said, when Paul had protested.

"We're ready for the sound check," Alle announced. She lingered just long enough to give Spook a kiss, then was off again. She was taking her role as Ulf's temporary replacement very seriously.

By the time they'd done the sound check, Jodi had

arrived along with their support band. She was looking slightly travel worn—a bit crumpled at the corners—blond hair caught in a messy knot from which most of the strands had escaped. The shirt she had on, what he'd describe as a peasant girl top—skirted the very tops of her nipples, almost but not quite revealing too much. She'd paired it with an oversized crocheted cardigan, which was only fabulous if you happened to love oversized crocheted cardigans of dubious origins, taste, and colour. He was neutral to *urgh* on the subject. It was periwinkle blue. It didn't lessen the uptick of his heart rate, or stop him heading straight towards her, at least until Xane caught hold of the back of his waistband.

"Don't fucking muck this up. The tour's going to be the pits otherwise. And if you hurtle over there—"

He switched off, and hence didn't absorb the rest, but he dutifully trooped to the dressing rooms with the rest of the band. Didn't mean he did it quietly, especially when the first thing Xane did when he got there was sweep his girlfriend up into his arms and kiss her senseless, which was precisely what he'd wanted to do with his wife.

"Are you glaring daggers at my partners for a reason?" Luthor asked, standing beside him and mirroring his crossed armed pose.

"It's okay for him to snog his woman senseless, but I'm not even allowed to say hello."

"Would you have just said hello?"

Obviously not.

"I'm not sure you're cut out for polyamory, or at least the current incarnation of it you're exploring," Luthor observed.

"What's that supposed to mean?"

"It means I can read your thoughts on the matter just by looking at you looking at my boyfriend and girlfriend making out. Here's the thing. The green-eyed monster doesn't visit when I see them like this. I'm just pleased they're happy. You on the other hand, are contemplating ways in which to part Nash's head from his shoulders."

"He's not good for her."

"That's not for you to decide."

Paul grouched. He was perfectly fucking aware of that. Otherwise, he'd be out there welcoming her with a full-body snog, not in here watching Xane turn Dani into a blancmange.

Spook clapped him on his other shoulder. "We're on your side, despite what you might think."

"That right. How are you?"

"Got an icebreaker lined up for tonight to get us all working as a big happy family."

"'cause that's not at all disturbing." He still hadn't got used to this new, more talkative, more proactive version of Spook. The guy still had plenty of moody-git days, but there were phases of gregariousness between them that he found disorientating. Also, Spook was a sadist, any activities he proposed required in-depth scrutiny before agreeing to participate in. His idea of helping them all get along likely involved roping them all together for the next forty-eight hours. Or worse, team sports. "Think I'll pass, mate."

"Even if it gets you full body contact time with the lovely Jodi?"

"What?"

"Please don't encourage him, Spook," Xane muttered in between kisses.

"I thought we agreed a forty-eight-hour ban on mentioning her," Ash said.

Spook shot him a grin. "Technically, only Paul's banned from mentioning her. I can say Jodi as many times as I like. Jodi. Jodi. Oh, Jodi."

"Stop it," Xane said, smirking.

"Okay, let's hear it," Paul could feel his blood

pressure spiking every time Spook said her name. Genuine time with her would make the inevitable bruises sustained in playing one of Spook's games worth it.

"It involves socks," Spook said cryptically. Then pushed ahead of them and disappeared into the bathroom before they could grill him further.

"Did he just propose a wanking game?" Paul asked.

Xane finally put Dani back on her feet and reinstated his shades. "Seems as likely as unlikely. I'm not sure how that involves you getting quality time with your missus mind—"

Xane was still talking about potential hurdles and difficulties, but Paul had stopped hearing him after the honorific—missus. He slapped their frontman on the back. "You can be all right, sometimes. Even likeable."

"Oh-kay. I'm still gonna offer to hold you still while Nash pisses down your throat if you don't stay away from her."

He reckoned he'd missed the first part of the threat when his hearing stalled over missus. Still, he got a kick out of repeating the word that made his cock excitable.

"You know threating him is totally the wrong approach," Dani said, from where she was now tucked beneath Xane's arm. "It makes him sixty per cent more likely to do the opposite of what you want."

More like a hundred and sixty, although, in this case, he was planning to show some restraint, but only because Jodi had requested it. Xane could swivel, even if he was all right sometimes.

As to Spook's sock game, he guessed they'd find out post-gig.

"How much longer till we can get out of here?" Ash asked.

A show had been played. Fans rocked. Showers taken. The two bands were now making a go of harmonising by way of some social drinking in a hotel suite booked for an after party. So far, despite the alcohol, and a medley of extras there for the prestige, it was all very stiff, with everyone divided into us and them camps. The only good thing about it was the free booze, which they were all knocking back to deaden the pure discomfort of being made to interact. Honestly, no amount of corporate nurturing would forge friendships out of thin air or dowse the tension that defined every interaction. Plus, Paul still hadn't had a chance to say hello to Jodi. She was nestled between the Ghost Boys, two of them on either side of her, like she was a mafia queen, and they were her muscle. Somewhat weedy muscle, but the analogy stood. He was sorely tempted to just walk over there and start things rolling by sayin, "Hey babe, wanna go somewhere I can worship your pussy", but Xane and Ash had already shoved him back into his seat twice, and Ronnie was currently sprawled across his, Alle, and Spook's laps doing... Actually, he didn't know what the hell he was doing. He gave him a push, which sent him rolling under the table.

Also, he wouldn't actually say that to Jodi. Too crude, and he was not a crude man. He did totally want to lick her out though.

"We done?" he asked.

Xane and Spook exchanged looks.

"Party time?" said the latter.

"Party time." Xane stood. Prompting the rest of them to do the same. "It's been lovely," Xane said to the Ghost Boys tour manager, an older guy who looked as if he'd seen some stuff, while Ronnie scrambled out from under the table.

The Ghost Boys exchanged bewildered looks with the suits, who didn't look pleased about the exodus. Xane put a hand on their blond guitarist's shoulder and said something to him too quiet for anyone else to catch. No doubt, the rest of the band would be grilling him for details the moment Black Halo were out of the room.

"How long?" Paul asked as they piled into the lift. Black Halo were up in the penthouse suite for the night.

"I said to give it ten."

"Ten what?" Dani asked yawning. "Man, I'm so pooped. It's gonna take me a while to get back into the rock star routine. My body's still on 9 o'clock tutorial time."

"Bonding sesh in ten minutes," Xane explained to his still yawning girlfriend. "I can't face another two days of awkward interactions, let alone months, and nothing's gonna ease while the suits are trying to buddy us up.

"So, you've invited them over?"

"'fraid so," he said in response to the wrinkling of her petite nose. "If you need perking up though, I can make time before they arrive."

"Hm," she rubbed her face up against Xane's chest. "I think I like that idea." They disappeared straight into the bathroom the moment they were through the suite door. No one needed to ask why, especially when Luthor followed them. The rest of them flopped across various surfaces as beverages were poured, and Ginny put some music on. Paul lingered on the periphery, so he'd be the one to answer the door and welcome them in. The wait was only a few minutes. He opened the door to the blond guy and their bassist.

"Lee. Balin."

They exchanged fist bumps as he ushered them in.

Jodi was next, along with the fiancé, who had his arm around her shoulders. "Welcome. Come on in," he said.

Fuck, he wanted to rip the guys arm off.

Luthor was right. He didn't want to share. He wanted every bit of her all to himself. Wanted time to explore and get to know her, make love, and grow old with her without interruptions. They ought to be honeymooning somewhere, not kept apart by some invisible force field of societal expectations that gave Nash the upper hand by virtue of having had her first. Except, that wasn't even true. She'd been his Jodi, long before Curtis Nash arrived on the scene.

"Appreciate the invitation, man," Nash said, brushing past him.

At least he'd let go of Paul's lady love. Entrance wasn't wide enough for them to get through glued together like conjoined twins.

"Castle."

"Rock Giant." She gave him a shy smile.

The final member of her fiancé's band, the one with the long, wavy brown hair, and eyes like Turkish coffee leaned around her. "Jez. Be good, guys. Now, point me at the booze."

Paul tipped his head in the right direction without taking his gaze off Jodi. "How've you been?"

"I'm good. How've you been?"

"Lonely," he said. "I got hitched, but it's still just me in my bunk listening to the rest of the wankers I work with get their rocks off of a night."

"I'm sorry." Remorse flooded her face. She touched his arm, leaned towards him. "I don't expect fidelity, if you wanna... I mean, we agreed we were just gonna be friends, and you know, I'm with Nash."

Oh, he knew that all right. Also, that wasn't quite what they'd agreed, but he let it fly for now. "Cute, Castle. Very generous of you."

Like hell was he going to be screwing anyone else. Just no to the nth degree. They might not have sworn fidelity as part of their vows, but that didn't mean he was going to diminish things by seeking comforts outside of their bond.

"Paul, please. I don't want you waiting around for me thinking something—"

"Jo-Jo, get your arse over here." Nash patted the spot on the sofa next to him.

She looked up at him. Paul smooshed his lips together into a smile. "Forever," he mouthed at her back as she crossed the suite and then sandwiched herself in between Nash and Jez.

Luthor emerged from the bathroom, looking rumpled. He took one look at Rock Giant and sighed. "Just no bloodshed, okay."

"She doesn't want me to do that, ergo, I'm not doing it."

"Who doesn't want you to do what?" Xane followed Luthor through the door, still zipping up.

"No one." Luthor distracted his boyfriend by squeezing his arse. "Let's go schmooze."

Chatter commenced. Drinks were drunk. Jez drank too much. Ronnie plied everyone with Haribo, and only afterwards mentioned they were vodka soaked.

Paul swallowed a few of them, mostly out of boredom when the conversation turned to logistics and industry gossip. He spent a while talking to Balin about pedal brands and pick-ups, but it wasn't exactly deep and meaningful. Throughout, he kept half an eye on Jodi. She seemed happy. She was smiling. Joining in with the conversation. All the Ghost Boys seemed pretty touchy feely with her. He guessed it wasn't just Nash she'd forged a bond with. He was looking at her "new" family. Jez was almost asleep on her shoulder, and Nash had a possessive hand on her thigh.

"Where'd you all meet?"

Balin, all dark hair and darker eyes, frowned at him over the top of his beer bottle. "They're happy, you know."

"I can see that."

"It'd be cool if you didn't fuck it up between them."

"If it fucks up, it won't be my doing."

"Dude, you've been eye fucking her since we arrived."

"She's hot. And more my thing than the rest of you, and what's up with asking where you all met?"

"Apparently you two hooked up one time in the past." Balin replied, still giving him nothing.

"She tell you that?"

"Nash. Nash told me that. I assume she told him."

"It was a while back," Paul confessed, happy to share that, if not the more intimate details of the occasion. "Weird night. Get you another beer?"

Balin swallowed what remained of the bottle in his hand. "Sure."

"God, the bus, the bus." Nash was expounding. "I cannot believe how much shit magically relocates. I mean, what is that about? You put something down, and next thing you know it's in a fucking cupboard, or the under-seat storage, or someone else's luggage."

"Or clogging the shower," Lee added.

"Truth." Nash pointed a finger at him.

"Twelve pencils all gone," Jez woke enough to contribute, before falling into a stupor.

"They're in the cupboard with the cat food," Balin said, walking over to join them.

Paul followed him, new drinks in hand for the two of them. He made use of the bottle opener, then found a perch on the edge of the coffee table alongside Ginny, who offered him a smile, then laced her fingers with his and gave his hand a squeeze.

"Who gives a shit about pencils?" Lee said. "All the fucking condoms magically vanished the other night. I had to finagle one out of Jez, who's like, 'I've only got a couple left, man', then this morning, I'm brushing my teeth and there's a full box of them nestled in alongside Jo-Jo's lady products in the vanity unit along with five random socks, a baby harmonica, and a packet of fucking feta cheese. Like, what? Also, ain't that stuff meant to be kept in the fridge?"

"Who the fuck bought it, anyway?" Nash added.

Jodi, clearly, based on the nibble she gave her lower lip. He'd wager she was responsible for the randomly migrating objects, too.

"Faeries," Paul suggested, half an eye still on Jodi, who began rolling a packet of love heart sweets— almost certainly from Ronnie's stash—back and forth along her thigh.

"Assuming you mean that's who's relocating stuff,

not buying feta. Although, maybe they can be blamed for both."

"If it's faeries, can't they do summat useful like tidy the empties away, or fumigate the bog?" Balin asked.

"Yeah, that'd be cool," Lee echoed.

"Clearly you've pissed them off." Paul knew his faerie lore. "Basically, means you're screwed until you make amends for the slight."

"Need a slash." Jez jerked awake and onto his feet. He stumbled over multiple sets of legs towards the nearest door and got redirected by Alle towards the actual bathroom. Paul took the opportunity to slide into the space he'd vacated alongside Jodi.

"Can I have one of those?" he asked, referring to the sweets in her hands.

"Um, sure." She offered him the packet. "I'm not really sure where they came from." Course not, his Castle was an object magnet. Things she passed magically stuck to her like in one of those running games that had been popular a few years back. Paul opened the love hearts packet and claimed the first one. He offered her the next. "Show me," he insisted, turning his sweet to her so she could see the message printed on his, which read, 'YOURS'.

"Not sure I should."

"Why not?"

She gave her fiancé a sidelong glance. "Not interested in causing ructions."

"It's a good 'un, then."

Cagily, she showed him. It read, "IT'S TRUE."

"Deffo," he agreed, chuckling. "Love Hearts never lie. Ask Ronnie, he'll tell you how prophetic they are. Aren't they Ronnie?"

Ronnie nodded, "Way better than an eight ball. Are they mine?"

"Jodi's," Paul replied, before she had a chance to

say otherwise. She looked down, fighting a smile. He passed Ronnie a single sweet.

"Let us have one," Nash stuck out a hand. Paul dutifully gave him one.

"Well, that's shit. I never get the good ones. HARD LUCK. What did you get, Jo?"

Jodi popped her first selection in her mouth and chose another. "YES, DEAR."

"Game time," Spook announced, entering the living area from one of the side-rooms, arms full of socks.

"Are they mine?" Luthor asked.

"You don't mind, do you, Luthor?"

"As long as I get them back undamaged."

"So, who's in?"

"What's the game?" Balin asked, eye cocked at the mound of sockage.

Ash roused from the sofa. "More importantly, what's the prize?"

Spook pointed at him. "Ah, interesting that you asked. That would be this here beautiful, 'Get Out of Jail Free Card.'" He showed them all the ancient orange Monopoly card. "Obviously, it won't get you out of actual jail, but it can be used in a range of circumstances to do-over, or defuse a situation, or simply to defenestrate your opposition."

Xane gave him a clap.

"Thank you." Spook gave a bow. "Now, who's in? It's a simple game. A very simple game. No complicated rules... Suitable for all ages and flexibility levels."

"I'm not playing Twister," Ash said.

"It's not Twister."

"I think we need to hear the actual rules." Lee was turning his head, looking at each of them, clearly trying to get a handle on what was likely to happen. "Is this an every man for himself game or a—"

"It's a team game. Black Halo versus the Ghost Boys. A friendly, obviously."

"There are six of you and only four of us," Nash pointed out. Fucking rules lawyer.

All attention turned to the bathroom and the sounds of heaving.

"And one of us isn't exactly at his best."

"I'm not playing, I'm adjudicating," Spook pointed out. "So Black Halo are down their best man too."

"Ooooh!" The sound was made by a combination of voices, disputing that claim. Although, depending on the measure, Spook was the best among them—best guitarist, best hair, best mediator, best at knots. Both tying and unravelling them. The list went on.

"I can play," Jodi offered, shuffling forward on the sofa, and accidentally bumping up against him in the process. Just that tiny bit of contact gave him an all-over happy glow.

"She is an honorary Ghost Boy," Lee confirmed.

"Yay, Jo-Jo." Balin raised his hand for a high five.

"That's not fair," Ginny complained. "I want to join in. I'm as much a part of Black Halo as she is the Ghost Boys. More so, even." She flashed her wedding band and engagement ring combo.

"Three teams," Spook proposed. "Black Halo, Ghost Boys, and the ladies."

"That still doesn't give an even number of players per team," Nash pointed out.

Yup, definitely a rules lawyer.

Ginny wasn't going to be thwarted. She nibbled her lip. Then her face lit. "Dani?"

Dani shook her head and waved her arms before her but was soon pulled from Xane's lap and drawn into a huddle with her best friend and his Jodi. "And Ronnie can join us and be an honorary lady," they declared after a quick conflab. "That's okay, ain't it? It makes the teams even."

Ronnie was promptly parted from a glass of what he called a Shoggoth, which was vodka, vermouth and on this occasion, crème de menthe combined with a bag of Golden Bears. Previous incarnations had involved peach schnapps, Tequila Rose, and Appletini. "Well, yes, I suppose. I mean, girls are cool. What are we doing? Is this a sock game that girls are even capable of playing?"

"Ronnie!" Ginny clipped him around the back of the head.

"What?"

"Everybody in the room is equipped with the requisite body parts for participation," Spook clarified. "And if you'll all fucking shut up a minute, I can get as far as the rules."

Luthor sighed as Alle began handing out socks.

"You had the biggest socks. And the biggest collection of socks. You have like forty pairs."

"A man can't have too many socks."

Xane leaned over and gave his boyfriend a kiss. "Especially when he has a girlfriend who steals them in order to read and drink tea in."

"Said girlfriend always puts them in the wash afterwards."

Spook clapped his hands together. "Okay, listen up. Rules." He got a familiar gleam in his blue peepers that sent a shiver of anticipation down Paul's spine.

"You guys should probably know that despite appearances, he's a complete sadist," he said to those in his vicinity. "Let's hope there's still some arnica in the first aid kit. Okay, go on, spill. We're listening."

"Rule One: everyone take your… shoes off and put a sock on one foot. No, I don't care which one, just as long as it's on a foot. Hands don't count, Ronnie. No, Rock Giant isn't allowed to put his on his extra appendage."

That earned him some side-eye from Nash, who maybe hadn't heard he had a big one.

Spook waited until everyone was done. "Aim of the game—remove the socks from the other participants. Winning conditions—be the last person still wearing a sock. Rule two" —he gestured, raising his index fingers on both hands— "you are not allowed to use your hands under any circumstances to remove the socks. You can use them for other purposes, like balance. Cheating will be met with severe consequences." Alle passed him a wooden-backed hairbrush, which Spook tested against his palm in a way that made a loud clap. "Okay, go."

Paul dived into the thick of things, avoiding the temptation to use the game to snuggle up against Jodi. He soon wrestled the socks off two of the Ghost Boys. A combined assault from Ginny and Dani soon put Ash out. Dani soon followed. Then Xane. Then Luthor. He noted the three of them slipping away into one of the bedrooms. No need to ask what for, all this wriggling about and grinding up against other bodies definitely got the blood pumping.

Ginny caught his gaze. Her sock was already wrinkled around her ankle. All he'd have to do to get it off her was pin her beneath him and use his toes to drag it off her foot. Easy peasy. He had both a weight and height advantage.

"Truce?" she mouthed at him and cast a glance at the other remaining players—Jodi and Nash were contorted around one another. Jodi's delectable arse in the air, Nash all elbows and legs. There was a lot of grunting going on.

"'kay," he mouthed back, already doubting the wisdom of the agreement. If he went after Nash, he couldn't rule out the possibility that the game wouldn't devolve into fisticuffs. Whereas, if he targeted Jodi, then...then Nash would likely see that as him making a move, and... bruises and bloodshed were inevitable. So, he was basically fucked whichever way he played things. He let Ginny dive into the melee first, before joining in. If things were going to kick off, they might as well happen now as later.

Goddammit, she was all curves and soft bits, and heat. Heat that spilled over him and rushed through his veins. It'd been ten days since he'd seen her. Ten days during which he'd been self-medicating with Ronnie's concoctions because it was fucking miserable thinking of her and wondering if they'd ever get a happily ever after, or if his punishment for overstepping the mark would be eternal solitude.

"Don't you dare." Jodi turned her head and bared her teeth at him when he grasped her around the midriff. Sitting with his back to her he used his heels to drag the sock down her shin. She twisted relinquishing her all fours position over Nash, so she could kick free of Paul's hold on her, while also drumming on his back with her forearms.

She smelled of autumn.

Nash, thinking he'd won a reprieve, succumbed to Ginny's ingenuity. She clamped her teeth around the toe of his sock and lurching backwards, took it clean off his foot. Unfortunately, she also fell on her arse right in front of Jodi, who used her forearms to steal her already floppy sock.

That left just the two of them. No. Wait. Was it just the two of them? Ronnie smirked at him from his seat on the coffee table. The bugger was still sporting a sock and apparently taking a breather while the rest of them battled it out.

"That's hardly engaging with the spirit of the game, Ron."

"Tactics," he responded.

Paul levelled a kick in his direction.

"Ow!"

"You could help," Jodi said to Ronnie. "We're supposed to be a team." On her knees now, she was leaning over Paul's shoulder, straining to reach his feet... his legs...some manner of purchase. Paul tucked his knees beneath him, and stood, lifting her up with him, so she was held in a reverse fireman's lift. While she squirmed and kicked, Ronnie finished his drink.

"I'm gonna give you a countdown," Spook told him. "Engage or I'm disqualifying you."

"If I go for his ankles, he'll fall over," Ronnie protested. "I don't think you should be making me do stuff that'll risk my teamie being dropped on her head."

"Then get him to put her down."

"Yeah, man, put her down," Nash added. He'd slithered back over to the sofa, where he was rubbing various sore spots. Someone handed him another beer.

"It's the game, Nash," his friends soothed him, patting various bits of him.

"He's fucking feeling my girlfriend's arse up."

Actually, he had a grip on the seat of her pants so that she didn't nosedive into his groin. Or fall. One of the two.

Ronnie started poking him. Nash rose from the sofa again, but Balin and Lee dragged him back into his seat.

"Do you want to end up on your head?" he said to Jodi. She wound an arm around his thigh.

Ronnie poked him again.

"Jesus Christ, what are you doing woman?" Having anchored herself and obviously realised he wasn't going to let her fall; she'd curled her fingers around the waistband of his leathers. A bit more wriggling, and she'd found his fly.

Do not. She was not going to unzip him. Fuck, she was. Button slid, motion and gravity did for the zip—

with a little help from internal pressure. He did have his favourite goddess wriggling about in his arms, while undressing him. Ronnie seizing on the situation, assisted his teammate by pulling Paul's leathers down to his ankles. Thankfully, he hadn't gone commando today.

"You're looking perky there, Paul," Ash remarked. He pulled out his phone and took a picture of the three of them dancing about. "One for the band's social media, me thinks."

Paul swung around to scowl at him. "Post that at your peril, Mr Gore. My arse ends up on the internet, and—"

"Nobody's arse is going on the internet." Spook snatched Ash's phone out of his hands and drummed him on the top of the head with it. "You can have it back when you've promised to be a good boy."

"I liked you better when you didn't fucking speak," Ash moaned. "And I am never promising *you* I'll be a good boy."

"Now what's your plan?" Paul asked an upside-down Jodi, who was still clinging to his thighs, and in increasing danger of slithering onto her face. He adjusted his grip on her arse, which did admittedly put his hand right over her crack, a place he'd like to visit in detail.

Behind him, Nash growled.

"What's your plan, Castle? How are you getting out of this?"

"You could be a gent and put me down gently. Not on my head."

He could. "And then what?"

"Which of us needs that card more?"

Fifty- fifty, he reckoned.

"Let me win, and I'll give you a kiss."

"Naughty, naughty... Are you trying to start a fight?"

"I'm negotiating."

"And I'm right here," Ronnie reminded them. "Also, with a sock still in this fight."

"Forfeit and Paul will give you a kiss," Jodi negotiated. He suspected the blood rushing to her head was addling her thought processes.

"He doesn't want to kiss me. He thinks I give shit bro—"

"Bro," Paul said loudly. "You can have a fucking kiss. Two if you shut your gob and take that sock off."

"Two kisses," Ronnie replied, a sly grin spreading across his chops. "One from each of you? Plus, I get to see pussy."

"What the fuck?" Nash barked.

"They're talking about cats," Balin said to him.

"That's right, isn't it? You want to see my kitties?" Jodi asked still upside down.

Ronnie shrugged and put on his sweetest expression. "As long as there's fur I can pet."

"I'm going to strangle you in a moment," Paul warned him.

"No need." Ronnie sat back on his haunches and offered up a foot.

"What am I supposed to do with that?" He wasn't allowed to use his hands, also he was using them to keep Jodi secure.

"Put your toes under my chin," Jodi said.

Ronnie wedged his foot between her chin and Paul's leg, then bottom-shuffled backwards so that the sock got left behind. "Oh, dear, looks like I'm out," he said, collapsing into a star-shaped sprawl on his back.

"Good, make yourself useful and open the door." Paul had decided the best option was the bed. It'd still be awkward, but at least he could lower her onto a soft surface. Only, he'd forgotten about the hogtie around his ankles. He tripped. Did his best to twist, so as not to fall on her, hit the corner of the side table which sheared across his abs, before flipping over and landing on top of him. Jodi was half under him still in his arms. There were voices all around him. "Shit, I'm sorry," he said, still dazed. "Castle?"

She kissed the inside of his leg, where the dragon wound around his thigh. "I'm fine." She gave him a push, and he rolled as best he could onto his back, while she rose onto all fours, then about turned to look at him. "You okay?" she asked, a grin stretching her face, and eyes watering with mirth.

Gingerly he lifted his shirt.

"Fuck," she mouthed, smile dissolving.

Paul looked down, but he couldn't really see what she was staring at. His skin looked a bit pink in between the lines of ink. Jodi gently touched his skin and winced when he hissed a breath in through his teeth. "You've sustained one hell of a scrape. Reckon that ought to make you the winner."

He shook his head. "I want my kiss."

She bent over him and pressed her lips to his boo-boo. "There, all better." She reached for his foot and tugged off the sock. "I win."

"Void," Spook declared. "No hands. Thems the rules." He took the sock off Jodi and handed it to Luthor, then dropped the orange card on Paul's chest. "Use it wisely my friend." He winked.

Paul closed his eyes. In a minute or two, he'd move. He heard Jodi rise, and people moving around him. Apparently, it'd been universally decided to call it a night.

"You staying there?" Ash asked him.

"For a bit."

"Blanket?"

"No, I'm good."

It went quiet. He didn't think he'd broken anything, except maybe the table, but his skin over his abs did knack. Someone—Ronnie? —sat down beside him.

"Not sure if it'll help, but I got some stuff for your scrape."

"Appreciate it."

Ronnie set to work gently applying the cream. He paused once he'd finished, looking at Paul's face. He hadn't opened his eyes; he could just tell.

"Are you about to demand your kiss?"

Ronnie startled out of whatever contemplative daze he'd fallen into. "Not just yet. Thought I'd save it for another day."

Whereas he'd prefer not to have it hanging over his head like the sword of Damocles. He crunched into a seated position, which put him practically nose to nose with Ronnie. Someone had dimmed all the lights, so that only the neon of the city outside illuminated the gloom. Ronnie's eyes shone in the dark. Paul cupped the guy's cheek. "There's nowt wrong with your blowjob skills, Ron, but it was a one-time thing. I feel like you're fishing around for something more and it's not going to happen."

"Because of her?"

"Because it was never gonna happen."

"Not so sure that's true." Ronnie pressed into his touch. Then he extended his arms into a stretch above his head and flopped backwards onto the floor. Paul lay back down too. They were silent for a good long while.

"Ever wish that people didn't get themselves wound into such major knots about sex?"

Paul didn't have an answer as such, not without more context.

"I just mean, I think we'd all be a lot happier if we didn't, you know? If it was okay to think, they're hot and do them. And afterwards, you could just carry on with your life. It wouldn't be awkward, and no one would have to adjust any other relationships they were part of unless they wanted to."

"Humans are jealous by nature. It's a survival thing."

"Yeah, but I'm saying, if it wasn't."

"I know what you're saying. Who would you shag first, Ronnie?"

He was quiet for far too long for his answer to be entirely honest. "Xane, probably. Reckon I'd work my way through the whole band, actually."

"Is that a roundabout way of saying you want to shag me?"

"Figured you knew that already."

"You kinda spelled it out when you waxed lyrical in the woods that night."

"Is that why you're being cagey around me?"

An awkward laugh rumbled in his throat. "Pretty sure you don't actually want my metalwork rammed up your arse." Also, if he was going to be plundering anyone's back passage, Ronnie's rump was not the one foremost in his mind. Nope, he'd take the very deliciously curvy, lady rump of his missus, thank you, and there was a vision to fuel his dreams.

When he woke, stiff and cold at four AM, Ronnie was curled around his lower limbs like a honeysuckle vine, and a thread of drool connected his lips with Paul's big toe. He disentangled himself from the huggy monster, put him in bed, and then crashed out on the adjacent twin.

"THIS IS AN invasion. Prepare to be boarded. We demand to see pussies." Ronnie yelled, as he mounted the steps onto the Ghost Boys tour bus. They were parked at a service station somewhere between last night's venue in Kristiansand and tomorrow's venue in Stavanger. "Also, we bring the gift of breakfast."

Breakfast, despite it being late afternoon.

Grumbles from towards the rear were succeeded by combinations of "gimme" and "please tell me you have bacon" and "take as many ruddy cats as you like, this one's just farted on my head. Get off, you fucking moggy."

Balin stumbled out first, beaten to the stash of breakfast offerings by their driver. "That's not bacon."

Paul shrugged. "We're in Norway. If you want hot food on the move, it's Bratwurst in potato bread or lump it. Seriously, man, they have like fifty-eight types of hotdog but not one of them contains British bacon. Get over yourself.”

“This is so good,” their driver groaned with delight between mouthfuls. “Honey mustard… That’s what it is, right?”

Jez wandered through evidently fresh from the shower, sporting a towel around his narrow hips. Ronnie shoved food offerings in his direction, prompting a juggling feat involving hotdogs and towels and a lot of unnecessary touching.

“Someone mentioned pussies,” Jodi leaned against the doorway, one such feline beast in her arms. Ronnie was thankfully still tangled up with Jez, leaving the pathway open for Paul to move in. “Flugwhump,” she mouthed at him.

“I remember. And the girls?”

“Hiding. They’re not so social.”

“Breakfast?” She passed him the cat so he could give her one of the *pølse i lompe*.

“Dude, stop trying to slide my fiancée your sausage,” Nash remarked, forcing his way between them, and snatching the food out of Paul’s hand before Jodi could accept it.

“Wanker.”

Jodi shrugged like it was no big deal. “There’s plenty more, right?” Jodi curled her hand around his wrist, which got his attention immediately. It was like an electric current passed through him. It made all his hairs stand on end and other less hairy bits get perky too.

Right. He released the cat to wind its way around various legs and got her another sausage before shitbag ate them all. He’d already claimed another two. Jodi accepted the second offering with a smile, before ducking back through the curtained doorway to where the bunks were. He’d have liked to have followed, but there was etiquette to be followed regarding tour bus bedrooms. You did not enter unless invited.

"Hope you're not peeking," she said, when he lingered on the other side of the curtain.

"How naked are you?" He figured she was taking the opportunity for some privacy to get dressed. Couldn't be easy for her living with four male slobs. Elspeth had never much liked touring with a bunch of guys, and she'd been part of the band, not just tagging along for the ride as someone's bunk buddy.

"Bra and knickers at the minute, but don't get excited. They're my ancient granny pants. Need to do some laundry, and my bra's seen better days too."

"Yeah, what's it like?"

"Grey. T-shirty. I think once upon a time it might have had pink spots."

"Comfortable?" he asked.

She chuckled. "Yeah. Yeah, it is." She emerged maybe a minute later dressed in a familiar jumper over a pair of jeans. It brought a score of memories rushing back all at once. Paul raked his teeth across his lower lip. "Your fiancé know you're wearing my clothes?"

She pursed her lips and looked at him primly. "Not if you don't snitch. Please don't snitch. This is the warmest jumper I own, and it's soft and snuggly."

He liked seeing her in it far too much to risk a scene, even if he would've got a kick out of seeing douche canoe's expression when he learned how close to her skin Jodi was keeping him. "Wearing my stolen boxers too?"

"They weren't stolen. They were loaned. And nope, not today."

Which suggested she wore them some days. God, the visuals that conjured.

"Granny pants, remember. What's that face for? Are you planning on calling in the loan?"

There was a thought, for a day when she was

actually wearing them. Then he could remove them from her with his teeth, after he'd sufficiently proved they needed laundering by making them thoroughly wet.

"Hey, can I have one of those coffees?" She darted past him, but the box Ronnie had arrived with was now sadly empty. "Damn."

"I was going to stretch my legs. I don't mind wandering over to the shop to get you one," Paul offered. Anything for his missus. Plus, he needed a few to clean up his thoughts.

"Really? Thanks."

"Not a problem." It really wasn't, and honestly, why weren't the twerps that inhabited this bus leaping up to right the issue? One of them had obviously snaffled two beverages. He suspected the douche canoe.

"Why are we being honoured with breakfast?" Nash asked, right as Paul reached the top of the bus steps.

Because they were making an effort, that's why. Xane had suggested it, and he'd liked the idea of bringing his lady breakfast so much, he'd volunteered. Ronnie had accompanied him, because, as he'd rightly pointed out, he was still owed a pussy visit. "Should we not have bothered?"

He was trying, he really was, but he just plain didn't like the tosser. The rest of them were all right, but Nash, he just... It was hard to put his finger on it. The guy just rubbed him the wrong way, and not just because he insisted on hanging onto Jodi like a fucking limpet and stealing her food. As he watched, turd brain stole multiple bits of her sausage, even though he still had the remains of the first one he'd nicked right there in his hand.

Paul took his irritation off the bus before he rammed his fist in the imbecile's face. Only most of them followed. At least they stayed beside the bus to eat and swig their takeaway coffees, while he did a temper cooling lap of the car park.

The service station was little more than a garage with basic amenities attached, but it was surrounded by breathtaking landscape. Rolling green hills, thick with trees, and that scent in the air, a unique mix of salt and pine. They'd driven up a stretch of coastline not long before they'd stopped. In places the road was right by the water's edge. Not here, mind. Here it was trees and rocks and winding, looping road. Troll country in his mind, but he knew that was really considered to be further north. He'd have to check the schedule again. See if they could find some time after the Bergen gig so he could take her to see one of the amazing waterfalls and stretch his legs with a decent hike. They were stopping within the Magma Geopark later, but it'd be too dark to take in the sights. Best they'd get was a nice view while they ate breakfast.

Having done his lap, Paul headed into the shop and picked up a coffee for his lady, along with some nibbles and another troll to add to his mum's collection. She had a thing about mythical creatures. They inhabited all the nooks and crannies of his parent's place. Hung their washing across the stairs, had doorways in the skirting boards and on mantlepieces. He'd found a three-legged crow lurking behind the washing machine the last time he'd visited, and a *tomte* peering at him from inside a jar of lentils in the pantry. It made it hard to believe they weren't living breathing entities, who just froze when you passed them by so as not to give the game away. The troll would fit right in.

Speaking of living, breathing entities. Jodi froze before him when she emerged from the ladies as he headed out of the shop door by the rear exit. It'd have made more sense to use the front door, but his brain logic adhered to the service station rule of same way out as in, else you could wind up who knew where. Maybe a whole different country, or a parallel universe, and while it might be nice to land in one where he and Jodi weren't engaged in the whole arm's length thing, other stuff might be different in that world too, and he was kind of invested in his current timeline.

"Coffee."

She accepted it gratefully, and he watched her as she pried off the lid and blew on the steaming liquid before taking a swallow and groaning in contentment. Cute. Plus, she still looked endearingly sleep tousled. Enough to want to push her up against the convenient wall and ravage her senseless.

"Did you eat breakfast, because you're looking at me like you're contemplating swallowing me whole," she asked.

"I ate. I could happily indulge in seconds, though." He licked his lips.

"Stop it," she warned, but she was grinning.

"Says the woman who undid my fly the other night."

The remark only made her grin wider. "That was a strategic move. It might have even worked in my favour if—" She frowned. "How are your abs?"

Paul lifted his shirt to flash her the damage. The scrape had bruised, leaving his skin mottled in shades of yellow, browns, and purples between the lines of his ink.

"Fuck. Ouch!" She reached out to touch but stopped shy of doing so. "Guess kissing it better didn't do the trick."

"You can give it another go, if you like."

"I think you'd like."

He absolutely wasn't denying that.

"You're thinking something. Not sure I want to hear it, but I kinda simultaneously do."

He considered the wisdom of speaking his mind, but ultimately figured, what the heck. "Just, how this could play out if there weren't certain barriers in the way."

"Ah! Oh!" She took another draw of her coffee, as heat flooded her cheeks giving her a rosy glow. "That sounds like something we definitely shouldn't discuss."

"You sure you don't want to hear? It involves tongues, and your leg going over my shoulder."

"What are you, six foot ten? Not sure I can get my leg that high. Not sure I can get it to half that height."

"Six six, and you could if I was kneeling."

"Oh," she said, hopefully picturing exactly what he was picturing. Her cunt open to him. His tongue exploring the contours of her slit. The taste of her thick on his tongue, and her towering over him. That coffee cup still clutched in her fist, and scores of bite marks around the rim of it.

"Well, this is a public place, Mr Reed, so that would be highly inappropriate." She waggled a finger at him as if she was giving him a stern ticking off, but there was merriment in her eyes, and he didn't think it was just down to her being flattered by his interest. The skin of her neck was pinkening too.

"I could carry you off into the woodlands, if you don't fancy security footage of the whole encounter making someone's evening."

"Hmm, think I'd better be getting back to my bus and away from your flirting. Normally I don't worry about anyone picking me up and carrying me anywhere, but..."

But he'd proved how easily he could lift her off her feet.

"Find me later," he called after her, letting her

return alone to the Ghost Boys bus. "I want to know all about how you wound up touring with that lot."

Over by the picnic tables, Lee was bouncing an empty cup off the top of Nash's head, while the rest of them lobbed bits of bread at him.

"It's not an interesting story."

"Reckon it is."

"Then maybe it's just not one I fancy sharing. I'm sure you have a few of those too."

"Aye. Maybe." Mind you, he'd tell her whatever she wanted to know. He'd given her his heart. His loyalty. His everything, really. Besides, openness was the key to a long and happy relationship. His parents had taught him that.

The phone in his pocket bleeped. Paul took a glance at it.

Dad: When are you coming home, son?

RG: I don't know when. I'll let you know as soon as I can.

THEY'D PULLED OFF the road, as far as Jodi could tell, in the middle of nowhere nowheresville. The boys seemed as baffled as her as to the reason, but the Black Halo bus was stopped right there ahead of them.

"I'm pretty sure this isn't Stavanger," Balin said, squinting to see the outside world through their combined reflection. A dozen or so moths landed on the outside of the glass, attracted by the lights. "Do you think they're having bus trouble?"

Brian was already on the phone to Samson. He made a few affirmatives and hung up. "Scheduled rest stop. I thought we were overnighting in central Egersund, but apparently, we're sticking to the outskirts and only the crew are heading into town. The guys wanted to wake up to a view."

"Outskirts." The pitch of Nash's voice matched what they were all surely thinking. This wasn't the suburbs. This was wild country. There wasn't a light in any direction other than upwards. That starscape, mind you, it looked impressive. Jodi got out her phone and opened up SkySafari.

"Where you going?" Lee asked, as she headed down the entry steps.

She turned the screen to him. "Says the Draconid Meteor Shower should be visible."

"Cool." He followed her out onto the gravelled area they'd parked up on. It appeared to be a maintained facility. There were a couple of picnic tables, though no amenities.

"Is this their idea of a joke, do you think?" Balin continued to complain, as the rest of them trooped outdoors, into the fresh night air. He rubbed his bare arms. "Where's the nightlife?"

Something howled in the distance.

"Look up, fuckwit," Lee replied, while lifting his own phone heavenward alongside Jodi's. It hadn't been visible from inside the bus due to the direction they were facing and the shadows of the mountains but hanging over the horizon were fantastic sheets of red and green, the starscape peeping through the gossamer strands. Having never witnessed the Northern Lights before, she was mesmerised. Black Halo were off their bus too, milling around in front of it.

"Sure, it's cool." Balin continued to sign and rub the goosebumps from his skin. "Anything else to do around here?"

Spook, who was nearest to them from among Black Halo waved an arm in a vaguely northern direction. Actually, was that north? Well, it was towards the pole star. "There's Trollpikken. It's about a forty-minute hike. Probably not a nighttime activity, mind."

"Hiking?" The way Nash said it made it sound like he'd never walked anywhere in his life. And to think they'd all met while fruit picking their way around Europe.

"Trollpikken. What's that?" Jez asked, sounding far more interested than he had in days.

"A rock formation that looks like a troll's prick," Rock Giant said wandering over to join them. "All mended now, after it's unfortunate dismemberment in twenty seventeen. Some people have no bloody souls."

"Like the morons that felled the Sycamore Gap tree." Ash contributed.

They were now surrounded.

"Exactly. Except I'm not sure they found out who did for the troll's cock."

"Humans haven't," Spook said, casting a sly look out of the corner of his eyes. "I imagine the culprit's been dealt with appropriately by other agents."

"You know trolls aren't real, right?" Ronnie said to him.

"Right," said Spook, fingering an iron pendant dangling from a thong around his throat. "The legends say they take the skinny ones and the goats first."

"We don't have any goats."

Spook grinned.

Ronnie sandwiched himself in the middle of the group between Rock Giant, Luthor and Allegra.

"I've been thinking about getting a pet goat," she heard him say to Allegra.

"Ronnie, you couldn't look after a hamster."

"Meteor!" Lee grabbed her arm, diverting her attention westward.

OCK GIANT LIT a fire, and the two bands settled around it. The drivers had gone to bed, as had Brian, but the few other crew members travelling on the Ghost Boys bus were lurking on the fringes. Beers got shared. Marshmallows toasted. Stories told. Jodi settled contentedly between Nash and Jez, her head resting on Jez's upper arm, Nash holding her hand. It was like it'd been in the early days back in Valencia, complete with constant ribbing, only with the addition of five super famous rock stars and their partners to the group.

The Black Halo gang were clearly loving the bit of downtime from being on the road. If she'd learned anything these past few weeks, it was that touring wasn't half as much fun as everyone supposed. Mostly, it was boring. It also involved a lot of being herded about like cattle, and lectures from Brian about where and what they were supposed to be doing, and some serious bollockings if they dared to deviate from the script.

For all that, she liked Brian. Brian was cool. The overall tour manager, though, he was fucking scary. Mostly he spoke to Brian though and let him wrangle the Ghost Boys. Black Halo were his priority. She wondered what they'd done to sweet talk him into this stopover. Or maybe folks were just more amenable to requests when you were a big-name band.

"I've missed this." Nash leaned over to whisper in her ear.

"Me too." She'd always loved the crackle of a campfire, and the swell of togetherness that came from sharing one.

"Come here." Nash reclaimed her from Jez. "Whoever made this call, it was a good one."

"Time out from the bustle."

"Yeah." He shared his beer with her. "Course I

might have to drag you off into the bushes in a bit for some private time."

"I might even let you." He looked pleased to hear it, and he gave her hand a squeeze.

"Let's stay awhile yet, though. I'm enjoying the vibes, and it's still early." Her guys and Black Halo were intermingled. The them-and-us feelings that had lingered even during the party of a few nights back had dissolved. She was nestled in between two of her favourite people. Things were pretty perfect.

"'kay." Nash claimed another kiss, his mouth gentle against hers. The scent and taste of hops lingering after their smooching was done. "Love you."

"I love you, too."

"Forest sex later though," he winked.

"Who's having forest sex?" Ronnie blurted from the opposite side of the fire. He had to have superhuman hearing to have heard them.

"Odds are, everybody but you," Xane replied.

"Don't tease him," his girlfriend said.

"Hey, I'm not the only single person here. Some of them are single," Ronnie swept his arm in an arc to indicate her boys, "And Rock Giant got mar—"

Ginny stuffed a smore into his open mouth. "You wanted one, right? Yes."

It wasn't really a question, but it was a more efficient way of shutting him up than kicking him in the arse. Jodi shot Ginny a grateful look, her heart now thumping over what had been about to come out of Ronnie's mouth, and how fast it would have soured the mood. The last thing she needed when things were finally chill was Nash getting a reminder about how she'd tied the knot with someone else.

Rock Giant was sitting between Lee and Balin and didn't appear to be paying attention to the conversation. She was grateful for that, too. So far, things hadn't been too testy, but if provoked, she didn't doubt he'd say something inflammatory.

It was a while later when someone suggested a game. All the campfire games she knew involved the sort of truth or dare scenarios that would guarantee a falling out or ensure they all had raging hangovers tomorrow. Neither sounded terribly appealing. She slipped her hand onto Nash's thigh, ready to suggest they take off and enjoy some forest fun together. The embarrassing catcalls would be worth it, if it meant it saved her from the greater evil.

But Xane put down his drink and leaned forward so that his long hair shrouded his face, and said, "Ah, guys, it's much too early in the relationship for that sort of kiss and tell. You're all still lil' baby rockstars. Let's revisit that idea a few months down the line when there'll be actual squirmworthy stuff we can hammer you with."

"You vetoing games all together?" Lee asked.

"Nah," Black Halo's prince of darkness replied. "I'm thinking maybe something physical rather than psychological tonight."

"No orgies," his girlfriend remarked. Xane leaned over Ash who was sitting between them and kissed her cheek. "With the current numbers, it'd wind up being a bit too gay even for my tastes." He sat back. "Hide and seek."

"Kids' games," Jez drawled. He'd downed at least six beers, even though she'd been trying to distract him from dissolving into the gloom he was carrying inside him.

"Kids play them for a reason. It's 'cause they're fun." Xane stood. "Seekers?"

"Me and Ash," Ginny volunteered. "And whoever evades us the longest gets the back bedroom for the night, to share or not as they wish."

Ash squinted up at his gorgeous wife. "What do we get, Gin?"

"No bugger protests when we opt to take the Danger Car out for a spin for the journey up to Trondheim next week, and you all clear it with Samson."

"Why do we have to clear it with Samson?" both Luthor and Rock Giant asked.

"Because he already turned them down," Spook remarked, demonstrating insight into the situation, or else a proficient guess. "Sam would rather he knew where they were. Meaning on the bus, rather than risk them being AWOL in the wild." It seemed the Black Halo guys were subject to the same level of micro-manging as the Ghost Boys.

"Honestly, just 'cause we turned up a tiny bit late one time on the last tour," Ginny grumbled while raking a hand through her long hair.

"Fine," Xane agreed on behalf of them all. "We'll let you make your escape and endure the absolute chewing out that'll result. Start counting. Everybody else, scram."

Jodi hadn't expected the Black Halo lot to leap into action so dramatically. They were all halfway to the treeline before her lot had even found their feet. "Shit. Shit. Come on," Nash dragged her along a few paces, her hand in his, but it'd always been difficult to run hand in hand despite what movies would have the world believe. She shook him off, only for Balin to scoop her off her feet, twirl her around and set her down facing the wrong way. "I need that bed more than you and Curtis."

"Balin, you git!" She tore after him, only for her foot to find a tussock, and then she was down. Splat! Face first.

"Oopsie!" Rock Giant helped her to her feet and dusted her down. "You okay?"

"Yeah, I think. Maybe." Her hands were scraped, her heart galloping, but nothing was bleeding, and her knees were sore. "Just humiliated."

"Falling over is just part and parcel of life. We'd better scarper."

She tried a step and pain sliced through her ankle and up her leg. "Fuck!" She tried again with the same stellar result. "You go. Looks like I'm sitting this one out."

Ash and Ginny had made it to the sixties. They were standing with hands over one another's eyes by the fire's embers. There was no sign of anyone else beyond the empty bottles and cans they'd left behind.

"Nah, I've a better idea." He scooped her up into his arms, making her squeal, but instead of running for the treeline as she'd expected, he about turned and carried her onto the Black Halo bus. She guessed no one had specifically said they couldn't hide there. That's if hiding was what they were doing. It was what they were doing, right?

"Paul." He carried her through the kitchen and upstairs. This bus was massive compared to the one she was staying on, and it was no pipsqueak. She wasn't sure she'd appreciated that during her prior visit. There were multiple rooms, not just two and the facilities.

"Where are you taking me?" Not his bed, she hoped. "Not the roof?" is what she said.

"Tempting but no, not on this bus, even if it is a nice night for stargazing."

He led her into the bunk room. One of two, he explained. This one is just for the band. Dammit, while everything was just as cramped, it felt different to the Ghost Boys bus, more like a home on wheels rather than a shagging shack. It smelled like it maybe got aired more regularly, too.

"Which one's yours?"

"Top, left-hand side."

"That cos of your long legs?" He was right up by the ceiling, and she could see he had things taped up there, but not the details. Also, it was too high up for him to be planning on depositing her there.

"Not so overlooked up there. The bottom has a similar vibe, but you're constantly confronted with arrays of feet traipsing past, and I'm not much for being kicked in the head."

"That happen much to whoever's down there?"

"No one in their right mind would do that to Spook."

"'Cause he's such a sweetie?"

"'Cause he'd a sadistic motherfucker, and he'd make you pay for it. Luthor's on the other side at the bottom, but if he's ever slept there, it's news to me."

"Him, Xane, and Dani squeeze into one bunk?"

"Nah, that's a bit too sardine like even for them. They tend to commandeer the back bedroom. Downstairs. Like the one on Bertha the First, if you remember that." Maybe Luthor would wind up in his bunk tonight, if someone else won the night in the bedroom.

Also, yes, she remembered the back room. She also remembered landing in a tangle of limbs with him on that bed when Bertha bus had decided to masquerade as a sailboat. Okay, that might have possibly been her fault.

Beyond the bunk room at the very back of the bus on the upper floor sat a small room containing U-shaped seating around the edges. A flatscreen occupied one wall, and various paperbacks and projects were jumbled together in the corners. Rock Giant lowered her onto the seat, then shuffled some stuff out of the way.

"Right, let's take a look at that ankle."

"Was it really necessary to carry me all the way up here to do that?"

"First aid kit's up here. Also, wouldn't mind winning the game. My bunk's not so bad, but I'd love a decent stretch out."

Just as long as he wasn't imagining them sharing it, like, for instance, she was.

"I've a Prince Albert piercing," past Rock Giant said in her head. "Wanna look?"

"Yeah. No. I mean that wouldn't be very appropriate." They had only just met.

It wasn't appropriate now.

"Let's have a look at this ankle." He felt around the bone above the top of her shoe. "Can't feel any... Hang on, what's this?" He pulled a teasel out from between her skin and her sock. "Try your ankle now?" Jodi put some weight on it.

"I think it might be okay."

Paul gave his chin a scratch. "Well, while I'm down here. Let's take a look at those knees, shall we?"

"I'm sure they're fine."

He ignored her and raised her trouser legs. Luckily, they were of the wide-legged linen variety so didn't get stuck on her fat thighs.

Paul pushed out his lower lip as he inspected her wounds. Long fingers gently probing the flesh. "Bruised, and they're going to be a bit scabby, but you should live."

"Sure I won't need an amputation?"

"Nah, think one of these should do the trick." He pressed his hot lips to her knee. Jodi's breath caught then released as a squeak. His hand was warm against her calf. His lips pleasingly moist. Cheekily, he slid his hand upwards to the underside of her thigh.

"Paul!"

"Just checking there aren't any scrapes I missed."

"No you're not."

"Fine, I'm copping a feel. Does it make you happier if I'm honest about it?"

She'd like it if he didn't present himself as a fucking ginormous ball of temptation. "I think you'd better stop it," she mouthed, hardly making a sound. She wasn't going to win any assertiveness awards for that whisper.

Paul eyed her, gaze full of mischief. His index finger swished back and forth another couple of times, riding perilously close to the apex of her legs, then he sighed and rolled back onto his butt, and crossed his legs. "Spoilsport."

"I shouldn't even be in here with you."

"My sweet, you should be sharing every damn minute with me. We should be nailing one another like the sky's about to fall and spending unholy amounts of time staring dreamily at one another and wondering how we got to be so lucky."

The reason they weren't doing any of those things really could be boiled down to one word. "Nash," she said.

"Yup, got the memo. Guess we'll just have to pass the time with a quiz instead."

"A quiz? What, like general knowledge?"

"Like ask me whatever thou wishes to know. Anything. Absolutely anything."

"Favourite pizza."

He made a dry scoffing noise and rolled his eyes. "Anything I say, and she asks me that."

"It's an important question."

"Only if you're planning on treating me to dinner. In which case I'd prefer a paella to pizza, but if we're going with pizza, mushrooms, and jalapeno. You?"

"Mushrooms are gross. And after the last lot of mushrooms you fed me, I'm never going near them again."

He leaned in, blinking at her in a flirty fashion. "I

can see this is going to be a point of contention between thee and me. It's not like anything bad happened."

She'd been about to say, it definitely had but stopped herself just in time. After all, he might not take it how she meant it. That it'd caused them both trouble, not that he was bad. He absolutely wasn't. In fact, he possessed, of all the qualities a girl could want in a partner, if said girl was free to take him thus, which she wasn't.

"You okay, Castle?"

"Fine."

"So, separate pizzas, when we order." Like that was definitely a thing they'd be doing at some time. "What are you having on your half?"

She cycled through the options in her head. "I'm mostly a garlic marguerita girl."

"So, you're telling me I have to put up with your garlic breath?"

"I have to put up with your 'shrooms."

His smile didn't waver. "They don't typically leave an aftertaste."

Last time they had. A bitter one she was still struggling to handle.

"No matter. I'll claim one of these as advance compensation." He grasped her hand and kissed her inner wrist, then sat back again, laughing at her outraged tut.

"Oh, Mr Reed," he said in a mock Regency upper class falsetto. "Such liberties you take. I'm quite overcome." He pressed the back of his hand to his head. "Deary me, I feel quite... faint.'" And he flopped onto his back as if he'd passed out.

"Mean," she complained.

"*Moi*?" He lifted his head and crooked a brow.

She tossed the nearest thing to hand at him, which

turned out to be a ball of wool that unravelled into a pastel yellow tail.

"Shit!" She caught the hook to which it was attached before it flipped onto the floor or lost the stitches.

Paul caught the wool ball and began rewinding it towards her until they met up. Him on his knees before her again. Her still clutching the crochet hook, with too much heat in her cheeks.

God his eyes were pretty.

"Sorry."

"No harm done."

"Is someone pregnant?" She'd realised what was attached to the hook. An array of delicate stitches.

"Um, no. Not as far as I know." He took it from her and tucked it away in a corner. "Everyone was drinking tonight."

"Then what's this?"

"It's mine."

"You crochet?"

He pursed his lips. "Aye, what's wrong with that?"

"I didn't say anything was wrong with it. I'm just.."

"Just what?"

"Pleasantly surprised." Intrigued. A little bemused that such a huge man would opt for such a delicate hobby. Then again, he was a practical person, why wouldn't he engage in a traditional craft? "What are you making?"

His shoulders remained slightly hunched, as if he was expecting her to mock. "Hats. Baby hats. They're for the neonatal ward."

Christ, her heart was going to burst if he kept presenting her with reasons to adore him.

"They need them for the teeny tiny preemies. I'm not very good though, and I'm slow. You're looking at a third of my output."

"A third, so you've finished at least one."

"Two." He mushed his lips together, considering, then reached over to where he'd stowed the hook and presented the finished articles.

They were both pastel yellow and bore cute ribbon detailing.

"Paul, these are amazing."

"You don't have to be kind. I know I'm not very good."

"Shut up," she smacked his shoulder, the nearest bit of him to her. "They're fab. Mind you, they do kinda look like something else." She demonstrated by stretching one of the hats over her left breast. "Bra cups."

Rock Giant groaned.

Jodi positioned the second hat.

"See. Just needs a bit to attach them together at the front and some straps."

"Oh, I can see, all right. I can see you're determined to spike my blood pressure."

"How?"

"How, she says." He levelled his gaze right at her breasts. "By being temptation incarnate, that's how. I'll have my hats back now, please. Unless you're going to be kind and whip your top off to model them properly."

"Ah!" She bit her lip but failed to stop her smirk, then passed him the articles. "It's not like these itty-bitty things would cover my girls."

Paul groaned again. Then his hand was behind her head, and their brows were pressed together and his hazel eyes looking straight at her. "You're making this difficult, Castle. I'm doing my best here to give you space, but it's hard when I want you, and—"

"I'm not intentionally leading you on. I'm sorry. Truly."

"I know. This is just you. You and your defensive banter and wandering hands."

"My hands don't—" They were clasped around the lapels of his fleece jacket, practically holding him in position. She cautiously willed them to uncurl.

"Jodi. I think you'd better order me not to kiss you."

"Didn't think you were much for orders."

"True." He recaptured her gaze. "But I don't want you to think I'm a dick, either."

"You've a nice one, but I don't think you are one." What the heck was she saying to him? "Sorry. I'm sorry, I shouldn't have said that. I'm gonna give you the totally wrong impression. We said we were just going to be friends. We both agreed that. I should go and find Nash."

His hold on her didn't release, nor had she quite left hold of his clothing.

He tilted his head.

Jodi's heart gave a kick. Don't kiss me. Don't kiss me. Nothing good would come of it. Nothing... "Don't."

The smile slid from his face. "Actually don't, or?"

She took a shallow breath. But the only proper answer sat on her tongue unspoken. It didn't help that he was sexy as hell and that she could remember the touch of his lips far too well. A week ago. Three years ago. The tickle of his tongue against hers. Against other places. For a moment she was back in that glass house that'd been their home for the night. He was there, licking mushroom pate off his fingers, while she drank all the tea. Him playing spoons, naming the kittens, and optimistically presenting her with a strip of condoms he'd pulled from that bag of tricks he'd brought along and calling them entertainment.

He moved her hair behind her ear. "Do you have any idea how much I want you right now?"

She didn't dare answer.

"How much I'd like to steal your top away, not so you can model my crochet, but so that I can cover you with my hands. Just sit with you in my lap, your back to my chest, your breasts in my hands. Just holding you."

"I think you'd get wrist ache." Again with her stupid quips. Why couldn't she just hold her tongue?

"It'd be worth it. You've the best rack I've ever encountered, and I've encountered a few." It wasn't a boast on his part, simply a statement.

His thumb swished against the bare skin behind her ear.

"Paul, we can't. God, I'm sorry. I'm so sorry. For all of this. For everything."

"Don't be."

"But I am. I know you must have regrets. I'm sure this isn't what you wanted when you gave your heart away."

"And you'd be wrong. I don't regret anything."

"You don't wish you'd chosen someone else to tie yourself to? Someone prepared to love you like you deserve? Who'd happily shag you silly and doesn't come with a prior attachment?"

"No. You're the only person I want. I knew it in the moment, and I know it now. I'm not saying I wouldn't mind you coming round to the idea of me shagging you silly, but I'll never regret the vows we made."

Her eyes were welling with tears over his words. What sort of defence was she supposed to mount against that sort of affirmation? "You're too good for this world, Paul Reed."

"Nah, just blindly optimistic." He raised his free hand between them and explored her lips with his fingertips. Then, he leant in and kissed the tips of them where they still rested against her lips, before releasing her. He pushed to his feet and turned to the door. "I hear voices. We should go down."

She followed him back through the bunk room. "Do you think they've found everybody?"

"Only one way to find out. Look, you go down first. It'll spare us awkward questions."

Them both emerging from the same bus would still raise questions, even if it was minutes apart. In fact, it'd look super shady.

"Don't worry, I've a plan. Fire escape and some army crawling." He obviously had it all mapped out in his head. "No one needs to know anything, Castle. It's none of their fucking business, anyway."

"Okay."

"Okay."

"Won't they think it's weird I hid on your bus?"

"Just say you were under the kitchen table 'cause you weren't sure you wanted to brave the woods alone in the dark. No one will think anything of it."

She nodded and headed down the steps. Most of the gang were back. No one even noticed she'd joined them from the direction of the buses. Nash, Jez, and Balin were by the fire, but Lee was still missing. He returned along with Dani and Ronnie a few moments later. Ginny following them.

"Still no sign of Rock Giant?" she asked her hubby, who had evidently already given up the search.

"Evading even my super-secret-agent powers."

"Guess that's another win to him, then. Backroom's his for the night."

"Like this was even a contest," Paul said emerging in their midst and making several of them jolt. Judging by the dirt now smeared over his face, and over his arms, he had indeed army crawled under the bus. "All yours, Castle." He gave her a sly wink. "Got to be some advantages to being my missus—"

She sensed Nash stiffen.

"—I'm good out here. But keep the noise down, so

you don't disturb the rest of them, right. No one needs an angry Cave Troll to deal with."

"Wait, you mean me and..." He was giving her and Nash his prize.

Nash's back remained broom straight, and he was eyeing Rock Giant like this was a trap despite his bandmates affectionately battering him with their knuckles muttering about accepting the gift horse.

Why are you doing this? Jodi wanted to ask, but Rock Giant avoided her gaze, and lingering around to ask while people were trying to steer her towards a cosy night with Nash in a double bed instead of their usual teeny bunk didn't feel like an option.

"HOW BLOODY MUCH?" Jez spat out most of the mouthful of beer he'd just taken. "That's insane."

"Twelve quid," Nash repeated.

To Jodi, the mad part wasn't the price tag, she'd realised days ago that Norway was expensive. No, it was the fact that despite the hour and the cost of beer, the club was thrumming. She was nestled between the two men, and thus managing to stay on her feet, but even that wall of muscle didn't protect her from all the jostling. If it'd been up to her, she'd have opted for a seat outside, overlooking the marina, where they'd at least have been able to hear one another without yelling, but it was late and drizzling, and the guys, still pumped after their earlier gig, wanted to be in the thick of things.

Or rather, they were looking for company. Balin already had his arm around the shoulders of some girl he'd met on the way through the door, and Lee was talking to a giggly trio that had followed them here from the gig. She reckoned he'd have already pulled one if not all three of them, except for the fact that one of them was wearing a Spook Mortensen T-shirt that stretched over her bust like a second skin and was clearly hoping she wasn't going to have to settle for the budget option.

"Are Black Halo joining us?"

"Some of them," Jez confirmed. "Ronnie, Rock Giant, Ash, and his missus. Xane, I think. Not certain though, he seemed preoccupied."

"We should attempt to find a table."

"Pretty sure there's one saved. Same as last night. Balin was going to check."

That's right, the guys had come here the previous night, too. She'd opted for a quiet night. Bus to herself, and the chance to shower and dry off in private. Well, after she'd completed the sixteen thousand tasks they'd left her with.

"Maybe we should just go find it, guys."

The three of them tacked their way through the packed bodies, eventually finding their reserved table not far from the stage area a local band were performing on.

The Black Halo party arrived right as they were about to sit. Various bodies slid into seats. Nash ended up offering to go to the bar with Ginny, since Ash had wound up trapped at the back wedged between Xane and Jez. Ronnie and Rock Giant filled out the remaining spaces. She'd need to find a stool to pull up to the end.

"Park your arse right here, sexy butt," Rock Giant gave his knee a pat.

Tempting, but... "Think my fiancé might have something to say about that."

"Alternative's sitting on the table."

"I can stand."

A group of passing Vikings bumped her off her feet. Rock Giant caught her before she splatted over the table and settled her on his lap. "Think you'll be safer here."

Nash would freak, she knew he would. On the other hand, there was something genuinely pleasant about her current position.

"I'll swap with you if you like," Ronnie offered, "Though I'm thinking we're all going to have to double up the minute they get back from the bar."

How would that work? Ginny on Ash, okay, but whose lap was Nash supposed to perch on? Except Ginny returned without him, some hulking bearded giant carrying a tray of drinks for her in Nash's place.

"Where's Nash gone?" she asked, as Ginny shuffled across multiple laps to reach her hubby.

"Gents'," she gave a vague nod toward the loos. "Xane, vodka and coke. Ronnie..." She slid a fluorescing green cocktail in front of him. Paul and Ash both claimed beers, leaving one for her, not that she'd finished the first, or was it for Nash? She scanned the crowd for him but couldn't see much beyond a few feet thanks to the wall of people, chatting and listening, and getting their sexy on, while bass and drums reverberated through the walls and floor.

Conversation slid into an analysis of the gig, before grazing over a variety of other topics. Jodi couldn't relax enough to focus. Why hadn't Jez sat on the end? Then she could have sat on his lap. Nash wouldn't make a fuss over that.

Ronnie took out a packet of jelly sweets and added half of them to his drink; the rest he slid onto his middle finger. For a couple of moments, she was distracted by watching him nibble at the rings, then more or less fellating his own finger.

"Ron, you need to get laid," Ginny said. "What about the fine chap sat next to you?"

"Gin, you don't even know if he's into guys. You can't just go matching us up." Ronnie levelled with her, all eyes, and smiles. He took a moment to check Jez out, letting his gaze rove in a spectacularly unsubtle way.

"*Pfft*, he's a rockstar," she replied, like that was an explanation everyone would understand. Evidently, most of the table did.

"I feel like I missed something," Jez remarked.

Yeah, her too.

"Don't encourage them," Ash replied, giving his missus a poke and then a squeeze when she stuck her tongue out at him. "They've decided rock stars are willing to hump anything. No offence meant."

"None taken." Jez turned to Ronnie. "Sorry, you're not really my type."

"Too male?"

"He likes blonds," Jodi blurted and regretted immediately as hurt lanced through Jez's expression. "Sorry."

"I don't exclusively like blonds just because my ex was blond. I think I'm going to see what happened to the guys."

Fuck, now she'd upset him.

Ronnie got up to let him out, then slid back into the space he'd vacated. It meant there was room for her on that side of the table. Except, Paul reached around her to pick up his beer.

"You okay, Castle?" His other hand settled on her bare upper arm and began stroking back and forth in an absent way that was far too delicious not to become her whole focus.

"Fine." It was difficult not to turn her head and follow the glass back to his mouth. He flashed her a grin.

"You seem twitchy."

Of course she was twitchy, she was sitting on his

lap, and her fiancé was going to blow a fuse if he caught them, but damned if a part of her wasn't enjoying it, too. Being a larger lady, she rarely got to perch on a guy's lap without moans about dead legs. Rock Giant didn't seem to be having a problem with that. He took another draw of beer, and her gaze snapped to the rim of the glass, and the way his top lip caressed it as he swallowed. It brought an unbidden memory of him looking up at her from between her thighs, triangular glass behind him, and beyond that a star-studded winter sky. This long after that event, the memory oughtn't to have been nearly so vivid.

"Were you here last night?"

"Nope. Took a scenic boat trip around the fjords and to see Hengjanefossen. It's a waterfall," he added at her squint of confusion. "You?"

She shook her head.

"Quiet night, just the two of you?"

Jodi gave another head shake. "Quiet night alone. It was pretty blissful. I got to take a shower without having to negotiate the usual gauntlet of observers."

"If I'd known you were home alone—" He crooked a brow.

She swallowed. He'd have done what? Come calling? What mischief could the pair of them have enacted in five spare hours. "I don't think—"

"—I'd have invited you to join Alle, Spook and me on the trip."

Okay, so it wouldn't have been just the two of them getting intimate on an otherwise empty bus. Still, the whole trip around the fjords sounded far too romantic. Far too easy to picture the panoramic, film-worthy scenery, the gentle lapping of the sea against the sides of the boat providing musical accompaniment, and the pair of them snuggled together to ward off the evening chill. Nothing like now. The club was sweltering, or maybe that was just her. None of that was to suggest she wouldn't have enjoyed the experience. She loved exploring new places, and unfortunately most of what she was seeing on this trip was the backstage areas of various concert venues, roadsides, and pit stops. "Was it impressive?"

"The water tumbles down the cliff face into the fjord. Yeah, it's pretty spectacular."

"I'm sorry I missed it."

"I'm sorry you missed it. If only I'd known, I could have stolen you away and had you back before anyone was the wiser." He grinned again, then pressed his lips to her shoulder.

It was barely pressure enough to register, but she felt it throughout her body. Her nipples tightened, an ache started lower down, and butterflies took flight in her stomach. They rose through her chest and finally escaped her throat in the form of a gasp. Luckily, it was too noisy for anyone besides him to have heard it.

"Paul!"

"Yes, my love."

"What are you doing?"

He wrinkled his nose. "Nibbling."

"Well, maybe don't." Her gaze darted across the crowd. Was Nash seeing this? Was he going to arrive any moment, a thundercloud over his head and murder in his eyes? Would it stop Rock Giant even if he did? She suspected not.

"But, Castle, I nibble all my friends."

The fuck he did. "I'm not sure that's true. Please, behave."

He gave her a wry smile. "Yo, Ronnie. Lend me your hand."

Without pausing the conversation he was now deep into with his other band mates, Ronnie thrust his left hand towards Paul, who clasped it around the base and then sucked the jelly rings off his middle digit and released it, so it made a pop. The sight made her insides dance in new and interesting ways. He flashed her a look that seemed to say, *see?*

"Paul." Ronnie fluttered his eyelashes and pressed a hand to his chest. "Did you just claim my ring?"

Paul showed him his tongue poking through the jelly ring's central hole. "Totally mine now." He winked.

Ronnie groaned. So did Jodi. "Why does that sound so utterly deviant?"

Paul leaned in so his warm breath heated the side of her neck creating yet more bewildering cravings. "Because you've a dirty mind, Castle, that's why." He chewed and swallowed. Jodi watched the muscles of his throat work, unable to refute his claim, or stop herself from imagining nibbling him back. There, right there at the edge of his jaw, where the line of stubble ended, and also lower, in the V-shaped indent where his neck met his shoulder.

Bad thoughts...bad thoughts. Honestly, the world stopped making sense when he was this close to her, or rather, it made sense in a way that was totally antithetical to her future happiness with the man she was engaged to marry.

Rock Giant dropped his chin onto her shoulder. "You're less handsy than you used to be. I'm kinda sorry for that."

"I'm sure I don't know what you mean." But she did, and now she was thinking about it, her hands were itching to stray. She clasped the table edge to make sure they didn't go roving places they shouldn't, like over his face, or his pecs, or his fly. It didn't work, not when she felt his lips against her bare skin again, this time followed by the exploratory flick of his tongue beneath the shoelace straps of her vest. Then, she was liquid. Immediately reduced to a puddle of want, desperate to be lapped up. Desperate to be kissed. Desperate to be touched. For him to keep on touching her. She grabbed her drink, knuckles whitening around the bottle as she took a long swallow.

"You're so fucking sexy." He breathed deeply of her scent. "I know I'm supposed to behave, but I can't help it. I want to do bad things with you. Real bad things..." He shifted slightly beneath her.

"Abduction? Bank robbing?"

"If you like." His arms wrapped around her middle and pulled her more firmly against him. They were close enough now that she could feel the thread of his pulse. It was hammering away at a pace not dissimilar to hers.

"I'm yours to command, Castle. Anything you want, you just name it. You want a partner in crime, I'm your man. Need someone to make it all better when you have boo-boos, then I've got ya."

She didn't doubt it, except who was going to save her from him? And, hello, there was something firm now poking her in the rear, causing the sort of heat in her that even draining her cold beer couldn't counter.

She needed to move. If she didn't...then what? Nothing was going to happen. They were in a public place, and Rock Giant wasn't Balin. He wasn't going to unzip his fly and pull her knickers to one side so he could screw her in full sight of the room and everyone they knew. She wasn't the sort of girl who would let any man do that to her.

Still, her breath kept catching in her throat thinking about it, imagining the bulbous jewellery-enhanced head of him aligning with her split, then filling that opening. Her body would have to stretch to accommodate him. She'd have to spread her legs wide. His hand would slide forward, delve beneath the skirt of her dress, fasten first around the plump tops of her thighs. Squeeze. He wouldn't need to wet his fingers before touching her. She'd already be stupendously wet for him.

She was already uncomfortably wet for him.

Maybe, a polyamorous solution to her current situation wasn't such a bad idea. It was working for at least one of the other people sitting at this table. Xane caught her glance and crooked a brow. Jodi turned away, cheeks flaming.

Ha, as if Nash would ever go for it.

Paul's hands settled on her hips. "You might not want to wriggle quite so much," he said into her ear. "That is, unless you're trying to make me embarrass myself."

"I'm not doing anything to you."

A soft chuckle rumbled against her ear. "Maid, if this is you doing nothing, then God help me when you decide to put some effort into it."

"I never took you for being quite so prone to exaggeration."

She shifted again, and he drew his next breath through his teeth. "Lady..." He exhaled. "In a minute, I'm going to throw you over my shoulder and take you to whatever dark corner I can find so I can maul the fuck out of you."

"Maybe you need to get laid."

"Oh, I definitely do. But I'm keeping myself chaste for you, sweetheart. My cock is entirely yours. The heart attached to it, too."

"I'm a little worried about your grasp of anatomy," she said. She needed to cool things down, before she was tempted to do more than just rub her arse against him. "I ought to go and see where Nash has got to."

It was a squeeze to get out, one that necessitated her planting one hand on the table and one on his brawny shoulder to gain her feet. She made the mistake of looking him in the eyes. "You're not going to follow me, right?"

"Only if you order me not to."

"We agreed we'd just be friends."

"Maybe we need to reopen negotiations."

"We don't. I'm still engaged. Still in love." Where the hell was Nash? "Don't follow, okay?"

Rock Giant gave a barely perceptible nod, then his lips whispered against hers. "Okay, but know that I'm right here if you change your mind."

He let her go.

Jodi staggered back a pace or two, before bolting into the crowd. She made a full sweep of the bar without spotting any of the Ghost Boys, and wasn't mad about that, other than in terms of wondering if they'd left without her. The sound of her pulse in her ears continued to compete with the thumping bass vibrating through the soles of her shoes.

What must everyone around that table think of her, canoodling with Paul, when she was engaged to Nash? Nothing kind, for certain. She certainly didn't have any kind words for herself. She'd never liked cheaters. Never thought she'd be the sort to wind up torn over her feelings for two men. It ought to be straightforward. A simple matter. She'd made a commitment to Nash. He was her security, and the platform on which the current incarnation of herself was built. Rock Giant...was a one-night stand she'd be wise to forget. Except, he made her heart wild, and he was hard to resist when he said stuff like, *I'll love you until the sun explodes* without any hint of irony.

Also, she never had any trouble locating him.

Where the hell had Nash gone?

She collided with Lee near the entrance, now lip-locked with the Spook Mortensen fan. "Have you seen Nash?"

He gave her a thumb's down, not bothering to break from the wet passion he was engaged in.

"Okay, I'll try outside."

He wasn't there either, but she found Jez alone in a dark corner, quietly puffing on a cigarette. "Thought you were packing those in," she said, slipping into the seat opposite him. He ignored her and kept on inhaling. "I can't find Nash anywhere."

"Surely that's a bonus."

"What? What do you mean?"

Jez blew out a long streamer of smoke. "What do I mean?" He laughed and crooked one dark brow. "More opportunity for you to indulge in what you actually fancy if he's not breathing down your neck and demanding shit."

"Excuse me?"

"Oh, knock it off, Jo. It's fucking obvious you're way more into Rock Giant. A toddler with permanency-blindness could fathom that, and if you're not already screwing him, you're at least contemplating it."

"I beg your pardon, I am not."

"Much." He laughed at the heat rising up her neck, creating a hot plate of her cheeks.

"I'm not fucking him." Only in the privacy of her thoughts. Thoughts, she was never going to act on. "I'm not trying to fuck him—"

"Then you're a fucking idiot."

"I love Nash."

"Sure." Jez agreed, managing to make it sound like he was doing the opposite. He leaned forward and stubbed out the ciggy, before settling back and lacing his fingers behind his head. "Do you, really? Is he not really just a means to an end? There are easier ways you could have stuck around, you know. You could have been part of the fucking band. Played the triangle or something. Or pulled a Bez and been our de facto mascot." He mimicked her shaking maracas. "You didn't have to tie yourself to him. And you're not going to lose anything if you wake up and tell him to take a fucking hike."

Not true. She'd lose everything. The cocoon of

safety she'd built. The security of exploring the world in company. A future with walls and Sunday dinners, and domesticity. But most of all, the friends, the family, she'd chosen for herself. If there was no her and Nash, then there'd be no her and Lee, no her and Balin, no her and Jez. It wasn't that they liked him more than her, it was just common sense.

"Where the hell is this coming from, Jez?"

"Guess I'm just done with playing nice and biting my tongue. Seriously"—Jez leaned forward and rested his hand on her forearm—"what do you even have in common with Curtis besides us and wedding plans neither of you are committed to?"

"What are you on?"

"What are you on?" He matched her glare. She looked away first. "Be honest, you don't want a marquee on the lawn, sherry flutes and a meringue dress."

"We haven't agreed that's what we're doing."

"Pretty sure him and his mum have it all planned out."

So, unfortunately, did she. She was sure Nash had dangled the handfasting in front of her as a way of saying, we did your version, now we're doing mine. Except, he'd stood her up.

"Rock Giant seems pretty goddamned sound," Jez observed.

Jodi retreated into the back of her chair. He was.

Jez lit another ciggy. She watched him smoke and occasionally brush a stray tress of his long wavy hair back from his face.

"If you dislike Nash so much, why are you in a band with him?"

Jez gave her a thin smile that planted grains of ice under her skin. "Wasn't the plan."

"You mean because you were supposed to take the

lead?" She'd always thought he'd been cool with the fact they'd voted Nash into that role instead.

"It's pretty darned difficult to play drums and sing lead vocals at the same time. No, I'm not sore. I just think he's a self-centred gobby wanker, and you deserve better."

"I'm happy with what I've got."

He outright laughed at that. "You're happy being ignored except for when he wants something? Babe, we've been here well over an hour now." He woke his phone screen. "Longer. And Nash has spent less than five minutes with you. You don't even know where he is. And he hasn't given a fucking thought to where you are or what you're doing, because out of sight, out of mind, right?"

Alarmingly, that was Nash described to a tee.

How many times had she slipped his mind because she hadn't been right there in front of him? His failure to turn up to their handfasting was only the most recent example of it. Looking back, there'd been others, like the time she'd spent three hours by a stage door in torrential rain because he'd forgotten to tell security to expect her.

"Fucking fool. In his position, I'd be glued to you. I sure as hell wouldn't be leaving the door open for a better man to walk through."

"Do you know where Nash is?"

Jez considered that with his fag dangling from his lower lip for perhaps half a second. "Like you need to ask. We both know where he is. Same fucking place he always is these days. With Balin." He tapped a bunch of ash away. "You should go do Rock Giant. Seriously. I'll cover for you if Curtis makes an appearance."

"I'm not going to screw Rock Giant."

"More's the pity."

"Have you always hated him this much?"

Jez sneered in a way that showed off the sharpness

of his canines. Girls were charmed by those vampire teeth, not that they were inches long or anything. He didn't have fangs, but they were pointy. "Wrong question."

He got up and bumped over the barrier dividing the bar from the street. What was the right question? "Why do you hate him?" What had changed? They had been friends, hadn't they? "Jez, why did you split up with Rune? Did Nash have something to do with it?"

"Do pigeons shit?"

Oh, God! She hadn't banked on it being the truth.

"What did he do?"

But Jez's long slim legs had already taken him halfway across the paved street. He didn't turn or respond to her call.

Jodi slumped back into her wooden chair. What had Nash actually told her? Wait, he hadn't actually told her. It'd been Balin...or was it Lee? Whoever it had been, had said they'd split because Jez figured it wouldn't work out due to them being set to tour so much. It'd seemed a flimsy excuse at the time. Now, she didn't believe it for a second.

"Jo-bill-o." Balin slid his arms around her from behind. He smelled of recently sprayed deodorant with an underlying thread of sex. She didn't need to ask what he'd been doing. "How come you're out here alone?" His lips grazed her cheek.

"I was with Jez, but he's..." She gestured in the direction of the quayside, with its colourful bobbing boats.

"Is he being a mardarse again?"

"Balin, do you know what happened between him and Rune? Has he spoken to any of you about it?"

He slid into the seat Jez had recently vacated. "Not to me. Figure he will when he's ready."

"But Nash didn't have anything to do with it, right?"

Balin pulled his legs up, so he was sat cross-legged in the chair. "Why would Nash have owt to do with Jez and Rune splitting? Did Jez suggest—"

Nash scraped a chair up to their table.

"You're here," she observed, an awkwardly bright lilt to her voice. She tipped her head up towards him, and he dutifully dropped a kiss on her lips. He tasted of mints. "Where've you been?" But smelled of the same anti-perspirant as Balin. They didn't usually use the same brand. She knew, she'd been doing the shopping, and they were all very particular about who liked what.

"I went to the loo, then it's taken an age to locate you."

The bar wasn't that big, which made it a shitty excuse for an excuse. He could have just admitted to being with Balin. It wasn't like she was unaware of his current fetish.

"But I'm here now." He folded one of her hands between the pair of his. "What's your desire? Do you want another drink? Shall I go to the bar? What do you want? Beer, again? Balin?"

"Yeah."

And off he went like he knew he'd wind up in the shit if he stayed.

Jodi drew her chair closer to Balin's. He had a dazed look about him, testament, she suspected to the fact he'd just got laid. "Was he watching you?"

"Ah, Jo—"

"Balin, just answer the question."

He sniffed. "Yeah, sure."

"Just watching?"

"Course."

"And what happened to the... to your hook up?"

He shrugged. "Went back to her guy, I guess." He was so blasé about it, at first, she was convinced she'd misheard him.

"You just shagged someone's girlfriend?"

"Wife, I think."

"What!"

He treated her to another of those loose-limbed shrugs. "It's hardly a first. What's the big deal?"

"Balin! You're screwing married women! You don't think maybe that might be detrimental to their relationships?"

He leaned over the table, bringing their heads closer. "Jo, their relationships are none of my fucking business. I make it a policy not to interfere in other people's affairs. I'm there for the good times. We have fun. I never disappoint. Everyone knows the deal and gets what they want out of it."

"Right." The word came out more clipped than she'd intended it to.

"Oooh, disapproving look," Balin crowed. He didn't seem in the least bit perturbed.

"And when the condom splits, or—"

"Shh!" He pressed his index finger to her lips while grinning. "Not your problem. Your job is just to keep me stocked up on jonnies and lube."

"Well, that makes me feel complicit."

His handsome mug scrunched into a frown. "Don't be daft. Look, is this because you're pissed off at me for letting Nash watch? Babe, if you've issues with it, you need to discuss them with him. You realise he's just watching, right? So, what's the big deal? It's not like he's cheating."

Right. Of course it wasn't. Balin wouldn't bullshit her over that.

"Is he just watching, though? Or is he getting off?"

Balin went all po-faced on her. So, that was a resounding yes, then.

"I'm just asking because if he is, that makes it sound an awful lot like you're having strings of threesomes with random married women."

"Not all of them are—"

"Not the point, Balin."

She rubbed her suddenly prickly eyes, and then at the stinging sensation in her nose.

"Jo, babe." Balin bumped his chair closer so he could sling an arm around her shoulders. "We're not having threesomes. Trust me on this. You don't need to get upset. Promise. He's just being an observant wingman for me. It's all harmless."

"Right," she snuffled into a napkin she didn't remember picking up. "But is it?"

"Yes."

"So, if I decided to, I dunno, go watch Rock Giant jerk off, would that be just harmless?"

"I'm not sure that's the same. Nash isn't watching me jerk off. He's not interested in me. Watching just gets him going. It gets him excited for you."

He was always hot for her after he'd been places with Balin.

"He's only interested in you."

"I know, but... Suppose I asked you to stop letting him—"

"Jo."

"Balin."

His gaze slid away from hers, so that he was looking into the middle distance.

"I thought we were friends."

"We are friends."

But not close enough friends that he'd make her that promise. A fact that hurt more than she liked, and cemented the precariousness of her position.

"I don't get involved in other people's relationships," he reiterated. "It's up to you two to make the rules of your relationship." He sat for a couple more seconds, no longer with his arm comfortably around her shoulder, then rose. "I'm gonna go see if Nash needs a hand with those drinks."

And off he went, probably to report everything she'd just said straight to Nash. Well, there was a truly smashing conversation to look forward to later.

It wasn't much fun stewing in the semi-dark alone, and while she didn't doubt there was a queue for the bar, she also couldn't tolerate waiting for them. Jodi relinquished the table to a bunch of thirtysomethings and crossed the plaza to join Jez by the water's edge. He was standing, gazing out to sea, his wavy hair lifted by the night breeze, hands in his pockets.

They stood in silence for several minutes.

"Do you ever wonder if you've made the right choices?"

Jez glanced at her from beneath half-shuttered lids, but didn't answer. After a moment, she rested her head against him. He yielded, and put his arm around her shoulders. "Sometimes."

"Do you miss Rune?" Stupid question, she knew he did. She'd watched him grieving, but she hadn't taken the time to ask him about it. She'd never dealt with a guy friend going through a breakup. All the lads she'd known growing up bounced from one lass to the next without standing still long enough to figure out if it hurt, and she'd never had a female bestie to nurse through a breakup with rom coms and ice-cream. Did Jez need rom coms and ice-cream? He'd probably prefer some psychological horror film that'd give her nightmares for months.

"Can't you fix it?"

"I'm the one who broke it off, Jodi."

"Right. Earlier, you implied Nash was involved."

"He wasn't uninvolved."

"But he didn't cause the... It wasn't because of anything he did that made you break up?"

He remained silent, a faraway look on his face. After a moment or two, his sullen scowl transformed, and a smile kissed his cheeks.

"What?" she asked.

"Nothing."

"I haven't seen you smile in like forever. It's something."

"I was just thinking maybe I should have a T-shirt made, or I could doctor one of the merch shirts. Or a Team GB one, graffiti on an R. No, wait, a Pokémon one. Instead of Team Rocket, I could be Team Rock—"

"Giant," she finished for him. "Please don't do that. Just because I'm mildly pissed off at Nash at the moment doesn't mean I want you to start trolling him."

He flashed her a look of those pointy teeth of his again. "I'm making no promises."

P

AUL HAD NOTHING against Bergen. Matter of fact, he quite liked Bergen, or at least its surroundings. He wasn't much of a city person, even if this was a comparatively tiddly one at about the size of Blackpool. What he didn't like about Bergen was that they'd arrived two hours ago to find Toys in the Attic had played a gig there the previous night and were hanging around the venue hoping for a chinwag before or after the Black Halo sound check. Paul promptly took himself off to the nearest bathroom, allowing the rest of the band to drop stuff off in the dressing rooms without him. Some days, you just didn't want to do the whole sociable thing and today happened to be that day. As luck would have it, his guitar tech came into the bogs right as Paul was washing his hands.

"Gonna take off for a few hours. You can handle the sound check, right?"

"Sure."

He liked Jake. Jake was always agreeable.

"The guys know?"

He mumbled something that might be construed as an affirmative but was really random noises. "I need to stretch my legs."

That was code the roadie would understand. When you were constantly living in the pockets of other people, everyone had days when they needed a few hours space, and it was always better to take them than hope the feelings would blow over. That sort of wishful thinking only ever led to explosions and bruises.

Granbakeen wasn't that far away. If he took a taxi, then he could get a good few hours of walking in. Breathe in some mountain air and be back in plenty of time for the show. Black Halo weren't even due on stage until half eight. Currently, it was only a bit after midday. More than enough time to take in some scenery and for the D'Amon brothers to get bored and piss off.

"Can't be easy seeing her with that prick all the time."

"He is a prick," he said, neither confirming nor denying the difficulty. So far, married life was kinda lonely. He'd anticipated more cuddle time, and less of a hollow zone in his chest created by her absence and the death of all the things he hoped such a bond would bring. Hard not to believe in soul mates and true love when you'd grown up looking at it every single day, yet here he was, the universe had spoken, he'd heralded the call, but... But his bed was cold and memories of three years ago weren't enough to sustain him.

He'd kept an eye on her during last night. She was struggling too. He could tell from the number of bar mats she'd slipped into her bag.

The prick entered the building along with his

bandmates as Paul hit the exit. He ought not to think of him in that way, but it was basically what popped into his head every time he clapped eyes on the man. He didn't see Jodi nestled among the group until they were on top of one another, trying to squeeze through the same narrow doorway.

"Where you off to?" she asked, flashing him the sort of smile that would have warmed him to his toes if he wasn't so eager to be gone and his mind wasn't still yelling "prick" at the top of its lungs.

"Shop." He didn't want his band mates learning of his actual plans until he was far enough away that they wouldn't attempt to change them.

The air outside was crisp. The sky was a typical Nordic blue and pleasingly cloud free. He'd crossed half the concourse before his ears caught on to the fact that Jodi was scurrying after him. As soon as they did, he slowed to let her catch up. "What are you d—"

"Need to get the guys some bits. You don't mind if I tag along, right?"

"With me? Unsupervised? Are you sure dork face won't—"

"Don't be mean to him. I don't want to hear it, and we're friends, remember. I can hang out with my friends if I wanna."

They weren't friends, but so as not to drive her away he continued to humour her. She, in a friendly way, linked their arms, possibly as an attempt to slow him down even further. Her cheeks were rather pink, and she did sound a bit winded.

"Yeah, um, what did you want?" He wasn't about to admit that shopping hadn't been his actual plan.

"Shower gel, mostly. And a couple of other things. Which way do we head?"

"Not sure." Immediately opposite was a local craft shop, but not far along from that they found a midsized grocery store. Paul carried the basket, while

Jodi picked up a dozen or so things. She had a list. He treated himself to a bag of apples, and a bar of organic chocolate, to give his shopping trip validity.

"Where were you actually going?" she said peering up at him with a smile on her lips once they hit the pavement again. He wasn't sure how she knew, so he didn't double down on the lie.

"A walk... A long walk."

"Something up?" Several things were up, but nothing that he wanted to talk about, so he repeated the line he'd given Jake about needing some air. It wasn't a lie, just maybe not the whole truth. "I'm feeling anti-social is all."

"Oh!" Her face fell.

"That doesn't include you. I always have time for you."

"You're sure you don't mind—"

"Castle, of course I don't mind. We're mar—"

She raised a hand and pressed her fingers to his lips. "Don't say it."

He huffed. "Sure you don't need to get back?"

"For what? So, I can stand around for the rest of the day like a spare part getting in everyone's way. The pre-show stuff is fucking dull. Besides, it's gonna take even longer than normal today because they're all in pissy moods due to lack of sleep. Hm, is that why you're out of sorts too."

"I'm not out of sorts." He wasn't. He couldn't stomach the emotional wringer the D'Amon brothers were likely to put him through, that's all. Especially not on top of having to watch her and Nash being all couple-y, when she was really his. "I got my beauty sleep."

"Wish I'd got mine." She indulged in an extravagant yawn. His soul mate did seem rather sleepy.

"Maybe stop partying until dawn," he advised.

She gave him a friendly punch.

"Ow!" It hadn't actually hurt, but he was going for a sympathy bid.

"Sorry." She gave it a rub. Hey, any sort of contact, he'd take it. "Weren't my idea. I'd have happily hit the sack sooner."

Then again, maybe he shouldn't encourage early nights. "When'd you get to bed?"

"5ish. But it was after six before I dozed off."

The Ghost Boys had obviously stuck it out at the club long after Black Halo left. "Explains why they all look so ghoulish today."

She gave another yawn, prompting another adjustment to his plans. Much as it'd be fun to jump into a taxi with her and head off to the mountains, a less arduous form of leg-stretching was in order. Also, practically speaking, neither of them were dressed for a wander in the Norwegian wilderness. He at least had a jacket, plus a daysack of essentials. She had a purse on a long strap across her body that served to emphasise her bust, and slip-on shoes that'd seen better days.

"There's a park with a lake just over the way. I thought I might do a lap or two."

"Swimming?"

"On foot."

"Right, I knew that. Sounds good."

She was wearing his old jumper again today. He remarked on it, earning himself another elbow to the abs, this time she hit him right on his bruise, causing him to suck in a breath. That damn table had done him more damage than first appeared. It'd heal though, if she didn't keep poking him there.

"I don't own many clothes, and stuff's still drying."

"Do you need to clothes shop?"

She looked him over, incredulous. "I can make do,

and you don't want to stand around while I try stuff on."

"It could be fun." Actually, it might be a lot of fun.

She shook her head again, insistent. "Clothes shopping is soul destroying. Nothing fits, and I look horrible in all of it. Plus, I can't afford it, anyway, and that wasn't a hint that you should offer to pay. I can support myself. I don't need charity. I've a decent paying job these days."

"PA to an up-and-coming band. Rather you than me," he muttered. Actually, his brain had stalled over the notion of her looking awful. She always looked fantastic to him. Still, he made a note to slip her another of his jumpers somehow, and to one day take her shopping and make sure she knew exactly how much he appreciated her curvy body. Not necessarily together. He wouldn't mind getting arrested for shagging in a changing room, but he guessed she might. From what he'd seen, she seemed to have put her bad girl past behind her, and was now attempting to pull off typical, nothing out of the ordinary, everyday citizen. He hoped she didn't think she needed to do that to make herself fit in, or worse, to fulfil Nash's version of an ideal wife.

A green area with bench-lined walkways surrounded the roughly octagonal lake, where an underwhelming fountain spurted jets of water into the air. They did a lap and a half of the circumference before making use of one of the benches. Paul ate his apples. Jodi polished off a sandwich and a can of cola. They shared the chocolate. After a few minutes debating whether to enter the museum opposite that had a Munsch collection, and agreeing they should, neither of them moved from the bench. An art museum wasn't where he wanted to take her. Nope, that'd be to the hotel he could see the roof of, and where they all conveniently had rooms booked for that evening. It might not stretch his legs, but they could get in a vigorous workout. He didn't suggest it. Couldn't face hearing her answer. Nor was he prepared to risk prompting her departure.

Being friend zoned was shit. He didn't want a platonic marriage. He wanted a physical one, a soul-deep spiritual one. Something that involved feels and connections across multiple planes of existence. Sadly, Luthor was right. He wanted her to himself. Wanted to be able to give her all the things he'd promised without overstepping the mark.

He let her ramble on about the stupid shit the guys did, nodding appropriately. It was predictable stuff. Her complaints were the same ones that Elspeth had often made about how guys were nothing but smelly oversized toddlers.

He shifted, the bench suddenly far too hard against his arse. That ring on her finger was fuck ugly. Clearly the man had no taste.

"Want to go get a tattoo?"

"Huh?" She goggled at him, a grin stretching her lips. "Right now? Do you even have space for another one?"

Tons. Also, he had something specific in mind, something he'd been mulling since their handfasting. The trinity ribbon symbolising their bond remained fastened around his wrist, but nineteen days on, it was starting to look rather grubby and frayed. There was plenty bare skin to ink three bands and a symbolic knot around his wrist though, and he really wanted her present for the occasion.

"Where would we even go?"

It only took a minute for the internet to provide the answer. There were numerous choices all within a five-to-ten-minute walk.

And still they didn't move.

"Are you mad at me?" she asked.

Where had that come from? "Never. Why the fuck would I be?"

She shuffled, so that she was sitting sideways, knees up against his legs. "Because this isn't what you want, not really. Us being friends, I mean."

"Doesn't mean I'm mad at you." He'd never be mad at her no matter how trying the situation was.

"I think you must be. At least a little."

"I promise I'm not."

"You must be, though. This isn't what you hoped to get out of it when you stepped up and promised me all that stuff. Why did you even?"

"I'm not mad, Castle. Disappointed, maybe, that the really hot chick that I wed doesn't want a happily ever after with me." As for why... Fate hadn't landed the same red-hot goddess in his lap twice for no reason. They were meant to be, clearly. The stars had aligned twice to make certain of it, and eventually she'd realise it. Leastways, he hoped she would. The possibility that they'd instead wind up being star-crossed lovers was too horrid to contemplate. How lonely would that be?

"But you don't love me. Paul, you don't. We hardly know one another."

He hushed her by pressing his ring-clad thumb against her lips.

"I'm not going to say it because I know you don't want to hear it, but time has sod all to do with it." Actually, he'd lied. He was going to say it. "I love you, Castle. Wholeheartedly. Undoubtedly. And I'm here for you."

"Shit!" She scratched at her face, causing the skin to pinken.

"You don't have to say it back."

"Please. Stop." She clapped both hands over her mouth. Her eyes a little too shiny as she looked at him. "Paul..." She remained contemplative a moment.

Avoiding his eyes but fixating on his mouth instead. "I'm sorry. The timing is all wrong. I wanted you for so long after that first night. I kept hoping you'd call, or you'd turn up. If you had then, I'd have been..." She shook her head. "I really wanted to be yours. I wanted the big strong man who'd saved me from myself, and been so fucking kind, and made me feel so wanted to come back and make everything right. But he didn't. You didn't. I wanted you to call so much..."

"I didn't have your number," he mouthed, while covering her hands clasped in her lap with one of his. With the thumb of the other hand, he rubbed away the tear that trickled down her cheek.

"It's too late now. I moved on. I had to move on. You understand that, right? God, if there was a way. If I could rewind time or split myself in two, then... Shit!" She pulled back, freeing herself from his touch. "I shouldn't be saying any of this stuff. What good will it do either of us? It's too late. I made other choices."

She could unmake them.

"It's too late."

He didn't agree, nor did he like to see her so agitated and be without a means of comforting her. While every instinct told him to throw his arms around her and pull her close, to soothe her with his hands and lips, he knew that wouldn't lessen the agony. It wouldn't be a magical fix. He wasn't sure anything would. It'd probably make everything worse.

Fucking hell! Rejection was a bitter pill, and that's what she was saying. You were too late.

He let his gaze drop to her lap, and her hands. The temptation to rip the ugly rock from her finger and throw it in the lake was near overwhelming. Perhaps intuiting his thoughts, she pushed her hands into the space between her thighs.

"When did you get engaged?" he asked.

She raised her shoulders. "Not that long ago. Start

of the summer." Her teeth raked her lower lip. "I guess it was pretty soon after Nash and I met, but lots of things changed fast what with the guys getting signed."

The way her shoulders rose as she spoke, and she curled herself into a smaller space said a lot about how defensive she was about it. People had obviously had opinions. They'd probably suggested all sorts of mean reasons why she'd insisted on him giving her a ring right on the cusp of hitting the big time.

"Didn't the rest of the band approve?"

"No. They were delighted for us."

"Right." He nodded. "You seem close with them."

"Yeah." Genuine warmth lit up her eyes again. "They're good friends. The best of friends. They've looked out for me. Been there for me. Continue to be there for me. I love them all to bits. Never want to be without them."

"So, Nash introduced you?"

Yes, he was digging. He was genuinely curious about her life between the time of their first meeting and now. Things had obviously changed, and not just in terms of her relationship status.

"Kind of. I guess. Not really. We all met at the same time, but the guys are a unit, what with being a band and all."

Was that what was keeping her with Nash? Belief that she'd lose the rest of her friends if the pair of them parted? He guessed it didn't help that the buggers had employed her, too, so there were multiple strings to cut to walk away.

"So, how did you meet?"

She sighed. "Can we walk?"

"Castle, is there something about your meeting that's—"

"There was this guy in Valencia. The site manager on the fruit farm we were all working at. He kept pestering me, and then there was an issue with stuff going missing and he thought... Someone said they'd seen me with some of it, so he..."

He risked a rebuke and curled his hand around hers. She let him. Even allowed him to lace their fingers together.

"Nash and the guys...mostly Lee and Balin. They interceded. The guy... He wasn't very nice. He kept threatening me. Saying that if I didn't do what he wanted, he'd have me arrested. All I kept thinking was who would take care of the cats?" Another tear tracked down her cheek. She hastily brushed it away. "I don't know why I get so wound up about it still. Nothing happened, and I met the guys. They kept me safe after that. It was like having five brothers."

"Brothers, not boyfriends?" He didn't much care for the idea of them all vying for her attention, bad enough that he had to put up with one of them making a prior claim.

"Brothers," she confirmed. "Except way better than my real ones." She made a face. "They were there for me, but I wasn't shagging them all, or anything. Although, I guess it wasn't entirely platonic either. We all shared beds."

Yeah, he definitely hadn't needed that factoid occupying space in his head. It was bad enough reconciling his feelings with the notion that she was intimate with Nash. Her plus four, wait... "Five?"

"Five," she confirmed. "Nash, Lee, Balin, Jez and Jez's ex-boyfriend, Rune. Actually, six, on the occasions Lee's kid brother Austen was around."

"They realise that you did take the stuff?"

She jerked her head to look at him. "I'm not a thief."

"Chill Castle, I know. You're just magnetic." He planted a kiss on the top of her head. "You only *steal* buses."

"You mean hearts, right?" she countered, giving him a playful shove.

He was prepared to give her that one.

She rested her head against the top of his arm. "Also, please don't say that too loud. I don't want to wind up in trouble. I've never told anyone about that, or about anything that happened that night."

"Me neither."

It seemed he'd surprised her, given the way she was peering up at him with a furrow in her brow. "You haven't? How come?"

Once or twice, he'd come close to saying something, especially in the six months immediately succeeding Bertha Bus's drowning, but something had always held him back. He liked having a secret...keeping her to himself.

"If your band don't know that it was me, then they must think that you—"

"Drowned Bertha. Yeah." He grinned. He'd taken and continued to take oceans of stick for that. "Don't you go telling them otherwise. You'll destroy my reputation."

"Your reputation for what?"

"Being a mad bastard." He pulled out his sunglasses and perched them on his nose. "Still want to walk?"

She nodded.

He noted how twitchy she'd become if she was confined to one place too long, the way her fingers would beat a nervous tattoo against the side of her thigh. Recognised it as a precursor to the hand wandering that happened when her anxiety truly kicked in. "Tell me what happened after you left that morning."

"I went to the vet. Then home. Realised sharpish that I couldn't stay there with the cats, so I moved out."

"On Christmas Eve?" He hoped that wasn't what she meant. He didn't much care for Christmas as a religious celebration, not being religious himself in the typical sense, but he did believe in it as a time to spend with family of all varieties.

"Seemed the best plan."

"To move out on Christmas Eve?"

"Yeah." She tried not to laden the word with too much ballast, but he saw through the false breeziness. The woman he'd met three years ago had a shitty home life, no job, no support, no real friends, and mental health problems that meant the previous things were unlikely to materialise.

"Where did you move?"

She chewed the inside of her cheek. "What does it matter? It was ages ago. I'm fine now."

It mattered. Terrifyingly, he had a vision of her alone in the glass house they'd taken refuge in after Bertha went down. All alone with three kittens and no survival skills. As to her assertion that all was well now... That was patently untrue. She was engaged to an idiot, and clearly still living pretty much hand to mouth.

"I went to Europe," she said, as they turned a corner. "Not directly, but once I'd got some cash together from some temping work. I explored a few places. Got work picking fruit and eventually wound up in Spain. You've already heard the rest. And now you're frowning."

"I don't like the thought of you being homeless."

She scoffed. "I'm not sure a tour bus counts as a permanent address, so that makes us both homeless, and you've been homeless longer."

It wasn't the same. "I have places to stay."

"I have places to stay."

He also had enough money and friends and extended family to never need to worry about shelter, or where his next meal was coming from, whereas he suspected she had barely enough to pay a deposit on a really shitty rental place for a month. Maybe it was time for him to put down some roots and get a place in case she ever needed somewhere. It wouldn't have to be much. Something the size of one of Xane's bolt holes would do.

There was an ice-cream seller a little way along as they headed seaward. Paul bought them both cones. Jodi licked the back of his fingers where it'd melted and run before he'd managed to hand it over. She gave him a cheeky grin when he raised his brows.

"Watch it, Castle. You might not approve of how I'll retaliate."

"Are you going to lick my fingers too?"

"There's ice-cream on your face."

"Oh." She rubbed the edge of her mouth with the back of her hand, thus managing to splodge ice-cream in her hair. "Bugger!"

"Come here. Let me." He got it out with his fingers, then threaded the same digits through the blonde tresses from near their roots. He wanted so badly to kiss her.

"Paul," she said, peeping up at him with those soulful eyes. "Were you going to lick my cheek?"

He did just that. She squealed and swung at him, but he easily darted out of the way. Way nippier on his feet, and with a vastly longer stride, he had no trouble dodging her attempts to smack him in retaliation. She gave up in under a minute, breathing hard, and set about licking all the dribbles off her hand, and around the outside of her cone. Paul tucked into his own.

"No more licking me," she said when he sidled up beside her and bumped their shoulders.

He could have offered to lick her places she might have liked him to lick, but he'd agreed to the friends thing, and he'd probably pushed his luck too far already over that. Maybe. He often licked his friends.

She turned away from him to look at the ducks paddling past and concentrated on her treat.

Once they'd finished their cones, they resumed strolling. Didn't take her long to loop her arm around his in the way girls did when they wanted him to check his pace. He shortened his stride, but not so much that she'd feel secure letting go. He liked her there too much. Liked the scent of her, and the curl of his fingers against his forearm, and the way those passing by looked at them.

"What happened to your band? You used to have a different lineup."

He nodded. "Steve died. Elspeth left. Luthor and Ronnie joined." It was a nice succinct summary. Wasn't much more that needed to be said, and he didn't want to waste his time with her dwelling on past events.

"Sorry. You must miss them."

Curiously, no one ever asked *him* that. They worried over Xane, but not the rest of them. Did he miss Steve? Their first drummer had been solid. He'd been a far better match for Elspeth than Xane had ever been. Did he miss Elspeth? All the fucking time, but even he recognised that the shit she'd done to the band had been too spiteful to easily forgive. Plus, Black Halo's current incarnation had a lot going for it. "E and I have known one another since we were little kids. It's weird touring without her, but" –he shrugged– "I still see her. Saw her at Equinox. She's doing okay."

She nodded. "You don't have your bestie with you anymore though. I'd find that hard."

He wanted to ask her who her bestie was, but suspected she'd say it was Nash, and frankly didn't want to hear his name on her lips.

"It's fine," he said instead. "Ronnie's a giggle."

"But not the same though, right?"

Right. All too perceptively right. He and E, they really knew one another. That said, he wasn't sure what she'd make of him getting handfasted. Probably wouldn't approve. No doubt he'd get an earful when she did learn of it. He imagined he was in for several earfuls from several quarters.

"It must get lonely. You must get lonely."

He wriggled his arm free of her grip so that he could wrap it around her, then bowed a bit so he could plant another kiss on her head and inhale the scent of her hair. "A bit, yeah."

"Is that why you did it, Paul? Hitched yourself to me because—"

"No."

Nor had it been anything to do with mixing alcohol and mushrooms, or the threesome with Ronnie and that beech tree. If he was entirely honest, he couldn't say what it was that had definitively made him step in and give himself to her, and ultimately, it didn't matter. Whether it was a gut thing or a spiritual thing, or just a moment of insanity, he wasn't sorry for it. He'd do it again, every time, without a qualm.

"How much longer can I keep you?"

She consulted her phone for the time. "A bit longer yet. They won't miss me. Are you sure your guys won't miss you?"

"Fuck 'em," he said with a shrug. "Let's get those tattoos."

"YOU GOT A tattoo?"

"Yeah, do you like it?" Lee grasped Jodi's hand to take a better look, though it was hard to see beneath the protective wrapping.

"Cats, right? It's cute."

She gave him an enthusiastic nod. The first tattoo parlour hadn't done walk-ins, nor did the second one, but the owner had recognised Rock Giant and wasn't about to leave a well-known heavy metal bassist standing in his foyer. Sure enough, when they'd been directed through to the studio, Black Halo were among a gathering of metal legends sprayed onto the walls life-sized, or almost life-sized. Wall Rock Giant was three inches too short. Paul had sketched out what he'd wanted for the guy, who'd agreed it was simple enough that it could be done right away. His design comprised three narrow bands around his wrist that were joined by a trinity knot. She hadn't needed to see him finally snipping off the ribbon they'd been handfasted with to know what the ink signified.

She'd tried to be mad about him permanently inking it onto his skin but failed. It was hard to dismiss that much conviction, especially when she'd given him no reason to hope for the future he wanted. Didn't matter, he claimed, he remained committed to her anyway. What girl wouldn't be a little swayed by that?

He'd saved that grubby ribbon too. Coiled it carefully around his fingers and then stowed it in a pocket, muttering something about a treasure box. It made her curious to learn what else was stowed in Paul Reed's treasure box.

Meanwhile, she hadn't set out to get inked. Nothing in the various design brochures she'd browsed while Rock Giant was in the chair called to her. It wasn't until she'd seen his design that the idea had come to her.

It was probably a mistake. The lead weights in her stomach certainly implied so.

People wouldn't understand.

Nash wouldn't.

While the handfasting didn't hold the same significance to her as it did to Paul, it did mean something.

There weren't many people in the world who put themselves out for her. Paul Reed was one of them. She wasn't sure why. It obviously wasn't just about sex, because she'd categorically told him that wasn't on the cards, and it hadn't chased him off.

The tattoo... Her tattoo consisted of three thin knotted bands that formed a bracelet around her wrist, along the top of which were silhouettes of three tiny cats in different poses. Why the fuck shouldn't she mark the intersecting of their lives if she wanted to? It was her skin. Her... their history. Considering the changes it had brought about, it was worth marking.

Rock Giant had nodded his approval. Lee wasn't making a fuss, so that was a good start. He was kind of her test case to see what the response would be like from the Ghost Boys.

"You're back." Nash entered the backstage room along with Balin, the two of them tucking into burgers and fries from a fast-food joint. Usually, she perked up at the sight of her future hubby, but he looked decidedly unwashed, unshaven, and unsavoury after their sound check. He was still dressed in the same clothes he'd fallen asleep in at the crack of dawn and that he'd worn on stage the night before. He needed a shower. Ketchup dripped from his burger and landed on him mid-chest.

"Fuck!"

"Here." Jodi held out a tissue to him. He looked at her through decidedly bloodshot eyes, but took it and daubed ineffectually at the mark, before swearing again and pulling the shirt off and chucking it onto the seat beside her.

"Where the fuck have you been all afternoon?"

While his tone was light-hearted, her shoulders still hitched. He took a perch beside her and continued to tuck into his meal. Jodi's tummy rumbled.

"I did the shopping and then explored a bit. I wasn't needed here, and you were busy. I didn't think it'd be a problem."

"Except I did need you."

He had?

Lee, on the left of her, made a noise in the back of his throat. "Don't be a dick, Nash. You wanting someone to fetch you coffee and snacks isn't the same as needing her. Why shouldn't she go look around Bergen? If it'd been an option, I'd have gone, too." He gave her a nod.

"Could have mentioned that you were heading out," Nash grumbled.

"I did. Guess you didn't hear me."

Nash cracked a can of lager and proceeded to tip most of it down his throat. She watched him swallow, feelings of guilt creeping over her at the fact she was comparing his unkempt currently antagonistic self to Rock Giant's earthy beauty. They were chalk and cheese. Nash a waspish wisp of a man. Nicely formed, but more boyish than manly. Paul was all ink, sculpted muscle, and stoicism. Nor did he seem to feel the need to draw attention to himself in the ways Nash did. When he was there, you knew it, whereas Nash, you could easily lose in a crowd if it wasn't for the fact he'd be making himself heard. It was why he'd ended up as the Ghost Boys singer, when in all honesty, Jez definitely had a way better singing voice.

Not that she'd ever upset Nash by saying that.

Not that any of them ever said that.

Well, Rune had once...

Anyway, it made sense for Nash to be their frontman. Jez was happy playing drums, and since Nash couldn't play anything beyond a couple of power chords, there wasn't another role for him to fit into.

Having finished both his burger, and the lager without even offering her a bite, he rested his damp and decidedly heavy head against her shoulder. "Where'd you go, anyway?"

"The park just across the way. There's a lake."

"On your own, for the whole afternoon? Didn't think you liked keeping your own company."

She frequently kept her own company.

"She went and got a tattoo." Jez, whom she'd assumed was asleep, piped up from the other sofa. He was lying on his back, occupying its entirety, and had a leather jacket pulled up covering most of his head.

"Is he serious?" Nash lifted his head in order to gawp at her. "A tattoo? Jo? Where? What of? What sort of dive did you go to that they—"

Good grief, you'd think she'd just tattooed a target on her forehead.

"It wasn't a dive."

"Wasn't it? How would you know? What do you know about tattoos? Were their needles clean? What if you've given yourself—"

Lee clipped him around the ear. "Give it a break. The correct response is, that's nice, sweetheart, would you like to show me your new ink? She's an adult. She can use her judgement over risk factors, same as the rest of us."

"Aye, but—"

Lee glared at him. "Adult, with bodily autonomy."

Nash frowned back, before returning his attention to her. "Let's see it, then."

Considering the attitude he was giving her, she didn't really want to. "It's still wrapped up. I'll show you later. It's of the cats."

"You put those fleabags on your skin."

Apparently that notion was hilarious.

"I happen to love those fleabags. Also, they don't have fleas."

"Unlike him," Jez muttered.

Nash aimed his empty can at his bandmate's head but missed.

He sat for a while, being fidgety, and picking at the sole of his boot. "Who went with you?" he asked when she got up, thinking she ought to find something to eat. "There's no way you went alone, and we were all here. Who else do you know?"

When she didn't immediately answer, he started nodding his head, and a hateful grin spread across his face. "You went with him, didn't you? That's why he missed their sound check. You fucking went with Rock Giant to get inked."

Jodi bristled at his accusatory tone. The way he

said it made it sound like a planned excursion, and it hadn't been.

"The guy's proper inked up. Best person to consult if you're looking to get some ink of your own," Balin said.

Thank you, Balin.

Nash glared at him.

"What? It's who I'd consult if I was looking to get some ink done."

"Do you now have matching tattoos?" Nash asked, ignoring Balin's attempts to dial the level of tension down.

"We bumped into one another. I don't know what you're implying, but there wasn't anything untoward about it. I went to get the stuff you all wanted from the shop, and he was kind enough to point me the right way."

"And after picking up some johnnies and snacks you thought, 'Hey, let's go get inked together'."

"Yeah... Sorta... No. I told you. I went to the park."

Nash scratched his nose. "With him?"

She was too shit at lying to even attempt to say otherwise. Not that it should've been necessary. She hadn't done anything wrong. She was allowed to hang out with her friends. But Nash levelled her with the sort of stink eye her father had been a master of. He'd look at her that way whenever she rolled home after curfew—a decidedly arbitrary time that was never communicated—before accusing her of being a little prossie, and telling her he'd throw her out, or worse if she ever dared to come home with a bun in her belly. And where the fuck was his tea?

Back then, she'd been far too busy borrowing cars to concern herself with mucking around with any of the racer boys she knew, and she'd not been their cup of tea, anyway. They all rode with skinny chicks.

Rock Giant was different. There was attraction

there. Attraction that ran both ways, but so what. She was also attracted to Lee, sometimes got gooey over Rune's beautiful soul, and indulged in celebrity crushes on members of both sexes and a few non-binary ones. She wasn't about to get off with any of them, because she wasn't a cheat.

"I suppose he's got a matching cat tattoo now?"

"No, he hasn't."

Nash gave a dismissive snort.

Jez sat, throwing off the jacket. "You sound jealous, Nash. What's the matter? Not feeling too secure? Worried she's going to dump your scrawny arse? Considering the way you treat her, she fucking ought to."

Her fiancé lurched to his feet. "The way I treat her!"

"Like chattel," Jez retorted.

"Shut the fuck up. Like you wouldn't ask questions if your fiancée had spent the afternoon with another guy."

"But I don't have one," Jez said, his lips curling into a cruel sneer as he held Nash's gaze.

"Guys, enough." Balin inserted himself between them. "Sit down, Nash. Quit provoking him, Jez. Jo, what ink did Rock Giant get?"

"A Celtic knot," she replied. The truth.

"See, not even vaguely the same. So, can we just can the pointless squabbling?"

Brian stuck his head around the door. "An hour thirty until show time, boys. We all good?"

"Fabulous, Brian," Balin said, conjuring up a convincing we're all delightfully untroubled expression.

The minute their tour manager left, Balin snatched the jacket from Jez's lap and stalked towards the door. "I'm going to go hang somewhere else... find some chill."

Jez catapulted off the sofa and followed him.

There was no need for Jodi to speculate about what they intended to do. Find some girls.

Willing girls.

The kind who were happy to suck off a couple of relatively unknown Brits in exchange for front row tickets to see Black Halo. Not that the Ghost Boys were without fans, but the crowds were here to see the main act.

Quiet descended after they left, to Jodi's relief, until she realised Nash was still scowling at her.

"You could at least fucking apologise," he said.

If there'd been anything to apologise for, then sure. "I haven't done anything wrong, Nash."

He gave another wounded huff and shook his head.

"We agreed you were going to stay away from him."

They hadn't agreed that. They hadn't talked about it, or him. Most of the time, it was like Nash took pains to excise Rock Giant from existence. Like any room he occupied, Nash patched over with an alternate no-Paul-Reed-present version. He'd yelled about the handfasting right after it happened, but they hadn't properly talked it out.

"Everything's been shit since he showed up."

Lee leaned around her. "Tone it down, Nash. You're being a git."

"It's okay, Lee." Jodi patted his knee where it was poking through the hole in his jeans. "Nash, if you're accusing me of something, then just go ahead and say what it is. Otherwise, get over yourself. I'm not apologising to you for getting some fresh air, or, oh my God, talking to another man. And if you can't trust me to be alone with one, then—"

"He's not just another man though, is he?"

Jodi shoved him away from her, blood pounding

in her head. "I'm really sorry if your afternoon wasn't as pleasant as mine, but that's not my fault. I've said all this to you already, but I'll say it again now, and maybe you'll actually hear me. If I wanted to be with him, I'd be with him. I'm not. I'm with you. God help me, I've agreed to marry you. Right now, the way you're behaving, you're making me feel like a fucking idiot for even contemplating that."

She left him chewing on that. Having slammed the dressing room door, Jodi slouched against the wall outside it, fuming. It'd been a nice day until this point. A blissful day. Why did he have to be so petty and spoil it?

"Are you trying to push her away?" she overheard Lee ask Nash.

"Stay out of it, Lee? It's bad enough having my bandmates constantly fawning over my fiancée without having the damn Black Halo yeti trying it on at every opportunity, too."

"You don't even know that's what was happening."

"I've seen him look at her."

"Yeah, and I've seen you look at Balin. And I've seen you look at Jez. Shall we talk about why Rune's not around anymore? Shall we? Because if we're going to play the accusations game, I reckon I've a few good grenades I can lob. That woman goes out of her way to make you happy, and you give her nothing but crap."

"I had nothing to do with Jez and Rune breaking up."

"And Jodi isn't screwing Rock Giant."

She heard footsteps coming towards the door.

"And only one of those things is definitely true."

Jodi shuffled along the wall. Lee came out. He caught sight of her and offered a rueful grin. "Wanna hug."

"I'd love one."

Lee smelled of woodsy cologne, and something

peppery. His hair got into her mouth. She wiped it away, while he ticked a calloused fingertip against her cheek. "I'm sorry about him."

"It's not your fault. I take it the sound check went well?"

"Oh, yeah. Amazingly well." He kissed the top of her head. "A shit ton of niggles that on another day wouldn't faze anyone, but today on too little sleep it was like we were being shat on by elephant birds." He yawned into his hands. "I need either an enormous cuppa or a power nap. Maybe both. Thank God we're just the support act. The crowd won't give a shit if we're shit. They're here to see Black Halo, whose sound check took a fraction of the time ours did, even accounting for their AWOL bassist."

They ambled along the corridor as far as the door to Black Halo's dressing room. Lee knocked. When there was no answer, he grinned and turned the handle. Silence greeted them as they stuck their heads around the jamb.

"Looks as if no one's home. I'm pretty sure they've gone out to get something to eat. Something more nutritious than a greasy burger or yet another hotdog."

Jodi's stomach rumbled again.

"I'm sure they won't mind us gatecrashing for a few." They claimed a sofa each. Lee stretched full length on his. Within minutes he'd dozed off. She hadn't had nearly enough sleep either, which meant she ought to be as tired as the guys. Evidently, there was too much nonsense tumbling around her head, because her brain refused to rest.

Was she being an idiot for sticking it out with Nash?

No. They'd been happy with one another until she'd screwed things up by hitching herself to Rock Giant. Their present discord was on her, and unlike all the previous times when she'd screwed up her life, she wasn't going to run. She'd stick it out. Figure it out. Compromise, like adults did. Work at it, and fix shit.

After another few minutes of fruitlessly trying to nod off, she rose and started poking around. This dressing room was far larger than the one down the corridor. It had a homely feel to it and wasn't littered with empty cans and food wrappers. A laptop sat on a counter before a well-lit mirror, various kohl pencils beside it, along with multiple cans of deodorant and expensive aftershave. She amused herself spraying them and attempting to work out which one she thought belonged to whom. By yet another mirror, she found an assortment of rubber bracelets printed with slogans, and a couple of bananas that someone had doodled on with a black sharpie. The best find, though, was Rock Giant's crocheting hook, complete with a tail of pale-yellow wool.

THERE WERE TOO many souls packed into the too small space, and the Ghost Boys dressing room was by no means small. Okay, it wasn't vast either, but it certainly hadn't been designed with this many occupants in mind. How the guys were supposed to get ready to head on stage with this amount of chaos around them defied reason. For the most part they seemed to be revelling in it. Balin had a girl on his lap. The guy beside him had a possessive hand on the small of her back. Boyfriend, she concluded. Giving his girl a treat and hawkishly wondering if he was going to be throwing punches before the night was done. He was right to wonder, considering.

Lee, freshly rested and showered, was attempting to blow dry his hair, surrounded by a group of six young women all sporting Vans and with a collective hemline of approximately six inches. "Your hair's so amazing," one of them said.

"Are you and Spook Mortensen related?" asked another.

They weren't even the same shade of blond.

"I love guys with beards. Yours is so soft."

"You okay, babe?" Jez bumped against her arm as he passed. In a show of pre-show nerves, he was pacing. Only he had a train of fans dogging his steps creating a tail effect that kept colliding with itself.

"Where's Nash?"

He waved vaguely. "Hogging the bathroom so he can doll himself up and look beautiful for the fans in the front row. Good thing the rest of us are beautiful already." He gave her a wink.

"Who's that?" the fangirl directly behind him asked.

"None of your business."

"Is she entertaining you tonight? I thought I was your number one for later."

"Only if you're not a drag."

Jodi found Nash in the bathroom sitting on the vanity unit by the sink surrounded by an array of sweets and deodorant cans. The former he appeared to be handing out to anyone with the forethought to ask. As she approached, he unwrapped one for a girl in fishnets and black lipstick then placed it on her tongue.

"Nash?"

"Jo-Jo." He bumped off the vanity sending various aerosol cans flying. "Babe." Seeking askance with his eyes, he sought her consent to get closer. When she nodded, he gave her a forehead kiss. "Sorry. I'm an arse. You know what I'm like when I'm tired."

"It's okay. I should've checked in and made sure I wasn't needed."

"Yeah. Give us some space, ladies, eh?" His fan club twittered and cooed "—we'll see you later,

Nash—" but dutifully vacated the room. Mostly. "That includes whoever's in the loo."

There were a few moments of shuffling, then the door latch clicked, and a girl with blue hair exited. She smirked at them both, then left. Balin followed her out.

"Didn't you literally have someone else on your lap three minutes ago?" Jodi asked.

Balin shrugged. "I'm popular." He zipped up, then pushed between her and Nash and used the sink. Then pushed between them again to reach the drier, which he used for approximately three seconds before wiping his hands against his thighs. Nash followed him to the door and locked it behind him.

"When did you all turn into such sleazeballs?"

"Ahem." Nash put his back to the door. "My dick hasn't been anywhere but your pussy."

Jodi rolled her eyes. "The rest of them."

"The rest of them were always sleazeballs. You just didn't realise, and luckily you wound up with me, not any of them."

She nodded. "Well, I'm glad you're feeling better for having had a nap?" she said changing the subject.

Nash pinned her with a sultry look. "I didn't have a nap. I had a couple of Monsters."

No wonder he looked bouncy. He turned to the mirror, pulling the remains of a packet of love heart sweets from his pocket. He smiled at whatever was written on it, then slid it along the countertop to her.

MAKE UP.

"Not sure how to interpret that. Are you asking me to apply your eyeliner or..."

He dragged his teeth over his lower lip, flooding it with colour. "I'm saying that I don't like being at odds with you, and it feels like you're not entirely onboard with us anymore."

"That's not fair, Nash. I am."

"Are you?" He drew her closer to him, one hand

hooked behind her neck. It didn't take a genius to figure out what he had in mind. Except a quickie in a bathroom wasn't going to smooth things over or fix things. It'd just mean he could convince himself he was the same sort of stud as his bandmates.

"Aren't you due on stage in like ten minutes?"

He caught a lock of her hair and twirled it around his finger. "Ten minutes is oceans of time. The door's bolted. Can't get much more private than that."

Someone banged on the door. "I'd like to use the facilities before we go on," Lee called.

"Find another one."

"There is only this one. Stop assaulting Jo, fuckwit, and open the door."

Nash rolled his eyes but relented. "I'm getting really tired of you cock blocking me, Murphy."

"Then stop trying to cop a feel in the bogs, then."

"Fuck off."

"Whatevs," Lee offered him a two-fingered salute, and headed towards the stall. He bobbed his head back out before closing the door. "Are you okay to give these to Xane for me?" He unhooked a pair of shades from the neck of his shirt and passed them to Jodi. "Ta, doll."

"I guess I'd better..." She offered Nash a shrug.

"Time, guys."

Back in the dressing room, Brian had appeared and was trying to hustle the guys towards the stage. Three girls immediately got in the way of Nash's exit. He signed posters and shirts and offered cheek kisses. Only at the last moment did he seem to recall her presence. "You and me, after the show. We're gonna find ourselves somewhere quiet. Kiss for luck?"

She dutifully did as asked.

THE BLACK HALO dressing room was considerably calmer than the Ghost Boys one. There weren't any fewer people, possibly more, but the atmosphere wasn't manic, more purposeful. One of their crew asked to see an ID.

"She's Rock Giant's missus," Spook called, prompting an apology. He gave her a nod, barely pausing in the act of pulling a brush through his acres of white-blond hair to gesture in Paul's direction.

"Actually, I'm looking for Xane. Returning these."

He pointed with the brush in the other direction.

Xane and Luthor were by the big mirror, Xane applying kohl and a death mask. Luthor sat on the dresser next to him, chatting, and feeding him bites of banana. She gave Luthor Xane's shades, after Xane waved her away when she offered them directly.

"*Tack till dig.*"

Two arms wound around her from behind and lifted her off the floor. She squeaked, "Paul?"

"Castle."

"Put me down."

He let go of her enough for her to turn around and face him, only to be engulfed by another swaddling hug. She tapped against his pecs. "Can't breathe."

"You're cute." He smiled down at her. A pair of goggles sat perched atop his shaven head, and he had one eye shell in that rendered that eye entirely black. Iris, sclera, the lot. It was freaky, but cool. "This is a fun surprise, but what are you doing hanging around these pair of reprobates?"

"Favours for Lee." She pointed to the sunglasses Luthor was holding. "Just delivering them. The guys are about to go on."

"Time to hang for a bit, then." He tucked her under one arm and guided her over to where he'd been getting ready. They passed Ash, who had a games device in his hands that was taking up all his focus. A squad of four young ladies were sat in an arch around him, but it seemed doubtful that he was even aware of their presence.

"I should really get to the wings."

"Five minutes," Paul insisted.

"What for?"

"So I can look at you."

"Stop it," she said, but he just grinned. "Did you get into trouble for skipping sound check?"

"Na." He fastened a leather cord hung with a pendant around his neck. "Guess I'm done. They can love me or lump it." He rubbed a hand over his scalp. "A lot less prep to do since this came off. You've never said what you thought of it."

"Whether I like you better with or without hair? Not sure." She reached up to feel, and he obligingly bent down so that she could reach. She expected prickles, but the new growth was soft. "You look good both ways. Not sure I've a preference. Whichever you're most comfortable with."

"Spoken like a true diplomat." He scooped a hand around the back of her neck, and she feared he was going to lean in and deliver one of those magic, knicker-soaking kisses he was capable of, but she raised a hand between them just in time. "None of that, now. Friends don't snog one another."

That earned her a laugh, and the slide of his thumb against her cheek. "Tell that to Xane sometime will ya? Come on, Castle, I'll walk you to your destination."

"Not sure I need an escort along two corridors."

"You'd be surprised by the number of people who come amiss in corridors," he said, utterly deadpan. "You can't be too careful."

What she feared was what he was capable of doing to her in a corridor, particularly, an empty one.

JODI GAVE THE dressing room a hard pass after The Ghost Boys left the stage, staying instead to watch Black Halo put on a show. Those guys knew how to rock. Xane had a way about him. He'd glide across the stage in a floating, almost ethereal fashion then electrify the crowd with something mean and sinister, only to switch things up again. His death growl eviscerated, while his clean vocals created the sort of frisson that painted goosebumps all over her body. Ash and Spook were goddamned perfect, especially when they'd torment one another by duelling. Luthor did an impressive job on drums, and while Ronnie was mostly confined to the keyboard, when they let him out to sing one of his solo numbers, multiple ladies in the front row swooned.

And then, there was Rock Giant. Larger than life. Never content to fade into the background. Besides, Black Halo's recent stuff had scores of killer bass lines of the sort that underpinned the lead riffs and the lyrics and inked their notes into your soul. Plus, it was hard not to be won over by that much raw sex appeal. The man oozed charisma of an earthy grounded variety, not the vampiric mesmeric sort exuded by Xane.

"You were fantastic," she spluttered, when he came off drenched in sweat and after an hour and a half of gothic-inspired metal mayhem, throwing her arms around his middle.

"You stayed for the whole show." He floored her with a dazzling grin and hugged her back in an equally dramatic fashion. "Castle, careful, I'll start believing you're into me."

She gave him a playful hip bump, and they wandered backstage. As they approached Black Halo's dressing room, one of the Ghost Boys roadies popped his head out from behind a stack of cases he was shifting. "They've gone back to the hotel to clean up."

"You mean they left without me? Buggers."

Paul dropped a sweaty arm around her shoulder. "It's fine, you can hitch a ride with us. Let me grab my stuff. They're onto something. The showers here are shit. Ash reckons there's something up with the water pressure. Plus, no waiting around to take turns at the hotel or the accompanying risk of standing in jizz."

Six sweaty guys and her piled into a chauffeur-driven people carrier. "Where are all the ladies tonight?"

"Allegra's still working," Spook said. That's right, she was part of their tech team. Sound and lights, or something.

"Ginny fancied a quiet night, and I think Dani stayed with her." Ash pulled his games device out and was instantly absorbed with the screen.

"New release," Paul explained. "He's addicted. The bottom wobble on this version is better than ever." She never got the name of the game and didn't ask.

Ronnie, who had been last to enter the vehicle, wedged himself into the space between her and Paul, snapped the strawberry lace necklace he was wearing and proceeded to suck it into his mouth. "Want some?" he asked, catching her watching.

Jodi shook her head. "I'm good." She did not need to eat confectionery that Ronnie Bush had been sweating on for the last two hours, although, if she'd been any kind of entrepreneur, she'd have taken it and auctioned it. There were definitely enough rabid Ronnie Bush fans out there who'd pay a fortune for sweated-on strawberry laces.

They were barely in the vehicle two minutes before they pulled up at the hotel entrance facing the plaza and lake she and Rock Giant had explored earlier. "That's us." Paul pointed up to a span of balconies above their heads. "Well, facing the other way. Fancied a sea view this visit. Where are you?"

"Not sure." She'd have to text and find out.

Having pulled several items out of her bag and pushed aside several others she had no recollection of acquiring, she found her phone and a message from Brian with her room number.

Brian: Concierge are expecting you.

Xane got out first. He'd been riding up front. Within seconds of hitting the pavement screaming fans emerged from the hotel foyer and ran across the road full of traffic from the plaza to engulf him. "Fuck," he muttered. "Hi, ladies. Yes, hello. Hello."

"Where's our goddamned security?" Spook asked no one in particular, before shouldering his way out of the vehicle and into the crowd.

"It'll be okay," Paul reassured her. He got out first,

then offered her his hand, and used his body to block her from the press of people. Nevertheless, several members of the crowd shoved phones in her face and snapped pictures.

"Is that your girlfriend?"

"Paul, please," she said, terrified that he'd say she was his wife. The last thing her relationship needed was the world press announcing her marriage to the wrong man.

Things weren't any better inside the hotel, which was largely open plan, and had windows in seemingly every direction. They were chased into the lifts, with no opportunity for her to collect her key.

"You can go down later for it. Or we'll send someone. Give security some time to calm things down."

"Is it always like this?"

"It is if people know where we are. Someone's let it slip. My money's on one of your boys. Our lot know better."

"It could have been someone from the hotel staff."

"Doubtful. It's bad for business."

He took her up to his room. A king-sized twin with a separate sitting area, and a broad balcony surrounded by glass railings.

"I'm gonna shower. Make yourself comfortable."

She pointed at the hanging egg chair.

"Go for it. I always figure they look more comfortable than they are."

Jodi shot off some texts to Nash as she waited. The edge of the swing chair dug into the back of her legs despite its padding, and it wasn't quite wide enough for her to curl up in comfortably. Maybe if she was as svelte as Mrs Ash, but she'd never been that. Even as a child she'd been chunky.

She kicked off her shoes and bent up her legs so that her feet rested on the basket edge. Better, except now she looked as if she was posed ready for a good railing. Was that the chair's primary purpose? In a hotel room, that was a somewhat disturbing thought. She relocated to the sofa.

Nash: Yeah, it was mental when we got here too. Glad you're safe. Gold star to RG, I guess. Sorry we abandoned you. All stinkified and in need of showers. Didn't want to disturb. Brian said you were enjoying the show.

Jodi: Shall I come down and scrub your back? Haven't managed to grab my key yet.

Nash: Not in our room. With Balin and Jez atm. Give me RGs number, and I'll find you soon.

Jodi: OK.

She knocked on the bathroom door. "Is it okay if I send Nash your room number? Paul?

Maybe he couldn't hear her over the noise of the water. She'd give it a minute, preferring to gain his permission before handing his room number out, even if it was just to Nash. It was unkind of her, but she could see her fiancé deliberately letting it slip to cause Rock Giant issues. She was especially suspicious of the fact he hadn't said anything negative about her being here. Maybe he figured other people were present.

Or maybe he was too busy watching Balin fuck some random woman to give a shit what she was currently up to.

She knocked on the bathroom door again. "Paul?"

Maybe if she cracked it open, he'd hear her.

It wasn't locked.

The shower had to have one of those waterfall

heads, for it was certainly pounding the base of the enclosure with considerable force. She hadn't counted on the mirror, or the extractor fan ensuring it remained condensation free, or the particularly beautiful curve of Paul Reed's arse being visible below the inked slope of his muscular back. Cheeks, high and firm, the muscles hollowing as he clenched and relaxed. Even as she watched he partially turned to rest one forearm against the tiles. The view was hazed by the water running down the glass but still gave her enough of a view to cause her to near choke when it became apparent what he was doing. He was... Heat washed through her body.

"Castle?"

She pressed her knuckles to her mouth. Swallowed in a futile attempt to get a grip on herself. No sense in pretending she wasn't here and attempting to close the door noiselessly. If she could see his reflection, odds were he could see hers.

"I know you're there."

She swallowed again. Croaked. "Just wondered..." Coughed and started over. "I just wondered if it was okay to give Nash your number... Your room number?"

"Yeah, if you give me your phone number."

"Not sure that's a good idea."

"Do you want to debate what is and isn't a good idea right now?"

"Not really." She was sure she'd lose dramatically. He'd stopped stroking, but his hand was still around his cock, not merely hiding it from her vision.

"I've seen it before, you know."

Why the fuck had she said that? Way to make it obvious that she was staring.

"Believe me, I know. I'm not sad about you seeing it now. Just frustrated that you've vetoed doing anything more than looking." A grin crinkled his cheeks. "That is unless you want to glide over here and engage in some intentional voyeurism. I promise, I'll put on a good show for you." He gave her a wink.

"Nash wouldn't like it."

That was her best defence?

"Castle."

"What?"

He made a noise right in the back of his throat, which sounded like it'd wriggled its way up from his knees. "You're killing me." His jaw clenched. Jodi's heart started pounding inside her ears so loud it practically drowned out the water noises. Droplets were clinging to his abs. Darker hairs at the tops of his legs were clumped together into wriggly strands. If she followed the dragon's tail to its end... She startled. Shook her head and got a grip of herself.

"So, can I give him your room number?"

He huffed. "Do whatever you must."

"Or?"

He grimaced and shook his head. Gave a dry little chuckle. "Or, she asks. Woman, you're torture."

She'd meant to say, or what?

"Or, Castle, you're going to wind up in this shower with me, and I can't promise I won't shag you senseless as a result. So, yeah, I guess you'd better invite ol' Joy Division over and maybe get out of here while I finish up."

Yep. Yeah, she ought to do that. Definitely...

"You mean the shower right, not..." She backed out of the room with her hands up.

Fuck! Jodi rested against the closed door to catch her breath, though the vision of him sparkling like he'd been painted with diamonds continued to loop in her head like an animated gif. And just like an old Tumblr gif, it stopped short of where she wanted it to go.

And that was a good thing. Wasn't it? Right? Yes. Of course it was a good thing, because she didn't actually want a close encounter with all those barbells, even if her lady bits were currently screaming at her in frustration to the contrary.

Well, they were just going to have to hush. She'd made her choice. Chosen Nash, and just because things were a bit testy between them of late didn't change that. He'd been there for her when she needed him. He was still here for her, even if he was distracted by his newfound fame. They were still getting married, and she wanted that.

Doubts were normal.

She was still excited about it, about him.

She sent Nash Rock Giant's room number pronto.

Accountability. The ultimate godsend.

Jodi: RG says you're good to come up and join us anytime.

Retrospectively, it hadn't been a good way to phrase it.

Nash: Join you? Doing what?

Watching him impersonate Neptune.

Jodi: Nothing. Hanging out. Just come up after you've finished watching Balin.

Nash: How'd you know that's what I'm doing?

Jodi: Are you saying it isn't?

Nash: Be there in a bit.

He was watching Balin.

And she... she wasn't even surprised enough to be bothered by that, just irritated, that the fall out of her doing something similar would have far-reaching consequences.

That was her fault though, too, because she hadn't kicked up a stink.

They all kept assuring her it was harmless, but was it really?

Her guts weren't so sure about it.

She'd made it as far as the lounge area again by the time Paul came out of the bathroom, mostly dry, but with a towel around his waist so all his ink was on display: the dragon—well, most of it—the many interlacing mythological and religious symbols, and of course, his newest tattoo, still safely hidden beneath a protective bandage. The towel was sadly a little longer than the one he'd been sporting the very first time they'd met.

He crossed to where his suitcase sat on a luggage stand and pulled out a pair of lounge-wear trousers.

"Unless you'd prefer me nude?" He flashed her a grin over his shoulder, before dragging a hand over his shorn scalp.

Jodi shook her head. Him nude was far too dangerous a notion. Him semi-covered already had her nerves ablaze. Her hands itched to touch. Her lips, to explore. He was literally three feet away from her wearing nothing but a white towel that it'd take zero effort to remove. She could see herself pressed up against his back. Her hands encompassing his arse, before sliding around his hips and... Yeah, was he still hard for her? In her head she was counting the rungs of his ladder with the tip of her index finger, while her lips explored the wings of his shoulder blades.

He sat on the edge of the right-hand bed, leaving the set of bottoms beside him on the comforter.

"I've been thinking."

"No."

He laughed. "You don't even know what I was about to say yet."

There were water droplets clinging to his shoulders. The dragon head across his chest had tears in its eyes. "Let's steal a bus and run away together?"

He barked out an even deeper laugh. "Okay, forget my idea, that's a much better one. Let me get some feet on. Wait, maybe shagging first, then bus stealing, then more shagging."

"No." She nervously wetted her lips. "I mean…no. I didn't mean to say that. I don't know why I said that. Forget I said that."

"I am never forgetting you said that. Any time, you just give me the nod, and I'll be ready to enact it."

"Stealing buses is bad."

"Well at least you didn't say shagging me is bad."

Shagging him definitely wasn't. It was simply forbidden.

Paul let his bent leg flop to the side, which dragged the edge of the towel around his waist apart, revealing the tail of his dragon curled around the inside of his thigh. The knot around his waist held… just about.

Unlike her.

"You don't need to use the force, Castle. You can just ask me to undo it, and I will. You can drink your fill, touch, tease. I'm yours to treat as you will."

The sad… unbearably… frustrating thing was that he meant it. Truly meant it. Providing she didn't compromise his core principles; he'd do anything to make her happy. She wasn't even sure what that looked like. Not so long ago, she'd been very certain what happiness was—hadn't she? It hadn't been a distant speck on the horizon that jumped position whenever she blinked. Why were her feelings running amok?

She'd chosen.

She did love Nash.

Nothing was going to change. So why did it feel as though she was stuck on a runaway train, hurtling towards a set of points? One leg of the fork led to a cliff edge and the other to utopia, but it was impossible to tell which was which.

Paul feathered his fingertips over the fold of the towel.

"Don't."

"Don't, what?"

Loosen the towel. Treat her to what her eyes were virtually popping out of her skull to see.

"Get dressed? I mean sure, I'll lay about semi-naked for you some more if you like, Castle, but didn't you invite your—"

"Yes. I mean, yes, you should put some clothes on before Nash arrives." She didn't need Nash putting naked man and his girlfriend together and reaching an answer that wasn't three...*fuck*...two. "I'd rather not have my relationship implode."

The way Rock Giant sucked his tongue suggested he'd have rather less issue with that.

"Paul."

He gave a sultry blink. "Old Joy Division gets jealous of you ogling other men, does he? That must make life tricky, given you're sharing a bus with him and three buddies."

Nash never worried about her looking at them. Maybe because they were his bandmates, and he trusted them. What did that say about their relationship, though? He trusted his bandmates, but not her? He wasn't threatened by his bandmates? He'd realised that rebuking her for catching the occasional glimpse of willy or naked butt cheeks would be hypocritical, considering his current favourite pastime was watching them fuck groupies? Not that he wasn't frequently hypocritical, if she thought about it. "Don't assume you know what our relationship is like."

He nodded.

"Please get dressed."

"I'm working on it."

But not in any sort of timely fashion. He reached for the joggers, drew them up his legs excruciatingly slowly. To his shins, to his knees, then thighs. Her heart hammered, anticipating the rap of Nash's knuckles on the suite door, then him entering to find her gawping at a still mostly naked man.

She squeezed her eyes closed as Paul undid the towel.

"All covered. You can look."

While he'd certainly covered his gear stick, that layer of thin cotton hid nothing. The soft grey fabric stretched taut across his abs. Dammit, she could count the sodding rungs of his ladder from the lowest barbell near his balls all the way up to near his navel and the Prince Albert through his tip. Nine. Damn! Nine.

"Put the towel back on."

"No chance."

"Put the towel back on."

"Castle, it's wet, and if you keep on looking at me like that something else is gonna be wet too. Babe, you're gonna make me leak."

She made a frantic noise in her throat, which didn't sound like a noise she usually made, but had to be her. There was only him and her, and he hadn't been responsible for it.

"Is something else wet too?"

She ticked her index finger from side to side. "You're not supposed to ask me stuff like that. Friends, remember. We agreed we're just friends."

Had they truly ever, and would they truly ever be just friends? There was something about the way they were when they were together, like they were opposite strips of a piece of Velcro, which meant when they got close, they stuck.

She had other close male friends. Fuck it, all of her close friends were men, but while she adored Lee, and Balin, and Jez, and would do until the end of time, there wasn't the same grippy feeling she felt when she was with them as when she was with Paul. And she never felt as if they possessed a part of her she was forced to leave behind when they parted.

"And yet, I'm asking, Castle. I'm asking because you're here, and you're looking, and I'm tired of not asking. Maybe it's about time we started being really fucking honest with one another, instead of hiding behind falsehoods. I don't want to be your friend. I don't want to sit back and watch you marry Curtis *fucking* Nash. I want you. I want to give you all the things I promised, not just a fraction of them—"

"I don't remember what you promised."

The way he looked at her, the green of his hazel eyes so bright, made it clear that it didn't matter if she recalled the promises he'd made. He did. He remembered, and he meant to deliver on them.

"I want all that silky heat you're generating all over my bare cock. I want my tongue on your cunt. Your thighs around my ears. I want to hear you scream so loud that every fucker in this building knows how good I'm making you feel. I want them to be so fucking aware of it that they make memes about it. Once wasn't enough. I want more, Castle. I want forever. And I think you do too, so the question is, are you ready to admit that yet, or do we have to keep playing this game awhile longer?"

ROCK GIANT WAS so done with being circumspect. If spending the afternoon with her had convinced him of anything, it was that it was time to stop farting about and at least attempt some sort of forward momentum. Enough with pretending they were only going to be friends, but more particularly, to hell with the idea of him standing in the wings and watching her live unhappily ever after with a man who didn't appreciate or deserve her.

Maybe Jodi didn't realise it, but crews talked. And he talked to the crew. Why the fuck wouldn't he? They kept the show on the road, and they had way more insight into what was going on at any particular moment than the bands usually did, especially a band as fresh as the Ghost Boys. They were carefully separated from reality by a management filter. But the point was, Curtis Nash's voyeuristic tendencies had garnered notice beyond the immediate circle of the

Ghost Boys, to the crew, to the Black Halo crew, to him, and more than likely to the growing number of fans turning out to see them all perform with offers of performances of their own ready on their tongues. He knew how the world worked.

"Paul, I'm sorry. I am, but I shouldn't have to say this. I'm engaged. We can't—"

"And how's that working out for you?"

She gaped at him. "You... You... Don't. You've no right to judge."

"I'm not judging, I'm asking a question. You tell me what the answer is." He didn't want her getting all defensive and staging a retreat, but he also wanted her to take stock and realise that maybe the world wasn't so rosy, and she had other options. They had other options. She didn't have to settle for shithead.

"I don't have to justify myself, not to you, not to anyone."

Too late, it seemed. Then again, it was easier to take offence than to take stock.

"I'm not saying you do. I just..." He spread his hand wide, palms raised as if he were ready to backpedal, but he wasn't. Couldn't. All this stuff was bubbling away in his brain, and he needed to say it to someone. To her. There wasn't any point in saying it to anyone else. "Here's what I see. He's promised to marry you but he's no fucking interest in you other than as a prize he won. You could have ended up with any one of those guys. Tell me that's not the case. Tell me I'm wrong. I've seen you with them. You've more chemistry with Lee, with Balin, even Jez than you do with him." He'd talked to them, too. "If I didn't know any of you at all, he'd be the last one I thought you were with."

"Will you stop?"

Not until he was done. He needed to make this point. Had to.

"If you marry him, he'll treat you like a doormat for the rest of your life. That's when he remembers you exist. Whereas I'm ready to worship you until the heat death of the universe. I'm willing to give you everything I have, and everything you need."

"Please... Please... don't do that. Don't say that. Paul..."

"I love you."

She sucked in a sharp breath. "You don't know me."

Not true.

He said it again.

He was pushing her, he knew that. Could see from the way she was twitching and reaching out for whatever was to hand that he was toppling all her defensive shields. He couldn't stop though, couldn't back down.

"I can't deal... I can't do this." Her hands were in her hair, and then in her pockets. "What was so bad about us being friends? I've had a lovely day. We had a lovely day..." Now she was fingering the room phone... the TV remote...

"And we can keep on having lovely day-days. We can be friends, the best of friends, and be way more than that too. This isn't lust talking. I want you. I...want...you, Jodi. Do you have an idea how much it hurts seeing you with him, and watching how he treats you? He's a git. You don't deserve it. He doesn't deserve you."

"And you do?"

He shook his head. That wasn't it at all. This wasn't about dishing out what was owed, it was about seeing the truth and acknowledging the connection that existed between them. A connection that would continue to exist between them forevermore no matter what happened tonight or any other night.

"Jodi, please."

"You always call me Castle." Her gaze hit him square in the face—frightened, flustered, needy.

"Fine. Castle, please." He crooked a finger.

"I can't." She shook her head. Crumpled the blank postcard she picked up in her fist.

"I'm not going to do anything bar give you the hug you obviously need." Noble intentions that would be quickly debunked if she could see inside his head. Maybe his thoughts were painted across his face, for she gave her head another shake.

"I don't think it'll play out well."

Because if she was in his arms, he'd be hard pressed to fight the voices telling him to do more than embrace her.

"How so?"

Her gaze flicked downwards, then back up to his face. "You're still..."

"Excited by your presence." Yeah. Yeah, he was. "Has a mind of its own. Doesn't seem to want to go down." Hardly a fucking surprise. He was struggling not to touch it... Not to shift the elastic waistband a little, so it wasn't quite so containing.

"I love him."

"Yeah."

"I said yes to him."

"I know."

"It might not be perfect, but... Why does this have to be so difficult?"

"Maybe ask yourself why it's difficult."

She gave a suppressed full-body shake. It was more of a tremor, he supposed, given how rigidly she was holding everything in.

"Come here, Castle."

Again, she shook her head but simultaneously took a single step forward.

"Nothing's going to happen," he promised. Nothing that she didn't want. But the misery twisting in his guts was evidently affecting her too. It was there in the furrow between her brows, in the cinched turn of her mouth, and the tight points of her nipples drilling against her top.

"I'm afraid I might accidentally sit on it."

The sudden bit of levity made him snort, until it dawned on him that might not have been her intention, and that those words had slipped out without permission. The blush that bloomed in her cheeks confirmed it. The way it then flooded the tops of her breast had him mesmerised. How far down did it go? All the way to the tips of her tits? Lower?

"Accidentally? You might accidentally sit on my cock? I don't think that's ever happened before… accidentally."

"I'm accident prone."

He nodded. "That so? Castle, maybe you'd like to put my wallet down."

"Wallet? I haven't got your—" There it was in her hands. "Sorry."

"Unless you want to take the condom that's in there out and come here with it. In case you accidentally sit on my cock."

Evidently, the gloves were off. The muzzle loosened.

She dropped the wallet like it was a grenade, or rather like the condom would magically tear free of the foil and unfurl over his joystick ready for her to slide her gloriously wet, plump pussy down over the top of it.

He got up and closed the gap between them, scooping the wallet up en route, saving her the effort of picking it up and putting it back down a dozen times or so. The more nervous or riled she got, the stickier her fingers became. She had his sunglasses in her hands now instead. He took them off her, too.

Her eyes widened. The blue of them brimful of

fear, while abject longing teased her mouth into an adorable pout. Damn, he wanted to kiss her. He really wanted to kiss her. To relieve the tension crackling between them. Just kiss her and push all the moralistic shit about this maybe being cheating to one side. It was only that if you looked at this from one particular viewpoint. A viewpoint he didn't share. She was his. He was hers. As the universe had witnessed it. Honestly, Curtis Nash was history, he just hadn't got the message yet.

"Breathe, Castle. It's okay. There's no scenario here where I do anything that you don't want, and explicitly say you want."

"Then why..."

He'd taken a couple of condoms out of the wallet.

"...torturing me."

It was a toss-up over who was torturing who here.

"Stop looking at me like that." Her voice was small and croaky, gave the impression of vulnerability.

"Like what?"

"Like you're going to eat me."

Their eyes met. Hers so blue. Afraid. Eager. They stayed locked into that stare. Each breath that wasn't made right into each other's mouths, abject agony.

"But, Castle," he whispered. "I would like to eat you. I'm sorry... I'm sorry... I know I shouldn't say it, but it's the truth. I want to lick every inch of you. Taste you. Worship you."

"Paul. Stop. Stop... We can't..."

They were inches apart.

"Even if we want to. I'm not going to cheat and make it worse. I've already screwed everything up so badly."

"Shh. You haven't screwed up anything." He touched her cheek, and she leaned into the touch with such desperation and torture lining her face.

"I don't know what to do. I love him. I do."

She made a sob, and he understood it completely. Funny how one tiny sound could convey so much nuance that it told him the agony gnawing on her soul was the twin of his own. Because, it was wrong, so wrong that they had to endure this. Wrong that he couldn't lean in, press his mouth to hers, breathe life into them both. Carry her to the bed, embed himself in the soft plumped folds of her opening. Get lost together, find bliss twined as they were fated to be.

"It's okay. It'll be okay." He brushed her hair back from her face.

"It hurts."

"Yeah."

"I'm so confused."

The glitter of tears clung to her eyelashes. He bent his head to kiss them away.

The knock came right as he leaned in. Jodi jumped. Her nose hit his chin at the same time that her knuckles grazed his hip. Paul caught her hand before she could drag it into her body and held it fast against his. "Do you want me to let him in?"

For at least a fraction of a second, she considered it. He saw all the possible repercussions play out across her face. Nash growing tired and walking away. Nash calling security and breaking down the door.

"Paul, what happens when you do? What are you going to say to him?"

He shook his head. Nothing. Sometimes fewer words served you better than a multitude, and until he had her permission to give Curtis Nash his marching orders... Well, he was just going to have to endure.

He kissed her knuckles, then released her to open the door.

Nash faced him, attempting to look chill, a pair of dark glasses perched on the bridge of his nose, that he pushed up into his hairline on seeing Paul. He shifted uneasily. "Jo here?"

"Yep." Paul about turned, leaving the door open for Nash to follow. The man's gaze rushed suspiciously from side to side, as if he expected to find a Dalek on the balcony or his woman tucked under Paul's duvet naked and flushed. In actuality, she remained exactly where Paul had left her, only looking twice as panic-stricken, and clinging to what looked suspiciously like one of his socks. The condoms were safely out of sight in his pocket.

"What's going on?" Nash resumed his arm folded defence measures. "Jo?"

"We've been hanging out, waiting for you, ain't that right, Castle?" Paul said.

"Yeah," she squeaked.

Ire immediately flashed in Nash's eyes, as if he'd caught them red-handed mid-bonk. If only! A few more minutes and maybe they would have been. That'd have been something for Curtis Nash to fix his peepers on.

"Paul took a shower," she blurted, like that would explain everything and somehow dissolve the ridiculous tension that now existed. Predictably, it did the opposite. That was his girl, guaranteed to enact the nuclear option in any scenario while attempting to do the opposite.

Nash's frown deepened.

"I didn't watch or anything," she continued, eyes growing wide. "Nash, I only meant that he... He was sweaty from the show. I stayed in here...while he."

None of this required explaining. Paul could feel those gulps she was taking between breaths. Flustered, she reminded him of Ronnie. He too had a habit of making his mouth run and blurting things that'd land him in increasingly deeper shit, rather than extracting him from whatever threat had presented itself. The difference was that Ronnie tended to blab other people's secrets over his own.

Paul let them eyeball one another, while he took a seat on the bed. Jodi looked at him expectantly, like he could dig her out of the pit she was desperately still shovelling dirt into. Nash didn't seem sure whether he should attempt to drag her from the room or take a seat.

"Yeah, we all needed to shower post show too. It's why we came back here." He opted for the seat, planting his skinny arse on the opposite bed to the one Paul had settled himself on.

"Black Halo gave me a ride back." Jodi remained on her feet.

"Yeah."

"We got mobbed as we arrived. Not me. I mean them. They did."

"Uh-huh." Nash's gaze ping-ponged between him and Jodi. He'd nod at her when she spoke, but every time his gaze would then dart back to Paul. Not to his face, mind. To his... Ah! Yes. Turned out that weird vibes didn't negatively affect his dick. It was still uncomfortably stiff and ready to party.

Boy was checking him out, counting rungs. Interesting.

"Nine," he said.

"What?"

Paul didn't bother to elucidate. If Nash wanted to play dumb, that was his business. Didn't mean he had to play along. "Want to watch me fuck her with it?"

Okay, he wasn't really sure where that question had come from. He was easily as surprised as Jodi and Nash. The pair of them gawped at him with twin open mouths. One he'd like to sock a fist into, the other possessed a tempting pink tongue his own was itching to duel.

"What the fuck, man? No." Nash peeled himself off the bed. "Why the fuck would you think I'd want to watch anyone fuck my fiancée?"

"Well, I've heard that you like watching."

"Excuse me."

Paul sniffed. "Is that not true? According to the grapevine you spend a significant portion of every day wanking yourself stupid while you watch your bandmates get off."

"That's not... bit of an exaggeration...so what if I do...not the same." Nash cleared his throat. "It's not the same. Anyway, she's not into that stuff." To Jodi, he said, "He doesn't seem to know you very well." And to him. "Can't even get her to—"

"Don't speak for me, Nash. Don't tell him I'm not into—"

Nash seemed so surprised by her speaking up, he actually sat down again. "Jo, babe, you hate having an audience, even an audience that's next fucking door, passed out drunk, or too busy getting off themselves to worry about us having a good time."

Or maybe, you fucking cockwomble, you just fail to make her feel safe.

"This is different to that. It'd be you watching."

Nash was back on his feet again, crowding her.

Jodi raised her hands. "I'm not saying we should do it. I'm just saying it's different. It wouldn't be like doing it and people accidentally overhearing. It'd... I'm just saying don't say no because you think I wouldn't be into it. Only say no if you think you're not."

Paul stirred, pulling his back away from the headboard. That'd been quite a determined speech. He might go so far as to say a promising one.

Nash pulled Jodi towards him, so she was hard up against his body. "So, you're saying you will if I want to? Why would you think that I'd want that?"

"I don't... I just... You're always watching Balin. I thought maybe one time you'd like to watch me instead. That maybe you'd like to include me. That I could do it for you."

Nash chewed on that like it was a piece of gristle. Guy kept on shooting him suspicious glances. Paul nonchalantly scratched his chin. All he'd done was proposed shit; where things went as a result was up to them.

"What you mean is that you'd like permission to shag him."

"Mate, if she wanted to fuck me, she could have done so a thousand times by now."

At any other time, that remark would probably have earned him a fat lip, if not from Nash, then from one of Paul's own band mates determined to ensure he didn't pickaxe the tour. Luckily none of them were around to intervene, and Nash betrayed an actual display of brain cells for once and didn't mouth off. Still, there was no blinking way he was going to let this happen. None.

"Look, if the pair of you aren't interested, feel free to mosey on off to your own room and get on with whatever plans you have for the night." Paul fought hard to make himself sound chill even though his heart was galloping, and he had more riding on this than was wise. He really wanted her to stay. He definitely didn't want her going anywhere with dickhead, who would probably punish her for Paul's temerity.

Nash clasped her hand. "Let's go, babe," he said proving Paul right. "Let's leave the sad bastard to wank off on his own."

"Okay." She gave a hurried nod.

They made it two steps before Nash brought them to a halt. "Then again..."

HEN AGAIN...

Jodi's heart lurched into her throat. She must have misheard. Or not, given the conflicted, half-strangled noise that made it past Rock Giant's lips. It made her turn her head, see him resting there, still propped against the headboard and pillows, all ink and muscle and... obscene bulge. There was a darker spot on the fabric now, up near the waistband of his lounge pants.

Embarrassed and alarmed, she jerked her attention back to Nash. This was a test, surely. It had to be. He wasn't actually going to let her... let them. Why would he? That made no sense, not considering how keen he'd been to minimise the contact between them and how anti-Rock Giant he'd been post-handfasting. He was studiously straight-faced as he returned her gaze. But Nash wasn't controlled in the way Paul was controlled. His moods determined his posture and changed his visage as if he were swapping masquerade masks, which meant there was something there, a crinkling around his eyes and a tilt to his mouth she couldn't quite interpret.

"Nash?" Her voice wavered uncertainly.

He dipped his head and grazed his lips with hers. "How seriously should I take your offer?"

Her offer?

"Are you actually ready to spread your legs and take his monster dick for my pleasure?"

"You..." She half choked just getting that first word out. "You want me to?" He sounded... he actually sounded aroused. Into the idea.

A glint of something hot and needy lit in the depths of his eyes. "I mean watching Balin's all right, but if there's another option on the table..." A smirk tugged on his lips. "You're what gets me going, sweetheart."

"I am?"

"Jo, seriously. I would hardly have put a ring on your finger if you weren't." He raised her hand and kissed her knuckle just above where her engagement ring sat. "I got off hard the other night when I watched you frig yourself, remember."

She did. She remembered how embarrassed she'd been, propped in the bunk, playing with herself as he watched her through the toy periscope. He had been fired up for her afterwards, though. That was true. What was currently being proposed was a major step up from that, though.

"What do you say, dumpling? Are you ready to take his dick and jiggle about on it for me? It's clearly a big one. I'm sure you'll appreciate that."

The size of Rock Giant's cock wasn't remotely important to her. "I thought you didn't want me anywhere near him."

Oh, God! He couldn't really mean for this to

happen. How could he spend weeks detesting the very earth Rock Giant walked on, cursing and complaining about him, but now announce it was okay for the two of them to have sex for his entertainment? This was a sick game. Had to be.

Nash gave a huff through his nose. "This isn't the same as if you were sneaking off with him. I'm going to be right here watching every move. I'll be watching your tits bounce and your cheeks get flushed. I'm going to see everything. And you're gonna make me come, baby. You're going to get me off so damn hard. You know how happy it makes me when you make me come that damn hard."

True. Plus, he was always so damned loving and giving after he'd got what he wanted. After the periscope episode he'd cleaned out the kitty litter tray unprompted. But this was something else, something big, something unlike anything they'd done before, or that he'd even suggested they do. What would happen afterwards? Would he still get shirty with her every time she so much as looked in Rock Giant's direction? Would it make him more suspicious or less?

Did he imagine that if this happened, it'd settle the matter, and Rock Giant would stop being an issue? Ought she to warn him the opposite was more likely the case?

And what about Paul? Did he really want this? He'd probably only suggested it to rile Nash up in return for all the shade he kept throwing, never imagining for a second that Nash would say, yes.

"You've gone quiet," Nash remarked, mouth turning sour. "Please don't tell me this is going to be like every other time anything mildly adventurous gets proposed, and you're about to tap out."

A part of her thought that was a very sensible plan. That she ought to veto the idea and drag Nash from the room, in the way just minutes ago he'd been ready to pull her out of here. They could go to their room, and maybe he'd grouch, but it'd be a molehill they'd get over. Especially if she offered to entertain him in other ways—offered to give him a lap dance, or something. Not that she had the faintest clue how one did that. Or they could try out a new position, or she could agree to them bonking where they might be overheard, or...or she could finally muster the nerve to slip him a finger while blowing him. All of those things would be safer options than this.

They wouldn't risk her heart getting bruised.

More bruised.

Dammit, Paul already had her questioning things.

And yet... She couldn't stop herself from being tempted. There was a connection between her and Rock Giant she wanted to examine. It didn't matter how much she tried to play it down or bury it. It existed. This would allow them the opportunity to explore that, to take it as far as they both wished. She wouldn't have to feel conflicted about it. They'd be doing it, not only with Nash's blessing, but his encouragement.

Again, her gaze strayed across the room to where Paul lay maintaining a tactful silence.

She'd wanted to touch him all night. Had wanted to touch him for days. Properly touch him, not just get by on the odd brush of skin. She'd been so desperate with longing right before Nash had arrived, she'd been on the verge of cracking. They'd been a hair's breadth away from doing something she'd have regretted. She had too much riding on her and Nash. She'd invested too much.

Was Nash truly about to allow this?

Was he really that into the idea of watching people fuck that he was ready to not just sit back and let his nemesis fuck her, but get himself off to the sight of them doing it? Shouldn't that set off warning bells?

Was him watching her better or worse than knowing he'd been out there watching other people? And doing it often enough it was now common knowledge among both bands and their crews.

What if watching her with other men turned into a thing, in the way him watching Balin was now a definite thing?

Nash bent his head to her ear. "You're bugging out, aren't you? Fucking typical. Even when I try and give you what you want, you're still chicken."

She didn't dare open her mouth to answer, afraid of what would come out. Both yes and no options seemed equally littered with potential pitfalls. She wasn't a chicken. She was trying not to set fire to their relationship. And this wasn't about giving her what she wanted, it was about what he wanted.

Nash made a rude scoffing noise. His breath puffed against her skin again. "Poor lamb, looks like he's not getting a taste of you after all."

She turned, so they were facing again and looked him right in the eyes. "Have you been drinking?"

"No."

"And this is truly what you want? You want to watch me? You want to watch me and him?"

The blue of his eyes seemed to swim with amusement. "Why's that so hard to comprehend? Look at him, Jo. Look at how he looks at you. He wants you. He's practically begging to devour you. He wants your curves, and your hands on him, and your tits in his mouth, and your hot cunt enveloping him, sliding over him, gripping him. He wants you all over him, and to be inside of you. To be grinding, fucking you." His hips mimicked his words, so that his loins bumped up against her belly. "But you know what the best part of all that wanting is? The bit that really gets me going about all this? It's that I get the say so on whether he gets it. He can only have you if I allow it. Look at him.

He's trying to be so composed. He's not composed. He's burning. Aching. His dick's straining those pants. It's probably got a pulse of its own."

Control. He was trying to exert control. That at least made sense.

"What about what I want?"

He gave a bemused chuckle. "Aw, Jodi. Jo. Please. Having fucked things up for us by tying yourself to this knob, the least you can do is indulge me over this and shag him when I ask you to."

"Right," she said. "Right." She had fucked things up between her and Nash by making those vows, and saying no suddenly seemed more likely to cause a detonation than accepting what she wanted. What they all wanted.

"Okay," she agreed.

"Good girl. That's my good girl. Now quit stalling and take your top off, so that he can admire what I'm loaning him."

Was he this directive when he was watching Balin? Something to ask him later. She'd kind of assumed he sat back and watched, as he'd been doing the first time she'd become aware of his habit, but maybe that wasn't the case. Maybe he was more involved than that and was merrily dishing out instructions to Balin and whoever he was with, while he rubbed himself off. That possibility further stirred the pit of unease in her belly but also cemented her resolve.

"Need some help to get you started?" Nash's lips tickled as they brushed against the side of her neck. He sucked hard. Too hard. No doubt leaving her with a mark. Paul's gaze fastened upon them. Torment flickered in his pupils, and his mouth became all grim and tight. While Nash might be happy to watch her with someone else, she was damn sure Paul didn't want to watch Nash maul her.

Sorry. She wanted to say. I'm sorry. I'm so sorry. I

wish you hadn't said anything. I wish you hadn't planted this idea in his head.

Paul returned her gaze. I'm not sorry, his expression told her. I'm not sorry. It might not be what I want, but I'll take the sliver that's on offer. Anything, if it gets me you.

Nash ringed a hand around her right breast and started plucking on her nipple. Paul's hand jumped from where it rested against his thigh, then formed a fist. She watched his knuckles whiten as Nash's exploration of her body continued, dropping lower to her arse, and then between her legs.

When Nash squeezed her pussy, she swore she heard Paul's knuckles pop.

Jodi wriggled out of Nash's hold and peeled off her top. The move had the desired effect of getting Nash to retreat and loosening some of the tension in Rock Giant's jaw. Thankfully she was wearing a blue butterfly-embroidered silk bra rather than her faded to grey comfy one. "You like?" she asked, attempting to sound sexy, and probably failing. She bit on her little fingernail.

Paul made a growling sound. "Oh, I like. I'd like to see more."

"Take it off," Nash said from behind her. "Let him see your naked tits. In fact, just get undressed. Both of you get undressed. If you're going to fuck, you need to be naked. I want to see naked fucking."

I F HE COULD'VE chosen the way in which he got Jodi back in his arms again, then this wasn't it. Hell, nope. Paul would have picked somewhere infinitely cosier, having first witnessed Curtis Nash being eaten by a land shark, or jettisoned into another universe never to be seen or heard from again.

Alas, sometimes you just had to roll with what you got.

And there were definitely good things ahead of him. His wife for starters. She was seriously hot stuff. All glorious curves, and exactly the right degree of nervousness and sass to get him going. Paul had seen more than his fair share of tits in his time, it came with the territory, but none of them as perfect as hers. None attached to someone who made him want to bury his head in her cleavage and lose himself there for days.

He didn't doubt Jodi would claim she was over-endowed. She was mistaken. Her breasts were the most perfect thing he'd ever seen, and so was the rest of her.

"Come here, goddess," he mouthed, which sawed off some of her nervousness. He couldn't quite tell if she was nervous about being with him, or the fact her dumbnut fiancé was watching them from the adjacent bed. He had a few reservations about that himself, and this wasn't the first time he'd been offered the opportunity to shag someone else's partner.

This wasn't like the time with Spook and Alle, though.

He'd understood *all* the rules of that game. Had known exactly what was expected of him. On a surface level what was expected of him now was clear enough. Fuck Jodi so that Nash could get his rocks off watching them. It was the deeper stuff he wasn't so certain of.

Actually, scratch that. Nash wasn't that fucking deep. His motivations were obvious. He was playing at being a beneficent overlord, while actually being a controlling arse. Doling out boons according to his whims.

Yeah, I'll let you have a taste of her, but make no mistake, she's mine, and she does what I say.

Fucking fool.

Yeah, this wasn't like with Spook and Alle. It wasn't like that at all.

For starters, he'd had no stake in that game, whereas he had a major one in this.

"Do I get to see now?" Jodi gave him a cheekily closed-mouthed grin, while her gaze raked over his upper body, then dropped to where his joggers were pulled taut over his erection.

The only part of that he didn't like was when her gaze shot over to Nash to check in with him that she was still making him happy and hadn't crossed any invisible boundaries. Why the hell she put up with fuckface and his irritating gob was beyond him. He was awful, but she didn't seem to see it.

Paul hooked a finger in one side of the elastic waistband and tugged it down a little. That got her attention back where it belonged. On him. He gave her a sultry look from under his eyelashes. In return her lips pursed.

Tease, said her gaze. *Tease...tease...big fat fucking tease.*

"Show me."

Paul obligingly hooked a finger in the other side of his waistband, then lifted his arse and let the elastic settle around his thighs. She'd seen it all before, but still.

"Jesus fucking Christ!" Nash spluttered.

Hard to say whether that was over his length or his adornments, and who the hell cared. Jodi...his Jodi was all smiles and eating him up with a grin that made him fill out a little more. There was none of the shying her gaze away she'd done the morning after their handfasting. Now, she was drinking in every detail, and he made sure to keep his hands out of the way so as not to impede her view.

It was probably a good thing that her fiancé couldn't see her face, or he'd have been calling a halt to this now. That was the grin of a woman who knew she was in for a treat.

He gripped himself. Jodi's gaze followed his hand, while her teeth dragged over her lower lip.

"You like that?" Paul mouthed enthused by her fascination. "You like watching me touch myself? It's all for you, sweetheart. All of it." All nine rungs of his shiny badass ladder, and all ten inches of his cock. "It's yours. You come and claim it whenever you're ready."

She made some sweet little groans in response. "Are they cold?"

Cold? No, his barbells weren't cold, not when they

were attached to a bit of him that was decidedly warm. "Why don't you come and find out for yourself?"

"You can touch him," Nash said, like his opinion was worth shit. He'd perched on the other bed and having peeled off his shirt and unzipped was now stroking his weedy cock.

It wasn't a sight Paul needed to see, and sadly couldn't unsee.

If it was possible to have negative degrees of attraction to someone, then he was negatively attracted to Nash. The guy made his balls want to retract up to his armpits. Jodi, on the other hand got his swimmers supercharged, and zipping about like superheroes, capes streaming behind them in the wind.

He patted the bed, inviting her to join him on it.

She put one knee on the duvet. Paused. For a moment, he thought she'd changed her mind, when she lifted it off again. But it was only to shimmy free of her jeans. Then she was beside him. Over him. Straddling his legs, as he leaned forward to meet her.

Her eyes were open, lips softly parted.

"No kissing," Nash barked at them.

Paul was all for ignoring him. Dictatorial little shit. He felt her breath whisper across his lips, then she buried her face in the crook of his shoulder instead.

Damn, he was going to miss her mouth. He'd been itching for her kisses for weeks. Dreaming of them. Then, she gave him a sly little lick on the side of his throat furthest away from Nash. Oh, okay. Okay, that he liked. He could work with that. The tingles she was creating with her attention to his hereto undiscovered major erogenous zone on his throat might make up for the lack of mouth-to-mouth action.

"I want to lick you all over," she whispered directly into his ear. "You're very lickable, Paul Reed."

"So I've been told."

She tipped her head back to regard him. "Who told you that?"

"Internet ladies…fans…Ronnie."

She laughed over the last one.

Then she pressed her palm flat against his chest and shoved him down onto the pillows.

Paul never said no to a woman on top, especially one who was also willing to dangle her boobs in his face. He put both his mouth and his hands to work. Half expected to hear a rebuke and was pleasantly surprised when Nash didn't manifest one.

Nope, sick fucking wanker was evidently loving this given the *swish-swish* noises his ears were picking up. Somehow, he needed to blank the bugger out.

He closed his eyes. Found a nipple. Sucked. And got lost in the act of pleasing her. Something he was quite honestly happy to do for the rest of eternity. She in turn, put her hands all over him. Leastways, all over his upper body, where her fingers gripped, and squeezed, caressed, and explored the lines of his ink over his pecs and his biceps, and his abs either side of his cock.

"It won't bite," he encouraged. He got her hesitancy, even as he despaired of it. It was like making out next to a crate of nitro-glycerine. If things got too hot, the damn thing was likely to explode.

Her gaze flashed towards Nash, who gave her a nod.

Yup, every action apparently had to be rubberstamped.

He forgot to be irritated a second later when just the sly trace of her little finger against the side of his cock was enough to wrench a gasp from him. The actual folding of her hand around him, midway between his crown and his base had his eyes rolling upwards into his head and his mouth falling open around groan after delicious groan.

Fuck, yes. He'd been waiting... and it was every damn bit as good as he'd imagined it to be.

She stroked upwards, rolled her palm over the glans making the ring there slide, then down, right to the root of him, where her little finger gave his balls a tickle. Then, up, and down, brushing against his ladder.

"Castle." Oh, God! With her hands on him he was hard pressed to keep it together and not slide into a rhythm of fucking her fist while bleating out her name like some sort of adorative prayer.

He needed to keep it together. He did not want to come now. Not before he'd got inside of her.

"Go easy."

"Why, am I getting you excited?"

"Now who's being a tease?"

"If I was teasing, I'd be rubbing you with a different bit of me."

Be still his rapidly beating heart.

"Oh, yeah. Which bit would that be?"

She grasped his hand and drew it to the juncture of her legs.

"Ah, I see." Was this allowed? Did he give a fuck? Only in so much as he didn't want to make trouble for her. There was no verbal slap, so he slid his thumb between her plump lips.

"Here, right?" He made circles around her clit, causing her eyes to sparkle and her to drag in her breaths between her teeth.

"Is she wet?" Nash asked. "How wet is she? You're gonna need to be wet to take the whole of him."

She was already plenty wet, but he didn't have any issue with making sure she was wetter. He was more than happy to put his tongue to work alongside his fingers.

Something hit him in the cheek. Jodi picked up the

foil condom packet from the pillow that Nash had thrown.

"Speed it up folks."

Seriously? What was the fucking rush? "We don't have to do as he says," he mouthed to her, as she tore open the wrapper.

"Maybe I'm just as eager."

"Are you?"

She got a firm hold on him and rolled the condom down his shaft.

And hell, if that wasn't hot. Most women sat back and let him dress himself for action.

"Little kiss first." She kissed the tip of him, causing shudders right through his body.

"The thought of my mouth on you get you going?"

"All of you gets me going."

She did it again, with the same effect.

"Extra sensitive there, huh?"

Nope, it was just her, and the crazy grin she was giving him, and her scent in his nostrils, and her body astride him, and her lips...her lips that he wanted to explore at his leisure, and her hands, and her very wet pussy, that he was so ready to fill.

She bent down again and encompassed his crown with her mouth.

Oh, hell, that was sweet. Unexpected, and sweet. Even through the condom it was nearly more bliss than he could handle. She started fellating him, moving her hand in time with her sucks.

"Hell, yeah!" Nash remarked. "Get it all in there. Take the whole fucking length of him."

She tried.

He hit the back of her throat, and she swallowed.

"Ca..castle... damn!" He meant to stop her, but his hands wound up in her hair, encouraging her instead. Okay, so as a matter of fact, he was sensitive, and he'd been hard for her and aching for her for quite some time now. He didn't want it to stop, but if she kept it up, they'd never get as far as being connected, and he wanted them connected. He wanted her heat around him and her breasts in his face, and the slip and slide of her riding him. God, yes, he wanted to be ridden.

"Sweetheart..."

She started caressing his balls, and his taint...and back to his balls. Dammit, it was like she had a map of all his most sensitive spots. How did she know? Had somebody told her?

She started an upwards climb again, still with her mouth on him, still with those appreciative groans happening alongside her kisses. Eyes closed, he basked in the sensation. Once she got to the tip of him, he was going to pull her to his mouth, and fuck what Nash thought.

One step, two step... His cock bucked in response to every kiss.

Unexpectedly, she grunted, as she was shunted forward against Paul's body. Her nose hit his chest, and she turned her head so that her cheek was against him.

Paul opened his eyes, figuring she'd lost her balance and slipped, only to find Nash behind her, hands on her arse, standing in the aisle between the two beds.

She gave a surprised moan. "Nash, I thought...."

"That I was going to sit back and watch. Change of plan. How can I resist when your arse is wobbling away like that and your pussy's dripping? Hold still for me now. That's it. Fuck, baby. Yeah. You're so slick for me."

Lead weights settled in Paul's belly. The bastard was inside of her, was fucking her like he had every right to fucking intrude. Seeing, hearing, feeling that. It was like someone was cheese grating his innards.

The wanker. The fucking wanker.

They'd been so close. He'd been about to kiss her, tell her exactly how much he loved her, and then give her every ounce of pleasure his body was capable of.

Idiots. They were fucking idiots.

They'd been so focused on one another they'd forgotten all about Nash, so of course he was punishing them for it. That was supposing he'd ever intended to honour the deal.

Paul's muscles twitched. He wanted so badly to rip them apart, but he was trapped beneath the weight of them both, being used as a goddamn pillow while Nash dirtied her with his cock. There was no way to punch the guy without dislodging her, and no way he could do that without risking hurting her too.

He wanted all that volcanic heat wrapped around him and sucking him in. Most of all, he wanted the noises leaving her throat to be entirely his doing. For them to be so raw and utterly filthy in their carnality that they'd wind up etched onto his eardrums the way the rest of her was already etched into his heart. Instead, he was stuck being used as a pillow while her beautiful furrow was being ploughed by an incompetent prick.

Scenes of gory, wanton dismemberment filled his thoughts.

It was a testament to how much Jodi turned him on that he stayed hard. Her hand still clasped around him probably helped, as too, most likely, did the sixteen...seventeen days of abstinence prior to this. Wanking in the shower didn't count.

Oh fuck!

Luthor had warned him. He'd told him.

Paul had dismissed it, because whatever, he'd had threesomes before, he'd celebrated May Eve and several other seasonal festivals amidst tangles of limbs. Those times had been fun. This wasn't fun.

This was agony.

He didn't want Curtis fucking Nash fucking her pussy, he wanted to be the only man with that right. The only man giving her the pleasure she deserved.

Fucking imps with their fucking hot pokers stabbing him in the chest.

If not for the matter of weights and angles, he'd tear the bastard a new arsehole and then drop kick him off the balcony.

"You feel so good, Jo-Jo. Always so good. Your pussy's coating me like a wet little glove. You were made for me honey. Gonna spill. Almost there." Nash kept on hammering himself home, slamming her against him.

"My precious buxom angel. Mine... Mine. All...fucking...mine.

He was going to puke.

Paul shoved his fist into his mouth and bit down hard enough the taste of iron flooded his mouth.

The mushroom cloud exploding inside his head at least spared him the full interactive experience of witnessing Nash flood her naked cunt and grunt his way through that release. He knew he was making sounds of fury and despair.

"Paul."

His gaze snapped to her face. Concern creased her brow. She was hot in the cheeks, a little breathless, but her attention was on him, on the heat pouring off him, and his punctured, bleeding hand, not Nash. Not the man who'd just come inside of her.

"Are you okay?" she mouthed.

"Fine." He was fine. Not really. At least some part of him knew something inside of him had snapped.

"I'm sorry."

None of this was her fault. None of it.

He was sorry too, for ever leaving her, and allowing her to fall into Nash's clutches.

Nash bent over and placed a kiss halfway along Jodi's back. "Love you," he said in a half-arsed way.

The fuck he did.

The fucker didn't love her. He didn't give a shit about her. Wouldn't know what love was if it fucked him with a shovel.

"Okay." Nash patted her still upthrust arse as he slid his already shrivelling cock free of her cunt. "Let's go."

"You fucking what?" Paul's emotions were addled, but not enough to prevent him being outraged all over again. Monster. The guy was a fucking monster in addition to being a dick.

Nash was already reaching for his shirt. "Mate, we're all done here."

"You selfish git."

"Come on, Jo-Jo, let's go. Fun's over."

"You really are a complete and utter wanker, aren't you? You're done, so the party's over."

"Like I give a shit if you get off."

Paul made a choking noise. "Wasn't me I was thinking about."

"Paul, it's—"

It was not okay, and he said so.

Nash fished around for his trousers. "She barely ever comes. Tell him, babe."

He was so nonchalant about it, that Paul figured his ears had to be malfunctioning.

"Castle?"

Not only did she refuse to look at him, she'd gone both very still and very quiet.

How had Jodi, his Jodi, ended up with a guy who couldn't get her off? Any minute the top of his head was going to blow off. "You can't make her come, and you're okay with that?" He lobbed the words like grenades at Nash, before scooting his attention back to her. "He can't make you come, and you've chosen that?"

"Fuck you, dude. She's not wired that way. Lots of women find it difficult."

Was that so? Was he supposed to conclude that his and Jodi's one and only time together had been an anomaly? "Funny, I don't recall any problems in that department."

Nash gave a nasty laugh. "Yeah, sorry to break it to you, man, but she was probably faking."

He didn't need to be reassured that wasn't the case. If you were inside someone when it happened, you could feel it. Fuck could you feel it. It was one of the best things about screwing, feeling that other person come apart. Not just seeing and hearing it but experiencing it right along with them. And if you'd ever felt that, well, then you could spot a faker.

Paul slithered down the bed so his head was right between her legs as she knelt.

"What do you think you're doing?" Nash demanded.

Paul ignored him. Only one person mattered, and their name wasn't Curtis Nash. Now, while he didn't claim to have superpowers, he knew a thing or two about arousal, and the woman he was feasting his gaze on was still plenty aroused despite the filthy trick her fiancé had just played. She shivered in all the right ways when his breath connected with her skin. Groaned in a way that made his cock twitch when he blew.

"Babe?" Nash tapped her arm but failed to draw her attention. "Let's leave."

"Stay awhile, sweetheart," Paul encouraged. "Let me take care of you."

"Paul, I... I should..." Her protests died as his mouth found her wet cunt. "Oh! Oh, damn..." The groan that came out of her mouth next nearly had him blowing his load, and made the irritating taste of Curtis Nash on his tongue worth it.

Paul blew again, making sure she felt it right where she needed to this time. "You're beautiful. You're so goddamned beautiful. Gonna put my tongue on you. Lick you clean of him."

"Now, hang on—"

"Gonna fuck you with my tongue, Castle. Gonna fuck you with my fingers. Gonna wring orgasm after orgasm out of you. Relieve all those needs that haven't been fulfilled."

"Mate, you're not fucking my fiancée. I've changed my mind. We're done here."

Wrong. They were not remotely done.

"I'm yours, Castle. We're meant for each other. Just say the word."

"Stop this, now!" Nash demanded.

"Say it, and I'll fuck you slow, and then I'll fuck you hard. I'll fuck you until stars explode in your brain, and not just once, but every time. Every fucking time."

His mouth met her skin again.

He watched the hectic flush crawl upwards, the exposure of her throat as her spine arched causing her head to fall backwards.

"Aah! Oh, fuck. Oh, fuck!"

He followed through with his tongue. Lots of it. In all the places she so obviously needed it. While he might not have been daubed with Ash's moniker as the King of Licking, he did know how to eat pussy. It was one of his favourite things. Nice pair of chubby thighs around his ears, hands in his hair, the taste of arousal on his tongue, what wasn't to love?

Her hands closed around his head, in exactly the way he liked, holding him in place, her nails digging into his scalp to the point of pain. He didn't care. She could hurt him as much as she wanted.

Paul concentrated his focus on her clit. Treated it

to his full complement of sucks and licks. He felt the spark leap between them as she came. It burned through his body and burrowed into his chest.

"Jo-Jo, let's go."

The flush of her climax was still glowing on her skin.

Nash finally succeeded in dragging her off the bed. He raked around for her clothing and wound up pulling Paul's discarded T-shirt over her head. Hand clasped firmly around her wrist, trousers on but still undone, he dragged her to the door.

"NASH, FOR FUCK'S sake let go of me."

Jodi dug in her heels bringing them both to a stop. Nash had dragged her into the hotel corridor in nothing but another man's T-shirt. Thank God, they hadn't encountered anyone, but it was only a matter of time and given the number of fans that had congregated outside, it was inevitable that some of them would have made it to the hotel interior. She did not want her naked arse on the internet.

"Stop, will you? Just stop."

He stilled. Finally. Jodi shook herself free of his grip and rubbed at the red mark around her wrist. "What is the matter with you? What is the fucking rush? I'm barely dressed. I'm not walking through the hotel like this." She about turned.

Horrified, he gasped, "You're going back to him?"

"All my stuff is in there. My bag, my phone, my

knickers. So, yes, I'm going back. I'd quite like my shoes too."

Nash, all pale goose-bumped flesh, did at least have all his possessions.

"Jo."

"No." She slapped away his attempt to pin her, which resulted in his key card winding up on the floor and his phone hitting a nearby door. "It was what you wanted. I was trying to give you what you wanted. To make up for..."

For what?

That *he* spent so much time watching Balin fuck random women... people? She'd learned from Lee only earlier that morning that Balin was doing almost as many guys as girls.

"We'll talk once I'm dressed."

They hadn't shut the door properly behind them on the way out, so she was thankfully spared the process of having to knock, but she hadn't thought about what she was going back to.

Rock Giant.

Still naked.

Still hard.

His head bowed toward his knees, while his fingers clawed at the crown of his shorn scalp. He looked up at her, jaw slack, his voice raspy, "Castle."

Hope, there in his eyes mixed in with the desperation. That she'd returned to him. That she'd made a choice, a different choice, one that made sense of what they'd so recently shared. One if there wasn't already a ring on her finger, she may well have made.

"I need to get my things."

Devastation, again.

It brought tears flooding to her own eyes, making the search for her belongings even more difficult. Having failed to locate her underwear, she pulled on her trousers and picked up her bag. Her shoes were over by the hanging chair.

He watched her every move, making non-vocal pleas.

"I have to go."

"Yeah."

"I need to talk to him."

"I get it. He's your fiancé."

That was right. Her future was waiting for her out in the corridor. The prickly sensation under her skin seemed determined to convince her otherwise, that in fact, leaving was the wrong choice. "I'm sorry." Hesitantly, she reached out, pressed her hand to his head, half expecting him to shy away. He pressed into the touch instead, creating an ache right through her core. "We should never have done this."

He knew it.

She knew it.

Nash was out there fuming about it.

"Don't say that. Never say that."

"It was a mistake."

Paul looked up at her, his eyes imploring, the green amidst the hazel luminous with woe. She could drown in that sadness. Couldn't allow it to infect her more than it already had, or she would never leave. How could she leave?

She had to leave. She'd chosen to make a future with Nash.

"Stay with me."

"Paul, I can't. You know I can't. I don't want to hurt you."

They were all fucking hurting.

"So, don't. Stay."

"I can't." She had to think about Nash, too. And herself. She couldn't tear her life apart again. She'd done it once. Wouldn't survive doing it again. It'd hurt enough the first time, and then she hadn't had the things she had now—a job, friends she adored, friends who meant more to her than her family ever had. She tore herself away from him, her heart cracking as she did. How when she stepped back it wasn't throbbing in midair between them seemed fantastical. "I'm so sorry. You don't deserve this. You don't." He was so kind. So loving. So precious. Absolutely deserved someone to love him wholeheartedly, it just couldn't be her. "This has to end, Paul. We have to end it. You can't keep waiting for me thinking it's going to happen. Whatever you promised me, I'm freeing you of that. I'm going to marry him. I made him that promise first. I gave my word."

"And we swore vows."

Vows she could barely remember.

"In a moment of madness."

"In a moment of complete lucidity. I meant every word."

That was the hardest part, his complete sincerity. It rang in his voice now and seared her soul right through. She might not remember what she'd promised him, but she remembered too much of what he'd promised her.

"Paul... Please... I can't deal with this. I don't know how to make this right. I'm trying, and I feel like I'm getting everything wrong."

That look in his eyes—adoration shot through with razor sharp pain, the glitter of his tears gathering—it was too much to bear.

"I love you."

"You can't love me. You can't be in love with me. You can't..."

His lips pressed to hers. Softly, if not entirely chastely. "I am. Profoundly. I opened my heart to you that night and let you pour right in. You don't understand. I put it out there into the ether for the universe to answer, and it did. It gave me you. Fate brought us together. It did it the first time I asked, and I foolishly let you go. This time, I'm hanging on and never letting go."

A tear slid down his cheek. Jodi raised a thumb to chase it away, but a second instantly fell, to replace it. Previously, she'd only ever seen one man cry. Her father the night he realised her mum had left. She wasn't sure she'd ever recalled that before.

Something broke inside her.

"Please, please, don't." The more she wiped his face, the quicker more tears spilled to replace them. The salt taste of her own distress trickled across her lips. She thought she'd been the only lost soul wandering the field that night, but hearing him now, that hadn't been the case.

She needed to fix this. Heal him.

She kissed his brow, meant only to kiss his tears away, but their noses bumped, and his breath whispered against her skin.

"I'm sorry. I'm so sorry. Please don't cry."

She kissed him again, and he kissed her back harder.

Goodbye, that's what sort of kiss it ought to have been. Only, it wasn't a goodbye kiss, nor an it's over kiss. It was an I can't take it anymore, I need this, and if I don't have this, I'll stop breathing kiss. A questing battle of tongues and drowning sort of kiss. A hello, there you are, I've finally found you, kiss.

"Castle?" He breathed her name right into her mouth, before enacting another collision. His hand on the back of her neck, pulled him to her. The other, in possession of her hip, soon glided to the small of her back. When and how her trousers came off she couldn't quite recall, but her head falling back, his hands beneath the T-shirt, him ripping it from her was crystal clear. Likewise, his mouth on her breast. Him claiming one nipple, then the other. Her pulse pounding in her ears. Her body awakening.

She touched him. Bit him. Wanted... Demanded more. Sensibility confined to the footnotes.

Their bodies fused together, in the way their mouths already had. It was wrong. Very wrong, while simultaneously, hopelessly, and impossibly right.

Afterwards, certain moments would remain crystal bright amongst the haze of clinging desperation. The sweep of his fingers along the lips of her split. His thumb on her clit, then dipping inside of her. The first feel of him hot and naked inside her.

His groan that accompanied that.

Riding him, forehead to forehead, looking him in the eyes the whole while.

The heat. The achy feel of him splitting her open. Begging for more. Begging that he give it to her hard. Him obliging.

"Castle, oh my God... Castle." Her scoring her nails across his back and breaking the skin. Skin she'd later clean from beneath them post-midnight.

"Never want to let you go."

"Don't let go. Want all of you. You never need to let go."

The tide of rising euphoria sweeping over her. All sense of control gone.

"You fit me so perfectly."

That fuzzy warm feeling expanding... expanding. Reaching the precipice. Balancing on the edge, muscles pulling impossibly tight all at once. Then, toppling over with a long cry. "God, oh God!"

Him, right there with her, making similar exaltations.

Him, driving into her that last few times, even as his cock softened. Neither of them ready for it to be over.

The stillness that followed. The cold horror of

having failed so catastrophically to do the right thing. Everything she'd sworn she'd never do. They'd done it.

Jodi brought her fist to her mouth but couldn't prevent the unstoppable sobs from erupting. She bit into the heel of her hand, but it didn't help. It didn't wake her from the nightmare of reality. *What had they done? They hadn't done this.*

Just a dream. Not the truth.

She'd wake in a moment on her bunk on the bus.

No awakening happened. She remained straddled across his lap.

Their bodies were still joined, and his hot skin pressed to hers. There was no option other than to touch him in order to break them apart. Everything was slick and wet as they did. His cock, free of her body, slumped against his thigh, wet and shiny.

No condom... No condom!

She closed her eyes to block out the image, block out the knowledge, even as additional panic alarms began ringing in her skull. They rang so hard it was difficult to hear him. Was he talking to her?

His hands closed around her upper arms. Steadying. Supportive. "Castle, are you okay?"

"No." She gulped. Opened her eyes. "I was supposed to leave. I only came to get my stuff. I have to leave. This is... this is wrong. We shouldn't have done this."

Paul gazed back at her. Stoic. Silent. Heartbreak writ through his face.

"I have to go."

She hauled the T-shirt back on. Pulled up her trousers, then bolted from the room with an assortment of items in her arms, some of which might have been hers. This time, she pulled the door firmly to behind her.

She'd made everything dozens of times worse.

Catastrophically worse. How would either man ever forgive her?

She'd never forgive herself.

Stupid. You're so fucking stupid.

She dropped half the items as she attempted to dry her eyes with her cuff. The salt tracks still made her skin feel tight, and the prickly sensation in her nose endured. Somehow, she put one foot in front of the other.

Nash was waiting just along the corridor, casually posed.

How long had it been? Minutes? Hours? She felt like she'd lived centuries in whatever time had passed. Did he know? Had he heard them? If not, he'd surely know when he looked at her.

Only, he didn't look at her or speak to her, simply turned towards the lifts, leaving her to follow in his wake like a gosling chasing a swan.

They rode the lift standing in opposite corners. Two levels down, their shared room was a mirror of Rock Giants. Smaller, and with a single double instead of two side by side, and no egg chair or balcony. Nash went straight into the bathroom and locked the door. He came out again five minutes later, freshly showered, his lithe body wrapped up in three bath sheets.

She turned away from the window to face him, her nails now chewed to the quicks.

Ignoring her, Nash crossed to where their suitcases sat side-by-side on the luggage stand and began rummaging in his for fresh clothes.

Every layer he pulled on felt like an additional barrier being erected between them.

Usually, he took pains to iron out the natural curl that caused his dark hair to form uneven waves, but having rubbed it over with a towel, he didn't even pull a brush through it before perching on the end of the bed to lace up his boots.

"Where are you going?"

Silence.

"We should talk about—"

He gave a huff through his nose. "Not sure what we'd say. I thought we were happy. I thought we had something. I really did, but since he turned up, it's like you're somebody else. I'm not sure I know who you are anymore."

She could have levelled similar accusations at him. He'd changed, too, or maybe she was seeing him more clearly than she previously had.

"You can have the room."

"Where are you going?"

He gave another snort. Okay, as if she needed to ask. Back to Balin's room most likely.

"Nash, stay."

He shook his head, while sucking on his teeth. "Nah. I can't do this now, Jo. I need to..."

"What?" He needed to what?

He raked a hand down his pretty face. "Process. I need to fucking process what it means that my fiancée comes... You know what, it doesn't matter." Right by the door, he swung back around. "You fucking came, Jo. You came for him. Just like that. No effort. No nothing. And...fireworks."

That was what had him rattled?

"I told you; we'd been together before."

"Right. And I'm supposed to believe that he fucked you once in the murky days of your past, and that makes him the authority on what it takes to get you there. Nah. Nah, I don't think so."

"God, Nash, it's not like it's never happened with you."

Maybe it would've been wiser to hold her tongue, because clearly, she'd said the wrong thing.

He took a hike straight out of the door, leaving her behind in the sterile, impersonal silence of their suite.

PAUL KEPT WAITING, expectantly listening for the tap of her knuckles against the door signalling Jodi's return to him. It was long past dawn when his faith in that happening finally collapsed. She wasn't coming. She was never coming.

He'd played his hand, given it everything, and he'd fucking lost. All that remained now was the lingering trace of her scent on his skin, and her fingerprints on the tabletop. The threads of fate hadn't led them towards the happily ever after he'd seen written in the stars.

Now all that lay ahead for him were endless nights of loneliness, because getting it wrong didn't undo anything. He'd still made those vows. Sacred vows. They didn't unravel because she'd rejected him and set him free of his promises. That wasn't how it worked. Forever meant forever, not until you didn't feel like it anymore or somebody gave you an excuse to fail.

In any case, his feelings hadn't changed. They were constant. Nope, the swinging pendulum in this relationship was Jodi. He'd thought when she'd let him inside of her... Well, he'd thought that meant acceptance. Fool him.

Christ! Fuckduster couldn't even get her there, and he sure as hell wasn't interested in her as anything more than a trophy he'd won.

At some point Paul ended up out on the balcony. There was his sea view, night sky meeting the equally dark ocean over the tops of the city's roofs, and below, late-night traffic crawling through the near silent streets. Easiest thing in the world to lean over a little too far. Swan dive his way to a different ending. Except, that wasn't who he was. He could never do that to those he loved. Black Halo didn't need that sort of shit to deal with, and his parents didn't deserve to have the remains of their only offspring scraped off a section of tarmac and shipped home to them in a box.

On the other hand, oblivion sounded like paradise right around now.

His phone beeped. Paul retrieved it and scrolled through the scores of unanswered messages. His dad again, pestering for dates. When are you coming home? When will we see you? We need to talk to you, son. The D'Amon brothers: Sorry we missed you. Hoped to catch up before we left town. Arrangements need to be made.

Eloise: What's this shit about you getting hitched? What happened to my fucking invite?

Elspeth: WTF Paul?!! Who is this bitch?

Ginny: Is Jodi with you? Ghosties are looking for her. Hope you're not doing anything naughty, Paul Reed.

Ginny: Scratch that. I hope you're giving her the ride of her life.

Ginny: She's cute. I like her.

Ginny: Approved for BH consumption.

Ginny: Alle says, J knows you're ribbed for pleasure, right? Guess we'll know if we see her sprinting through the foyer like a giant cock monster's about to stab her in the pussy.

Ginny: And we'll know about the riding part if she's walking funny.

Ginny: Huh? No response. You must be busy. I sometimes think you must be as sadistic as Spook to have put all that metal in your knob. Anyways, happy shagging.

Allegra: The boyfriend's heading your way.

Lee: What just went down? Nash went up to yours to get Jo, and now he's back in the bar downing shots like he's been shat on by the world's fattest pigeon. All I can get out of him are grunts, and Jo's not replying to calls or me hammering on her door. Is she still with you?

If she was, he wouldn't be looking at his fucking messages.

Ronnie: Can I come to your room and hang?

Ronnie: Right, figured why you're not replying.

Ronnie: Does she suck as good as me, man?

Ronnie: Are you fucking her tits while he's in her cunt?

Ronnie: Ooh! What did you do? He just threatened to shove a metal straw up my urethra. Should I come up?

No. What he needed was for everyone to piss off and leave him alone!

He threw the phone, but instead of the satisfying fracturing of its screen and a final bleep before it succumbed to digital death, it bounced and landed on the carpet with not so much as a dent to show for his efforts.

Fucking thing! Fucking with him, same as everything sodding else.

He picked it up and bounced it off the floor another couple of times. Bastard thing evidently possessed forcefield technology, because nada when usually all you had to do was smile the wrong way and the fuckers cracked. He locked it in the mini fridge as punishment.

The two beers he removed to make space for the phone went down his throat smoothly enough. The following shots with a variety of grimaces. Then again, by the time he got to the peach schnapps, the fact that it tasted like fruity nail polish barely registered.

The whole cocktail came up again less than an hour later in one gloriously cinematic fountain, most of which hit the toilet bowl. The rest he dropped a towel over, before crawling out of the bathroom and passing out on the floor in the aisle between the two beds, still stark naked, her knickers making for a pitiful pillow.

❧

AUL DIDN'T MAKE it down to breakfast, and he only got into the car meant to ferry them back to the tour bus because Samson nearly beat his door down after a stream of minions had failed to get Paul's arse out of bed.

"Well, you look like shit," Ash observed. Naturally, Ash looked like he'd been fanned by angels all flippin' night. Hair perfect. Eyes all smiley. The bastard was even freshly shaved. Paul's jaw felt like twenty-four grit sandpaper.

"Rough night?" Ginny asked, attempting to nudge Paul's sunglasses off his nose for a closer look at his face, but he shied away from her attempt to expose him. Bad enough he was sporting a nine o'clock shadow equally composed of burst capillaries as fuzz, he didn't need the fact that his eyes were so bloodshot and swollen they'd work as an advert for the next big zombie game being observed and remarked upon. "Allergies kicking your butt?"

He gave a huff. Sure, he'd just developed a virulent bullshit intolerance.

Ronnie got in on the other side of him, meaning he was squashed into the middle seat, a position he never cared for, and the last position he wanted to be in right now. What was worse than scrutiny from one ace interrogator? How about two? One of whom had a 99.99% success rate. And, here in the middle seat there wasn't even a convenient place to rest his screaming head while they did a double act on him.

Gawd, he should have insisted on riding with Spook and Allegra. At least they wouldn't have pried while drawing conclusions. When Samson climbed into the front passenger seat, and barked at him about holding them up, Paul almost insisted on being let out. He was already leaning over Ronnie to reach the door handle when the Ghost Boys exited the hotel and started piling into the third of the waiting vehicles. And there she was.

His Jodi.

Or rather not his Jodi.

Not his anything, according to her.

He didn't want to look.

He couldn't not look.

Even when he closed his eyes she was imprinted onto the backs of his eyelids, and not just any version, nope, he was treated to the mouth wide, eyes molten, tears streaking her cheeks as she surrendered to bliss in his arms version. The version that his whole goddamned body remembered.

Well, tough shit, because that taster is all we're ever getting, skin cells.

Apparently being a source of pleasure wasn't enough.

Caring about her wasn't enough.

Being ready to put her first and love her until death do us part wasn't *e-fucking-nuff*.

Seemed those things were all a terrible inconvenience to her getting on with her painfully average romance with a self-centred prick. Not that he was bitter or owt.

Paul scratched under the lower edge of his glasses,

which surreptitiously allowed him to smear another salt tear across his cheek.

That bullshit allergy was really doing a number on him.

"Feathers," Ginny suggested. "I had a friend who was allergic to down. Did you notice all the pillows here were authentic goose down?"

He hadn't, his head never having touched any of them. In any case, feathers weren't the issue.

"Gin, babes, leave the man alone, he's clearly hung over."

Thank you, Ash.

Ronnie's head came up. "But I didn't even make vodka bears. How can you be hungover? You spent all night in your room."

Ash spluttered, "Bushie, there's more than one way to get smashed. Gummy bears aren't a requisite for the activity. Don't believe me, try drinking a couple of pints of Guinness through a straw."

"Oh...Oh, is that good?"

The chatter moved on to various experiences of slurping alcoholic beverages through straws, and Ronnie recounting knobwhistle's threat of the night before. Paul tuned out to the best of his ability, eyes closing behind his dark glasses. The minute they reached the tour bus, he was climbing into his bunk, and God help anyone who disturbed him for the next forty-eight hours.

THE DIRECT ROUTE to Trondheim equated to a ten-to-fourteen-hour drive, but since the next gig wasn't until the following weekend, there was time to take the journey at a more leisurely pace, including a three-night stopover. Or there would be if they got on the road with any sort of alacrity. Five minutes pacing the tarmac the tour buses were parked up on rapidly turned into ten. Seemed the roadies hadn't got the departure memo.

He could have had another hour or two of floor time.

"What's the fucking issue?"

The Ghosties' driver turned up, and they got underway.

"Driver regs," Samson informed them. "Your rotaed driver is sick, and Troels is on a scheduled break until twenty past."

"So, we're just supposed to twiddle our thumbs for fifty fucking minutes." They couldn't even get on the bus, because it was all locked up, and Cave Troll presumably had the keys.

Paul stomped his way over to a nearby grassy verge and parked his butt. He did the hunched over the knees thing for a bit, before figuring what the heck and adopting a supine pose. The ground was hard, and the sky monstrously blue. His shades failed to take more than the faintest dazzle off the sun. He was thirsty, and the ground kept vibrating beneath him as if a mountain troll were taking a morning constitutional a few miles away.

Someone squatted on the grass next to him, and worse, didn't fuck off when he failed to respond to their presence. "Not in the mood for company."

"Did you guys have a threesome?"

"Fuck off, Ronnie." He clapped his hand against the ground in dismay.

"Yeah, but you did, didn't you?" Captain elastic grin settled in beside him, his skinny legs folding into some sort of esoteric yogic anomaly. "I thought it was a possible last night, and now, it's the obvious explanation for why you're all out of whack this morning. Emotional hangover: that's the phrase. Luthor says lots of people get antsy after the fact. It's all fun in the moment, and then their anxieties kick in, or they get jealous."

"I'm not anxious, and my hangover is alcohol induced."

He might as well not have spoken.

"I figured you'd been there and done that before, so it must be them not you having regrets, and hence getting you stressed out."

Yay, psychic super sleuth strikes again!

How the fuck was it obvious that anything had happened? Other than when they got into the cars, he hadn't even seen Jodi or Nash this morning, and he doubted either of them had had a heart to heart with Ronnie about what had gone down. The man was a walking security breach. Besides, if either of them had talked, Ronnie wouldn't be here attempting to tease answers from him. Every bugger on the tour would already know every intimate detail of the encounter, right down to how many strokes it'd taken each of them to get off, and who they'd cried out to in exaltation as they came.

"Was it at least good in the moment?"

None of his business.

"I'm peeved that you didn't offer me the chance to join in. Seems only fair. They're a couple, we're a—"

"We're not a couple."

"Fuck buddies."

"We're not fuck buddies. It was one time, Ronnie. Pretty sure I made that clear then."

"I know but never say never."

He sat and whipped the shades off. "Ron, no. I'm absolutely saying never. I don't want or need you all over me like a rash. We're not a thing. We're never going to be a thing. You need to get this into your skull." He made a half-hearted attempt to knock on

Ronnie's skull. The last thing he wanted was for anyone—Jodi—to think he had a side project. "The only person I'm interested in is Jodi." God, it hurt to say her name. His throat closed even as he was trying to force out the syllables. "I got hitched to her for that reason."

"Yeah, but she's marrying the other dude."

Paul pinched the base of his nose as his rising blood pressure caused a spike of pain to pierce his frontal lobe and exit through his nostrils. *Cheers, Ronnie. I really needed that reminder.* "Doesn't mean I'm interested in your skinny arse as a substitute."

"But you luvs me." Ronnie made a dramatic swoon in his direction, clearly expecting to be caught.

Paul roughly shoved him away.

"Everything okay over here, kiddos?" Xane intruded, his long shadow falling over them both. Paul squinted, the sunlight hitting him right in the eyes, while Ronnie continued rubbing his arms and looking like a kicked puppy.

"Piss off, Xane. It's none of your business."

Xane's pierced brow slowly arched. "That right?" He crouched, so he was on a level with Paul's head. "I'm in a band with the pair of you. That makes any sort of discord my business."

"There's no discord."

"Why are you fucking shouting, then? And why did I just watch you shove him off his feet?"

He wasn't shouting. He may have very slightly raised his voice to make sure Ronnie got the message, and he might be on the verge of raising it a tiny bit more so that Xane got it, too, but he had not shouted.

Shouting would hurt his brain too much.

"What's the deal, Ronnie?"

"There is no deal." Paul flipped onto his feet before Ronnie had a chance to launch into a spy cam blow-by-blow account of all the shit Paul didn't need sharing.

"Nothing fucking happened." Leastways, nothing that anyone had any right to know. It wasn't like he needed every bugger on the tour to know he'd been rejected in favour of lazy dick. "I emptied the minibar, end of. Not a story. Fucking move on and give me some fucking space."

Of course, Xane did precisely the opposite. "Why'd you need to empty the minibar, Paul?"

"Felt like it."

"Why'd you feel like it?"

"I just did. You never just feel like that?" He knew for a fact Xane did. That sex addiction of his wasn't borne out of nothing.

"Sure," Xane agreed. "We all have down days. What worries me is what I'm hearing about you having taken another man's fiancée up to your room last night. We don't need any shit with the Ghost Boys."

"Fuck off, Xane. I never crawled up your arse when you were busy screwing us over with your bedroom antics—"

Xane made the sort of noise that sounded like a laugh track had got stuck in his voice box. "Oh, no. No, you never had any opinions over any of my 'antics'." He made inverted commas with his fingers. "You were nothing but opinions. You weren't happy when I was with Elspeth and Steve, and you weren't happy when I told them to fuck off after they screwed me over, and you still weren't fucking happy when Elspeth screwed us all over with that shit she fed to Bang!. 'Aw, she's just misunderstood.' Christ, you still think she's the injured party because we decided against putting up with any more of that shit."

Where the fuck was this coming from?

"She lost her—"

"I lost my best friend."

Right, so that's what this was about. Not him.

Xane was wobbling because their former band

mate's birthday was a couple of days away. No doubt Elspeth would remind him of that, too. Maybe she'd already dropped that into his inbox, alongside the scores of other messages he was planning on deleting unread.

"Are you fucking her, Paul?" The question came from Allegra, not Xane.

Jeezus, all he'd wanted was a bit of peace and a pillow to settle his thumping head on. Instead, he was apparently both the celebrity guest and topic of conversation on Question Time.

"I hope to God the answer to that isn't an affirmative," Xane muttered.

"Why, because it'd kill you to know I was having some fun for once? It's not as if we're not both grown adults capable of independent thought and reasoning. Whatever decision we make about our relationship has fuck all to do with any bugger else. We got hitched, maybe you forgot that bit. I've as much right to shag her as beetlebreath."

"He shagged her," Ash announced, raising his hands in a display of defeat.

"And is her fiancé aware of that?"

"They had a threesome," Ronnie said.

Paul lurched towards Ronnie intent on wrapping his hands around his mouth to make sure he didn't contribute any more dumb remarks that would magically transform into gospel if he didn't supply all the actual ruddy facts. "Will you shut the fuck up? That is not what happened."

"Jeezus, Paul!" Xane started trying to pry his hands free from Ronnie's mouth. "I don't know what your game plan is, but if you screw up this tour, so help me God, I will bury you six feet under."

"Right." He nodded, still determinedly muffling Ronnie. "What happened to being on my side, guys?

What happened to it's your call; we're behind you whatever you decide?"

"Will you stop trying to fucking smother him?"

"Will you all get off my fucking back?"

"Let Ronnie speak."

Nope. Capital nope, he was not going to do that. "There. Was. No. Threesome!"

"But there was something." That contribution arrived courtesy of Spook who until this moment had been obligingly staying out of the fracas. "If there wasn't, you wouldn't be rattled by the hint that there might have been. So maybe simmer down with the theatrics and spit it out and get it over with. Whatever it is, we're gonna find out soon enough."

Not likely. He wasn't blabbing, and he didn't see Jodi doing that. Nash would likely enough relish the opportunity to act all wronged, but did he really want it advertised that he couldn't get his woman off? Did he even know what had happened when Jodi came back? Would she have blabbed? Paul wasn't sure. Sometimes there was a line you had to draw between honesty and self-preservation.

"Jesus Christ, he's going to pass out."

And all of a sudden, it'd turned from a spat into a rumble.

P AUL ROUSED TO the sensation of the air slapping his cheeks, and a thumping bass competing with the percussive force of the wind. He was folded into the passenger seat of the Danger Car. Ash occupied the driver's seat. Around them lay nothing but empty roads and snow-capped mountain peaks. "Where are we?"

"Heading north towards Stryn, where I've a room booked for tonight."

Stryn. It wasn't a place he'd heard of, and definitely wasn't on the band's itinerary, even as a stopover point. They were booked into an Airbnb in Flåm for tonight, then a lodge in Dombås.

"It's on the banks of Nordfjorden, on the edge of the Briksdalsbreen glacier."

That was a polite way of Ash telling him he'd booked a room for him and his missus to enjoy a bit of sightseeing getaway away from the rest of them for a night or two, which Paul had now cocked up. He therefore tactfully held his tongue rather than doing any grumbling about the prospect of sharing a bed.

At least his head didn't have an axe embedded in it any more.

"On a scale of one to ten, how pissed off at me is Ginny?"

Ash gave him a fleeting glance. "This was her call. She's concerned about you, mate. We all are. Figured some time away from the bus might help."

Time away from anyone he might recently have punched is what he meant, and maybe time away from Jodi and the Ghost Boys, too. That hurt, but maybe it was a good thing. It wasn't like he needed to see her and Nash being all couple-y. And he could definitely live without Nash flaunting his win in Paul's face. He just wished he understood what she saw in him. Her loyalty to the guy didn't make sense. If it'd been Lee she was engaged to, then he'd get it. Hell, even Jez. Balin maybe, at a push, but Nash? He didn't love her, and deep down she had to know that, right?

Paul chewed over that fact for a mile or two more as the scenery rolled on past. Green upon green. Fields and forest. Norway was fucking breathtaking. He just wasn't in the right frame of mind to appreciate it. Still, being here did mean he could avoid the inevitable face to face with reality that kept trying to squeeze its way onto his agenda.

No thankee, he did not need another major downer fucking up his equilibrium.

Know what else he didn't need occupying space in his skull? The possibility that last night's shit might have prompted bollockbrain to slide a gold band onto Jodi's finger alongside the ugly engagement rock.

Did Norway have quickie marriages?

A quick google confirmed not. All praise the Goddess. They required paperwork with a processing time of four to six weeks, so even if butt trumpet had applied the moment they crossed the border, he still wouldn't have the necessary document to get them as far as I dos.

"You owe both Xane and Ronnie apologies."

Did he, now?

"You remember what happened, right?"

More or less. Some of the details were a little fuzzy, like who had put him out and how.

"Spook," Ash informed him after he'd stewed for a bit longer. "You clocked Alle, albeit by mistake, and earned yourself a knuckle sandwich."

"Fuck, I never meant—"

"He knows. So does she. There are no ill feelings there."

"Didn't realise Spook had such a mighty right hook." Now that he thought about it, he did have a sore spot on his temple that was surface level, and not down to the knots in his grey matter.

"Yeah, well, Spook's nothing if not full of surprises."

"I figured Cave Troll, or maybe a Xane and Luthor combo."

"Not sure throwing punches is really Luthor. He's way too laidback." And thus, perfectly countered their vocalist's more highly strung nature. "Cave Troll scooped you up and moved your gargantuan bod into this here vessel."

That'd explain the other bruises he could feel. Troels wasn't exactly known for gentleness.

"Xane has a bust lip that he's probably not going to forgive you for before the century ends, and even if he does, Dani won't."

Yeah, and he was honestly more worried about that lil' hellcat than he was Xane.

"I know you all think that I'm fucking nuts."

Ash slid him another sidelong glance, before

returning his attention to the windy road. "I don't, actually. Leastways, no more than normal. You've always been a bit unhinged. Tying the knot with some lass on a whim's hardly the wackiest thing you've ever done, and a deal less life-threatening than most of them. To be honest, I kinda anticipated the current situ at least a week ago. The whole keeping it in your pants and taking your lead from her thing was never going to last. You might be mostly chill, but you're also fucking possessive over some shit. Mostly pint-sized lasses."

"I'm not possessive." And Jodi wasn't pint-sized.

A smile crooked Ash's lips. "Not over meaningless shit, no. You're never gonna have a meltdown over a missing bit of kit, but when it comes to people you care about, that's another matter. Then you're pure grizzly. And before you go denying it, I'll remind you that I saw at least six seasons of the Paul and Elspeth show. You still can't shake the hold she has on you, even now, after all the shit she pulled."

"She's a friend, and she lost—"

"I know. I know all the ins and outs of the story, Paul. Point I'm making is that considering you're like that with her; it was always a given you were going to be a downright mean fucker regarding your missus."

"She's not my missus." It made his stomach ache to assert that and brought an uprush of acrid bile to his mouth.

Ash chuckled. "Is. Even if she hasn't realised it yet. And I'll note you now have the ink to prove it."

Paul's gaze settled on the newly inked trinity knot encircling his wrist, as he recalled how intently Jodi watched him as the artist worked. Then, the feel of her smaller hand in his as he kept her still while she had her own variation on the theme inked onto her virgin skin. He thought that'd meant something to her. Clearly, he'd read too bloody much into it. Symbolism might be woven into the warp and weft of his being, but that evidently wasn't the case for her.

"Dare I ask what happened?"

He shrugged. "What makes you think something did?"

"Mate, you don't have to tell me if you don't want to."

He chewed that over. After Spook, Ash was probably the least likely to blab. "It doesn't really matter what happened. She's his. She made that plain." Had done so every time he'd presented her with a choice. Every time, she chose Nash. Every fucking time. And fuck if that nonsensical fact didn't make his nose sting.

He wondered what had happened to his shades. They were no longer tucked into his top pocket.

"Tough break."

"Yeah." He sure as hell didn't care for it, but it wasn't like there was anything he could do about it. He was wise enough in the ways of the world to get the message when a woman told him to naff off. Sure, she might not have put it quite so bluntly, and her actions didn't exactly pair up with what she'd said, but—.

"What did Ronnie say to set you off?"

Paul shook his head. "He was just being Ronnie."

"You guys have seemed a bit... I dunno, not off exactly, but scratchy with one another since Equinox. He say something about your missus that's got your hackles up?"

Paul let the missus reference go, seeing as she remained the mistress of his heart, even if she wasn't on board with them getting all connubial. "I let him blow me, okay. And that stays between you and me, Ash. Don't you even share it with Jeopardy Mouse, okay?"

Ash took his hand off the wheel to scratch at his jaw and then demand a sweetie from the dashboard tray. Paul obligingly unwrapped it and popped it in his mouth. Ash kept his counsel until he was done with chewing.

"At Equinox?"

"Yeah."

"Why?"

Paul shrugged. "It was on offer, and I'm not exactly getting balls deep every night like the rest of you."

"There was a field full of lovely ladies a few hundred metres walk away."

"Yeah, well at the time that was a few hundred metres further than I fancied wandering."

"Right," Ash drawled, clearly sceptical. "So, you did what multitudes of BushBabies dream of doing and popped the Bushie cherry."

Paul irritably scratched his scalp. "I didn't pop crap. Him being an innocent is a total myth. His sucking skills are almost on par with Xane's, and blowjobs, regardless of what porn and the average romance would have us believe aren't an innate talent you're fucking born with."

"Reckon having a big gob probably helps."

"Well, there's no denying Ronnie has that."

They both shared a largely humourless laugh.

"Hey, we're just about over the halfway mark, fancy a comfort break."

"I'm not Ginny, you can say you need a piss."

"Fine, piss break okay with you? And you know Gin would probably call it a piss break, too?"

"Yeah." At least around Ash she probably would. Ginny was a bit of a ledge. "Sorry I've fucked your mini break."

Ash hit the right indicator. "There'll be other mini breaks." See, that was where Ash's future had a rosy glow his lacked. There were no couple-y mini-breaks awaiting him in his future, just an eternity of loneliness.

"Okay, let's piss and see if we can find some scran before we head to the ferry."

CHAPTER 35

NASH COULDN'T LOOK at her. Leastways not when she was looking at him, something Jodi found herself doing a lot during the journey north. They didn't talk, and when they had to interact, a cold edge tainted his words that left her permanently on edge. It didn't take long for the rest of the Ghost Boys to clock on to their disharmony.

"Something going on?" Lee asked her over hotdogs in Flåm.

Jodi shook her head, not wanting to share the details, even though she'd have loved Lee's wisdom.

"You know you can talk to me."

But she couldn't. Not about this. Not about her screwing up so badly. All the details kept churning inside her head. Everything she ought to have said and done. The fact she ought to have stopped it. Should have left with Nash right after Paul propositioned them. She'd known that staying would create issues, but she'd buried those thoughts, buried them deep in favour of satisfying the itch there in her brain that made her want Rock Giant instead of only wanting Nash.

Even now, that need still hadn't gone away.

All her indulgence had confirmed was that she was every bit the monstrous screwup she'd ever been.

You couldn't hide from yourself forever.

Bonus: no doubt both men now hated her, and everyone else would hate her too once they found out.

She hated herself.

All that time she'd spent raging against the labels her father and younger brother had accredited her with, and now she'd gone and proved them right. "Worthless, lying cheating cunt." The last words her father had ever said to her rang in her ears again. "If you leave, you'd better not show your fat arse around here again."

She hadn't. But that was all in the past, and there was trauma enough in her present that she didn't need to open old wounds.

Did Nash even know the full extent of what she'd done?

Would his seething eventually lead him to break up with her? She could hardly blame him if he did. She'd done this to them. She'd proved she wasn't decent wife material. But then, if he did, what would she do?

She couldn't lose everything again, and if they split, she would—job, friends, family, security, all the support that kept her sane. It'd be back to the tent, and much as she loved her tent, now she'd grown used to it, she loved the bus more. There were definite benefits to solid walls. Plus, this was where all those who were important to her were.

If he dumped her, there'd be no more touring. No more Lee cuddles and Jez pep talks. No more Balin making her laugh until it hurt. No more family and feeling like maybe she'd found somewhere she belonged. It'd be back to relying on herself, and she was shit at that. Left to her own devices, she always screwed up—faster than she did in company—her and the cats had barely got by the first time, scavenging and living on hedgerow produce.

"You okay, babe?" Balin sidled over while she was tidying her undies drawer and rested his head on her shoulder. "There a reason you're stowing tea in your knickers? Hey, are you the one responsible for the toothpaste in the fridge?"

She couldn't handle his closeness, even as she craved it, hence couldn't bear to shake him off. "Did I do that? I'm sorry. My head's a mess at the minute."

She scooped the circular bags out from one of her bra cups and placed them on the edge of Lee's bunk. Now she was looking, at least a dozen bottle tops, a staple gun and a phone charging cable had also somehow ended up in the drawer. Plus, one of Rock Giant's baby hats. She'd have to figure out a way of returning that. Babies would suffer otherwise, and she didn't want the emotional burden of some tiny premature baby in the NICU suffering because she'd stolen its hat.

Balin seemed to be hovering around like he was waiting for her to say something. She didn't have those words ready. He shifted. His movement making the floor creak.

"Yeah, we've kinda noticed, you're a bit off. Are you going to tell your uncle Balin what it's all about?"

He made it sound jokey, but she knew him well enough to detect the difference in tone between now and when he was actually mucking about. He was genuinely worried, and Balin rarely worried about anything.

"I take it the pair of you had an argument?"

"That obvious?"

God, her throat hurt.

"It's the silent treatment and the wide berths you're giving one another that's the giveaway. And you know, the separate beds. Can you not just fuck and make up?"

Fucking was what had landed them in this position, and she didn't just mean in terms of the other night. Because really the problem was that they didn't talk about anything. The last weeks had consisted of blow up after blow up, followed by sorries and sex, but no discussion, no analysis, no time spent together working shit out. Hence, nothing changed and nothing got resolved. They just got shittier and the knots inside of her more complicated. So complicated, that it never seemed worth the effort of picking at them to see if they could be unravelled. It was easier to pretend they weren't there. That everything was peachy, and if they said, 'I love you' and talked about wedding dates, that would be enough.

But it wasn't enough.

Not when she'd started to see how different things could be, but she didn't see a fix either, other than attempting to talk to him, but honestly, that seemed like a conversation that was rife with landmines and Nash blew up over the slightest thing. Irrelevant, anyway, given he wouldn't occupy the same space as her for more than five seconds.

So, she was both stuck and fucked.

"Jo, please? Seriously, please. Can you not just forgive him for whatever shit he's done? He's our frontman, and we need him on top form. The next gig's only a couple of days away, and he's completely off his game. I know he's always a scrappy little bitch, but Christ, I don't need my head bitten off every time I so much as look at him. Jo-Jo, please. If we attempt to wow a Black Halo crowd at the minute, we'll be laughed off the stage."

"I'm not sure sex is going to fix it, Balin."

He scoffed. "Of course it will."

Sorrier than he'd ever know, she shook her head. Was it nice living in a land where you didn't have to worry about complex emotions or anything outside of the here and now, like he did? Balin never seemed burdened with the same sort of emotional baggage as the rest of them. But it had to be lonely, too, right?

Dammit, she knew it was. She'd lived that life. Him having his fun was the exact same thing she'd done back in her past. Taking off with something that wasn't hers and putting it through its paces, only to abandon it and walk away at the end of the night. Problem was, once the fun was done, and the adrenaline high wore off, you were still alone.

"Then just forgive him. Let him say, sorry, or whatever."

"What should I forgive him for, Balin?" She closed the drawer. Further organisation could wait until later.

Balin lifted his head from her shoulder and rested his chin there instead. The point of it dug uncomfortably into her shoulder. "Ain't this about him watching me? I figured it was, and he implied it was about him watching me."

Evidently Nash was being circumspect with the truth. Perhaps that oughtn't to be so surprising given the circumstances.

"I've told him that he should cool it for a while—"

"It's not about that."

"—maybe concentrate on. Wait. It's not?"

"No."

"You're not mad at him and me over what went down in Bergen?"

She stilled, gaze fastened on her hands and the hat she'd stretched over them, flashes of that moment upstairs on the Black Halo bus intermingling with the present. She shoved the piece of crochet into the drawer and closed it tight. NICU babies had more than one source of hats, one going astray wouldn't matter.

"I'm mad at myself."

"Huh?" Balin circled around her and squeezed in between her and the bunks. That close there was no avoiding his presence. She let her gaze fall to the easy viewing that was his chest. It was never difficult to figure out why people went for him. He was exactly the right mix of groomed and rugged. Pretty, too, with his dark hair and even darker eyes.

"Jo? I'm not following. Unless you're saying you overreacted. In which case sorry will fix it. Did you? You know him having a fetish isn't any sort of slight against you?"

"I know that, Balin."

She also knew in her soul that was a lie. That she was having her emotions manipulated by Nash, and—possibly unwittingly—by Balin.

"Good." He flashed her a smile, which faded just as fast as it'd appeared. "Are you sure you know that? I promise he loves you, and I know we had that earlier conversation, but he's not cheating on you."

No. The cheater was her. Nash just got off on bending the rules and her to his will.

Would Balin be so eager for them to fix things if he knew the truth? What would he say if she mentioned they were in this position because Nash had decided watching her and Rock Giant was a fantabulous idea and she'd foolishly agreed, and then when Nash had lost control of the situation and changed the rules, she'd gone a step further and took a hammer to the very idea of them by shagging his rival?

"It's been forty-eight hours. Isn't that enough wallowing?"

Two days. Was that it? It felt so much longer.

And honestly, she didn't know what was worse, Nash being present and ignoring her, or Rock Giant's suspicious absence. They'd been staying in different apartments, but she'd seen the rest of the Black Halo contingent out and about around Flåm, but not Rock Giant. There'd been no sign of him at all, and he was a hard man to miss. Clearly, he was avoiding her. Hardly a surprise, given she'd metaphorically socked him in the teeth.

He probably never wanted to see her again.

Surely, she ought to feel a little bit relieved at that, not as if she'd had her soul snipped from her.

"Balin." She risked an upward glance. "What is it you think happened in Bergen?"

Her question etched two deep grooves between his eyebrows. "Ah, yeah. I was kinda hoping we weren't going to have to get too heavily into the details." He took a breath, then plopped himself down on the lower bunk. "Okay, so, a fourway in my room. Two lasses, a guy, and me." He raised his hands, then pressed one of them to his heart. "Nash wasn't involved. I promise. He categorically did not participate. He barely even watched."

"Right."

It wasn't any sort of news to hear that Nash had gone straight from watching her to watching Balin. His actions did leave her infuriated, but simultaneously strangely cold, almost indifferent to the fact. She felt detached from the event, as if it hardly mattered anymore.

"Honestly, babe. He spent most of the night in the bathroom hurling. Said his stomach was off from the burgers we got, but my guts were fine."

He wrinkled his elegant nose as if the stench of vomit were assaulting it, but the bunkroom didn't smell any different to usual, namely the familiar scent of worn socks and residual farts.

"He was verifiably bad, though. He spent the night in the bathtub 'cause he didn't want to risk shuffling any further than that away from the loo."

"I wasn't aware that he'd been ill."

"Aye, yeah, he was proper sick. Lee was talking about fetching you at one point, but Nash insisted he didn't disturb you."

But not because he'd wanted to spare her the sight or effort of having to look after him.

Her silence deepened Balin's frown. In fact, he started to look downright worried.

"He loves you."

"Yeah. You said. I know."

"Thing is, the way you're looking at me right now, I'm not sure you do know. You guys aren't going to split over this? Come on. No, that's dumb. You're solid. The two of you are getting hitched. I've already got my best man speech written."

Had he?

"Jo. You're scaring me." He reached out and grasped her hand between both of his. "Doll, don't do this. It's bad enough dealing with Jez and his heartbreak. If you dump Nash, you're going to fuck up the band."

Jeezus, was that true? She didn't need that burden on her head. Bad enough that doing so would make a mess of her own life.

"I'm not going to dump him."

"You're not." He squeezed her hand. "That's right. Course you're not. You're gonna take your Uncle Balin's advice, and fix this."

"He's going to dump me."

Balin stood and wrapped her in an embrace. "The fuck he is. I'll kick his arse if he even thinks about it. I'll go kick his arse for you now if you like for making you suffer."

Quiet tears slid down her face as he crushed her

against his shoulder. He smelled good. He always smelled good, but no amount of distracting herself with that thought could distract her from the truth. Life was about to pivot. Unless some sort of miracle occurred, she was going to lose everything. She curled her fingers into the back of his shirt and held on tight.

They spent the rest of the journey together on his bunk watching a movie on his phone. Leastways, Balin was watching. What was playing in her head was the last few weeks.

When the bus finally rolled to a halt, Lee poked his head around the bunk room door. "Last stop until Trondheim. Guys, you have to see this. We're staying in real log cabins. There's grass on the roof and everything."

"Sounds cool, right Jo-Jo?" Balin stood. He was upright for all of a second before Lee hooked his fingers through the belt loops of his jeans and started tugging him towards the front of the bus.

"I'll tell Nash you're not mad," Balin said to her as he was dragged towards the doorway.

"Please don't."

He caught hold of the doorframe. "Wait. So, you are mad?"

"No. I'd just... I'd rather you didn't say anything."

"Stop fucking tugging, Lee."

"How about listen to the lady and stop meddling, Bayley-boodle-oo," Lee said, continuing with the tugging. "If the lady wants to be pissed at her darling dick-for-brains fiancé, then let her. He probably deserves it. Has cuntface been a cunt to you again?"

"Jeez, Lee, undo all my hard work why don't you." Balin twisted, aiming a swat at Lee's head, who pre-emptively ducked, then rose, his fingers still hooked through Balin's belt loops, and lifted Balin off his feet for a second before the loops snapped, throwing them both off balance. Lee's back collided with the toilet door, throwing it open. Balin fell over the top of him and wound up with his hand in the bowl. "Jesus, shit!"

Balin lurched towards the sink and started fiercely pounding the lever on the liquid soap. "I just bought these, you stupid fucker. You owe me a new pair, Murphy. And I did not need to shove my hand down the bog." He started scrubbing his nails hard.

Lee patted his friend's calf, while he remained on his back laughing. "Should have stuck to quality Primani, instead of Armani."

"I don't do sweatshop wear."

"Aw, is that why you're nearly always walking around with your tackle out?"

"That's 'cause he thinks he's still in Sri Lanka," Jez called from the lounge area.

"People don't walk around naked in Sri Lanka, Starlord," Balin yelled back. "They wear sarongs."

"What's that, thongs? Sheesh, I thought all the panties lying about around here were dropped by young ladies, not that they'd caressed your smelly bollocks."

"My bollocks are not smelly."

"Not what she said," Lee quipped, from where he was still spreadeagled between Balin's legs.

Balin aimed a kick at his band mate's head, and yet again missed thanks to Lee's lightning reflexes. "Excuse me while I throttle him," he said to Jo, before chasing Lee out into the grassy valley that housed their lodge for the night.

Jodi followed only as far as the bus's main lounge area. The lodge was exactly the sort of place that she'd normally have gushed over. It was also the perfect spot for a romantic getaway or a holiday with friends. Sadly, right now all she wanted to do was get away. Away from the questions and Nash's butt hurt silences. Away from the pious imps in her head that were flagellating her with tiny whips for her heinous sins, and far away from the possibility of running into Rock Giant and wondering what to say. That was assuming she could even summon the courage to look at him without breaking apart at the seams, or that he'd acknowledge her.

He'd offered her everything. All the love she could ever want or need, and she'd turned him down.

And why?

Not because of Nash.

Well, yes, because of Nash.

But mostly, because he deserved someone better than her.

Someone who didn't fuck up everyone and everything.

"Are you going to take Balin's advice?" Jez asked her. She turned to find him cross-legged in the corner of the banquette, his long wavy hair shrouding his face, and his dogeared notebook on his lap.

"I guess." That was the only way to make things right and not fuck up the band.

On the other hand, spending forever with Nash seemed less and less like a comfortable plan, and more and more like a recipe for heartache.

T HE CABINS WERE a curious mix of chintz and old-world charm. The outsides blended into the surrounding farmland, the verdant roofs housing the same meadow flowers as the grass underfoot. Inside the wood was brightly painted in earthenwear colours, but the furnishings were all plain wood, benches, tables, and chairs of the kind Victorian children sat on at school. A large grandfather clock stood in one corner, and a rustic shelf hung between two windows housed a row of delicate china teacups and saucers. It looked like the sort of abode a spinster hippy aunt would occupy, alongside her two lesbian lovers and their pet cockatiel.

"Three rooms," Jez said, lowering his overnight bag from his shoulder. Jodi dropped her bag too, and released the cats from their carrier, while the rest of the guys raced ahead to claim rooms. She didn't feel she had a right to stake a claim on any of the spaces.

Obviously, she'd be expected to bunk in with Nash. They were a couple. The booking had been made on that assumption. Except with everything so fraught, she was tempted to about turn and get back on the bus. Stay there for the night. Heck, if that'd been an actual option, she wouldn't be standing here.

Jez curled a hand around her shoulder. "I don't mind sharing if you need a—"

Nash swaggered into the lounge. "There's no bathroom. Only shared facilities in a bathhouse in the main house somewhere."

"Sauna time," Balin yelled from inside one of the rooms where a lot of creaking and groaning of the wood seemed to be taking place. Lee stuck his head out of a doorway, "Yo, Curtains," he addressed Nash, who was regarding her with his lips pursed. "Are you joining us, or sparing us the sight of your twig-like physique?"

Jez gave her shoulder another squeeze, then brushed past her fiancé and claimed the last unoccupied room.

Jodi wasn't good with silences. She didn't know what to do with silences. Silences in her life were indicative of solitude, not discord. Arguments resolved themselves into slammed doors and revved car engines, and hurtling along roads at speed, the car stereo volume turned up loud enough to batter even the most egregious hurts into submission. They weren't prolonged measures of time, demarked by the ticking of clocks, nor tallies of offences. They weren't a familiar part of the relationship she and Nash had.

Usually, he blew hot and loud, stormed off and came back sweeter. Eager to paper over the issue and move on. Based on that schema, things ought to have been right again between them the morning they'd left Bergen.

"You can take the bed, if you like," he said.

She peered at him awkwardly, "What will you do?"

He shrugged. "I don't know." His voice remained soft, conciliatory. "Pitch a tent on the roof."

She had a tent. Maybe she ought to do that. Pitch it, that is, not necessarily on the roof. Why hadn't she thought to retrieve it before the tour bus left?

"I'm not serious, Jo. God, you take everything so literally. I'll be sleeping next to you, obviously."

Obviously, like they were the same couple they'd been this time three days ago.

He cocked an eyebrow, turning his statement into a question. He'd extended the olive branch, now it was up to her to accept it.

"It's a nice big bed. We won't have to squish up like in the bunk."

Like he hadn't spent the last two nights on the banquette, and the one before it in Balin's hotel room bathtub.

Her call. All she had to do was agree, and everything would be right again. She wouldn't have to worry about breaking up with her boys or losing her home and overwintering on the streets with three cats again. So why was it so difficult to say yes? Why did it feel as if she was throwing herself off a ledge by doing so?

Reconciliation meant she got to keep her life intact. That was good. For fuck's sake, that was good. This was exactly the outcome she'd been praying for.

"Great," she croaked, forcing the word out around the boulder in her throat. Then said it again, attempting to inject positivity into her tone. It was the right thing to do. The only sensible choice. "Which room is it?"

"Straight down the hall. The door facing you." She bent to pick up her bag, but Nash caught the carry strap and swung it over his shoulder. He stuck out his free hand, indicating she should go ahead.

The room was painted an odd shade of pink, somewhere between cinder rose and salmon. In contrast, the insets of the shutters and all the cabinet doors were shamrock green and stencilled with traditional rosemaling. The bed was made up with a patchwork quilt. An iron stove sat centrally along the wall that housed the door they'd entered through, and a rocking chair occupied the corner by the window. Eerily, it began to rock itself as they moved into the room.

"Good, eh?"

"Yes." She thought she'd rather be camped on the roof right now.

Nash made to lower her bag to the bed but paused with it still dangling an inch above. "Where do you want this?"

"Anywhere, I guess."

"Right side or left?" He nodded at the bed. They hadn't shared a double bed often enough to have assigned definite sides.

"Which do you want?"

"I don't mind as long as you're in it with me."

Like he'd missed her.

Heck, maybe he had.

He finally put down her bag on a nearby chair, then he was coming towards her, arms open wide, expression all reconciliatory.

She was outside of herself as he put his arms around her. Not really present in her body, more like a dust mote circulating in the air beside them.

"I've spent a lot of time thinking over the last few days. We shouldn't let one mistake wreck us." He rested his chin on the top of her head. "I'm not going to pretend I haven't been mad at you. I've been fucking furious, but it'd be a mistake to call quits on us over one dumb decision. We're good together, Jo-Jo. Much too good to let it fall apart. You and me, we complement one another."

Did they? Well, in so much as they took on opposite, but not oppositional roles.

"Say something. You're alarming me being this quiet. You're never this quiet. You can't really be mad at me for being hurt."

"I'm not mad at you." Not for that.

The fact they were still hugging made it easier to lie than if he'd been looking her in the face.

"You're not? That's good. We need to put this behind us. What do you say we spend tonight together just the two of us? We could go out for a meal, or order in. Maybe do something fun. What do you think? What would you like to do?"

"Are you coming with us or not?" Balin stuck his head around the door. On seeing them locked together in an embrace, he gave her a thumbs up and a grin, and mouthed, "Stability restored." Then, "So?"

"Don't think so, mate," Nash replied. "Think Jo-Jo and I are going to do stuff, just the two of us."

"'kay. Right."

"Are they not coming?" she heard Lee ask Balin. He sounded surprised.

"Sloppy make up time. Let's go, Quilly, you're coming too. They don't need any eavesdropping gooseberries."

The three of them left, ushering in another uncomfortable silence the groaning joints of the lodge failed to fill.

Nash eventually stepped back, breaking their close embrace in favour of a looser hold on one another. He clasped her hands. Raised her knuckles to her lips. "What do you want to do? Dinner? Go out, order in?"

"I'm not really hungry yet, and I don't really want to leave the cats." It'd be wrong to dump them in a new place and run out the door. They needed time to settle.

She needed time to settle. She hadn't set up their litter tray or anything yet. She wandered back into the living area, intent on that task. It gave her hands something to focus on. Less chance of them relocating random objects that way.

Nash followed along. Even helped squeeze food out of a pouch and distracted Flugwhump from eating it all before Mel and Zar had even seen it by tossing his catnip-infused toy mice around.

They acquired drinks. Maybe resorting to booze wasn't the best plan, but the craft beers were waiting for them there on the table, alongside an artisanal loaf, brown cheese, and chocolates.

And drinking at least filled the void.

After days of stewing and imagined conversations—okay, confrontations—she didn't know what to say. Shouldn't they be confessing their sins and seeking apologies? Rehashing the events wasn't something she was eager to do, not considering the guilt she was carrying over where it had led her, but simultaneously, not talking it through felt like moving forwards with grenades in her pockets, and who knew when one of them would accidentally snag the pin.

"Balin said you were sick."

Nash tapped the bottle against his lips, then lowered it to the table. "Yeah, I was."

"Because of what...what we did?"

He lifted the bottle, took another long draw. Then wiped his hand over his lips. "I forgive you, okay. Let's just move on."

"Are you saying we should just forget—"

"Yeah, exactly that."

Jodi scratched at the bottle label and began systematically peeling it from the glass. "Okay, but—"

"There's no but, Jo. Okay, so that night shouldn't have happened, but that doesn't mean we have to let it define us."

"—you're still touring with Black Halo." Thus, Rock Giant would still be a permanent fixture in their lives for the next seven-ish months. There'd be no way of avoiding him, and God help her, she wasn't even sure that she wanted to.

Fool! Here she was being offered a lifeline, and she was being her own worst enemy, refusing to give up what she'd already cast aside. She'd told him. Right afterwards... She'd told him, and she'd made her choice. Walked away. Left the room. Because her relationship with Nash mattered and giving that up meant giving up everything else that mattered to her too.

Rock Giant wasn't going to forgive her for that.

"Rock Giant's irrelevant. Just don't fucking speak to him." There were the sharp shards of Nash's hurt she'd expected. He turned and took a walk away from the table, only to retrace his steps, his expression smoothed of anger. "He's only a problem if you make him a problem. Look, everything until now is forgiven. It's forgotten." A robust swallow made his Adam's apple bob. "Agreed? Fresh slate." One hand got shoved towards her. Jodi stared at his outstretched palm. All she had to do was accept it.

"And you'll stop watching Balin," she tacked on, shy of their palms making contact.

"For fucks sake," he hissed under his breath. Then, more of that smoothing out of his features and swallowing his irritation happened. "Deal." A robust shaking of her hand happened. Rather than letting go once the pact was agreed, he lifted her hand towards him, and turned it over, exposing her inner wrist and the interwoven lines of her recent ink.

"Which one is which?" he asked of the cats running along the black strands of the design. So, she told him, and he nodded, and he asked if it'd hurt, and she told him it was an odd sensation, not painful and not entirely unpleasant, but odd. And after that, somehow, he ended up with his arms around her, and kissing her, and then they were back in familiar territory heading towards their room to make up how they'd always made up after a fight.

Nash left the door wide open.

First test. He didn't say anything, but she knew he was waiting for her to complain. She didn't. It didn't make any sense to give him a reason to erupt again, not when they were busy fixing things. She did want to fix things. And God, he was giving her a chance, when there wasn't any reason for him to do so. His voyeurism wasn't remotely comparable to what she'd done.

Did Nash know everything that had happened? She was sure he must do. He'd been right outside in the corridor. And his silence the last few days made far more sense if he did. So much more sense. What she'd done in those moments were far more unforgiveable than her unexpectedly orgasming on Rock Giant's tongue during their ill-thought-out threesome.

Why had they done that?

Why had any of them done it?

Foolish. So goddamned foolish.

And now this, heartbreaking gentleness, that nevertheless felt scratchy. Nash guiding her, but not in his usual ham-handed way that was all about gratification now, now, now. No, this was tenderness in a hereto unseen way, even if the door was open.

It was fine. The guys would stay away. Give them space. Wouldn't they?

Balin had practically marched Lee and Jez from the cabin.

They would. They'd stay away. It was important to them as a band as much as it was to her and Nash as a couple. They needed Nash in the right headspace to perform.

She ought to be as into this as he was. So why did she feel so goddamned detached as he tugged the shirt from her back and peeled her panties down?

Sticking with it, was the right choice. The only choice if she wanted to keep her life together. It's what she concentrated on as he wet his fingers and teased them along her split.

This was how they made things right.

"Want me to go down?"

He usually never...

God, he was trying. Trying so hard to make it right. But didn't seem to see that putting his tongue there was just releasing an onslaught of memories while simultaneously highlighting his...not ineptitude, that made it sound bad. It wasn't bad. Cunnilingus was pretty hard to get wrong, but it wasn't his forte, thus he was unskilled, unlike the man who'd last put his tongue there.

Shit! She needed to stop thinking about him. They weren't ever going to be, and his presence in her head now was reinforcing the barriers between her and Nash, that the latter was working so damn hard to tear down.

Only Nash deserved space in her thoughts right now.

This was the future.

The one she'd chosen for herself.

The one they'd chosen together.

The one that didn't divorce her from everyone she loved.

"Getting tongue strain."

"It's okay," she assured, reaching for him, cupping his cheeks. He crawled upward, bringing his mouth to hers. "We're good, yeah? We're good. Did I do good?"

"Nash—"

"Just let me." He brought a hand down between them, lined them up. "Lift your legs a bit."

He made a sharp inhale as he entered her. The one she made as an echo, prompted more by muddled emotions than anything physical.

"You're so special. I love you, Jo. Say you love me too."

"Of course, I love you."

"Of course you do." He kissed her again, then braced his forearms either side of her head and started thrusting. She stroked his arms and tried to stay grounded in the moment, even as tears leaked from her eyes. She made all the noises he expected of her. Cried out in faked ecstasy, mimicking the sounds that tore open his mouth and made his chest arch away from her as he came.

In contrast, the tears that dribbled down her cheeks and that he kissed away so tenderly were all too real.

"It's okay, I forgive you. I forgive you, Jo. I forgive you. It's all fine now. We're together. All fixed. We're getting married. We're getting married soon."

"Soon?"

"Yes, soon." He wiped her cheeks dry. "Can't wait to make you wholly mine. Let's give notice the moment we're back home and book a venue."

How soon was that? A few days?

"Yes?" he prompted.

So, in a month and a few days, she'd be his wife. She'd be secure.

"Yes, okay. Okay."

It was the right choice. The only choice...

TRONDHEIM

"NO HEADACHE TODAY, I trust."

Paul looked up from his crochet to find Xane resting against the sink unit in the tour bus kitchen. "No," he said. "Not today. Sorry about the lip." Whatever swelling had resulted had gone, but there remained a nick in Xane's lower lip about half an inch left of his piercing.

"Forgiven. It got me at least a dozen sympathy shags."

Paul and Ash had rejoined the tour as they'd rolled into the outskirts of Trondheim late the previous evening, past the point of the night when anyone was up for talking. Even given the hours they all regularly kept, some conversations were better left until daylight.

"I'm assuming that face isn't down to the folk museum being closed today?"

Direct it wasn't, but in over a decade of band life,

Paul couldn't recall Xane ever having asked him anything quite so prying. Sure, it sounded like a simple observation about Paul's demeanour due to one of his favourite activities being off the agenda, but it wasn't. It was more than that. The clue being the hesitation in their lead singer's pale eyes. No contact lenses yet; he'd only recently rolled out of bed and was now wandering about in a pair of beaten-up black jeans, bare-footed, and nursing a brew strong enough to induce angina.

Paul set down his crochet hook. He still had to concentrate on what he was doing to not to constantly muck it up and drop stitches, but it had kept both his mind and his hands busy these last few days. Ginny or one of the girls had thoughtfully packed it for him when they'd thrown his survival bag into the boot of the Danger Car for his road trip with Ash. He'd manged a hat a day during their sojourn and was aiming to maintain his record. Crochet, it turned out, really helped with keeping his mind out of his Bergen hotel room.

"Haven't seen your girl around much."

He, of course, hadn't seen Jodi since they'd left Bergen, though she was in his thoughts pretty much constantly.

"The rest of the Ghosties have been around plenty, but not her."

"Do you know if she's okay?"

Xane sighed and scrubbed a hand over his face, before finding himself a perch on the bench on the opposite side of the kitchen table. "I've not specifically heard anything to say she isn't."

Paul wasn't sure that meant much. And given that he wasn't sure what anyone knew, it was impossible to gauge what they might or might not tell him.

"How are you?" he asked, changing the subject.

Xane tilted his head, while his lips became pursed. "Elspeth remind you?"

"Yeah." Today would have been their former drummer's birthday. Paul didn't routinely make a big fuss over birthdays, especially the birthdays of people who were no longer around to celebrate them, but this one tended to have a melancholy pull on at least two of the people he knew. He'd had a short Zoom chat with Elspeth a few hours ago. She'd been subdued but was holding up better than she'd done the previous October seventeenth. Not that that guaranteed future improvements. That wasn't how grief worked. There weren't any neatly delineated stages you could work through and emerge fixed. Rather it was a constant rollercoaster. You could drift along fine for years, then wham—loop the loop—and you were mired in the raw loss again exactly as if it'd just happened.

"I'm okay. Okay enough. Have to be. Are we going to talk about what happened?"

"I had a hangover and lost my rag."

Black hair swished against his bare shoulders as Xane shook his head. "I'll rephrase. Are we going to talk about why it happened?"

Paul followed the ends of Xane's hair to the bars through his nipples. Funnily enough he'd never fancied piercing that part of his anatomy. "I didn't need anyone in my business."

"Yeah, I guess that explains you trying to choke the living daylights out of Ronnie."

"Is he okay?"

Xane took a long sip of his brew, then he sucked on his lip ring, making it rotate. "A bit hoarse. Bit subdued, which isn't such a bad thing. He told me a rather garbled story about the pair of you exchanging bodily fluids at Equinox."

Well, he guessed it had been inevitable it'd come out. Stuff always did.

"Sounds like he read into it more than he should've."

"Not gay," Paul muttered. He and Ronnie were never destined to become a thing. He was a cool friend, but it was never going to be more than that.

"Nor's Ronnie."

"I like tits and arse, Xane, and even if I'd been remotely interested in it becoming something more than a one off, which I'll point out I categorically stated wasn't the case at the time, I'm definitely not interested now I'm hitched."

Xane's dually-pierced eyebrow arched impressively, then eventually sank back to normality. "Ronnie hasn't known you as long as the rest of us. I don't think he's got any real understanding of what makes you tick. That, and he gets fixated on stuff. It was me. Now it's you."

"Yay!" he groaned, loading his voice with insincerity. On top of everything else, he'd screwed up a really good friendship at a time when he needed to be hanging on to his friends. He'd have to attempt to straighten things out with Ronnie for the sake of the band, and because his own code of ethics demanded it. Hopefully, they could bounce back from the current upset. "Are you planning on holding a vigil tonight?"

Xane sighed. "Constantly changing the subject isn't going to distract me. But to answer you, I might take myself up to the roof with a bottle of something for a bit, but I'm not looking to sit around sharing stories."

"Fair enough." The roof was the only quiet location on the bus, and for the most part, you could only get away with sitting up there in the dead of night while you were parked up somewhere quiet, otherwise, people wound up gawping at you, or commenting, or getting pissy about the health and safety aspects of it and calling the police.

"You know if you want to talk—"

"I don't, Xane. There's nothing to say. Do you want to?"

They both knew that if he did, he wouldn't be cosying up to him. Maybe he'd talk to one of his partners, but more likely, Xane and Spook would have one of their weird telepathic conversations and then go and screw their respective loved ones. Paul didn't exactly get it, but he missed having someone around he was that comfortable with. Ash had done his best, bless him, on their road trip, to help him work through his shit, but outside of a love of music and a few common references, they weren't anything alike. He missed Elspeth. He missed the D'Amon clan. And Jack and Gloria, his parents' pygmy goats, who always had the answers to everything, which was to chew on it. Hell, he missed his mam and dad, mad buggers that they were.

They'd understand all this. They wouldn't just tell him he was an oaf for interfering with an established relationship. They'd get the significance of cosmic signs and the handfasting. They understood oaths. Had sworn lifelong ones of their own that they'd stuck to through countless ups and downs. Were determinedly sticking to them now in a way he wished they wouldn't. He understood. Christ, he understood. Still, did they have to take the until death us do part bit quite so literally?

"Paul?"

Xane had slid out from where he'd been sitting and was now crouched down to the side of him so that they were on a level. "Are you going to be okay for the show tomorrow night?"

"I'm fine." Even if he wasn't, there were too many people relying on him to consider pulling out of a gig at this short notice. "Can I get out, please?"

He waited for his band mate to shuffle aside, then

bolted down the bus steps into the sunlight. The arctic wind took the heat out of his skin. It didn't do shit for his mushy innards.

Okay, so maybe he wasn't entirely okay, but he would be. Everything was going to be all right. He just needed to practise acceptance. Sure, he'd had his heart bruised, and that meant he was feeling everything a bit more sharply than usual, but it'd pass. Bruises healed. He'd get through this. He'd endure. Of course he would. The wheel of fate would eventually rotate.

It always did.

And then, maybe, he wouldn't feel so alone.

He'd seen a happy future written for them in the stars and had listened to the wind between those standing stones whisper their names. All he had to do was persevere and in time... In time all would be well.

That was how the wheel worked.

A wan face looked down at him from the back window of the Ghost Boys bus. Paul's attention snapped to it—Castle.

She looked as if she hadn't slept for days or even brushed her hair. His own was easily an inch longer than when the tour started. If he was going to keep it shorn he'd have to get the clippers out.

He almost caught Jodi's gaze, but she staged a hurried retreat. Was dick spanner giving her hell? He hoped the cats and the rest of the Ghost Boys were providing some comfort. Wished he could be there to do so, too.

His arms ached with the need to embrace her and make everything right.

But she'd chosen dickweed, not him.

FOR THE LAST few hours Paul had been fixated on one particular thought. In all honesty, he was surprised it hadn't beaten him around the head sooner. It ought to have done, because he and Jodi hadn't just had sex—yes, he'd been reliving the details—they'd had unprotected sex. Very, very messy, very spontaneous swimmers at the ready sex. Obviously, he'd known that. It just hadn't sunk in until he was going through his bag, sorting out what needed a wash, and found the condoms in the pocket of the lounge pants he'd been wearing that evening.

Then it sunk in.

That they'd both been fools in a multitude of ways. Consequently, as much as he was doing his best to adhere to her wishes and keep his distance, this was a valid reason to talk to her.

He wasn't worried about diseases so much, they

were all regularly tested. Pregnancy, on the other hand...

His tongue hit his upper front teeth. The probability wasn't high, but the universe did like to play the odd cosmic joke.

She had to be on some sort of birth control, right? Right?

Nash had definitely fucked her bare, because he'd got an unfortunate taste of the bugger on her. In the moment, he hadn't cared about anything other than taking care of her. Then again, did that mean anything? Dipshit was exactly the sort not to give a shit about knocking her up. It'd be another thing he could manipulate her with. Also, thinking back to the morning after their handfasting, she'd been manic until he'd assured her, they hadn't in fact done the dirty deed. It could just have been because of cockwomble, but equally... she was essentially homeless, and probably wasn't registered with a GP.

Shit! He wasn't sure he was ready for a little Rock Giant appearing in the world.

It probably wasn't going to happen, and he was worrying about nowt, but on the other hand, maybe he needed to think about branching out from just hats. Kid would need more than its head keeping warm.

Rock Giant decided the most sensible time to corner Jodi for a quiet word was while the Ghost Boys were on stage doing their set. That would give him a window of an hour and a half, and Nash wouldn't be aware of their interaction because he'd be busy warming up the crowd. Next, he needed a location. Backstage during a show was a hive of activity. If a member of his band didn't interrupt, then one of their partners or a member of the crew almost certainly would. Maybe they could step outside. There was a bouldering wall at the rear of the building. Except, why would she go there?

Other than to do some bouldering, obviously, but his Jodi wasn't exactly a sporty type.

Ginny flopped into a chair beside him in the green room. "Fancy giving me a hand with something?" he asked.

She patted his thigh and laughed. "Paul Reed asking me for help? What is the world coming to?" Her hand having met with muscular resistance, she gave his thigh another good prod, that she followed with a squeeze. Then she simmered down her playfulness and looking him right in the eyes, asked, "Okay, who are we killing? And do we need a getaway driver, because your driving sucks, and I barely know where the ignition key goes."

He fell ever so slightly in love with her at that moment. In a platonic way, obviously. Everything else was reserved for Jodi.

"No killing required. Stealth mission. I need to talk to—"

"Your girl," she finished for him. "Got a reason, because correct me if I'm wrong, but I think she's avoiding you, and usually, I'm an adherent of the school of life that says if a lady's told you to keep your arse away from her, you keep your arse away from her."

"It's important."

"Honey bun, it always is."

"I'm serious, Ginny. I've potentially screwed up badly and I need to know..." He bit his tongue; not sure he wanted to share the details. He hadn't even gone into the weeds of it with Ash. Honestly, the fewer people that knew, the easier it'd be for everyone. "I need to know that she's all right, and that she's not experienced any complications as a result of our last.. .of when we last saw one another."

"Right, care to explain that again, without resorting to code? Sorry, while I'm an epic super-secret agent, as you know, I left my cryptography specs at home today."

Not really. "The night you texted me asking if I was, you know," –he lifted his brows— "I was?"

She shook her head. "Nope. Still need a decoder."

"Fucking her," he said under his breath, as he bowed his head. "I was. I mean, I did. But not deliberately. I mean, yes, deliberately, but not in a... planned fashion. Stuff happened, and it... Do I really need to explain this to you? I'm just concerned, because we didn't use anything, and..."

Ginny put her curled fist to her mouth. It took him a moment to realise she was trying to hide a smirk.

"It's not funny, Gin."

"No," she agreed her whisky gold eyes gleaming. "Definitely not funny. It is a little bit funny."

It wasn't. It really wasn't. Okay, if it'd been someone else telling him they'd screwed up, he might have thought it was a bit funny. Living it, though. That wasn't funny. It was fucked.

"I don't fuck people bare. I don't take those sorts of risks. Not ever."

She sobered and patted him on the back. "Oh, that's what you're worrying about, not the actual shagging part." Her pats gradually slowed, before transforming into circular rubs. "Okay, so what is it you're thinking of asking her?"

Was that not obvious? "If she's okay? If there's anything she needs my help with, or that I can do?"

"Paul, are you seriously worried you've knocked her up? You realise if you have it's too early to tell, and too late to do anything about it."

"Yes, but…"

Ginny gave his back another comforting pat. "I always liked you. You always recognise actions have consequences, even if you ignore them most of the time."

Not true. He calculated risks and acted accordingly.

Paul squinted at her from out of the corners of his eyes. She'd stuck one thumbnail in her mouth and was thinking aloud. "Well, she's in a long-term relationship, so she's probably using some form of birth control. Ergo, you're probably worrying unnecessarily. It's sweet that you are, though, even if you're doing it approximately seven days too late."

"Yeah, well I got whisked off to Stryn with your hubby, didn't I? And it's not seven days, it's five."

"Do you not have the lass's number?"

"No." And even if he did, he wasn't sure she'd answer if he called. Nor was he about to send her incriminating text messages.

"I'm gonna go out on a limb here and say her fiancé doesn't know that you're fucking her?"

Paul rubbed his suddenly extremely itchy nose. "I'm not fucking her." Much as part of him very much wished he was regularly fucking her. "It happened once. Accidentally, in a moment of…of high emotion. You know what, Gin, I'm not sure it matters. He's pissed off with me anyway and pissed off at her as a result. And if he knows, then he knows, and if he doesn't, I'm not about to tell him. It's up to Jodi whether she does…has."

There was a distinct possibility she'd confessed, it'd be a very Jodi-esque thing to do. Her self-preservation instincts were decidedly lacking. "I just need a quick word, and I don't want that to cause a nuclear explosion. You gonna help me, or not?"

Ginny crossed her arms, making him sweat, while she considered. "Ahh, yeah, okay. Since it's you."

Paul let some of the tension melt from his shoulders. "Thank you."

"But I'd like it acknowledged that I'm only doing it because I know you equate your handfasting to a legitimate marriage. Otherwise, I wouldn't approve. It's not cool hooking up with someone who's in a relationship behind their partner's back. It hurts people."

"Like I said, it wasn't planned, Gin. I've been keeping it in my pants." Which had not been fun. Usually, he managed to get laid reasonably regularly while on tour. "And it's not about to happen again, because she's categorically chosen him."

There it was, the truth that had been slapping him around the head the last few days and turning him into a bugbear.

"Wait." Ginny turned towards him, rising onto her knees. "She shagged you and then chose him? Paul, sweetie." She crushed his nose against her shoulder pulling him into a tight hug. "Darn, that's not fun, tiger. I'm really going off this girl. Are you sure she's the one?"

"She's scared," he said. It was the most plausible reason he could come up with for why she kept rejecting him. He wasn't buying a profound attachment to Nash. "She's frightened of turning her life upside down again and losing everything that matters."

"Aye, but she'd gain you, and a whole new family."

"I'm just telling you what I think she thinks, Gin, not agreeing with her reasoning."

"Gotcha. Okay, do you want me to hunt her down now, and if not, when? Also, whereabouts were you thinking of this covert meeting taking place?"

J ODI HADN'T EVEN planned to go to the gig. She'd decided staying out of sight on the bus was a wiser option, but then Balin had texted her demanding she bring him his favourite pick.

Balin: No, not the orange one. The one with the chainsaw-wielding hamster on it.

And once she'd delivered that, Jez had bemoaned the fact he was having a bad hair day and begged her for help taming it before everyone decided the Ghost Boys were shit because of his frizz. No amount of pointing out that he was sitting at the back of the stage behind a drum kit would convince him that a) no one would notice, or b) give a shit. So, she'd been forced into ringlet-taming measures and a long conversation with him and one of the Black Halo roadies about the benefits of silk sleeping hats for those of the curly-haired persuasion. Not a problem she possessed.

Thus, when Ginny planted a crate of beer in her arms and insisted she help schlep them over to the Black Halo bus, she did it. It wasn't as if she was at risk of running into Rock Giant; the Black Halo guys were chilling in their dressing room.

The buses were parked at the back of the arena, just a short walk from the building. They left the beer stacked behind the driver's bay in a slot they honestly looked as if they might have just come from. No matter. She was merely the hired muscle. Then, on the way back to the building, Ginny spotted the bouldering wall and insisted they needed to give it a try.

While Ginny practically ran up the surface, clinging to the fingerholds as if she had Velcro fingertips, Jodi failed to get more than ten inches off the ground. Fact was, she had minimal upper body strength when compared with her lower body mass, and she'd spent her youth nicking cars, not climbing trees.

She'd managed to get her feet into a V shape about a foot up and had her butt sticking out when the crunch of footsteps snapped her attention towards the arena's rear exit.

Oh shit!

Her left foot slipped, her fingers failed to support her, and gravity did the rest. She landed on her arse with a thud, which prompted mister heroic to come striding over to her aid.

He was dressed to go on stage. Heavy boots with a multitude of buckles and spikes. Leather jeans that laced up the sides and encompassed his long legs like a second skin. No belt. Then, a raglan-sleeved top that was due a second life as a dishcloth. Probably going to wind up being thrown to the audience mid-set. He'd completed the ensemble by spraying a black stripe across the bridge of his nose and his eyelids and adding freakish UV reflective contact lenses.

"Castle." He stretched a ring decked hand towards her.

Dignity already lost in the dirt; Jodi scrambled backwards away from him. "Paul, no."

"Hey, how are you?"

"No, this is a bad idea. He can't see us together."

"He's on stage. He's not going to see us. I just want a minute."

Right. So, this had been a setup.

"What is it?" Avoiding his help, she found her feet and stood facing him with her arms crossed.

"Are you okay?"

"I've a well-padded arse." Except he clearly hadn't meant had she hurt herself slipping off the climbing wall. She considered lying, but he'd always seen through her. Instead, she dropped her gaze. "Of course I'm not. I wasn't before I screwed up..." She couldn't say it. "Nash wasn't speaking to me. He is again now. We made up." She sighed and let her arms flop down by her sides.

"He knows about...?"

She raised her shoulders, then dug her teeth into her lower lip. "Can we not? I feel sick enough as it is."

"You feel sick?"

Realisation made her splutter. "I'm not sick because I'm pregnant, Paul. I'm sick because all this is stressful and fucked up, and I don't know how to make it right, or if I've managed to make a single sensible choice since the first day of Equinox. I do know that us being seen together will make things infinitely worse. I had everything mapped out. I finally had my life together, and then you...then this... God! You need to just leave me the fuck alone before you completely fuck up my life."

"Jodi."

She shook her head.

A group of people came outside, vapes and cigarettes already in their hands.

"Seriously. Thanks for being concerned, but you needn't be. Now stay the fuck away from me."

THEY'D SPOKEN. Paul had been given the confirmation he'd sought that he didn't need to worry. Too bad it didn't make him feel any better. Worse even, it felt like he'd added another loss to the ones he was already mourning. How was he supposed to stay away from her, when she so obviously needed rescuing?

He wasn't in the proper headspace to go on stage, but that was the life of a performer. Sometimes you had to plaster on a smile and deal, even when you felt like poo and the only thing that appealed was the idea of taking a very long walk in the wilderness, living on berries and mushrooms for a few weeks, and actively avoiding hearing anything but your own voice.

Spook patted him on the back. Ronnie offered him a meek smile. Paul was pleased to note that the latter didn't look any different to usual. Well, perhaps a little less elastic grin, but same amount of sugary insolence.

"Sorry," he huffed, simultaneously with the same word leaving Ronnie's mouth. "I'm sorrier."

He got offered a sticky jelly strawberry.

Chewing it filled an uncomfortable gap and gave his jaw a workout.

Ash joined them with his guitar already slung by its strap around his shoulders. "We ready to melt some faces off?" He produced a pick and readied it between thumb and finger. Ash normally announced them with a few opening riffs.

"Ready," Paul agreed. The energy would come. It always did. He bounced onto the balls of his feet a couple of time to loosen up.

The show was running over ten minutes late, so Samson had shaved time off the interval between the bands, endeavouring to get them back on track. Venues liked that. Meant the locals didn't voice excessive noise complaints. On the downside, it meant Black Halo were already in the wings as the Ghost Boys were saying their farewells. The last notes of their final track were still reverberating, and roadies were already rushing on, barking information back and forth between themselves through their headsets.

Lee and Balin came off first, sweat soaked and bubbly. Nash lingered, dragging the mic stand as he bantered with the crowd. Jez got out from behind his drum-kit and the roadies swept on to move his set off and bring Luthor's forward. Paul braced, ready for the inevitable dirty look he'd get when he and Nash passed. Happened practically every show. This one was no doubt going to be extra vicious given the boy had had a week to stew, and things were obviously dicey between him and Jodi.

Luthor and Ronnie went on. Paul turned his head to ask Spook to repeat what he'd just said, something about a locally brewed beer. He got a millisecond warning that something was coming courtesy of the horrified contorting of Spook's face. Wasn't long enough to do anything about it, before the stand smashed into his left shoulder, bounced upwards, and struck his Adam's apple, stealing his ability to breathe. For several bewildering moments his head rang, and his vision danced in and out of focus. All he could hear was the rush of his own blood. Then an explosion of voices battered his eardrums.

He got hit again, across his thighs, narrowly missing his kneecaps. The third time, he was still reeling, but ready for it. He blocked the stand's arc with his forearm, then stepped to the side of it, which got him in close enough to launch a retaliatory swing at its wielder.

Nash seemed genuinely gobsmacked at the fact he'd been punched. He flew backwards, bowled off his feet by Paul's right hook, crashed into Jez, and the pair of them toppled onto their arses in full view of the paying audience.

Laughter flooded the arena.

"No!"

Someone grabbed Paul from behind but failed to arrest his forward momentum. He pulled them along with him. Nash was on his knees when he reached him. Paul led with his foot, and put him down again, even as the bastard was gearing up to make another jab with that mic stand.

He got in another few kicks.

Audience laughter turned to alarm. Cameras picked up the scuffle and broadcast it. On the big screens shifting shapes mimicked his actions. He wrestled the pole from Nash's hand and chucked it away. He didn't need weaponry. He had two perfectly good fists.

All around him, people were screaming.

Multiple hands clawed at his back and arms.

Another series of explosions went off inside his ears. His knuckles were bleeding.

"PAUL... FUCKING HELL! Don't kill him. What is with you lately?"

Hair both black and blond swished across his field of vision. He swung his fists and his left shoulder screamed as if something inside had ripped. Someone dragged his arms into his back, then sat on him. He rolled, attempting to throw them off. Succeeded, and crashed into one of the guitar pedals. Something heavy fell across his legs. He tried to push himself up, but his left arm refused to support his weight. No matter. He pulled his right beneath him instead and used that as a lever. Around him lay a tangle of bodies and wires. A patch of yellow striped hazard tape was stuck to his sleeve.

There were too many people in too small a space. Both bands. A countless number of backstage staff. He saw Jodi screaming, fist shaking. Lee pulling her back, trying to shield her with his body. Who the fuck had hit her? Her nose was bleeding twin streams over her lips and chin.

Paul ripped off the tape and gained his knees. "Get her out of here," he yelled.

The audience were riled into an equally frenzied bloodlust, fists in the air, yelling.

Xane seized the mic. Started improvising some bullshit dialogue that implied this was all part of the show, and their audience lapped it up. Balin and one of the roadies dragged Nash into the wings. Jez scurried in the same direction on hands and knees. The roadies went to town on their equipment. Spook helped him to his feet.

"Not sure I can..." Fuck, his shoulder hurt.

"Dislocated?" He could barely hear Spook, but he could lip read.

He tried a shoulder roll. "No." It just hurt like buggery.

"Do what you can?"

There wasn't really an alternative; they had a show to put on. He pulled off his shirt and used it to wipe his face, then hurled it into the crowd. The psychos would probably love the fact it was blood-spotted as well as sweat soaked this evening. Then he claimed his bass, and ignoring the pain, did what was expected of him.

"DO YOU EVER think that maybe you chose the wrong man?"

Jodi peeled her gaze away from her image in the mirror to stare at Lee beside her, holding an equally blood spotted tissue to his nose. They were in the tiny tour bus bathroom, crowded before the mirror.

"Lee, he's your friend."

"Yeah. He's also the clown responsible for this, and I'd like to ring his scrawny neck right now." He lowered the tissue and inspected the crust of dried blood around his left nostril. Satisfied that it was no longer dripping, he aimed the tissue at the toilet, missed and had to scoop it off the floor. "You realise he's just cost us the tour, if not our bloody careers."

She hadn't really thought as far as consequences. Her head was still smarting from the smack in the face she'd sustained. Adrenaline was still pumping through her veins, and unlike Lee's, her nose didn't seem to want to stop leaking red stuff.

"Pinch," he advised. "Not there, a bit further up."

"You know this is all my fault, not his."

"Nope. Wasn't you that took a swing at Rock Giant with a mic stand."

She still couldn't quite wrap her mind around that fact even though she'd damned well witnessed it.

"What I did led to it."

Lee gave a nod. "I'm sure Nash'll be happy for you to take the blame, but fuck that. And fuck him. Christ, Jo, wake up. The man's a tool. A complete and utter tool, and you deserve better. I'm sick of hearing you make excuses for him. Are you not sick of making them?"

But...Nash had been sweet, and they'd agreed to put all the disasters of the last few weeks behind them and make another go of it.

"Jo. Gawd." Lee knocked her hand aside. "Stop letting go or it'll never stop." He pinched for her.

"Do you really think Black Halo will dump you?"

Pain shot across the surface of his eyes. "Of course they're going to ditch us. Nash just attacked their bassist in front of a live audience. We'll be lucky if we play another gig, let alone open for Black Halo again. The whole rock star thing, it's over. We're done. By the end of the night, I expect I'll have had my arse handed to me by Brian, Samson, Harry and probably Black Halo's manager too." He let go of her nose and nodded when the blood trickle didn't resume. "Be a miracle if the words assault charges don't get thrown around. If they don't, it'll only be because the lawyers haven't had their say yet."

"You really think it'll be that bad?" Why did they all have to suffer, when it'd been Nash who'd taken the swing? It wasn't fair to tarnish them all with the same brush. Then again, it had turned into a full-scale rumble with everyone in the vicinity involved.

Lee had taken the sort of breath that filled up his cheeks. He released it in one long puff. "Truth. I think it's gonna be worse." He laced his fingers above his head, then dragged both hands down his face. "Believe me, I'm praying otherwise, but my guts say we're sunk. Christ, even if by some miracle we don't get booted, we're going to get dogpiled on social media. I guarantee footage of what happened is already circulating. And Black Halo fans are completely rabid."

"I'm sorry, Lee. I'm so sorry. Fucking, shit!" She yelled the latter part while taking a swipe at a stack of paper towels. They scattered like a hundred disabled butterflies.

This wasn't right. It wasn't fair. Lee, Balin, Jez, they didn't deserve to have their dreams snatched away from them like this. Not because she'd fucked up. Not because she'd been incapable of being honest. She looked up and met Lee's anxious gaze in the mirror, then turned to face him again. "I'm so sorry, Lee. I should never have come on this tour."

"Would you stop it?" He shook his head, making his long hair swish against his shoulders. He reached out to her, and pulled her closer, one hand behind the back of her neck and reeled her in until their brows were braced against one another. "You need to ditch the martyr routine."

"You say that, but if it wasn't for me getting handfasted to Rock Giant, then none of this would ever have happened. The tour would have run smoothly."

"If Nash hadn't stood you up, you'd never have got handfasted to another man."

"I shouldn't have got high."

Lee sandwiched her head between his hands. "You're still not listening. He shouldn't have stood you up. There's no fucking reason why you should shoulder the blame for all of this. It's time the annoying fucker took some responsibility for his own actions."

"Maybe if I explain to Brian...to Samson, to Harry."

"Explain what?"

"That I cheated on him, and that's why he was angry. Why he attacked."

Her heart was fluttering like a caged bird inside her chest. Her lungs felt tight, like someone had bound them with a dozen rubber bands. Her nose hurt where she'd been hit. Her eyes were stinging too, and it was getting harder and harder to see Lee through the filter of tears gathering in them.

"Breathe, Jo. Breathe." He stroked a gentle hand through her hair. "Babe, no one gives a shit what the reason was. It only matters that *he* did what he did."

"Wait, are you not angry at me? I thought you'd be. .. How are you not angry with me?"

His jaw worked open and closed a couple of times without explaining.

"I don't understand. He's your friend. Your bandmate."

"He's also a colossal arse, and maybe...maybe I hoped—"

"Hoped what?"

"Murphy, you back there? Get your arse out here." It seemed Samson had arrived along with the rest of the band if the jolts to the bus's suspension were anything to go by. It was shit hitting the fan time.

Lee fished a clean T-shirt out of the cupboard by his bunk and pulled it on, leaving the blood splatted one behind on the floor. He took a step towards the door. Jodi caught hold of his arm.

"Hoped what, Lee?"

He offered her a tortured smile. "That you'd come to your senses, babe."

"I... What?"

His hand stalled on the door handle. "He doesn't deserve you. I'm not even sure he really likes you. I mean, he likes ordering you about, but that's not really the same thing, is it?"

"You don't think he likes me?" her voice rose into a squeak.

Lee wetted his lips and shifted uncomfortably from one foot to the other. "I have to go, Jodi."

"Don't you dare." She clamped her hand against the door. "Explain what you mean. And then explain why you've never said it before."

His mouth twisted, causing his nostrils to thin. He looked almost longingly at the wood separating them from the front of the bus. With a sigh, he bowed his head. "Just that it's become increasingly obvious since we hit the road that what he values about you most is the opportunities it affords him to crow about shit. 'Ooh, look at me. I have a girlfriend. Ooh, look we're getting married. Take a gander at the rock I got her, guys.' And then there's the fact that he wasn't remotely interested in you until I was. Until Balin said you were cool, and Jez and Rune were ready to adopt you—"

"You were interested in me?"

"Murphy," Samson yelled from the front of the bus.

Lee flashed her a sad grin. "Come on, you knew that."

"No." She hiccoughed. "I didn't."

Lee's lips stretched open so that his teeth were showing. "Cute little cupcake like you, of course I was."

"Murphy!"

"Was?"

"Was." He pulled her into a tight hug. "You're still cute, Jo-Jo, but I'm not looking for a relationship now, and even if I was, there's already a man out there with his heart set on you."

"Nash."

"No, dumbo. Rock Giant."

When she gulped, he patted her on the back.

"He said he loves me," she whispered into his shoulder.

Lee teased her away from his body, so they were looking one another in the eyes again. "If you mean Rock Giant, I don't think he says much he doesn't mean. If you mean Nash, I hate to say it, but I think he's talking crap. If he loved you, he wouldn't have stood you up, he wouldn't spend his time watching Balin screw, and he'd be ready to put you ahead of his own interests instead of using you as a convenient scapegoat for his own shortcomings."

A cry wriggled its way free of her throat. Lee pulled her fast against him, entwining her in a more aggressive hug.

"Lee, I'm frightened you're right."

"Nah. You're frightened because you know I'm right."

"Murphy, so help me God, if you don't—" Samson wrenched the door open. He stared at the pair of them entwined, then made a thumbing motion indicating Lee needed to move up front. "You stay here," he barked at her. "I don't want to hear a peep from you. Got it?"

"Yeah," she squeaked, cowering away from his rage.

Lee caught hold of the doorframe with both hands as Samson attempted to shove him over the threshold. He looked back at her. "I'm sorry I put the band ahead of our friendship. I should have said all this before."

JODI WOKE WITH a raging thirst and her mind cobwebby. She'd dreamed she'd been driving a succession of cars through labyrinthine lanes that kept getting narrower until she was certain she was going to wind up embedded in the hedgerows.

The vibrations through the bunk told her they were in transit. Presumably, on the road south towards the port and back to Britain to whatever fate the Ghost Boys awaited. She'd heard bits of the conversation between her boys, Samson, and Brian, but not enough to know the outcome. When three of the four had trudged into the bunk room long after midnight, grim-faced and tight-lipped, she'd asked, "What happened?" but Balin, Jez and Lee, had all crawled straight into their bunks without answering. Nash hadn't appeared. Whether that was because he'd been arrested, disciplined, or simply sent to Coventry by the rest of them was unclear.

Flugwhump, who'd been settled by her shoulder, jumped down from the bunk and started scratching at the door to the lounge area. "It's too early," she told him. The square of sky visible through the skylight confirmed it was still hours before dawn. Her girls, Mel and Zar, were cosied up with Balin, one on his legs, the other tucked against his side. Lee's curtains were drawn across his bunk, but a yard of blond hair spilled from beneath them, proving he was in there. The bunks belonging to the crew had their curtains drawn too.

"Meow," her little bestie complained, followed by the scritch-scratch of his claws against the door.

"What is it? Do you need to pee?"

So did she, but she didn't want to move, and more likely Flugwhump just wanted to sit on the back of the banquette and watch the world roll by from the window. Jez's eyes glittered in the dark from up near the ceiling, but when she returned his gaze, he rolled out of sight.

"Mee-ow!"

"Okay, I'm moving."

Flugwhump trotted through the door the moment she cracked it open. She could see straight through to the front windscreen. They were on a narrow grey road, sandwiched between pine forest and rolling snow-topped mountains. There was no other traffic, and no illumination besides the headlights.

Nash lay asleep on the left-hand side of the leather banquette, still dressed in last night's clothes including his boots, a leather jacket pulled over his shoulders, and his head on a pile of merch shirts.

He stirred while she was unlacing his boots.

"Jo?" he enquired, cracking one shadowy eyelid.

"Thought you'd be more comfortable." She kept on with the task and pulled his foot free of the boot, avoiding making eye-contact. "The bunk's free if you'd rather..."

"Aren't you going back there?"

She shook her head, now wide awake, even if she was yawning into her sleeve.

Flugwhump jumped up and occupied his favourite spot by the window.

"I'm not sure I'm welcome back there."

"They're all comatose."

"Still."

He closed his eyes again.

Jodi dropped onto her butt, and leaned her back against the opposite bench, unable to tug her attention away from him. She'd been too worried about what was going to happen to the band earlier to think straight, but now it was imperative that she did. Whatever the outcome, she couldn't continue along the trajectory she'd been travelling. Couldn't keep making excuses for Nash to ensure her security. It'd been a false security anyway.

There were creases in Nash's cheeks, and the remains of kohl smeared around his eyes. He looked so boyish, lying there. Harmless. An overgrown child, hardly a man at all. It made it all the harder for her to open her mouth and say what she needed to say, but they needed to talk, and now, in the dead of night, they at least had the privacy to do so.

How to begin was another matter.

Jodi imagined herself pulling off the engagement ring and not saying anything at all, simply placing it on his chest and walking away. Returning to the bunk room and delaying the consequences until daylight. Was she really that much of a coward?

Perhaps...

"There a reason you're staring at me?"

"Why'd you do it?"

He peered across at her from under his dark

fringe, eyes unfriendly, then pushed into a seated position, dislodging the jacket. It crumpled in his lap. The T-shirt he was wearing was torn at the collar, and face on, she could see that not all the shadows around his eyes were down to smeared kohl.

"I'd have thought you were the one person other than him I didn't need to explain it to."

"We'd agreed to put it behind us."

"We had, yes. But then you planned a little rendezvous with him the moment I was busy."

"That's not true."

"Fucking is. Krista told me. The second we were on stage; you were out back canoodling with him."

"That's not what happened."

She'd kicked Rock Giant to the kerb.

"I gave you the benefit of the doubt, and you fucking betrayed me," Nash said. "You didn't mean any of what you said to me the other night. You must think I'm a fool."

Jodi bit her fingernail, unsure how to defend herself, or even if it was worth the trouble. Nash obviously had his version of events all worked out, and no matter how much she argued to the contrary they wouldn't change. All that would happen was that the thread of their conversation would gradually shift from the truth to him forgiving her, to him making her feel as if only he could save her from herself and all her bad decisions, when in reality, the one genuinely bad decision she kept on making was believing all the hogwash he fed her.

"And now the band's screwed because of you and your inability to keep your knickers on."

"That isn't why the band's screwed." She got to her feet. "It's screwed because you attacked a man in front of a huge flippin' audience because some bitch who's had it in for me since the tour began whispered a load of shit in your ear, and you believed it. Not only that, instead of asking me what happened, you decided I was guilty and that the answer was to take a pop at him. Why the fuck did you do that, Nash? You had to know there'd be consequences."

He leaned forward, snarling. "Well maybe when it comes to my fiancée and the guy she keeps screwing behind my back, my brain doesn't exactly fire on all cylinders. Jeezus, Jo, there are limits to what I can take, you know. Was it not enough that you got fucking high with him, then tied the knot with him, and came on his face and all over his monster fucking cock? Why say all that stuff to me the other night, if you were already planning to sneak off for a repeat the second my back was turned?"

"That is not what happened. I just told you that?"

Nash stood. "Bullshit! It's exactly what fucking happened."

"No, Nash, it isn't. It's just what you want to believe to justify your actions, but it's not the truth, and even if it were, it still wouldn't make what you did right. I was ready to give us another chance. I believed you when you said we could put it all behind us and move on, but we can't, and we shouldn't. Maybe the truth is that we don't belong together."

I felt like ripping off a limb to finally admit that fact aloud.

"More like you've realised we're fucked. The Ghost Boys are fucked. You fucked us, so now you're moving on to more fertile ground. I'm sure it doesn't hurt that he's loaded."

"It hasn't anything to do with him. He's done with me anyway. No, Nash, the truth is that I'm breaking up with you because you're an arse. You've always been an arse, and I've been too fucking stupid to realise it."

"You're breaking up with me. You're...breaking.. .up...with me. The fuck you are. You're mine. You're wearing my fucking ring."

The bus came to an unexpected halt throwing them against one another. They fell hard against the seating.

"Fag break," their driver announced.

She'd entirely forgotten they weren't alone, and that Raoul—or was it Ray—had been privy to their every word.

"I'll give you kids five." The driver's cab door slammed.

On top of her, Nash grabbed her face and forced her to face him. "You're not ending us. You're not, Jo. We're not breaking up. You're not ending anything." He slammed his mouth against hers.

Jodi shoved against his chest. "Get off me."

"No. No. We're not over. You're not dumping me for that prick. We can figure this out. We can—"

"I don't fucking want to figure it out. Stop touching me. Stop—" She couldn't get her arms free and into a position to shove him off despite a weight advantage, but then he'd always had spaghetti arms, and an unfailing ability to know exactly where to apply pressure.

A shadowy form dropped onto his back.

Nash yelped, his eyes going wide. He twisted away from her attempting to reach over his shoulder. "Fucking cat. I'm going to wring its fucking neck!" He let go of her and made a grab for Flugwhump's hissing form now a metre or so further along the leather.

Jodi scooted into the corner of the seating away from him. Blood stains were leaking through the cotton covering his back where Flugwhump's needle-like claws had lacerated him through his shirt. Nash made a dive towards her cat, resulting in a mad scramble. Her shadowy baby's nimbleness was unfortunately eventually overcome by Nash's size advantage. He grabbed Flugwhump by the scruff of his neck and held him aloft as if he'd just claimed his opponents head on a battlefield of yore.

"Let him go."

"Oh, I'm going to let him go, all right."

Keeping the squirming cat at arm's length, he made his way to the bus steps.

"Put him down, Nash."

Nash hit the door release, then hurled her saviour down the steps.

Jodi's heart lurched up her throat and practically out of her body. He had not just… She hurtled off the seat with the velocity of a bullet and hit him with the full force of her fury, driving him with an impressive thwap up against the dash and windscreen. "You fucking monster. You fucking…evil…" She cracked his head against the glass again for good measure. "I can't believe you hurt my cat." Then she was flying down the steep steps towards the tarmac where Flugwhump had landed in a squalling heap of black fur.

"That's right, chase after the fucking cat. That bastard animal just ripped my back open."

Aye, in defence of her. Jodi didn't bother wasting her breath making that point.

Flugwhump spat at her when she tried to pick him up. He arched his back and his tail stood erect as if he were about to shoot poison darts from it. "It's okay. It's okay baby. Did he hurt you? Are you hurt?" Was he avoiding putting a weight on his back leg? Oh, God. Oh, God. What if he needed a vet?

"You always loved that fucking moggy more than me."

"Is that any wonder considering what a bastard you are?" She stilled a moment, arm outstretched, then pulled it into her body and tugged the engagement ring from her finger. "Here, take your shitty love and shove it up your arse. I don't need you and your fucked-up manipulative crap. I was a fool to think I ever did." She threw it at him and noted with grim satisfaction the score the diamond left across his cheek when it hit him.

"Bitch!" Nash gripped the handrails and swung himself down the steep entry steps. Jodi didn't wait for his feet to hit the tarmac. She bolted alongside Flugwhump, the pair of them heading straight for the nearby building.

Whatever service station they'd stopped at was unfortunately closed. It was only as she ran, she realised there were no other vehicles, and the lights were out in the building that claimed to be a hotel.

A missile sailed past her shoulder. What the actual fuck! Was he throwing rocks?

"You're fucking irrelevant. You're irrelevant, Jo. You were only ever part of this tour because of me. You wouldn't have got near Rock Giant if it wasn't for me."

This wasn't anything to do with Rock Giant.

She hadn't torn that ring from her finger because she was ready to ride off into the sunset with another man. She'd done it because she deserved better than binding herself to a shitty excuse for one. A man who didn't love her and never would, and who thought far too fucking much of himself. Christ! She'd spent her teenage years being lorded over by an arsehole of a father and two chips off the ol' block. How had she been so blind as to believe her future security was dependent on another copy from the same mould?

"So, we're over, are we? Fine. Well, if we're over, you can just fuck off then, can't you."

She'd reached the edge of the parking area, where the tarmac gave way to the grass of a children's play area. Ahead of her, Flugwhump paused beneath the toddler swing, his form a solid black silhouette against the nighttime shadows.

"You can fuck off and go back to being the pointless thieving waste of air you were when we met.

Bet you thought I didn't know that, you sad bitch. Juan-Luis was right about you; you are a *puta ladrona británica*. Rock Giant know that about you, does he?"

Happened that he knew a heck of a lot more about her than Nash, but that's because he saw people, and didn't only look at them in terms of what he could get out of the relationship. Not that it mattered. She wasn't doing this so she could be with him.

Out of breath, Jodi sagged against the metal A-frame of the swing. A moment later her little bestie was rubbing up against her calves. This time when she reached for him, he let her pick him up without making a fuss and nuzzled his soft furry face against her cheek. His little pink tongue lapped at the tears coursing down her face. "It's okay," she said. "It's okay. It'll be okay." The guys would still be there for her, even if her and Nash were done. Lee had said as much. No matter what happened with the band, they'd stay friends. They'd work something out. This wasn't a parting of ways between all of them, only between her and Nash.

She could live without him dictating the terms.

The shock of it was starting to sink in. She'd finally told him. "I told him," she said to the cat. "I told him. You gave me the strength. I couldn't stay with him after he did that to you." She'd been planning to tell him it was over, but, "That was the final straw."

Across the lot, the bus's engine made a sputtering start. Ray had evidently returned and was eager to get going again.

Her foot had only just hit the tarmac when the bus began moving.

Jeezus, what? "No!"

In her surprise, she squeezed Flugwhump too hard, making him yowl and squirm out of her arms. He landed lightly on his feet, while her bare foot came down hard on a spiked stone. The automatic wince and withdraw routine left her off balance. Her other ankle gave, and she went sprawling to earth, scraping open her palms in the process and jarring both her shoulder and knees.

For a crawling span of seconds, she lay wounded and winded, tears clouding her vision, but even through that veil she could see the bus's taillights moving towards the slip road. They winked out completely as the road curved to join the main carriageway.

Did Ray realise he'd left her behind? He probably didn't. Maybe he didn't even realise that she'd left the bus. What had Nash done, given him a nod, and offered no explanation to her whereabouts? The roadie would assume fight done, she'd retreated back to the bunkroom. The bunkroom she ought never to have left.

Slowly, she peeled herself off the ground and looked around. She was alone in the dark. Her and a cat. Barefoot, wearing her sleeping shorts and a tatty vest top. No phone, no money, no passport. No clue where she was, let alone how far away the nearest town or village lay. She wasn't even certain what time of night it was.

And now that she was no longer running, her skin registered the nip of the wind.

Oh, God. Oh, shit!

White noise futzed up her hearing and tunnelled her vision.

She'd screwed up again. Dramatically.

PAUL HAD FALLEN asleep with his head on Alle's lap, while she massaged his stiff shoulder. He had numerous welt-like bruises across his body, but none of it pained him more than the realisation that Jodi had left with the Ghost Boys, and without even stopping to see if he was all right.

He woke to his phone's choral wail, and grumbled when having silenced it, the damn thing burst into a second rendition immediately. Who the hell was calling him at 5am, and why?

Unknown number.

Yeah, they could fuck right off.

It hurt to roll over. Someone had inserted at least a dozen iron spikes into his shoulder and his neck felt as if he'd spent the night as a blood donor to Lestat de Lioncourt. He managed to press out a couple of painkillers someone had helpfully left on the pillow of the bed at the back of the tour bus, and grimaced as he was assaulted by a third wail. He really needed to change his ringtone.

"There'd better be a bloody good reason you're calling me," he grouched at the caller without bothering to look to see who it was.

"Is Jodi with you?"

Lee.

"Please don't hang up. I know you have no reason to speak to us—" He wasn't pissed off at the rest of them, only their vocalist. All the rest of the band had done was try to stop him. "—I just want to know if she's there. You don't need to put her on. I'm just worried."

Paul's head wasn't as online as he'd have liked, or he might have extrapolated more from what Lee was saying than his sleep deprived brain managed.

"She's not here, mate," he drawled. "I don't know why you think she would be." Jodi had made her feelings entirely too clear. She wanted nothing more to do with him. "Didn't she leave with you?" He didn't bother asking how they'd come by his number. Nothing stayed private these days, and equally likely Jodi had given them it.

"Yeah, but I figured, maybe when we stopped, she must have—"

"Have we stopped?" He didn't think they'd stopped. Wasn't any real call for them to have done so. They'd only been on the road a few hours, and they wouldn't swap drivers until they reached the drop off point across the border in Amål.

In any case, he'd spent years travelling around on buses, and he always woke when they stopped, even if it was only for a handful of minutes. Still, he did a quick once over of the room, just to be sure he hadn't missed her sitting in a corner. No such luck. There was no cherubic Jodi-angel watching over him.

"Have you checked the loo?" Maybe she'd just needed a few minutes of peace.

"The bog's right next to me. She's not there."

"Pretty sure Flugwhump's missing, too," a background voice said. Balin, he thought.

A feeling of deep unease swept through Paul's aching body, adding a layer of pain he could have done without. He eased himself into a more upright position, back to the headboard and pillow. All was quiet around him. No voices, only the vibration of the bus in motion. Everyone was obviously asleep. "Have you talked to your driver?"

"On it," he heard the same background voice say. Followed by, "Driver says he thought she was back here in the bunkroom. We did stop about forty minutes ago. Her and Nash were arguing."

Rock Giant was suddenly as wide awake as if he'd just had a thousand volts zapped into his skull. "What's missing other than her and a cat? What about the other cats? And where's cunt face now?"

If that bastard had done something to her, so help him Goddess, he was going to—.

"In my bunk," Balin said. Lee had obviously put him on speakerphone. "I mean the cats. Nash is asleep, upfront. I think he's taken Nytol, because I've prodded him and he barely gave a grunt."

"Have you tried calling her?"

"Yeah, we've tried."

"Try again."

"I'll do it," Jez said, "She has different ringtones set for each of us and mine's the loudest." A faint purr sounded in the distance, followed by some muffled sounds of motion.

"What's going on?" Paul demanded.

"Her phone's here. Likewise her bank card," Jez informed him. He could picture the Ghostie's drummer, items in hand, standing over Lee holding the phone.

"She wouldn't bail without those," the latter said.

"She wouldn't bail without all three cats." Come to think of it, she wouldn't bail at all, not like this. Not in the dead of night, not without a means of transport or her passport. Leastways, not by choice.

"Wake that fucking bastard up now," he growled. "And find out what the fuck he's done to her. And talk to your driver again. He must know something. Find out where and when you stopped."

He wanted to believe that Nash wouldn't abandon her in the middle of nowhere, but he didn't trust the bastard. Not a bit. As for the driver, either he was an accomplice or plain old thick. What sort of moron drove off without making sure all his passengers were onboard first? It was literally part of the driver's job to make sure they were all there before pulling off and reporting to the tour manager if they weren't.

"Guys," he heard Balin call at some distance from the phone.

"What's up?" Paul demanded.

It took far too long for Lee to answer him, and when he did, there was a definite clip of panic to his voice. "Balin just pried Jo's engagement ring out of Curtis's hand."

"I'm going to fucking kill him."

"Not sure you're gonna need to, mate. I think he might have overdone the sleeping meds. We can't wake him up."

I T HURT TO move, but Rock Giant got out of bed despite the devil's pokers prodding him in a dozen areas at once and made his way to the front of the Black Halo bus.

"We need to make a stop."

"That right?" Cave Troll replied from behind the wheel. He gave Paul a brief glance, and taking in the fact he was naked save for his boxer briefs, added, "You need a doc or summat?"

"Nah, I'm good. I need to pick up my wife."

"You mean the one whose fiancé has probably taken a hit out on you, and who didn't even bother to see if you were okay after you got wanged with a mic stand? Sorry, mate. Ferry to catch and a bunch of annoying arse wipes to drop off."

"Troels, I'm asking nicely, but it's non-negotiable. I've got a location. We need to stop."

He was ready to hijack the damn bus if he had to. He rattled off the details Lee had managed to extract from the Ghosties driver, but Troels began shaking his head before he was even halfway through them. "Can't mate, sorry."

"Fuck the ferry."

"T'ain't that. Your location's about twenty minutes back that way." He raised a thumb over his shoulder.

"You're fucking joking me."

"Wish I was, man. Best I can do is pull over at the next convenient point and let you out."

Paul wasn't exactly sure how that would help. It wasn't as if he could walk the fifteen or so miles back to where Jodi had been stranded in any reasonable sort of time. Not that he wouldn't do it if another option didn't present itself.

"Has the rust-bucket passed that point?"

The roadies' bus was almost as nice as theirs this tour, but old habits died hard, hence the nickname for the crew bus remained. "Call them and ask."

He did. They were past that point, too.

"Shit!" He aimed his foot at the dash but thought better of it. He needed a means of getting to her. "You gonna have to turn around."

"That," —Troels assured him— "isn't happening.

Road ain't wide enough to be pulling U-turns even if I was of the mind to do one."

He had a point, the road was currently only two lanes and most of what was off to the sides was grass and mountainside, with the occasional farmstead dotted among it accessible via dirt and gravel tracks. "Fuck!" He did thump the partition between the driver's booth and the tour bus kitchen. If the buses couldn't stop then... "Who's driving the Danger Car?"

Troels gave him another sidewards glance. "Tony and Sam, I think. Leastways, they've got the big van."

The big van housed most of the stage equipment but also played transporter for Ash's car he insisted on ferrying places with them. For the second time in recent history, Paul was thankful for that fact.

He tried both men, Sam picked up. They were ahead on the road. Finally, a bit of good karma. He gave a quick explanation of the situation and arranged a rough location for them to pull over and wait for them.

Troels whistled through his teeth the moment Paul hung up.

"You're not going to be an arse about stopping, are you?"

"I'll stop. It'll have to be a quick drop off mind. That's not the issue. You know they're not going to hand you the keys, not without a written affidavit signed in blood and witnessed by every member of the band."

Good point. He'd have to get on with negotiating that. Sure, he could attempt to argue the toss with Tony and Sam, but it'd waste precious time he'd rather prioritise for the task of finding his lady love. What state was she in out there alone in the dead of night in a foreign country?

His shoulder needed an icepack, but he bypassed the fridge-freezer without opening it.

"Go away," Ginny moaned when he stuck his head beneath the curtains of the bunk she and Ash were occupying.

"Can't. I need Danger Mouse for an urgent mission."

"It's too early, Paul."

"I need the car."

"Fuck off," Ash muttered.

Paul slapped a creased orange card down on the centre of Ash's bare chest. "Get up, goth boy. I need a ride, and I'm cashing this in, so shift your arse."

Groaning reached him from across the aisle. Xane stuck his head out from behind his curtains. "What's going on? What are you stomping around for?"

"I need Ash and the Danger Car. The fuckers have left Jodi stranded by the roadside."

"Say what?" Ash squinted at Paul, his handsome face irritably distorted, but his brain coming online.

"Her fuckwit fiancé's kicked her off the bus and left her stranded. I need to go get her. You can drive, or you can give me permission to do so."

"You're not driving my car. Not even if it is a rescue mission." Ash propelled himself into a sitting position and swung his legs over the bunk's edge. "Let me grab some clothes and get some feet on."

At least he hadn't lobbed any moronic questions about why Paul needed to run to the rescue. The shit with Nash, the rejection, none of it mattered. Of course it hurt, but none of it changed what he'd promised—that he'd always be there. And he was going to be there, just as fast as he was able.

"Paul," Ginny said, looking him over from her horizontal position beneath the duvet. Only the top half of her face was peeping out. "You might consider doing the same. Not that the view isn't pretty, but it's October in the wilds. Might be a bit nippy out there."

True. Good point. He saw to that, even though it

knacked to pull a jumper over his head. By the time he and Ash stumbled down the stairs a couple of minutes later, Cave Troll was signalling to pull into a layby where Sam and Tony were already backing the Danger Car out of the truck.

"Thanks, guys," he remembered to say, before Ash pulled a U-turn across the carriageway and pointed them north. Only then did he wish he'd had the foresight to pick up a spare fleece or something.

AT FIRST, JODI convinced herself that Nash would punish her for a few minutes and then turn the bus back to collect her. He could be a callous and vindictive knob, but he wasn't heartless. At least that's what her jittering, held-together-with-elastic-bands faith in his core values told her. It took ten minutes of shivering alone in the dark, to realise maybe Nash was in fact twice as big of a knob as she'd ever imagined, and how much evidence of that did she really need to get with the picture. The bus wasn't coming back. At least not before daylight arrived and the rest of the band awoke. That was likely hours off, and consequently, the bus would be hundreds of miles further south if not on a ferry by the time it happened.

Conclusion, she was screwed. Properly screwed.

Help didn't seem readily available. Traffic along the road was sparse, and there hadn't been much of a hard shoulder, which meant standing out there trying to flag someone over ran the risk of her not being seen until it was too late, thence, *splat*, pancake time.

Hell no! Being stranded was bad enough without the prospect of becoming roadkill.

There was also the matter of Flugwhump. The mighty devil refused to be restrained and kept disappearing into the undergrowth. She could only hope he wouldn't stray too far, and that if someone did come along, he'd come when called, and they wouldn't drive off convinced she was mad when they realised she was in her pyjamas and prattling about her black cat she couldn't catch.

The longer Jodi sat, the deeper the wind bit into her flesh, turning the exposed parts blue. The pair of them needed to find some shelter or build a fire or something. Alas, she was no Paul Reed. Conjuring flames from two rocks and a bit of moss wasn't in her skill set.

Why had she told him to keep his distance? She ought to have said, I'm yours. I've always been yours right from the very first moment we met. I'll always be yours. Can I please be yours? Instead, she'd blinded herself to reality and stoppered up her ears to anything that didn't affirm the illusion she'd been blithely inhabiting.

Well, it was too late for that now. There were no knights in shining armour coming to her rescue.

With the wind still nipping at her, Jodi headed over to the deserted building. Maybe she'd get lucky and find the door unlocked or a window that she could shimmy through. She tried the door, but it was fastened tight. The windows were all boarded, leaving only the shallow indent of the doorway to shelter inside.

It wasn't the first night she'd spent alone outdoors, and likely wouldn't be the last, unless she froze to death. Comforting thought. Norway, even in October, was significantly colder than the UK, especially after the sun dropped. Here, the land was on the cusp of winter. Right on cue, a flurry of snow arrived.

God, she was such a fool. Why had she ever imagined Nash would be reasonable about her calling quits on them? When had he ever been reasonable about anything? Also, why had she stuck it out this long when she knew they were doomed?

She was such a moron.

Unfortunately, the answer was as simple as it was cynical.

Because it'd been better than this. Living with Nash, putting up with Nash and his whims and tempers had been better than this. Being his girlfriend beat the hell out of the misery of surviving winter on the streets.

The dumb part was that she'd been blind to the obvious and significantly better alternatives to both of those options. Foremost: Paul Reed. Secondly, that her friendships weren't dependent on Nash. Hell, maybe they were even despite him.

So, while she'd forfeited Paul, the guys would come back for her. They would. They'd talk to Nash. They'd talk to Ray. Figure something out. Nash might be willing to dump her in the wilderness, but not the rest of them.

They'd do something, even if they couldn't turn the bus around and collect her.

If she just endured. Sat tight, waited for however long it took, one or all of them would appear. Or they'd arrange a pick-up, a taxi, something...

Her bare feet were like blocks of ice. She rubbed them, trying to offset the numbness setting in, then folded herself up small by pulling her knees against her body, and drawing her pyjama top over them. Damn it was bitter! And to think it'd only been a week and a half ago that they'd all sat outside around a campfire. Mind, that'd been a stretch further south than she currently was.

She imagined being swaddled inside Paul's oversized jumper, the threads ticklish against her arms, and the faint trace of his scent still captured amidst the fibres. He always smelled so good. Earthy, but clean. Snuggly, not that snuggly described a scent, except it kinda did.

How far off was dawn? Two, three, maybe four hours away. That wasn't so long, really. She'd endured sound checks that lasted longer than that.

At least her position here gave her a vantage point from where she could watch the car park for arrivals. Someone might stop. She could ask to use their phone. She wouldn't ask for a lift, not unless it was a family, not while she was dressed in skimpy nightclothes. That sort of thing was risky enough all buttoned up and with pepper spray in her pocket. No, she'd just ask to use their phone. Not that she knew any numbers.

She could phone Paul. She did have his number, or rather Flugwhump did. She'd been wary of storing his number on her phone given Nash's attitude, so she'd filed it on a curl of paper inside the little capsule tag on Flugwhump's collar.

Okay, so, she'd phone Paul, but would he answer?

He would. She was sure he would. Even if he hated her. He'd still answer. That was who he was. He kept his promises, and he'd promised her all those things— that he'd take care of her, be there for her. She needed him to be here for her now. Not that there was any way for him to know that. Yes, he'd help if, or rather when she called.

He would.

God, he would, wouldn't he?

Tears trickled down her cheeks. Jodi rested her damp skin against her knees. The snow had stopped, having only glazed the surroundings. She'd stopped shivering too. Maybe the temperature was warming up as dawn approached.

Damn, she blinked to stop her eyelids falling. It wasn't half hard keeping herself focused on one spot when it was so unchanging.

J ODI WAS BACK in the glass dome. The remnants of her message to Paul still smudged the glass by the door. She'd been trying to light a fire for an hour now, but the collection of twigs refused to catch. The night before he'd made it look so easy. The former pub dining shelter contained most of the same comforts it'd provided the night before, all except the vital one, the one that'd turned the temporary shelter into a palace.

She hadn't expected him to still be here when she'd returned, but she'd not been prepared for his absence either. It had left a funny lump in her throat and an ache in her chest that no amount of massaging would shift.

They'd lain, there. He'd sung to her, there. Handed her the best cup of tea ever brewed, there.

The kittens were back in their trough, their three little pink noses peeping out from their fur. The vet had said they were maybe three to four weeks old, and that she could start offering wet food alongside cat milk. At least they could lap that up. No need to bottle feed. It was going to be too cold for them, though, if she didn't get this fire lit.

Why…wouldn't…it…just…bloody…strike. Increasing the pressure she used to scrape it along the striking surface caused the match to snap. Jodi dropped it into the bundle of twigs with a cry of frustration. Why hadn't she joined the Girl Guides instead of wasting her youth hotwiring cars? Then maybe she'd have some useful practical skills.

Catch. Please. Oh, fucking Christ. Just catch will you.

The tiniest of tiny flames formed around the edge of one of the twigs. "Please," she begged, pushing more of her bird's nest of kindling towards it. "Please...please...please."

It caught.

It finally caught.

"Impressive, Castle." She turned to find him sliding open the glass door to her shelter in a way that had definitely never happened.

⁓

"CASTLE? Hey, wake up."

Her sluggish brain took a while processing that Paul Reed was standing over her. His face was rimed with shadows, and for a moment, she thought they were in the glass dome the morning after she'd drowned his tour bus. Then he shifted enough for her to see the stars behind him, and she remembered. They were in Norway, three years on from that event. And it was impossible for him to be here. He was just a hypnagogic bit of wish fulfilment. She blinked, but he remained. Crouched now, and peering at her in obvious concern.

"You here with me, Castle?"

"Yeah." She lifted her head from her knees. Her neck and all her limbs were stiff. Her fingers screamed for mercy as she straightened them. "How?" she croaked, still staring at him, almost certain that he'd blink out of existence if her attention lapsed even for a second.

A smile tugged his lips away from his teeth. "Got a call from some friends of yours a bit frantic about your absence."

So, the rest of the Ghost Boys had realised she was missing and acted. Yet, it wasn't daylight. Wait, Jez had been awake, hadn't he? She'd glimpsed him right before she'd climbed out of her bunk. So, they'd called Rock Giant when they realised she wasn't onboard. And he'd come. Exactly as he'd promised her, even though she'd given him no reason to.

They stared at one another for a moment, while she let that fact sink in, and then once it had, while she embraced him in her head and took back all the things she'd said to him hours before.

"I told you I'd always be here for you, no matter what." He touched her arm but winced at the contact. "Cripes, come here, you're half frozen."

He took off his jumper, exposing his chiselled torso to the bracing night air, and wrapped it around her shoulders.

"Paul, I'm sorry."

"Hush, there. You've nothing to be sorry for." His arms did encompass her then, drawing her towards the solid wall of his chest and the intense heat he was radiating. "Are you hurt? Did that fuckwit hurt you? I'll skin him alive."

The way he was eyeballing her, she figured he'd been planning to already. Because while he was a big cuddly teddy bear, he also happened to be composed of barbed wire and gristle.

"I told him it was over."

"Good girl." He patted her back.

"He threw Flugwhump off the bus."

"Fucker."

"Left without us."

"Yeah," he acknowledged, cradling her closer, so that she was breathing in the earthy comfort of his skin. He was so solid, and warm. So, present. She could be content here, if she never moved again.

"What do you say to leaving here with me?"

She wanted that more than anything. So much so, that the prospect of it made her cry.

"Hey, none of that." He nudged up her chin and swept away the tears with his thumb.

"I don't deserve you."

"Well, you got me anyway." He followed up the thumb sweep with gentle kisses to her eyelids. "And more importantly, I've got you. I've got you, Jodi." He eased her to her feet, supporting her rise. When she wobbled, he bent as if about to lift her.

"We need Flugwhump," she said, staying his hands.

"Aye. Aye, we do. So where is your little black demon?"

Said tiny panther emerged from the gloom at the first call of his name. He rubbed straight up against Rock Giant's leg, purring like he'd just won the kitty cat lottery.

"He likes you."

"Of course he likes me. I rescued him from a plastic bag, and he knows I'm gonna score him some premium catnip later. Don't cha, mate." Paul scooped up the cat, who happily flopped in his embrace like he was a baby. When he then pulled her in closer to his side, her feline monster walloped her across the chin.

"Hey, we'll have none of that, mate."

He planted a kiss where the paw had hit her. "Better?"

"A little."

He lovingly offered another.

She didn't deserve his concern or his gentleness,

but she craved both and was never ever saying no to them again. She'd been a fool to ever do so.

Flugwhump yowled as he was sandwiched between them and succeeded in squirming his way free of Paul's arms. It left the path open for their bodies to meld together. His, so solid, and so much bigger than hers. Comforting, surrounding her like a protective cage, while her hands reached up and clasped the sides of his shorn head, drawing him to her mouth. To where she wanted to feel the softness of his lips against her own. To where she felt the hot hunger of his desire that made her shake and warmed her from the inside.

It wasn't only his kisses that brought her back to life, it was the realisation that she was free to accept them. The past was done; a new dawn sat on the horizon. "I'm not his anymore," she gasped, energised by that fact.

The admission scored her a ferocious grin. "No, Castle, you're something much better. You're mine."

Their mouths melded once more, hands wandering this time, hers determinedly pulling him closer.

"I don't deserve this," she whispered when they surfaced for air.

"You deserve more than I can ever give you. You deserve love, and you have mine, for now and for always, exactly as I promised." His voice was a sexy rasp weighed with sincerity. "You're my everything, Jodi."

"Castle," she automatically corrected. He always called her that, and he was the only one who did. Also, it reminded her of Doctor Who and Matt Smith insisting, 'Come along, Pond,' before they embarked on some wild adventure. Paul held that sort of pull to her. One that was so much more than sexual attraction, though that was an evident factor, it wasn't the limit of it. It was also the heart and beneficence of the man. The care with which he moved through the world, and the sense of wonder and adventure he brought to everything.

"You're my everything, Castle." Paul kissed her again, this time sliding his tongue between her lips and effortlessly making himself the king of her heart.

"Hey, can we hurry this up? I'm not one to complain, but I was pulled from my bed, and now I'm freezing my nads off here."

They turned their heads simultaneously. It hadn't dawned on her that Paul wasn't alone, though it ought to have been obvious. It wasn't as if he'd *poofed* himself here like a brother from one of her favourite books.

Black Halo's lead guitarist stood leaning against the side of a bright yellow sports car, an easy grin on his handsome mug. "You two lovebirds want a lift somewhere with a bed?"

Paul exhaled some of the tension that she hadn't realised he was carrying until she felt the release in his shoulders. "Damn straight, we do." He looked back at her, all grin. "That plan cool with you, Castle?"

When she gave him a nod, he tugged her towards the waiting vehicle and got her settled in the passenger seat. Then he scooped up Flugwhump and deposited him on her knee, before squeezing his bulk into the tiny bucket seat in the rear. For a wonder, he actually fit. It certainly hadn't been built with a man of his stature in mind. It meant his knees were threatening to collide with his nose, but he didn't gripe.

Jodi kept her head turned, still afraid that if she let him slip out of her field of vision, he'd be gone forever.

"It's okay." He settled a reassuring hand on her shoulder. Jodi put her hand on top of his, and Paul laced their fingers. "I'm not going anywhere without you."

On which subject, "Where to?" Ash asked.

"Rendezvous with the guys and your missus in Amål."

Jodi didn't recall anyplace named Amål from the itinerary, but honestly, he could have told her they were hightailing it to Jupiter and she'd have gone along with it.

Ash gave a nod and woke the engine. He slid the car into gear. "It's a good job I love you, man, because that's a five-hour drive and I've not had a brew yet."

J ODI WASN'T SURE where she was geographically. Usually, that would have sent her into a full-scale panic. She felt none of that as the shower spray hit her upturned face and chased off the last of the chill that had penetrated her bones.

She was safe.

Her very own knight protector was standing guard outside ready to see off demons, vampires, spiders, stalkers, ex-boyfriends, and any -one or -thing else that had the discourtesy to wish to disturb her.

After Paul had tucked her into Ash's Danger Car, and they'd hit the road with the car heater on full, she'd quickly drifted off. Her exhaustion had kept her comatose for most of the multi-hour journey. She'd woken on the far side of the Norwegian-Swedish border on the approach to the rendezvous point with the rest of Black Halo. That reunion had lasted mere minutes before Paul had bundled them both into a waiting hire car and brought them to this here lakeside cabin. Theoretically, that ought to have helped her pinpoint her position, but Sweden being a country of almost a hundred thousand lakes, she might as well have just stabbed a random area of the map and drawn a hundred-mile radius around it.

Truth was, it didn't matter. All that mattered was that she was here with him. A man so good, he hadn't taken her to task over all the shit she'd said and done to him. Nah, he'd shrugged it off, grinned, and said, "You've always been a walking catastrophe. I knew when I signed up it was likely to be a bumpy ride. Now, eat. And marshmallows, cream, or sprinkles with your hot chocolate, or all three? Also, I've fed the cat."

After plying her with the best cuppa on the planet and thick-cut slices of crusty bread spread with butter and honey, until the hollow in her stomach was well and truly filled, he'd turned her towards the shower, where she'd now been for some time judging by the enquiring knock on the door.

"You okay in there, Castle?"

"Yes," she said, only to repeat herself louder realising he probably couldn't hear her over the thud of the rainfall shower. Although, actually, "No."

"No? Fuck, what's up?" Genuine concern scored his vocals.

Curious how the timbre of his voice could have such a direct effect on her body. Pleasure tickled beneath her skin. "You're out there and not in here with me."

Maybe that was forward, but she'd been holding her feelings for him in check for so long that she had no intention of doing so now that it was no longer necessary. She just wanted him close. Heck, she just wanted him.

"Aw, that so, is it?"

"It is."

The creak of the door hinges alerted her to him sticking his head around the door. "Wasn't sure if I was welcome," he said, voice husky with hope. "Thought after everything, you'd maybe prefer some space."

"I'd prefer your company."

She hoped that made him grin. There wasn't an easy means of confirming since she couldn't see much besides fuzzy shapes through the hazy glass of the shower surround.

An awkward silence followed.

"Are you saying... Should I—"

"Plenty of space for two in here," she sang out.

Through the hazing she could just about make out that he was undressing. Well damn, that was something she'd have liked to watch.

He cracked open the door, releasing a cloud of vapour. Jodi shuffled backward, making space for his bulk in the enclosure. Okay, so maybe it'd be a squeeze after all. He was a giant and she was the opposite of dainty. A smile painted itself across his face as water drops caught in his eyelashes. Damn, he was something, all carved definition, ink, and washboard abs. Plus of course the bejewelled pleasure stick that had given him his moniker. Jodi let her gaze eat him up. There'd been few other opportunities in their acquaintance for her to do so.

Shame, because he truly was a piece of art, and deserved admiration.

He was evidently also excited to see her, given his cock was jutting out from his body at a forty-five-degree tilt. A fact he wasn't even attempting to hide but also wasn't trying to tackle her with. She felt her cheeks heat realising she was staring and dragged her gaze sidewards.

"Nah, you drink your fill all you want." His thumb

grazed her chin and turned her back towards him. Jodi opened her mouth to him and kissed him. It's what she'd wanted to do ever since she'd woken, but the moment had never felt quite right. Firstly, because there were too many other members of his band around hurling questions at them, then because he was driving, and then feeding her. Now all that noise was gone. It was just them.

Jodi moaned as his tongue pressed to hers. The current between them was probably dangerous in a shower, given how well water and electricity mixed, but she wasn't about to pull the plug. Nah, she was all for turning up the voltage not down. So what if bits of her ached, and so what if she'd literally stopped being engaged to a different man less than eight hours ago? This had been a prospect for far too long. It was time to make it real.

As he crowded her against the tiled wall, and lifted her against him, his strong arms supported her effortlessly, skin so smooth, muscles concrete as he anchored them.

"Paul," she gasped.

"I know. It's in your eyes. And the answer's yes. It'll always be yes. I'm yours for eternity."

"I want you."

His grin said he still needed convincing. Jodi caught his hand, intending to guide him to where he could feel her readiness for himself, but he slipped down onto his knees before she got the chance, putting his tongue to work.

"You don't have... That's not necessary." Her hand played over the centimetre or so of his hair that had grown back.

"Aye, but why would I deprive myself and you of the pleasure of it. I've got a taste for your pussy, and now I intend to indulge it."

The spray continued to rain over them as he kept his promise and did just that.

He didn't just go down on her. He worshipped her with an intense focus that ensured she lapped up the rewards. Thus, one orgasm was rapidly followed by a second chaser that left her weak-kneed and mushy-brained. And even then, he held her to him so she was practically mounted over his shoulders, and continued to tease her nub with the flat of his tongue.

"Come up here," she commanded, sounding almost drunk.

"If you're sure my work down here is completed to your satisfaction?"

Was he kidding?

He rose, like Neptune rising from the waves. Jodi pulled him to her and caught the taste of herself all over his mouth.

"I'm not sure my limbs are stable enough to take matters further right here." Shower sex could be a tricky affair. She made to open the door, but Paul hit the shower off with his elbow as he picked her up off her feet and carried her out of the bathroom and into the attached bedroom with its A-line sloped roof and low set windows. They fell onto the bed together, damp, and slippery, bodies aligned and eager, hips, curves, and muscles perfectly moulded to one another.

"Let's do this right, this time. Let me get—"

She clasped his hand as he made to rise, pulled him back to her. "I want to feel you." The last time, back in Bergen had been too emotionally fraught and frantic to truly appreciate it.

"You'll still feel me, promise." He kissed her wrist. "I'm not ready to risk sharing you with anyone yet, I've only just got you to myself."

True to his word, he was back in seconds, condom already out of the packet. He stood by the side of the bed and rolled it down his length while she watched, biting her lower lip to contain her grin.

"What?"

"Nothing."

"What?"

"Just all that's mine."

He chuckled as he straddled her legs and folded himself over her, trapping her beneath him and sinking them deep into the eiderdown. "You betcha it is."

She folded her legs around his hips as she kissed his face, and raked her teeth over his chin, then down the slope of his neck to the intriguing dip by his collarbone.

"You're something special too, Castle."

Back as far as her teenage years, Jodi couldn't recall ever looking at herself naked and believing she was anything other than too big and too wobbly, but the way Paul looked at her, revered her, suggested it was another thing she'd been wrong about. His hazel eyes shone, eyelids falling to halfway as he closed the remaining inches between them.

"Goddess," he hissed, as his cock slid against all the slipperiness he'd created with his care for her. She groaned in turn, caught in a delirium of anticipation.

"Paul."

"Yeah," he rasped.

"I want you."

"Ah, God, I want you too." He made an *mmmn* noise deep in his throat that made his skin vibrate against her lips as the tip of him notched against her entrance. "Damn!"

He clasped her hands, so they were palm to palm, and folded his fingers tightly around her, squeezing, as he gave inch after precious inch of himself to her. "You feel amazing. So wet and silky."

"You feel like you're mine."

His smile stretched broad, swallowing up all of his features, and penetrating deep into the hearts of his eyes. "I am so totally yours."

PAUL LOCKED HIS fingers tight around Jodi's hand as he eased himself into the heat of her body. He wanted to look at her the whole while, stay right there with her, watch her expression, feel everything along with her, but there was a curling sense of urgency thickening in his blood that warned him anything tantric wasn't in their immediate future.

He allowed himself only an inch or so before he withdrew, so he could make the same entrance again. Of course, that didn't necessarily help, given that the head of his cock was the most sensitive part and even relaxed and as ready for him as she was, the friction on his shaft, against his piercings still had him seeing stars with every shallow stroke. When he bottomed out, it was going to be murder, but only in the sense that he didn't want it to be over too fast. This was a moment worth savouring, the one in which they finally got to cement those vows they'd made thirty-five days, thirteen hours and forty-seven minutes ago.

"I love you. And you don't have to say it back," he said, before scooping her hair to one side and bowing his mouth to the side of her neck, while his cock filled her. The sensation of that caused him to make a sound unlike any he'd made before. He wouldn't have been sure it was him, but there was only the two of them here, and she was chanting his name like a mantra.

She rocked against him. "I love how you feel inside of me."

Near enough.

Breathless, Paul chuckled and kissed the tip of her nose. "Yeah, me too." Then he lost his grip on his restraint, his arousal overtaking everything, distilling the world into the space they occupied. All the outside noise gone. Just them, hot, damp, delirious. Emotionally and physically bound.

He was trying not to be rough, trying his best to pleasure her with the care she deserved, but his nerves, his muscles, tendons, his whole motor system was countermanding any thoughts he had about tenderness and slowing things down. Then again, maybe softly wasn't what she wanted either, given how tight a grip she had on his arse, and how forcefully she was both pulling him to her and lifting her hips to meet his.

Damn, she was something else. This woman, this curvy goddess who was finally his to love, and serve, and devote himself to body and soul. He wanted to take her in every position; in all the ways it was possible for two people to bond. It was so good. So good. She was pounding her body against him, matching him stroke for stroke, and fucking hell, she was coming. Her muscles spasmed around him, pulling him deeper, milking him, and as a result he was coming as well. Damn, they were coming together.

That launched him off the planet and into outer space. He felt it in every molecule of his body, felt her molecules singing alongside his, the pair of them perfectly twined.

The come down was meandering. His bones liquid, and his mind inclined towards indolence. He was good, thank you universe, lying here still inside of her, hopefully not squashing her, savouring the tremors and aftershocks that were still making her sheath flutter around him. Eventually, there'd be no choice. He'd have to move. Deal with the practicalities like the condom, but hell if he was going to rush to it.

"How soon can we do that again?" she asked, when he eventually lifted his head and gazed down at her all pink cheeked beneath him. Not half as soon as he'd like, but soon enough that he reckoned he'd at least a hope of satisfying her. Her nipples were furled into two tight points that were just begging him for attention. So, obviously he gave it. He sucked one, then the other, making her moan and causing her inner muscles to make more of those delicious flutters around him.

"I think I'd better deal with this." He anchored the base of the condom, doing his best not to touch her while he did it, else he might get lost in an exploration of those slick and delightfully plump folds.

She hissed through her teeth as he pulled out and pouted over the loss.

"Was that a request to fuck you again this afternoon?"

"More an expression of hope...that you'll fuck me as many times as you can get it up this afternoon."

He tied off the condom and lobbed it into the bin, before settling to the right of her shoulder. "Might need to swallow some egg whites," he said against her ear.

Jodi rolled onto her side to face him. Paul lifted his

arm, and she snuggled in close, resting her head in the indent between his pec and his shoulder. It felt unbelievably right, like that was where she was always supposed to have been, and now she was, he couldn't fathom how he'd got by before. Her hand splayed over his heart, then she started running curious fingers over his chest, along the swirls of his ink, and up and down the hills and indents of his abs.

"What?" he asked, sensing questions brewing between them.

"You're not like any other man I've ever been wi... .like any other man I've known. Certainly, none I've slept with. I don't mean physically. I mean, yes, physically, but mentally, emotionally..."

"Well, maybe they just didn't appreciate you the way I do."

She sniffed and went quiet a moment as she considered that. "Paul, I'm not sure I understand why you do. I love that you do, but..."

He squeezed her shoulder, and brought his other hand to her face, so that he could gently tilt her chin up enabling him to reach her lips and bestow a kiss. "Why does anybody fall for anybody else? Sometimes the stars just align, and you know that it's right. That's how I feel with you. It doesn't matter if it makes sense. Only that it is. I love you, Jodi. And you still don't have to say it back. I think I have from shortly after we first met three years ago—you did kill Bertha, but even then, I kind of loved you for that, or at least for the circumstances of it. You're like mayhem on legs, and that does something to me."

"Gives you a headache."

"No, not that. It makes me want to cosset you. Look after you. Protect you."

"Make mad passionate love to me?" Her hand strayed down towards his cock.

"Ahem." He caught her hand and brought it back

up to the centre of his chest. "We're still on a scheduled rest break, missy."

"So, I'm not allowed to play with your jewellery?"

If he hadn't just had an out-of-body experience, that question would likely have got him perky. He did get all tingly around the root.

"Question." She raised her hand as if they were in class. "Is it okay to blow you with them in?"

Paul's lips peeled back off his teeth. Oh, she was a menace and adorable all rolled into one, and damn, those tingles were spreading. Buckaroo might be ready to kick again pretty soon. "Uh, yeah, but I'd never expect that—"

"In a bit," she said, cheekily cutting him off. "It's cute that you won't demand it. I might like it if you sometimes demanded it." She rolled onto her tummy and lifted herself up on her elbows, so she was looking him in the face, "It's something I do actually like doing, same as you seem to like licking."

"I do like licking. I especially like licking you." He licked her forehead, which was as far as he could easily reach without straining his neck.

"I like doing it best when it's soft to begin with and my sucking wakes it up and it thickens in my mouth. That's kinda…" She wriggled, rubbing her legs together and making her bottom wobble in a way that turned those growing tingles into developing perkiness. "It's nicer than when a guy is like take my whole length in one go with no build up."

"That so? Note taken."

"Mmm." She nodded. "Tell me something you like, and don't just say me. Tell me something specific. If Paul Reed could have any sort of sex he wanted, what would he choose?"

He lifted his hands up to behind his head, elbows pointing outwards. "I'm not sure the answer to that is the same as what I think you're asking me. Positions aren't relevant to the answer. I'd choose sex with an emotional connection, every time. Sex like we just had. But faves on par with your admission..." He made a soft *hmm* as he thought. "So many good options to choose from." His gaze strayed to the fullness of her breasts, but then he shook his head. "I like a girl who's not afraid to slip me a finger while we're at it."

She opened her mouth in mock shock and swept her tongue over her front teeth. "And have many girls you've been with done that, Mister Mighty Rock Star?"

"Is that a sly way of asking me how many partners I've had?"

"How many partners have you had?"

"A fair few. You?"

"A few."

"Not many of them have ever done that, though." He scrunched up his nose, thinking back. "Like two... And neither of them were women."

"Ah!"

"Ah?"

"Ah, I didn't know that about you. I mean, not for definite. Not that it's a problem. Obviously, I've seen you fooling around with Ronnie, but I figured that was just—"

"The Ronnie thing is just messing about. He's not my type. Look, I'm bi by virtue of not being a hundred per cent straight, same as most of planet Earth's population, but I'm like ninety per cent there, and a hundred per cent into you, so anything else is now irrelevant."

"Sweet talker."

"You betcha." He clasped her around her upper arms. "How'd you feel about coming up here and dangling your tits in my face?"

His irreverence made her snort, but she shifted readily enough, and straddled him, then shuffled upwards a bit so her tits were dangling right over his face. "Well, hello," he said before diving in and lavishing both their fullness and her nipples with his full attention. It was only a few minutes later she was crouched over him facing the opposite direction, the pair of them sixty-nineing so she could suck him into complete wakefulness. After that, the rest of the afternoon glided by between bouts of urgent thrusting and catnaps and eventually resolved into evening.

It was dark again out when Paul's phone lit up and wailed at him while he was rustling them up halloumi burgers naked but for an apron, while Jodi watched him from the sofa, snuggled inside one of his jumpers and a pair of his socks, making occasional remarks about the bounciness of his arse.

Dad: Any chance you could make it over this weekend?

RG: Sorry, no can do. In Sweden. But soon. There's someone I'd like you to meet.

Dad: That why you're avoiding us, son?

RG: I've no idea what you mean.

RG: We'll see each other in Ireland. I'll be there for the fire festival.

Dad: Samhain?

He replied with a thumbs up.

Dad: Not sooner?

RG: I'm on tour. Sorry, can't get away.

Besides, Samhain was right around the corner. Less than two weeks away.

"Problem?" Jodi asked when he looked up.

He shook his head and turned back to the grill. "Family stuff."

"I wondered if the guys had contacted you about my cats?"

He was about to toss her his phone and suggest she message Lee herself for an update, but thought better of it. He didn't want to wreck things by burdening her with the knowledge of Nash's overdose. Guy was fine, pending a heart assessment, and probably a lengthy lecture from a cardiologist. Her cats hadn't been mentioned during the update Lee had sent earlier, but it was the work of seconds to ask about them.

The photograph that came back, he instantly turned to her, knowing it would make her smile. Balin was sitting on the tour bus bog, trousers around his ankles, one cat in the sink beside him and the other perched on his shoulder. Lee had captioned it, the pussy whisperer.

"They'll take care of them until we can collect them." Meanwhile, Flugwhump was stretched out on his back on the rug by the log fire swatting invisible invaders. "Burgers are done." He dished up and slid hers towards her across the kitchen table.

Jodi joined him on the perch stools. "Looks great. I love squeaky cheese."

"Me too," he agreed tucking in.

He'd cut the halloumi slices thick, so they were extra squeaky, and matched them rather perfectly, if he did say so, with sweet chilli mayo, avocado, and lamb's lettuce. Plus, a side of mushrooms for him.

The sound of a car outside caused them both to look up. The cabin was set back from the main road down a dirt track driveway. Paul's brows furrowed.

"What?" she asked, mirroring his concern.

He rose, heading towards the window, muttering under his breath. "He better fucking not have. I told him not to." A lanky figure humping a large holdall was approaching the door. "You have got to be kidding me." Sure enough, a rap on the wood followed.

Maybe if he ignored it...

No, there it was again. This time a little more aggressive.

"Should I answer that?" his beloved asked, already putting her burger on her plate, and moving her leg to slip off the stool.

As tempting as it was to pretend they weren't home, he knew their visitor wasn't the sort to give up and go away. Fuck it! "Why, Ronnie?" he asked, swinging the cabin door open to admit his bandmate.

Tone-deaf as usual, Ronnie swung his bag off his shoulder and left it by Paul's feet, before sweeping past him and flopping onto the sofa. "Hey guys. I'm finally here. It's taken forever."

"Ron," Paul muttered through gritted teeth. "Didn't you get the message?"

"Xane did give me a message, yes. And Alle and Ash suggested I could maybe rethink my plans and go to Spook's, but I didn't see why I needed to change plans. Not really. By the way, do you realise your arse is hanging out?"

Paul covered his face with his hand and squeezed his temples. Jodi snickered into her food.

"That's because my wife was appreciating it." Also, he'd volunteered to remain naked for the whole of his stay if it pleased her. "You're not supposed to be here, Ronnie."

"I am, though. We booked it together, and I really wanted to see the lake."

"You could have gone to Spook's and still seen the lake. It's the same lake. It's a really fucking big lake."

"Is it?" Ronnie said innocently. "Well, yeah, I suppose it might be, but..." He got off the sofa. "I'll make myself scarce. Promise. You won't even know I'm here. Oh, hello, little fella." Flugwhump leaped onto the table, attracting Ronnie's immediate attention. He dived straight in with the ear scritches.

"Ron," Paul prompted.

Ronnie held up his hands. "Making myself scarce. Doing it right now. Look, see. I'm going." He scooped the cat up and headed towards the bedrooms. "Oops, no, not that one," they heard him say from down the corridor. "Guys, you need to air your room. This one across the way, maybe? I'll be across the hall from you guys," he yelled.

"Great," Paul replied.

"You told him not to show up?" Jodi remarked, eyebrows hiked.

Paul pursed his lips. He had in fact told him both to his face and through every member of the band not to show up, but here he was anyway, all green and prickly.

"So, I guess we won't be fucking in the lounge or on the deck, or—"

"We are so doing those things. He's staying in his room." He raised his voice. "You're staying in your room, right, Ronnie?"

"I'm staying in my room," his bandmate replied.

There was no fucking way he was going to stay in his room. Paul wailed. His wife came to him and wrapped him in a comforting embrace.

"I'm not supposed to be sharing you with anyone besides the cat," he complained. "But of course Captain Oblivious doesn't comprehend that."

Ronnie came out of his room again and grabbed his bag. He made it about four feet with it before he dipped into a pocket and produced a bag of jelly sweets. "Worm?" he offered.

"Ronnie!"

He side-eyed the pair of them. "Okay, no worms. Ooh, what are you having, burgers? Nice."

"Ronnie..."

"Say," Ronnie leaned towards Jodi's ear, while chewing on the mouthful of Paul's burger he'd just stolen. "Has he flashed you his purple worm yet?"

"Don't answer that, Castle."

"It's mega, right?"

Paul clapped a hand to his own head.

"Still can't believe I managed to fit the whole of it in my gob."

Paul and Jodi (and Flugwhump) will return in
Rock Solid.

Having turned the final page, you may have noticed that Rock Giant is the anomaly among the Black Halo boys. He's the least screwed up of them, and while he does exhibit some major tunnel vision with regards to Jodi in this here book, he doesn't carry around the sort of personal hang-ups his band mates suffer from. On this basis, he was a bastard to get to know. Boy have we had a time together, the pair of us, trying to figure one another out. Our communications haven't always been the easiest, but having reached this point, I can say without a doubt, he is a top bloke. Also, we had lots of fun coming up with his increasingly vitriolic names for his rival. If you're the sort of person who likes to tab your books, maybe that could be a fun exercise, and if you happen to have a favourite from among them, do let me know.

Thanks, as always, to my editor and proof reading

peeps. You're the best. And no, I'm not promising not to hurt Ronnie in future books. How about I promise that if I hurt him, I'll fix him afterwards. Deal?

Madelynne. October 2025.

About the Author

MADELYNNE IS A New York Times & USA Today bestselling British author of angsty bisexual romance featuring bad boys who desperately need someone to love them unconditionally.

Madelynne wrote her first novel after discovering Black Lace Books in the 1990s but had to escape the Hotel California before she could dive into storytelling full time. She's been described as a cool mum, a full-time geek, and plain old weird. Some of those might even be accurate. She lives in the UK near the Welsh border, where you can find her surrounded by books and rapidly cooling mugs of decaf coffee, dogs at her feet, listening to loud music.

To keep up to date with her releases, join her newsletter using the QR code below.